Edward Mathews

The Autobiography of the Reverend Edward Mathews

Edward Mathews

The Autobiography of the Reverend Edward Mathews

ISBN/EAN: 9783337413040

Printed in Europe, USA, Canada, Australia, Japan

Cover: Foto ©Raphael Reischuk / pixelio.de

More available books at **www.hansebooks.com**

THE

AUTOBIOGRAPHY

OF THE

REV. E. MATHEWS,

THE "FATHER DICKSON," OF MRS. STOWE'S "DRED";

ALSO A DESCRIPTION OF THE INFLUENCE OF THE
SLAVE-PARTY OVER THE AMERICAN PRESIDENTS,
AND THE RISE AND PROGRESS OF THE
ANTI-SLAVERY REFORM;

WITH A

PREFACE BY HANDEL COSSHAM, ESQ.

~~~~~~~~

London :—HOULSTON AND WRIGHT. Bristol :—THOMAS
MATHEWS. New York, United States :—THE AMERICAN
BAPTIST FREE MISSION SOCIETY: OFFICES, 37,
PARK ROW.

PREFACE.

THE following pages are from the pen of an earnest worker in the cause of human progress, civilization, and religion. The Rev. Edward Mathews passed several years of his life in the United States during the time that the pro-slavery party of that country were in power, and when it was dangerous both to person and property to advocate practically the doctrine on which the American constitution is based, namely,—"That all men are born free and equal, and are entitled to life, liberty, and the pursuit of happiness." Thanks, however, to the Providence of God, and the efforts of that truly heroic and noble band of men and women, who, after years of toil, misrepresentation, and discouragement, have at last succeeded in freeing the Great Western Republic from the foul curse of Slavery, and removing the great obstacle to the progress and prosperity of the country; the day of darkness has passed, I trust for ever, in America, and henceforward, I hope and believe, she will continue to advance in material and moral greatness.

It is twelve months ago to-day since I left the shores of America, and as the outline of Boston harbour faded from my view, I could not but breathe a prayer that the country I was leaving—(where in connection with Sir Morton Peto and others with whom I had been privileged to visit many of the most interesting spots in the States, and where I had also received so many proofs of hospitality and kindness)—and the mother country, to which I was then sailing, might always cherish for each other feelings of generosity and respect, and that no "root of bitterness" might ever arise to trouble them.

I confess I am one of those who think that during the late war we did the people of the Northern States great injustice and wrong in the way in which we, to a large extent, misrepresented almost everything they said and did,—and in the stupid and unreasoning sympathy we showed for the Southern rebels; who were not only traitors to a Government whose worst crime was that it had been too friendly to their "Peculiar Institution," but they were also guilty of the greatest crime that ever stained the character of any party—namely, the desire to overthrow all representative and constitutional Government, to subvert a free press, a free platform, a free pulpit, and a free school, and establish on the ruins of these glorious institutions, the most inhuman and accursed system that was ever set up in opposition to the will of God, and the true interests of man.

The result, had they succeeded, would have been neither more nor less than the entire degradation of that middle and trading class that in every country, has always been the best defenders of liberty and the truest advocates of justice.

There are, no doubt, many great problems yet to be solved before the political and social relations of the coloured race will be fully and finally settled in the States, and placed on a satisfactory basis; but I have faith in the good sense, the patriotism, and the religious character of the American people. I believe they are resolved to settle at once and for ever this great question of the relation of the two races; and that in doing so they will prove the possibility, and the advantage of doing justice to a weak and dependant race, and show to all the world that in this, as in everything else—"Honesty is the best and soundest policy."

I also beg to congratulate the American people, and in fact the friends of humanity and freedom on both sides of the Atlantic, on the evident failure of President Johnson in his unwise attempt to bully the American people into the admission of the Southern States to the Union without some satisfactory and constitutional guarantee as to the relation in which the coloured race are to stand for the future. It is for the interest of North and South that this relation should now be definitely and clearly understood—so that the Stars and Stripes shall hereafter equally protect the men of all races and colours.

To our disgrace be it spoken, that when we abolished slavery in the West Indies, we left an Anti-slavery policy to be worked out by the Pro-slavery party:—and hence we now hear of the "failure of emancipation," and have lately had to blush for our country through the atrocities permitted by that weak and worthless representative of the British Government in Jamaica—Governor Eyre —who has, however, fortunately been recalled and disgraced, and who will I hope, like Jefferson Davis, be shortly placed at the bar of his country,—tried—and then condemned to perpetual banishment.

For these reasons, I hail with pleasure, every book that will tend to beget in England and America a sense of the obligations under which we lie, and the duty we owe to the coloured race, and that will also tend to beget kindly feeling between the two countries.

I believe the following work from the pen of Mr. Mathews, whom I have long known and highly esteemed, will help to promote both these results, and I therefore venture most cordially to recommend it to the attentive perusal of every lover of liberty and right on both sides of the Atlantic.

HANDEL COSSHAM.

Hill House, near Bristol,
October 11th, 1866.

CONTENTS.

THE PRESIDENTS.

COMPARISONS AND CONTRASTS.

FROM THE "AMERICAN BAPTIST," NEW YORK, U. S. A., MAY 1, 1866.

WE have received the first sheets of an Autobiography of Brother Edward Mathews, the original Father Dickson of 'Dred.' It will be a very interesting work. The first chapter discusses the American Constitution; compares Washington and Jefferson; the Adamses, father and son; Madison and Monroe; and traces the aggressions of the slave-party and the motives of their course, with that clear and close discrimination which characterises every thing that proceeds from Brother Mathews's pen.

FROM THE "AMERICAN BAPTIST," AUGUST 21, 1866.

We have received the closing sheets of this memoir, ending with page 444. The work has been constantly growing in interest since the first chapters. The whole is admirably written and shows a perfect insight into the characters and policy of the men who precipitated us into our civil war. We copy on our first page an extract from one of the early chapters. Brother Mathews intends to print an edition for this country, and it will probably be published under the auspices of the Free Mission Society. We are sure that all Free Missionists will want the work, especially those who with him bore the burden and heat of the day, when to be an abolitionist was to be a social outcast. Brother Mathews thus sharply draws the distinction between Lincoln and Andrew Johnson. "Lincoln tried by every means that his sense of duty permitted to save the country from war; Johnson has pursued a course calculated to awaken the war feeling. Lincoln was anxious to do his duty; Johnson is anxious to stand well with the ruling classes of the south. Lincoln had right impulses but in shaping his policy yielded to his cabinet. Johnson has southern impulses, which direct his policy and that of his cabinet. Lincoln's great difficulty was slavery; Johnson's great difficulty is equal rights for all."

We shall be happy to receive subscriptions for the work, and will, as soon as practicable state the price at which it can be furnished.

FROM THE "ANTI-SLAVERY REPORTER,"

—*October* 1, 1856.

THE ORGAN OF THE BRITISH AND FOREIGN ANTI-SLAVERY SOCIETY.

"In her delineations of the ministerial body, Mrs. Stowe has produced pictures which will be easily recognized. The temporizing do-nothing policy of the Northern divines, and the open criminality of those of the South, in their participation and advocacy of the peculiar institution are properly and unsparingly laid bare. In Father Dickson we have an abolitionist minister-martyr. Unfortunately, the vile deeds of Tom Gordon and his reckless drunken associates, find frequent parallels in the States. The Rev. E. Mathews, now in England, and whose case is recorded in the *Key to Uncle Tom's Cabin* can bear personal testimony to the unsparing severity of Lynch-law in Kentucky. We presume, from this reference to his case, that he stands for the original of Father Dickson."

INTRODUCTORY CHAPTER.

The American constitution—principles—compromises. The Presidents from 1789 to 1828. Washington and Jefferson com-- pared—their official acts pro-slavery and anti-slavery—su-premacy of slavery—their anti-slavery sympathies—retribution follows slavery. The two Adams', father and son, compared— their official acts pro-slavery and anti-slavery—payment claimed of England for refugee slaves at the close of each war—anti. slavery influence of both father and son—aid of the latter to the anti-slavery reformers.—supremacy of slavery. Madison and Monroe compared—the slave-party dictates the embargo and non-intercourse acts—the war with England—and the Missouri compromise—anti-slavery sympathies of each Presi-dent—supremacy of slavery.

AMERICAN institutions and their influence in forming the American character, have recently become pro-minent subjects of thought and discussion in England. This is owing, in great part, to the American war. Before the commencement of the war a discussion had been carried on between the slaveholders and the abolitionists for a period of thirty years. This con-flict of principles preceded the conflict of armies; and a knowledge of the principles involved in the dis-cussion is not only essential to an understanding of the origin of the war; but also to a correct appre-ciation of the influence of American institutions in forming the American national character.

To impart information on so interesting and practical an inquiry I enter upon this work, premising that I resided for nineteen years in the United States; advocated publicly emancipation for eleven years; and learned by experience the tender mercies of Lynch-law as dispensed by the slave-party in Kentucky.

I became a resident in the United States during the presidency of Andrew Jackson. In my labours as an anti-slavery advocate I found, in common with all my co-workers, that the pro-slavery policy of the American Presidents had placed formidable obstacles in the way of emancipation. The policy was founded in the compromises of the constitution; and the Anti-slavery struggle can only be fully understood by a clear view of this policy and these compromises. I propose, therefore, to explain the one and to describe the other in this introductory chapter.

Among the slaveholders who were members of the Convention that framed the constitution of the United States in 1787, were some who regarded Slavery as the highest question, if not the highest good; and, unhappily, they obtained from that Convention four concessions in favour of slavery. This was the greatest victory they achieved, being the groundwork of all the rest. These concessions, usually termed the compromises of the constitution, were the following:—first, that slaves escaping from one state to another should be returned to their masters; second, that in the representative population every five slaves should be counted as three free white people, though no slave was to vote; third, that if the slaves rose to obtain their liberty the military forces of the United States were to be engaged in subjugating them; and fourth, that the slave-trade between Africa and America was not to be suppressed for twenty years. So that, although the constitution of the United States was established to secure justice and the blessings of liberty, these being its professed principles, they were ignored by the compromises just recorded, and, as the result—four millions of persons groaned in chattel-slavery under a constitution framed to secure justice and the blessings of liberty.

In proceeding to trace the influence of the compromises on the policy of the Presidents the following table will be useful for reference :—

George Washington was President from 1789 to 1797
John Adams   ,,   ,,   ,, 1797 to 1801
Thomas Jefferson   ,,   ,,   ,, 1801 to 1809
James Madison   ,,   ,,   ,, 1809 to 1817
James Monroe   ,,   ,,   ,, 1817 to 1825
John Quincy Adams ,,   ,,   ,, 1825 to 1829
Andrew Jackson   ,,   ,,   ,, 1829 to 1837
Martin Van Buren   ,,   ,,   ,, 1837 to 1841
William Henry Harrison }
John Tyler   } ,,   ,, 1841 to 1845
James K. Polk   ,,   ,,   ,, 1845 to 1849
Zachary Taylor   ,,   ,, 1849 to July 9, 1850
Millard Fillmore   ,,   ,, July 9, 1850 to 1853
Franklin Pierce   ,,   ,, 1853 to 1857
James Buchanan   ,,   ,,   ,, 1857 to 1861
Abraham Lincoln   ,,   ,,   ,, 1861 to 1865
Andrew Johnson   ,,   ,,   ,, 1865 to

Respecting the Presidents, their policy may, perhaps, be best shown by comparisons and contrasts, of Washington with Jefferson; John Adams with John Quincy Adams; Madison with Monroe; and so of the other Presidents to Andrew Johnson. Commencing with GEORGE WASHINGTON and THOMAS JEFFERSON—both of these sanctioned the extension of slavery to the territories of the United States, or the unsettled land—the common property of all the states, which was held in trust by the Federal government. Washington admitted to the Union the slave-states of Kentucky and Tennessee, and the free state of Vermont; Jefferson admitted to the Union the free state of Ohio, but no slave state, because none applied.

Washington signed the law establishing slavery in the District of Columbia, which made the city of Washington the chief slave-mart of the United States; he signed the law which excluded from citizenship coloured foreigners; and the law which excluded coloured citizens from training in the militia.

The latter precedent, probably, induced President Lincoln to refuse the aid of 100,000 coloured men for the army during the former part of the civil war.

Washington made no effort to exclude slavery from the territories; Jefferson proposed a law to exclude slavery from almost the whole of them—which eventually resulted in making five free states northwest of the Ohio river.

Washington as a member of the Virginia legislature made no effort to abolish slavery in that state; Jefferson, when a member of that body, proposed such a law, but it was rejected by the Virginia legislature. In the messages of Washington to Congress, the only reference to slavery is a complaint against the British government for not paying for the slaves, who by taking refuge under her flag in the war of 1776, obtained their liberty. In the messages of Jefferson to Congress, the only reference to slavery is a congratulation that the time had arrived when the compromises of the constitution no longer prevented a law from being passed to suppress the slave-trade between Africa and America.

A law was passed during Washington's administration prohibiting Americans from conveying slaves from one foreign port to another; but a better law for the same object was enacted during Jefferson's administration. Under Washington the home or inter-state slave-trade was practised but not legalized; under Jefferson it was both practised and legalized. Under the former the African slave-trade was continued; under the latter it was prohibited; and preceding its prohibition a law was signed by Jefferson forbidding the carrying of African slaves to any one of the United States that had, by its laws, prohibited their introduction. Washington signed a fugitive slave law in 1793, which was the parent of the fugitive slave law of 1850; and in its chief characteristics equally infamous with its offspring. Washington made an unsuccessful attempt to regain one of his escaping slaves—a woman. Jefferson, though making no effort to repeal the fugitive slave law, approved of the flight of some of his slaves. Washington, however, did not stand in the twofold relation of master and father to any of his slaves. Jefferson sustained this two-fold relation and one of his own slave daughters was publicly sold in New Orleans.

Washington by his will emancipated his slaves. It is a disputed point whether Jefferson did so. Washington was not susceptible of French influence; Jefferson, through his sceptical views, was greatly so, and hence signed the embargo law. This gratified the slave-party because it destroyed New England's commerce; and gratified Bonaparte because it injured Old England's interests, and thus led to the second war between England and America in 1812. Washington subdued an insurrection led by Shau, arising from the tax on whisky; Jefferson prevented the success of a formidable conspiracy to invade Mexico, extend slavery, and break up the Union, organized by Aaron Burr. (This conspiracy repeated itself in the acquisition of Texas, and was successful in extending slavery. It thenceforth secretly gathered force and in 1860 displayed its power in the secession and the Southern Confederacy.)

In the Congress of 1774, Washington gave a pledge, as did every other member, to promote the abolition of the African slave-trade. In the Congress of 1776, in the Declaration of Independence, Jefferson proposed to commit the Revolutionary movement not only to a separation from England, but also to the abolition of the slave-trade and slavery. A paragraph to this effect in the Declaration of Independence was stricken out by the slave-party. Washington purchased for the government no slave territory; Jefferson purchased of Bonaparte the

Louisiana Territory of which were formed three slave states ; thus paving the way for the annexation of Texas, and the war with Mexico. His object, probably, was to benefit the nation by the acquisition of the land—not to strengthen the slave system. Had Washington resisted the slave party he would possibly have lost South Carolina and Georgia—but would have made an anti-slavery nation. In making the attempt he would have had fewer difficulties than Jefferson, had he tried to do so. The slave victims were not so numerous; the slave party not so well organized ; while the anti-slavery sentiment was stronger and more general than when Jefferson came into power; Jefferson, therefore, would have had to contend with a slave-party made vigorous by the continued concessions of his two predecessors, Washington and Adams.

Washington, as the first President, strengthened the slave-party by the pro-slavery precedents he established; and which were followed by each succeeding President to the time of Lincoln. Jefferson strengthened the slave-party by the land he acquired and the democratic party he organized and led. (The federalists desired a strong central government and feared lest too much power should be held by the government of each state ; the democrats desired that each state should have a strong government and feared lest too much power should be held by the federal government.) The sanction given by Washington to slavery told more against the anti-slavery reform than that given by Jefferson ; because he was held in such estimation for his abilities as a general, his dignity as a statesman, and his wisdom as a ruler. Many an audience in America has been infuriated against an anti-slavery lecturer who denounced slave-holding as man-stealing by the response, by a pro-slavery man " Washington was a slaveholder !" and the inquiry "Will you libel Washington?"

Comparing them in private life—both had anti-slavery sympathies. The correspondence of Washington shows his desire for the abolition of slavery ; his resolution not to purchase another slave ; his regret that petitions for the abolition of slavery were not more favourably received by Congress ; and his belief in the final success of the movement for the emancipation of the slaves. The writings of Jefferson show how clearly he understood and defined the rights of man ; how intelligently he discerned the evils of slavery ; how strongly he denounced those evils ; and how emphatically he warned both statesmen and people against them. Yet both yielded to the demands of the slave-party, Washington from his devotion to the Union, and Jefferson from his devotion to his party. Washington with his hundred slaves aimed to have a model plantation. Having done much to see his high purpose accomplished he died in 1799, emancipating his slaves by his will. His plantation, however, affords a melancholy and remarkable instance of the ceaseless vigilance aud unerring certainty of Providence in pursuing, overtaking, and punishing injustice. His nephew, Judge Bushrod Washington, succeeded to the estate, which he re-stocked with his large family of slaves; yet though receiving a salary of four thousand five hundred dollars, as Judge for life, from the Federal government, in 1819, pleading necessity, he sold from thirty to fifty of his slaves, being about one half. In 1828 he died, and his nephew, Colonel John A. Washington succeeded to the estate. He died in 1840, and in 1842 his widow and her children were through poverty driven out from the estate. A son of Colonel Washington being an officer in the Confederate army, was killed by a Federal sharp-shooter. He was walking out, supposing himself to be beyond the reach of the rifle of the Federal soldiers. But he was discerned by a telescope to wear the uniform of a confederate, and hence was fired at; and though the distance was very great, the shot was fatal.

Jefferson sold his large library from necessity, and contemplated, for the same reason, selling his estate at Monticello, when he also died. Could Washington and Jefferson have foreseen the Confederacy and the war, would they not at every sacrifice have resisted the slave-party! O slavery! the greatest of thy victories is not over the slave, as he writhes on the plantation, under the whip of the overseer; but over statesmen possessing some of the highest gifts for their position—yet bowing to the imperious will of the slave-party and making such laws as I have described.

JOHN ADAMS AND JOHN QUINCY ADAMS.

It is remarkable that John Adams, the only one of the first five Presidents of the United States who had a son, should have lived to see his eldest son, John Quincy Adams, elected to the Presidency of the United States. Both father and son were natives of Massachusetts; and were non-slaveholders. The father supported the war with England in 1776; the son supported the act of non-intercourse with England in 1809, which led to the war of 1812. The father in his effort, was governed by his regard for human rights; the son in his effort, by his deference to the President, Mr. Madison—a slaveholder. The father, with the gallows looming in the distance, attempted to form a great nation ; the son, with the Presidential chair looming in the distance, gave a vote that offended the free state of Massachusetts, for which he was senator. The father gave his reasons for his course in the Declaration of Independence ; the son gave no reason except this—" The President has recommended it—I would not deliberate, I would act." The honours of the Federal government were higher than those which any State could bestow, and they were at the disposal of slaveholders. Though John Quincy Adams offended his constituents and resigned his seat, he was soon after named by the President, minister to Russia, and was almost constantly in federal service till having been made Secretary of state by Mr. Monroe, a slaveholder, equivalent to nominating him as his successor—he came into the Presidency in 1825. After this the most gifted sons of the free states, who began their life, like Daniel Webster with anti-slavery promise, yielded to the influence of the slave-party, and had their reward in high federal offices.

The father, John Adams, was one of a commission to conclude a treaty of peace at the close of the first

war with England; the son was one of a commission
to conclude a treaty of peace at the close of the
second war with England.   In each treaty the stipu-
lation was the same, in reference to the carrying
away of refugee slaves.   Under the first treaty England was asked to pay for the slaves who, having
taken refuge under the British flag, had been carried
away by the British forces; but no payment was
obtained; the reply being that the slaves were free
and did not belong to anybody.   Under the second
treaty payment was similarly asked for slaves carried
away under similar circumstances; and after a persevering negociation—conducted at Washington, in
the Chesapeake Bay, at Bermuda, in London, and at
Petersburg, in Russia, during twelve years—the
British government paid the full market value for
the freed-men.

In the messages of John Adams to Congress, no
reference is made either to slavery or the slave-
trade.   In the messages of John Quincy Adams to
Congress, three references are made to the African
slave trade, strongly condemning it; and two references are made to the slaves who sought refuge under
the British flag; but none to those still held in
bondage.   The first reference states that the prospects of success in obtaining payment for them are
exceedingly dubious; the second reference is all
joyous and sounds the praises of England for its
honor and magnanimity in handing over the price
of the slaves.   The father sanctioned slavery in the
territories; the son offered to Mexico a million of
dollars for Texas, when slavery existed in that state.

Under the rule of the father the African slave-trade, not being unlawful, was carried on; under the rule of the son, it was carried on, though unlawful. The father did not attempt to prevent the abolition of slavery in Cuba; the son did attempt it —and held in check both Colombia and Mexico, powers favouring its abolition in that island. The father discouraged no foreign nation in its efforts to abolish the African slave-trade; but the son did so. The delegates of the South American Republics who were about to meet in Congress at Panama, proposed to attack the African slave-trade; but John Quincy Adams sent them an intimation that they must do nothing of the kind. The father made no effort to obtain from Canada the slaves that had escaped; the son did,—but England refused to give them up. The father made no attempt to obtain from Mexico the slaves that had escaped; the son did,—but Mexico refused to surrender them. The father signed a law prohibiting Americans from carrying slaves from one foreign port to another; the son severely condemned Americans, who, in violation of law, continued the African slave-trade. The father was Vice-President for eight years under the Presidency of Washington, a slaveholder; the son was Secretary of State for eight years, under the Presidency of Monroe, a slaveholder. The father approved of the pro-slavery laws of Washington; the son, those of Monroe. When the father was President, Jefferson, a slaveholder, was Vice-President; when the son was President, John C. Calhoun, a slaveholder, was Vice-President. In the election of the father two slaveholders, Jefferson and Pinkney, competed with him. In the election of the son, three slaveholders, Jackson, Crawford, and Clay competed with him. The father after being President four years—one term—was succeeded by a slaveholder, who was twice elected. The son, after being President one term, was succeeded also by a slaveholder, who was twice elected. No state applied for admission into the Union during the Presidency either of the father or son. To the father, before he became President, is Massachusetts chiefly indebted for its constitution, which gave liberty to its slaves; to the son, after his Presidency, are the United States chiefly indebted for the right of petition, which the slave-party attempted to destroy. The father, after being President, was not elected to Congress; the son was, and became the real, but not the recognised leader of the Anti-slavery party; as he did not advocate immediate emancipation. He secured the right of petition for that party. It was essential to their progress. The father was not threatened with assassination by slaveholders; the son was. The slave-party made no attempt to expel the father from a deliberative body, but they attempted to expel the son from Congress and failed. The father expressed no opinion as to the power of the Federal government over slavery; the son declared in Congress that in time of war, that body could set free all the slaves. His speech on this subject was not sent to the press by any one of the reporters, but John Quincy Adams wrote it out HIMSELF, it was published, and was a guide to Mr. Lincoln, and led him to emancipate the slaves. The father though making no proposal for the abolition of slavery, said :— "I have through my whole life, held the practice of slavery in such abhorrence, that I have never owned a negro or any other slave, though I have lived for many years in times when the practice was not disgraceful—when the best men in my vicinity thought it not inconsistent with their character; and when it has cost me thousands of dollars for the labour and subsistence of free men, which I might have saved by the purchase of negroes, at times when they were very cheap." The son proposed a plan for the prospective abolition of slavery, through an amendment of the constitution. His proposal at the time received no favour either at the north or the south, but recently that very mode has been adopted, and by it slavery prohibited in every state in the Union. In speaking of the influence of the slave power, John Quincy Adams said it entered into and pervaded all the acts of the Federal government. He opposed the annexation of Texas, and the war with Mexico; and his efforts, in resisting the slave-party, inspired with fresh courage and warmer zeal all in America who were labouring for emancipation.

His son, Mr. Adams, is now the ambassador from the United States to England.

JAMES MADISON AND JAMES MONROE.

Both Madison and Monroe were natives of Virginia, were slaveholders, had some degree of Anti-slavery sympathy, but yielded to the slave-party. Madison was sincerely opposed to the African slave-trade, and in the Convention that framed the Federal Con-

stitution he endeavoured, unsuccessfully, to obtain
its suppression without a delay of twenty years.
Monroe was professedly opposed to that traffic, but
his correspondence, while President, with the British
government, shows no such desire, but instead of
it, a persevering and settled duplicity. It sufficiently
explains this policy to observe that John C. Calhoun,
the high priest of chattel-slavery, was a member of
his Cabinet. During his Administration, the captain
of a ship engaged in the slave-trade was sentenced to
death, but Monroe pardoned him. When the constitution was framed, Madison was determined that
no words in it should sanction the idea that man
could be the property of man ; and he succeeded in
his purpose. When Monroe was a member of the
Virginia Convention, he said of slavery, " We have
found that this evil has preyed upon the very vitals
of the Union, and has been prejudicial to all the
states in which it has existed."   Madison was a timid
man, but he was forced into a declaration of war with
England in 1812, by the slave-party, under the leader-
ship of John C. Calhoun; who claimed the paternity
of the measure, and drove it furiously through both
Houses of Congress. When Mr. Madison was a
candidate for re-election to the Presidency, several
members of the democratic party, including John C.
Calhoun and Henry Clay, both slaveholders, waited
on him and informed him that " War with England
was now resolved upon by the democratic party, that
unless a declaration of war took place previous to the
presidential election, the success of the democratic
party might be endangered, and the government

thrown into the hands of the federalists; that unless
Mr. Madison consented to act with his friends, and
accede to a declaration of war with Great Britain,
neither his nomination nor his re-election could be
relied on.   Thus situated, Mr. Madison concluded to
waive his own objections to the course determined on
by his political friends, and to do all he could for the
promotion of a war for which he had no taste; and
he pretended to no knowledge of war as a profession."
The above extract I copy from the " American Statesman's Manual."

Monroe in a similar way yielded to his party,
and extended slavery to Missouri, conscious that it
was an " evil preying upon the vitals of the Union."
When the war with England, of 1812, was raging in
all its fury, commissioners were appointed to make
peace.   The only condition on which they were to
insist was that Great Britain should send back the
slaves who had sought the protection of her flag.
Peace was made, the slaves were not returned, and
payment for them was demanded.   It was not made
to Madison or Monroe, but his successor John Quincy
Adams, received the large sum of one million two
hundred and four thousand dollars; the full market
value of each slave was paid; and there being a
surplus, it was divided among the slave claimants.

So ended the slaveholder's war.   It inflicted a
measure of suffering on Old England; but, as
designed by the slave-party, a much greater amount
of suffering on the free states of New England.   The
war lasted nearly three years, and cost the republic
thirty millions of dollars per annum, which was chiefly

paid by the free states—the price of their disgrace
as well as of their subjugation. Senator Benton of
Missouri, says of this compensation for slaves,
"that the example and the principle were the main
points, and the enforcement of such a demand against
a government so powerful, and after so much resistance." He also predicted that no other government
would make the liberation of American slaves a mode
of warfare. He was mistaken. His own son-in-law,
General Fremont, declared as a war measure, in
Missouri, that the slaves of rebels were freemen: a
declaration that was eventually re-echoed by President
Lincoln; and had not Senator Benton been a Unionist,
his own slaves would have been emancipated by this
very mode.

Madison admitted Louisiana, a slave state, into
the Union, but no free state; Monroe admitted three
slave states, Missouri, Mississippi, and Alabama, into
the Union, and the free states of Illinois and Maine.
By the war with England, Madison offended the free
states, hence a Convention was summoned at Hartford,
with a view to the formation of a Northern party.
By the admission of Missouri into the Union as a
slave state, Monroe offended the free states, and
aroused some spirits to anti-slavery action who never
rested till slavery was abolished. Under Madison,
General Jackson was sent into Florida, then belonging to Spain, to break up a fort which was a refuge
for escaping slaves. By order of Commodore Pattison,
a gun-boat fired red-hot shot upon the fort, the
magazine exploded, and nearly 300 Indians and
negroes, men, women, and children, were killed or

mortally wounded. Under Monroe, Florida was purchased for five millions of dollars. The reasons were,
that the President was harassed with numerous letters
from Georgia slaveholders, declaring that their slaves
were escaping continually into Florida, and finding
an asylum there, and if the province was not secured
by treaty, the Georgians would take it by force.

Madison signed a law prohibiting any coloured
person from being employed either as a post-rider or
driver of a carriage carrying the mail. Monroe
signed a law authorizing the white citizens of the
city of Washington to elect white officers, and prescribe the terms on which any free negroes and
mulattoes might reside in the city. The terms were
prescribed, and among other iniquitous regulations,
coloured people were required to register themselves
or be imprisoned, and any one who could not prove
his freedom was to be sold as a slave to pay his jail
fees. In 1816, a law was passed for a high tariff.
It was forced upon the reluctant north by the same
John C. Calhoun who had dictated the war of 1812.
Northern capitalists demurred, they desired no
capricious change. But the north was over-ruled,
Calhoun again triumphed. Yet, he tried at a later
period to take South Carolina out of the Union on
account of the tariff.

In his messages to Congress, Madison complains
of American citizens who carried on the foreign slave-
trade in violation of the law, and asks for measures
for its suppression; he complains also of abuses connected with the home slave-trade, and asks for
measures to regulate it.

In his messages to Congress, Monroe complains that one of the islands of Florida, then belonging to Spain, was used for the illicit introduction of African slaves to the United States; and also was an asylum for refugee slaves. He complains that absconding slaves had found an asylum at Pensacola and St. Augustine in Florida, and states that the Federal government and Great Britain had referred the question of payment for war-emancipated slaves to the umpirage of the Emperor of Russia. Twice he announces that effectual measures had been taken to suppress the African slave-trade; he also observes that he believes no Americans are engaged in the traffic; and finally, he expresses his regret that no plan of joint co-operation had been arranged with England for its suppression. Meantime, however, President Monroe refused to allow to England the right of searching suspected slavers—a right which England was prepared to concede if it could be reciprocated.

Madison was willing that the civilized Indians should remain on the land they possessed; but Monroe's policy was to send them west of the Mississippi. White slaveholders entered on the lands of those who were removed, and the number of slaves was increased. The Indians also thus removed to the west were several of them slaveholders. So that their emigration increased the extent of slave territory and the sway of slave-law. Both Madison and Monroe died leaving their slaves in bondage.

CHAPTER II.

President Jackson and the Anti-slavery Struggle. My Birth and Parentage—Father Mathew, a kinsman—Family history—a Sunday Scholar—a Baptist—a Preacher. Voyage to New York—Contempt of colour—a Scene on Board—New York—Sunday School Teaching—White and Black Scholars—Rev. Dr. Cone and the Burning of Richmond Theatre—Gift of a Scholarship—Journey to Hamilton—Rev. E. Kingsford—An Anti-Abolition Sermon — Hamilton — The Students — Anti-slavery Agitation—View of its Origin—Pioneers—Benjamin Lundy—William Lloyd Garrison—Rev. George Bourne—Rev. John Rankin — Formation of American Anti-slavery Society — its Peace Principles—Visit of George Thompson to the United States.

As PRESIDENT, Andrew Jackson succeeded John Quincy Adams. His predecessors seem to have yielded reluctantly to the demands of the slave-party; but Jackson inspired its zeal, marshalled its forces, and led them to attack the dearest rights of the citizens. To resist him, organizations were needed, with members possessing talent, zeal, knowledge, strong faith, and a self-sacrificing spirit. The slave-party was a despotism—Washington was its centre—but its ramifications extended to every hamlet in the free, as well as the slave states. Then were formed the American Anti-slavery, and kindred Societies. The hour came and the men. There was a remedy for the evil. These organizations resolved to agitate till the rights of the coloured population were secured, equally with those of the white. The reign of terror existing in the slave states was extended by Jackson to the free states. So commenced the struggle between the slave-party and the anti-slavery party. At this period I went to America unconscious of the struggle, or of the part which in the future I should take in it. I will now trace my history from my birth to this period.

My grandfather, William Mathews, was a native of Leckwith, near Cardiff. When about twenty-one years of age, becoming dissatisfied with country life and its pursuits, he endeavoured to find more congenial scope for his energies in a city, thereby incurring the lasting displeasure of his father, who, in common with the landed gentry of that day, heartily despised city life and trade. Undeterred by threats of disinheritance, in 1770 he apprenticed himself to a printer; and shortly after the period of becoming free, entered into business, adding an s to his name of Mathew, and commenced the publication of the "Bristol and Clifton Directory," which has been continued annually by his sons and grandsons till the present time. I may here mention that he was of the same family as the much honoured Father Mathew, their great grandsires, William and George Mathew being brothers. William continued to reside on the estates at Rhadyr, while George went to Ireland soon after the Restoration, where he held positions of trust and honour, founding the Irish branch of the family, one of whom was created Earl of

Llandaff, (an ancient and once an important city, near Cardiff), in 1798, and died at Swansea in 1806; the funeral cortege was accompanied to the ship by Anthony Mathew, of Leckwith, and my grandfather, as chief mourners, the corpse being forwarded to Ireland for interment. The following characteristic letter from Father Mathew to my late lamented cousin, Edward Hazard Mathews, of Bristol, will be read with interest :—

" Cork, July 9, 1849.

" My dear Friend,

" Your very kind letter has afforded me much gratification, and I feel proud of being able to claim a relationship with one to whom I am so deeply indebted. As yet I am unable to say when I shall leave Ireland, but my first visit to Bristol will be to your family.

" The present state of the country renders my presence absolutely necessary. Our teetotallers are exposed to many temptations.

" With most respectful compliments to your parents and grateful acknowledgement of your unvarying kindness.

I am, dear Mr. Mathews,
Your affectionate kinsman,
THEOBALD MATHEW."

My father, William Mathews, was the eldest of four sons, he was married at Clifton Old Church, Bristol, and afterwards settled at Oxford. In the *Oxford Chronicle* a brief notice of his life and labours appeared with his obituary, as follows :—

"Jan. 28th, at Oriel street in this city, aged 85, Mr. William Mathews, engraver, and on the same day at Cardiff, aged 79, Catherine, wife of Mr. Matthew Mathews, brother of the above.

"Our obituary contains the announcement of the death of a well-known townsman, Mr. William Mathews, the engraver. Between fifty and sixty years since, he matriculated on his removal to Oxford, having been recommended to the managers of the Clarendon Printing House by Lord Stanhope, and he was for many years engaged in connection with the old foundry in perfecting the stereotype plates, the art then being newly discovered. Mr. Mathews was subsequently instructed to go to Cambridge University, to teach there the plan he had adopted with so much success here. He afterwards commenced business in his own profession. When a student at Somerset House, Fuseli took particular notice of him, as his drawings from the antique were remarkable for correctness of outline and character. In later years he published outline engravings from the figures in the Radcliffe Library. He also engraved 'The Schools of Athens,' now in the University Galleries; and (by permission of the Duke of Marlborough), the cartoons of the Titian Gallery at Blenheim. He had an extensive knowledge of the different schools of painting, and had some ability in modelling, and a piece of his sculpture may be seen in front of a house near Folly Bridge, or it was there some time since. He was as remarkable for perseverance and industry, as for his love for everything that related to the fine

C

arts. His early ivory miniatures were painted with great delicacy and care. In after life he preferred oil painting. He understood something of anatomy, and attended courses of lectures on that subject, making a great many coloured drawings from nature for his fellow-students. Bewick, the father of modern wood engraving, made the drawing of his card (an illustration of Sterne's 'Maria,') for him, when he turned his attention to that art. Before leaving his native city (Bristol) his kindly feelings were enlisted on behalf of the sufferers from the ravages of the small-pox, and he was an active member and secretary of the Vaccination Society, was well acquainted with Dr. Jenner, for whom he made many coloured drawings of the various stages of the cow-pox; and after a round among the colliers of Kingswood, to induce them to have their children vaccinated, would return disfigured with mud, and hardly escaping rough usage. He informed the writer some years since that he was the means of getting between four and five hundred to be vaccinated. From a cast of his head taken by Papari, Dr. Spencer Hall on one occasion read off his character, and the Doctor's description agreed most remarkably with what were known to be the tastes and social bias of Mr. Mathews. *Feb.* 3, 1866."

The sixth of a family of seven sons and three daughters, I was born at Oxford, March 12th, 1812. At ten years of age I became a member of the Sunday School at St. Ebbe's Church, and of the class taught by the Rev. W. Hodgson, then a student at Queen's College, now the Perpetual Curate of St Peter's, Cheltenham. By committing to memory a chapter

in the New Testament weekly, I learned the four
Gospels, the Acts, the Epistle to the Romans, and
some other portions of scripture. This has been an
invaluable advantage to me as a minister and missionary. I regard Mr. Hodgson as having been the
means of leading me into the way of peace; and he
gave me as a parting gift "Doddridge's Rise and
Progress of Religion in the Soul."

When eighteen years of age, I was baptized by
the Rev. James Smith, of Cheltenham; and united
with the Baptist Church at Eynsham, of which my
brother, Rev. Henry Mathews, has been for many
years the pastor. Afterwards I supplied regularly
the pulpit of a chapel at Chalgrove, near Oxford.
At the completion of my apprenticeship, I took
passage in the ship President for New York. Mr.
Freeman, a relative and a Wesleyan local preacher,
saying as the ship moved from the shore, "Do all
you can for the poor blacks!" An occurrence on
ship-board, a few days before we reached New York,
illustrated the American contempt of coloured people.
The crew were Americans, and the sailors, who were
white, had heard that the cook, who was coloured,
had threatened to put poison in their food. Taking
the law into their own hands, they hastened to the
caboose to wreak their vengeance upon him; but he
seized a ladle, and by a free use of scalding water
kept them at bay. Turning from him they happened
to meet the steward, an intelligent and gentlemanly
mulatto. Instantly they felled him to the deck, and
commenced beating him, when Captain Moore rushed
to the rescue and saved him. He went to the cabin

pale, feeble, injured, and bleeding, and I understood
went to the hospital on reaching New York. The
passengers conversed upon this; and one who had
been to Virginia said—that to kill a coloured person
for an insult offered by him was quite allowable in
Virginia.

On reaching New York, I was struck with the
pale complexion of the people. Having obtained a
situation as clerk, and united with the Oliver Street
Baptist Church, of which the Rev. Dr. Cone was pastor,
I became a teacher in the Sunday School. The white
and coloured children were separated. The former
were taught in a fine attractive room; the latter in
one gloomy and dark. The coloured people were not
allowed to sit with the whites in the chapel; not even
when the Lord's Supper was administered. This rule
was followed with but few exceptions in all the places
of worship throughout the states; but—as I shall have
occasion to show—it was more marked and odious in
the slave states.

The early religious impressions of Dr. Cone had
been received in the slave states. When a young
man he was an actor on the stage. In 1811, there
was to be a performance on the evening of the day
after Christmas Day. His mind, however, was under
religious conviction, and he obtained permission of
absence that evening. There was a large attendance,
and during the performance the theatre caught fire,
and between sixty and one hundred persons were
burnt up in the conflagration. Amongst these were
the governor of the state, George W. Smith, Mr.

Venables, the President of the Virginia Bank, Mr.
Bott, who was counsel for Aaron Burr, at his trial,
and many others both young and aged.

My business engagements afforded me but little
opportunity to gain information respecting the great
struggle that was going on in reference to slavery.
I found that there was much excitement in the city,
which, at a later period, I fully understood. Occasionally, I preached for Dr. Cone and other ministers.
There was a scholarship at Hamilton Literary and
Theological Institution in the gift of the Baptist
ministers in the city; and as I desired to study for
the ministry, they kindly placed me upon it. Thus
after spending about two years in New York, I set
out for the Institution, in the western part of the
state, by way of Albany.

Reaching Utica on Saturday night, I remained
over the Sunday, and attended worship at the Baptist
Chapel. The pastor was the Rev. Edward Kingsford,
an Englishman. Afterwards he became pastor of the
Baptist Church at Harrisburg, Pennsylvania. On
the 8th of February, 1838, he preached a sermon
against the anti-slavery reform, which was published
by request of several of the members of the Senate
and House of Representatives of the Legislature of
Pennsylvania. It was popular because it reflected
the popular feeling. It awakened suspicion against
the abolitionists, and aided to expose them to the
fury of the pro-slavery party, who soon afterwards
raised a mob and violently assaulted them. It will
throw light on those times if I quote the heads of
the sermon.

The text was John xviii. 36. "My kingdom is not of this world." The subject, "The claims of abolition on the Church of God." The ground assumed in the sermon is that "Abolitionism is entirely incompatible with, and entirely subversive of, the great and distinguishing principles of the kingdom of our Lord Jesus Christ. 1. As it respects its constituent elements. 2. In its attitude, like the two-faced god, looking at the same time towards the capitol and the altar. 3. From the spirit which it breathes. 4. The delusive and anti-evangelical form and modes of action in which it operates; this last head was subdivided thus: (1.) The physical bondage of the slave, his helpless and hopeless degradation, the sufferings and wrongs which he is compelled to endure at the hands of his oppressor, with all the incidental and consequential evils of slavery, are urged in justification of the measures which are employed to effect his freedom. (2.) The indiscriminate admission of all characters into the ranks of abolition it is contended may exert a salutary influence upon the profane. By an association with the pious, the ungodly may be led seriously to examine and at length embrace the noble principles which called the godlike enterprise into existence. 5. The denunciation of God's anger against the Jewish nation for their general iniquities, or for specified sins, by the mouth of the prophets, is no warrant for a national appeal against the sin of slavery. 6. The appeals that are made to American citizenship to sustain abolitionism are unscriptural in their character and dangerous in their tendency." Mr.

Kingsford afterwards went south and became a slave-holder; still claiming to be a follower of Him who came "to preach deliverance to the captives." (The people advanced beyond the above teaching long before the battle of Gettysburg, which is a town not far from Harrisburg. A friend from America informs me that when President Lincoln saw the carnage after this battle, he was profoundly impressed. He recognized the war as a retribution for slavery, and resolved to promote its removal so far as he could.)

On Monday, I proceeded to Hamilton by stage-coach. It was a day's journey. Arrived at the village, I observed it was well-laid out. There was a park in the centre, and various churches of different denominations, each with a spire and bell. The Institution consisted of two large, plain, but substantial stone buildings, on the brow of a hill, a mile from the village. The dining hall and steward's house were detached. The Faculty received me kindly. The students were diligent in their studies. They numbered 160. In the morning the first bell rang at half-past four, and punctually at five o'clock Professor Taylor attended with the students at chapel for prayers. There was a good library. The students were from the free, and the slave states. Those from the latter were the sons of slaveholders. As a rule their opportunities for mental culture had been greater than those from the free states, and both time and money were more at their disposal. Several of the New England students turned their hours of relaxation into profit by making the pendulums of clocks, or engaging in some other remunerating work. In the rooms the slavery question was discussed, but not in the debating societies, and the Faculty would not permit an anti-slavery society amongst the students. One had been formed, but the Faculty urged each member to withdraw his name, and two refusing to do so were expelled the Institution. I conversed with the Southern students and referred to the cruelties which some of the runaway slaves stated they had endured. The Southerners contended that no confidence should be placed in the statement of any slave who had left his master. Sometimes they would lose both temper and argument, and say "In the name of God let us alone!"

The agents of the American Anti-slavery Society were calling public attention to the horrors of the slave system. The Rev. Beriah Green, President of Oneida Institute, came to Hamilton to lecture, but the mob drove him from the village. James G. Birney, who had emancipated his slaves, came and was patiently heard. Gerrit Smith came, and by a public discussion rendered valuable aid to the Anti-slavery movement; the rise and progress of which I will briefly describe.

The progress of the slave-power from the time of Washington to Jackson, though very rapid, was scarcely perceived. Faint and few were the rays of light thrown upon it, even in the Free States, by the press, the pulpit, or the platform. In 1820, scarcely a minister in the slave states defended slavery by the Bible. The admission, however, of Missouri into the Union as a slave state greatly increased the political power of the slave-party. Some consider that up to

that period the American nation though fearfully
misled by slaveholders, still held to its liberty creed
—but that by agreeing to the Missouri compromise
it apostatized and took a slavery creed.   One thing is
certain, that at the end of ten years from that compromise, scarcely a minister could be found in the
South who was not a defender of slavery by the
Bible ; and in the next ten years, so had the heresy
spread, that there was scarcely a college in the north
but was an auxiliary to the slave-party.   In the
south the minister who defended slavery found it the
path-way to wealth and honour ; whilst he who
preached against it as a sin was liable to be hanged
by Lynch-law on the nearest tree.   A similar spirit
was diffused throughout the north by means of the
various religious and other connections in which both
the south and the north were united.   The contest,
however, with reference to Missouri partially dis-
turbed the slumbers of the north; and amongst those
who were thoroughly awakened was Benjamin Lundy,
a member of the Society of Friends.   In 1821, he
commenced the publication of a monthly Anti-slavery
paper, the first ever published in America, named
The Genius of Universal Emancipation, and in
the next ten years he sacrificed several thousand
dollars of his own hard earnings, travelled upwards of
five thousand miles on foot, and more than twenty
thousand in other ways, visited nineteen states of the
Union, held more than two hundred public meetings,
made two voyages to the West Indies, by which
means the liberation of a considerable number of
slaves was effected, and the way prepared for the

liberation of many more. He published his paper successively at Philadelphia, at Baltimore, and at Washington city. At one time he traversed the free states, lecturing, collecting, obtaining subscribers, writing for his paper, getting it printed, monthly, wherever he could conveniently have it printed; stopping, himself, to read proofs, to direct and post his papers, then proceeding with his journey another month, conveying in his trunk his direction book, column rules, type heading—with the date of Baltimore, to facilitate the publication. (At that time the periodical press in all the free states was to a great extent, controlled by the slave-party.) All this he did, though small of stature, feeble in health, and afflicted with deafness partly arising from the ill-treatment he had received from Woolfolk, a slave-trader, who had thrown Lundy down on the pavement. "Then," says Lundy, "with a brutal ferocity that is perfectly in character with his business, he choked me until my breath was nearly gone, and stamped me on the head and face with the fury of a demon. One of the blows from his heel was given about the middle of the forehead, with such violence that it stunned me exceedingly; and I am confident that had it not been a glancing stroke, it must inevitably have fractured my scull, if it had not caused immediate death. As soon as I could release his gripe from my throat, and recover my breath, I called for assistance, and he was taken from me. It was with some difficulty I rose to my feet, and my face was literally in a gore of blood." Woolfolk was tried before Judge Brice, who fined him one dollar, and indicated that he wished *The Genius of Universal Emancipation* could be put down.

This was the first case of inflicting brutal violence on an abolitionist. It has been practised ever since, and by a recent paper I see that an anti-slavery missionary has been thrown into a river in Virginia to compel him to leave the state.

In Mr. Lundy were combined the qualifications of several of the early labourers in the anti-slavery cause, belonging to the same religious body. He had the pen of Anthony Benezet, the moral courage of Sandiford, the tenderness of conscience of Woolman, and the benevolence of Lay, without his eccentricity. His humanity and strong faith made his purpose indomitable, and these with his great patience and self-denial qualified him to be a pioneer in the Anti-slavery Reform. It was chiefly to communications from Benjamin Lundy that John Quincy Adams was indebted for those astounding disclosures concerning the Texas plot, with which he so suddenly electrified Congress and the nation in 1836.

In 1828, a copy of *The Genius of Universal Emancipation* fell into the hands of William Lloyd Garrison. The perusal of it brought to his view the great wickedness of the national sin, and he vowed to consecrate his life to the deliverance of his enslaved countrymen. Many who became leaders in the Anti-slavery cause had been led to make a similar vow, but it was known to Him only before whose mercy-seat it was made. Garrison united with Lundy in conducting the *Journal* advocating emancipation. He was, however, fined fifty dollars for condemning the home slave-trade, by a packed jury in Baltimore, and being unable to pay that sum, was imprisoned. The forty-nine days he spent in the cell strengthened his courage, instead of weakening it, as the following lines evince, which he wrote upon the prison-wall :—

" Prisoner ! within these massive walls close pent,
　Guiltless of horrid crime or trivial wrong,
　Bear nobly up against thy punishment,
　And in thy innocence be great and strong !
　Perchance thy fault was love to all mankind ;
　Thou didst resist some vile oppressive law;
　Or strive all human fetters to unbind,
　Or would not bear the implements of war.
　What then ? Dost thou so soon repent the deed ?
　A martyr's crown is richer than a king's !
　Think it an honour with thy Lord to bleed
　And glory 'midst intensest sufferings !
　Though beaten, imprisoned, put to open shame,
　Time shall embalm and magnify thy name "

Arthur Tappan, a merchant of New York, who was active in the Anti-slavery movement, paid the fine. Mr. Garrison was released from prison, and visiting England, checked the progress the pro-slavery party were making under the guise of the Colonization Society. Returning to America, he established the *Liberator*, which was continued until the slaves were emancipated.

The Georgia Legislature offered five thousand dollars for the arrest and conviction of the publishers of the *Liberator*. This offer ought to be removed from its statute book before Georgia again takes its place as a state in the Union.

The Rev. George Bourne was an early labourer in the cause. For seven years he was pastor of a Presbyterian Church in Virginia, and was fiercely persecuted for his faithful testimony against slavery. In "*American Slavery As It Is*," it is stated that Mr. Bourne's book, "*Pictures of Slavery*," is acknowledged to be true by William Handborough, of Culpepper County, Virginia, the owner of sixty slaves. The book was handed him to read by Lindley Coates, a member of the "Society of Friends." After reading it, he said that all the sufferings of the slaves therein related, were true delineations, and that he had seen all those modes of torture himself. In the discussion on slavery at Hamilton, I heard a northern lawyer, who afterwards became a judge, deny the truthfulness of Mr. Bourne's book. To this, however, I will again refer.

Among the early pioneers of the cause should be mentioned the Rev. John Rankin, a Presbyterian minister of Kentucky, now of Ohio. In 1824 or 1825, he published his "Letters on Slavery," maintaining its inherent sinfulness and enforcing the duty of its present abandonment. Through his influence an Anti-slavery Society was formed in Kentucky, at that early period. It was afterwards, however, "laid asleep" by the illusive pretences and seductive influences of the Colonization Society. I learned the following when I was in Kentucky:—Mr. Rankin's house being on a high hill on the Ohio state side of the Ohio river, can be seen from Kentucky. It was often pointed out to the slaves, and they were informed that if they could reach that house on the

D

hill, they would find a friend who would help them forward to Canada. On the Kentucky side of the river there was a boat, and it became known to the slaves that its owner had no objection to their using it to cross the river. Thus several slaves escaped. The slaveholders suspecting Mr. Rankin's aid to them; sent him word that they would cross the river and burn his house. Mr. Rankin is not, as I am, a member of the Peace Society, and he returned them this answer,—that if they attempted to burn his house, he should feel it to be his duty to shoot them.

The slave-party was thwarted in many of its plans by the work of the American Anti-slavery Society. When this Society was formed, no war was thought of except the possible uprising of the slaves, and this—it was pledged never to countenance. It will be seen that the pulpit, the press, and the platform were the means to be employed to change public opinion. The slave-party had to decide whether they would meet argument by argument, tract by tract, press by press, and lecture by lecture, or whether they would endeavour by violence to prevent the use of the above means by the Anti-slavery party. Being conscious that if the question were carried to the arena of public discussion—as all great questions are in America—they could not possibly retain the popular favour and support, the slave-party determined to resort to violence. They sowed the wind, they have reaped the whirlwind.

A National Anti-slavery Convention was held in the city of Philadelphia, December the 4th, and two following days, 1833, consisting of upwards of sixty members from ten of the free states. Beriah Green, a Congregational Minister, and President of Oneida Institution, was chosen President of the Convention ; and Lewis Tappan, and John G. Whittier, the Quaker poet, Secretaries. The Convention organized the American Anti-slavery Society, of which Arthur Tappan was chosen president, Elizur Wright, jun., Secretary of Domestic Correspondence, and William Lloyd Garrison, Secretary of Foreign Correspondence, A. L. Cox, Recording Secretary, and William Green, jun., Treasurer. The following is from the declaration of sentiments adopted at the above meeting:—

" We have met together for the achievement of an enterprise without which that of our fathers is incomplete; and which for its magnitude, solemnity, and probable results upon the destiny of the world, as far transcends theirs, as moral truth does physical force.

" In purity of motive, in earnestness of zeal, in decision of purpose, in intrepidity of action, in steadfastness of faith, in sincerity of spirit, we would not be inferior to them.

" *Their* principles led them to wage war against their oppressors, and to spill human blood like water in order to be free. *Ours* forbid the doing of evil that good may come, and lead us to reject, and to entreat the oppressed to reject, the use of all carnal weapons for deliverance from bondage, relying solely upon those which are spiritual, and mighty through God, to the pulling down of strongholds.

" *Their* measures were physical resistance—the marshalling of armies—the hostile array—the mortal

encounter.   *Ours* shall be such only as the opposition
of moral purity to moral corruption—the destruction
of error by the potency of truth—the overthrow of
prejudice by the power of love—and the abolition of
slavery by the spirit of repentance."

When Mr. Garrison wrote the above sentiments
he no more dreamed that his own son would, as a
federal officer, lead coloured troops into South Carolina,
than did the Georgia Legislature dream of such an
event, when it offered five thousand dollars for William
Lloyd Garrison.   His son, however, when Charleston
was taken, was the first to enter the city leading his
coloured troops.

The declaration further states that they intend to
send out agents, circulate tracts and periodicals, enlist
the pulpit and the press and the churches in the cause,
and spare no exertions to bring the whole nation to
a speedy repentance; and they add that the abolition
of slavery will remove the chief danger of the dissolution of the Union.

The Executive Committee was located in New
York City, and the operations of the society were
prosecuted with vigour.   The *Emancipator*, a weekly
paper, under the editorial charge of the Rev. William
Goodell, became the organ of the society.   Tracts,
pamphlets, and books were published and circulated,
a large number of lecturing agents were employed,
conventions were held, and state, county, and local
Anti-slavery Societies were organized throughout the
free states, auxiliary to the American Anti-slavery
Society, and contributing to its funds.

The agents were mobbed, their lives were threatened,

their characters calumniated, and their work ridiculed; but converts were multiplied.

In 1834, the act for the abolition of colonial slavery. passed in England. At this critical period that most devoted and eloquent advocate of the slave, George Thompson, paid a visit to the United States. His arrival and labours formed an era in the history of the cause, and in proportion as that cause spread, the more fierce and unsparing grew its adversaries, yet at the close of the year the auxiliary Anti-slavery Societies had increased from sixty to about two hundred.

Thus commenced the Anti-slavery struggle. The quiet village of Hamilton was soon to be the scene of one its conflicts.

CHAPTER III.

At HAMILTON Institution it was announced that Beriah Green, President of the Oneida Institute, would lecture on Slavery in the Baptist church in Hamilton village. I went to the meeting, as did many other students. The lecturer, a man of great ability, commenced his address; when, lo! the doors were darkened by a mob, composed, as all mobs are, of certain lewd fellows of the baser sort; prepared to meet facts with cabbage-stalks, and argument with sheep-plucks. President Green was driven from the pulpit and the village; on his way, meeting one of the Professors of the Hamilton Institution, he said to him, " Ah! you are the cause of all this!" For the remainder of the evening the streets were filled with knots of people, of all classes, discussing the rights of the white man as well as those of the black.

I drew near to one of them. The disputants were a villager, and one of my fellow-students, Mr. Everts, now the Rev. Dr. Everts, of Chicago. The villager contended that Mr. Green had no right to come and disturb the peace of their quiet village by lecturing on Slavery. The student looking him steadily in the face, made this reply, "This mob's doings will not read well in the history of your village. We live under a republican government, and if any evil exists we have power to remove it by legal means. If it is necessary for this purpose to change the laws, the people have power to elect legislators to do so, therefore there is not the slightest excuse for the scene of disorder which has disgraced the village this evening."

This meeting was followed by another. James G. Birney, who had emancipated his slaves, had attempted to establish an Anti-slavery newspaper in Kentucky. For this the people were about to take his life, but he escaped to the Free States. He came to Hamilton, and lectured on Slavery in the Church from which President Green had been driven. The meeting was an orderly one. In replying to the question, " Are you going to set the Slaves free all at once?" Mr. Birney said :—" Each State must emancipate its own slaves, and this will not be done till the public opinion of each respective state is prepared for it ; and this will be done state by state. We shall begin, first, say with Kentucky, as a border slave state, and aim by the press, the platform and the pulpit to create a public feeling in favour of abolition. We shall urge her people to petition her state Legislature to emancipate the slaves of that state. When public opinion is prepared for it the Legislature will yield, and Kentucky will be free. Next we shall take Delaware, or Maryland, or some other border slave state; and by the same means bring about emancipation. Then we will go farther south, and changing the public feeling of Tennessee and other states, will obtain emancipation, state by state, and tier of states by tier of states, till we reach Florida and Louisiana, and thus labour till all the slaves are peaceably emancipated like those in the West Indies." Such was the plan. But the slave-party would not allow it to be pursued. For Mr. Birney's persuasion they threatened his life, and put him out of the south. One of his sons, however, sent them a messenger, which could not be put out so readily. He is said to have invented the Greek fire used at the attack on Charleston in the war. Two of Mr. Birney's sons were in the federal army, and one of them was a general.

Subsequently, Mr. Birney undertook the editorship of the *Philanthropist*, the organ of the Ohio Anti-slavery Society, published weekly at Cincinnati. The journal had reached its fourth number when a band of men, at midnight, broke into the printing office, and destroyed his press. He was afterwards nominated by the Anti-slavery party for President. He was a member of the World's Anti-slavery Convention which assembled in London in 1840; and his work, " *The American Churches, the Bulwark of American Slavery*," was published by the " British and Foreign Anti-slavery Society."

A third meeting at the Baptist Church at Hamilton

was announced. Gerrit Smith was to discuss the question of slavery with Mr. Gridley, the leading lawyer of the village. Mr. Smith was a fine specimen of an American gentleman, he was a practised debater, and had a voice of great depth and melody, over which he had perfect command. He was a large landholder, and when the state of New York required each coloured person to be a freeholder as a condition of voting, though the whites had manhood suffrage, he divided among the coloured people one hundred and thirty thousand acres of land. His conversion to the Anti-slavery cause was chiefly through a mob at Utica. A convention to form a State Anti-slavery Society met at the Bleeker Street Presbyterian Church, on the 21st of October, 1835, in that city. The meeting was broken up by Joseph Kirkland, C. Hayden, S. Beardsley, W. G. Tracy, E. Hart, and others. The first named, who thus trampled on the law, was the Mayor, the two next were members of Congress, and some others held seats in the legislature. Witnessing this, Mr. Smith said it was easy to see on which side Satan was ; and invited the audience to Peterborough, where he resided, promising them protection and a place to meet in. Coaches, traps, and every available conveyance were procured forthwith, and the audience hastened to Peterborough, where the work of the convention was completed without molestation. He was afterwards elected to Congress.

Mr. Gridley was a man of ability and tact, fluent in words, in person short and stout, and quite prepared to fashion his doctrines to the " varying hour." The prospects of his promotion brightened in proportion to the boldness with which he defended slavery; for the President of the United States was a slaveholder. The time came for the discussion. The Baptist Church was crowded. Each speaker did his best—the one for enslaved humanity not allowed to plead its own cause—the other for office. Mr. Smith showed that the Bible was against slavery, and contrasted the condition of the Hebrew servant with that of the American slave. Then he came to the facts of slavery. *"Bourne's Pictures of Slavery"* was presented as evidence. He described a variety of horrid atrocities perpetrated upon slaves: such as brutal scourging and lacerations, with the application of pepper, mustard, and vinegar, etc., to the bleeding gashes; also maimings, backs torn with the claws of cats, and similar tortures. Mr. Gridley, taking the book in his hand, and holding it up in a somewhat theatrical manner, said loudly and deliberately, " I pronounce this book a libel on the south." All eyes were now turned to Mr. Smith. He rose, and with a very complacent expression of countenance said, " Lawyer Gridley has pronounced ' *Bourne's Pictures of Slavery* ' a libel on the south. I endorse the whole and every part of that book."

The discussion greatly strengthened the Anti-slavery feeling of the community. I have already mentioned, on page 37, that a slaveholder had stated that he had himself seen all the modes of torture the book describes. So great was the sympathy of Gerrit Smith for the sufferings of the slave, so deep an interest did he take in every effort to secure emancipation, and so earnestly did he desire the speedy success of those efforts—that when Captain John Brown was arrested, his health was prostrated by the intelligence; and when John Brown was hanged, Mr. Smith endured the most extreme anguish of mind, but in a short time was able to resume his Anti-slavery labours.

Mr. Gridley had his reward, he was made a judge; while Judge Jay, eminent by birth and for judicial knowledge, as well as for piety and philanthrophy, was removed from his office, as judge, by means of the slave-party, through the agency of Mr. Bouck, a pro-slavery governor of the State of New York.

There was a revival meeting at the village of Hamilton. The Revs. J. Knapp and J. Swan, baptists, were invited to assist the Rev. A. Perkins, the pastor of the Baptist Church. Among the people there was great activity in the cooking department for the purpose of largely entertaining strangers. Every morning there were prayer-meetings — and a sermon each afternoon and evening. Mr. Knapp had a series of sermons, which he had preached and revised again and again. Commencing with the evidence of the being of a God—of his moral government, and of the inspiration of the scriptures—he proceeded to take up in succession the great truths of the Gospel. They were able sermons. At the close of the evening sermon, those desiring to be prayed for, were invited forward to occupy the front pews; prayer would then be offered; and short addresses would be given by various members of the audience relating to their own religious experience or urging the unbelieving to come to Christ.

Soon after the meetings commenced the mechanics
laid by their tools, the farmers their winter work,
the shopkeepers closed their shops, and even the
recitations of the students at the institution were
suspended—and all attended the religious services.
At the close of some two weeks, thus spent, about a
hundred persons came forward, relating how they
had found peace in believing and were accepted as
members of the Church. The ice was thick on the
river, but it was broken and removed, and they were
baptized. Each one on coming up from the water
being wrapped in a buffalo skin and driven in a
sleigh to a house near by, to change their apparel.
None of them took cold. Shortly afterwards, however, the general zeal was followed by general apathy.

As a rule in the American revivals, people united
with the Churches without repenting of their pro-
slavery and slaveholding sins. In one revival embracing the south as well as the north, two hundred
and fifty thousand persons joined the Churches—yet
I did not hear of one slave having been set free
as the result. Religion is love to God and man, and
he who loves his brother will not sell him in the
market ; yet a line was drawn between the revival of
religion and the emancipation of the slaves. Some of
the revival preachers were anti-slavery men—but they
failed to give the emancipation question its relative
share of importance. It is due to the Rev. Jacob
Knapp that I should relate an instance of his faithfulness. He went to Richmond, in Virginia, and
commenced a revival meeting. The people were interested and began to close their shops and attend

the meeting. He preached one evening from the text, "Thou shalt love thy neighbour as thyself," and contended that the command included the coloured, as well as the white members of the human family. This, too, in Richmond—which was second only to Washington as a market for slaves. After the sermon the slaveholding ministers gathered round him and asked him what kind of doctrine that was? and whether he was an abolitionist? and required him to give a pledge never again to preach in Richmond, that the command, "Love thy neighbour as thyself," included the coloured people. He refused to give any pledge of the kind. They then told him he must leave Richmond at once, as the mob were gathering to take away his life; and that night he fled to the free states. So they rejected the gospel. One of Mr. Knapp's sons entered the federal army, and fell in the war. It would have been well, however, had Richmond accepted the gospel, instead of clinging to slavery; for there is scarcely a family in that city but has had to mourn for the loss of a member slain in the war. Had Richmond emancipated its slaves it would not have been the seat of government of the Confederacy, and would not have been besieged.

Before I left Hamilton Institution, there was yet another meeting in relation to slavery. One day in looking over the papers in the Reading-room of the Institution, I observed that the *Friend of Man*, an emancipation paper, published at Oneida Institute, was printed in mourning columns. The Rev. E. P. Lovejoy had been slain by the mob for his anti-slavery efforts. He was a native of Maine, a

E

graduate of a college, and conducted a religious paper at St. Louis. In this station he advocated the right of free discussion in opposition to the persecutors of Dr. Nelson. When a free coloured man was burned to death near St. Louis, Mr. Lovejoy rebuked the savage outrage. For this he was driven from the state. He afterwards published the *Christian Observer*, at Alton, Illinois; and advocated emancipation. This raised against him a storm of violence. Three several times were his press and office destroyed; and three times were they replaced by the friends of liberty and law. On the 7th of November, 1837, an attempt was made to set fire to the warehouse containing a new press for Mr. Lovejoy. He went out to prevent it, and fell pierced with balls. It was announced at Hamilton that a funeral sermon would be preached on the occasion at the Baptist Church. Threats of violence were made against any who should attend. I was present with many other students. The sermon was preached by the Congregational minister. It was a faithful one. There was no opposition shown. The Rev. Owen Lovejoy, brother to the martyr, a congregational minister, was an able preacher; and a leader of the anti-slavery party. I have had the privilege of hearing several of his addresses. He was afterwards elected to Congress from Illinois; and till the day of his death, was one of Mr. Lincoln's most cordial supporters. He began the anti-slavery movement designing to carry it through on peace principles, notwithstanding the death of his brother by the violence of the slave-party; but as that party proceeded in its measures, he changed his views and supported the war.

Having mentioned the name of Dr. Nelson, I will briefly refer to him as an anti-slavery leader. He was a slaveholder, and one of his slaves was smart. In America this means clever in the English sense ; in the American sense a clever man is a good-natured easy sort of person. This slave convinced her mistress that it was wrong to hold slaves. Mrs. Nelson convinced her husband, and he emancipated his slaves. He was a professor in Marion Institute, Missouri. A public meeting was held to hear an address from Dr. Nelson—a statement of his reasons for emancipating his slaves. The people assembled—but just as he was about to commence—a slaveholder rose and stated that it was dangerous to the interests of slaveholders for such an address to be given—and that it should not be done. He then pulled out his bowie-knife, (a name taken from Colonel Bowie, one of the men who perished in 1836 at the defence of the Alamo, in Texas.) A friend of Dr. Nelson's, who was on the platform, contended that the Doctor had a right to be heard, and declaring he would defend him, pulled out his pistol. He then asked the Doctor to commence. He did so. The man with the bowie-knife approached the platform, the other presented his pistol, a report was heard, and the slaveholder fell mortally wounded. Dr. Nelson was then charged with causing his death, and was driven by lynch-law from the state. While hiding himself from his pursuers, he commenced to write " The Cause and Cure of Infidelity," a work of whose merit I need

not speak, as it has been extensively read in England.
The Doctor was president of a Missionary College in
Illinois; and one night when the Mississippi river
was frozen over, the slaveholders crossed on the ice
from Missouri, and burnt down the Chapel connected
with the Institute. Neither the murderers of Lovejoy
nor the burners of the Chapel were ever punished.
The pro-slavery course taken by the Faculty at
Hamilton was followed by a large proportion of the
students. Those who were sons of slaveholders clung
to slavery. Some who were natives of free states
went south, and became pastors of slaveholding
churches; married the daughters of slaveholders and
became slaveholders. A still larger number became
pastors in the free states, but, till the war broke out,
were silent on slavery. A similar pro-slavery influence was exerted by all the colleges, except Oberlin,
and Oneida. At that period, the fate of the nation
was in the hands of the college professors. Had they
taken sides with the liberty-creed of the United
States, their example would have been followed by the
northern students and the people; and by them the
slave-power would have been overthrown.

The southern students would have divided, some
would have joined the Anti-slavery cause, others
would have returned to the south. Unhappily, the
college professors joined the apostacy in favour of a
compromise with slavery. At a later period the
colleges sent their professors to the war, and their
students by hundreds. The previous pro-slavery
course of the college professors was brought to my
mind in reading the following article in the " *British*

Quarterly Review," from the pen of Dr. Vaughan, describing his visit to America since the war:—

"At Wheeling, Ohio, [Virginia I presume], I saw one wounded soldier resting upon his crutch at my hotel door, waiting for the conveyance to the railway station. I found him, as I found most Americans, willing to converse frankly with an Englishman on public matters. I learned from him that he had been a student in Jefferson College, and was one of forty who decided to close their books and go to the war; that two of their professors, one their professor in Latin, joined them, prepared to act as their officers, and that they had kept together to the end. He had been wounded seven times, had a ball lodged in the back of the jaw, under the ear, which could not be extracted; another ball had passed through his leg, and he had suffered from that wound many weeks before medical aid could be obtained. Scores of colleges did the same. Harvard boasts of having sent some five hundred of her former students to the conflict. Yale not less than seven hundred. So did the best culture and lore of the United States make contributions to the national cause. Who shall estimate the relatives' anxieties and griefs, or tell the hearts literally broken by the sacrifice."

One of the visitors to the Institution was the Rev. John Clark, a Baptist missionary from Jamaica, who, with his wife and daughter, came to the United States seeking health. He gave me a full account of the working of emancipation in the West Indies, which, in view of the abundance of misrepresentations made by the slave-party, was exceedingly valuable. His reception by the Faculty was not as cordial as it would have been had he been a slave-holder. He strengthened the Anti-slavery movement in all his intercourse with the Americans.

In 1838, I completed what was termed the shorter course of studies. Before leaving the Institution each graduate gave an oration, at a meeting similar to the annual commemoration at Oxford, on a subject chosen by himself. Popular ministers and celebrated scholars addressed the audience which crowded the large hall of the Institution on the occasion. The choir, composed of the students, sang special pieces. In the dining hall there was an abundance of provisions prepared for all the visitors, whose carriages waited without in extended lines. In my oration I embraced the opportunity of referring to the cause of the slave. My subject was that "In the moral world effect follows cause as uniformly as in the material world." In showing that evils were inseparably connected with ignorance, I noticed the enforced ignorance of the slaves and its consequent evils; also the evils necessarily resulting from prejudice, as evinced in the case of those who refuse information on the slavery question, lest they should be induced to become abolitionists; and I described the effects of truth on the mind when received, as invariably beneficial. In closing my discussion of the theme, I observed that to examine and decide upon great moral questions was one of the chief ends of our being; and that these decisions tell not only upon the welfare of the community, but also upon the moral history, for both worlds, of the person by whom they are made.

I offered my services to the American Baptist Home Mission Society, and was appointed a missionary to labour in Wisconsin, then a frontier Territory. In connection with the appointment, a public meeting was held in the lecture room of the Oliver Street Baptist Church, in New York city, at which there were ordination services, and addresses from several Baptist ministers. Receiving many tokens of kindness, including a good library, from the friends of missions, and an expression of best wishes for the success of my labours, I left New York, September the 21st, 1838, to labour in the great West.

The trip up the Hudson was pleasant; I stayed at Albany over the Sabbath and preached at the Green Street Baptist Church; and visited Whitesboro and Palmyra, spending a Sunday and preaching in each place. On my way to Buffalo I visited Brock's monument and the falls of Niagara, obtaining my first view from the Canada side, as being far the best. There was in the view less of the terrible and more of the sublime than I had anticipated. The next Sunday I preached at the Baptist Church at Buffalo, for the Rev. Mr. Choules, an Englishman; on Monday I proceeded by a Lake Erie boat to Milwaukee, about 900 miles from Buffalo, where I arrived safely.

CHAPTER IV.

WHERE Milwaukee now stands, a city of 100,000
people, there was in 1834 but one house, in which
resided Mr. Juneau, a French Canadian, his wife,
who, on her mother's side, was of Indian descent,
and their children. He saw a city spring up around
him, and was elected its mayor. As his children were
not white, though nearly so, the prejudice against
coloured people extended to them; and but few white
people associated with them. Mrs. Juneau was one
of the invited guests at the first wedding at which I
officiated. It was the marriage of Mr. Corbin to
Miss Walker, sister to Mr. Walker who was elected
to Congress from Wisconsin. The bridegroom gave
me as a fee an English sovereign because I was an
Englishman. In the United States places are not
licensed for marriages, and persons are usually married
in the parlour of their own house. Before any minis-

ter can perform the ceremony he must file a copy of his ordination certificate with the County Clerk, who then furnishes him with a license. The gentleman about to be married applies to a magistrate, and makes oath that there is no legal impediment to his being married. A license, costing a small amount, is then granted him ; without this he cannot be married. Before the marriage he must pass this to the minister. When the wedding has taken place, the minister sends to the clerk of the county a certificate to that effect, and transmits with it the license he has received from the bridegroom. The non-performance of any one of these requirements is visited with a very heavy penalty.

The members of the Baptist Church in Milwaukee were few in number, and they had no place of worship. They chose me as their pastor, and the Court House was kindly granted as a place for our worship. In Milwaukee there were two other congregations—the Independent and the Methodist Episcopalian. As there was much drinking in the town, it was arranged that every alternate Sunday the three congregations should meet together, and that the ministers should, in turn, preach on temperance. The Rev. Mr. Crawford, who preached to the Congregationalists, the Rev. Mr. Thompson, who preached to the Methodists, and myself, were abstainers from intoxicating drinks. Several came forward after each service and signed the temperance pledge. The population of Wisconsin rapidly increased, and I visited various parts of the Territory to aid in forming churches. The land, divided into 160 acre lots, was expected soon to be

sold by auction, and the best portions were eagerly
sought.   I was present when the auction took place ;
each acre was sold for a dollar and a quarter.   Among
the settlers it was pre-arranged that each person who
had commenced to cultivate a lot should bid the above
price, and no one should bid against him.   That all
disputes should be laid before a committee, and settled
by that mode.   This was carried out.   Now, however,
in the Territories land is granted to settlers without
charge.

The eastern shore of Wisconsin is laved by Lake
Michigan, the northern, by Lake Superior, the
western, by the river Mississippi, and on the south
it is separated from Illinois by an imaginary line.
The shore on the east was skirted by a forest.   Iron-
wood, birch, black walnut, bass-wood, the sugar
maple, and the tamarisk flourished, but the tall and
stately pine predominated.

Milwaukee, built on the Lake-shore at the con-
fluence of the Milwaukee and Menominee rivers was
the chief city—but Southport, (now Kenosha),
Racine, and Sheboygan, which are also towns on the
eastern shore, grew up rapidly.   West of the border-
forest were the oak openings, the trees in their
distance from each other reminded one of an
English apple orchard.   These openings were beau-
tified by numerous lakes—from one to ten miles in
circumference.   This land was excellent for wheat.
West of the openings were verdant plains— the
prairies—stretching to the horizon without a single
tree.   Intervening between the prairies and the
Mississippi river, were high mounds and deep ravines,

furnishing the lead ore ; while an abundance of copper was obtainedfrom the north. Raspberries,straw berries and plums grew wild. Occasionally the attention of the traveller would be arrested by a herd of startled deer. There are no game laws in America, and the people shot them in large numbers, and caught and tamed the delicate fawns. They were favourites of the children, and ran round the room, adorned with a red collar or a small bell. Wolves were disagreeably numerous and traps were set for them with good effect. The calves, as well as the sheep and deer, became their prey. Some of the missionaries thought that at the voice of singing the wolf would flee away. Crossing a small prairie, in my sleigh, one winter's day, I observed a wolf in the distance, sitting and eyeing both myself and my horse. I tried the experiment of singing ; but whether my voice lacked melody, or his ears appreciation, or whether the theory was a mistake, he failed to move. I held the whip ready in case he should make pursuit, hoping to be saved by the speed of my horse. Looking back I perceived that the wolf, instead of pursuing me, seemed engaged in quietly pursuing his own reflections, and I hoped that they might not be interrupted. One wolf alone, however, will seldom attack a man. In journeying to Beaverdam to preach, one Sunday afternoon, I observed in the sleigh track before me a lame wolf, and overtook it, it lay down like a cat and looked at me imploringly. I divergd from the road, saying mentally, "If you will let me alone, I will let you alone." I re-entered the road in advance of it—and it moved slowly after me. After the ser-

vice at Beaverdam, I mentioned the subject to the
friends, who went out and killed it.   Bears, also,
when the snow was deep at Hudson's Bay, came from
the north for food; to kill one was an honour chronicled
in the newspapers.   Pigeons—in the season came in
clouds.   A Wesleyan minister, an Englishman, had a
trap in which he caught numbers.   In inviting me to
dine he would say, "We have plenty of pigeons."
Squirrels, of different colours disported themselves in
the branches of the trees, and cranes, wild ducks,
prairie chickens, whip-poor-wills, and other families
of the feathered tribes gave to the settlers the advantage of their residence in the Territory.   The
population represented every state in the Union, and
nearly every nation in Europe.   In purchasing land
unions were often formed, so as to form a Welsh, an
Irish, a Norwegian, or a Dutch settlement.   Passing
once through one of the latter, I enquired at several
houses for Turk's mill; but in each case the response
was " Can no fosh stand."   A few of the matrons now
consulted, and despatched a messenger for a little girl
who could speak both languages, and through her
services as an interpreter, I was soon on the way to
my destination.

    There were Indians, civilized and uncivilized.   Of
the latter class were the Menominies, Pottawottamies,
and Winnebagoes.   These wandered through the
country, hunted the deer, caught fish, or in the
season, tapped the sugar maple trees, and brought to
the towns sugar; or wild honey; or they might be
seen in their canoes, among the wild rice which grows
on the edges of the river, shaking the stalks, and

letting the rice fall into the bottom of the canoe. They lived in wigwams, and wore blankets and deerskins; and indicated the death of a relative by broad black marks painted across the face. Sometimes in meeting them, they would offer me whisky, which they had procured, although it was illegal to sell strong drink to an Indian, recommending it by saying, ne-sha-sheen, that is, very good. My reply would be, Cowin ne-sha-sheen, Aynishanaybay squibee, it is not at all good, drunken Indian! The rejoinder would be, petit squibee, I am a little drunken. From the French traders they had picked up a few French words. Several of these Indians had pitched their wigwams on the east side of Rock river. One Sunday, in connection with the Rev. Richard Griffing, I had held a meeting on the west side of the river at Aztalan. At the close, the entire audience proceeded to the river, as Mr. Griffing was about to baptize three young persons. The Indians on the other side of the river seeing us approach, were stricken with terror, hid themselves behind the trees, and sent their chief to learn the reason of the movement. It was explained to him that it was a meeting for a religious purpose. He listened most attentively, and at the close, evidently with a relieved mind, he said ne-sha-sheen—very good. I learned afterwards the reason of the alarm. A white man had sold the Indians some whisky. On becoming sober after the debauch, they regretted the loss of their blankets and guns which had been exchanged for the whisky, and going in a body to his house they assaulted the barrel of whisky, poured its contents on the ground,

F

and destroyed some other portions of his property.; hence the Indians seeing the audience approaching, feared we were coming to take vengeance upon them.

A white man who had lived many years among the Winnebagoes, stated to me their views of rewards and punishments after death. The Indian who has left this world sets out on a long journey—and arrives first at the sun, and proceeds to the moon, which they imagine to be farther off than the sun. Continuing his journey he arrives at a place where three judges live in three wigwams. Now his trial takes place. He crosses a deep abyss on a very narrow bridge. If he has lived a good life—he crosses in safety, and reaches a fine hunting ground, where the deer are fat, the water pure, and great happiness is enjoyed. But if he has lived an ill life —he is certain to fall from the bridge into the abyss, which is a place of great misery. The deer are lean, the water bad, and as to the wood it must be fanned continually with the wing of a duck to make it burn.

The civilized Indians are settled on the shores of Lake Winnebago, comprising the Oneidas, the Stock- bridges, and the Brothertowns, numbering altogether about fifteen hundred persons. The two former wear the blanket and speak their own language, but cul- tivate the land and reside in houses. The Brother- towns speak the English language, and dress like white persons.

I was amused upon one occasion, in listening to a discussion which was held between a Brothertown and a Stockbridge—as to the relative merits of each nation. The former referred to the language, dress, and citizenship of the Brothertowns as evidence of their superiority to the Stockbridges. "True," said the Stockbridge, "I acknowledge this—but I still think my nation is more improved than yours, because, on the Sunday, the sound of an axe or a gun is never heard in our borders; but the sound of both are heard in Brothertown."

At De Père, near Green Bay, the Roman Catholics have a large church, and many uncivilized Indians are Catholics.

In 1660, René Mesnard, a jesuit missionary, was charged to visit Green Bay in Wisconsin, and Lake Superior. He laboured, for eight months, among the Huron Indians. In his travels, while his attendant was engaged in the labour of transporting the canoe, Mesnard was lost in the forest and was never seen again.

Three other jesuit missionaries, Alouez, Dablon, and Marquette, were employed in 1668, in confirming the influence of France in the vast regions that extend from Green Bay to Lake Superior. The two former bore the Cross through Eastern Wisconsin, visiting the Indians on the Milwaukee. The latter, with Juliet, discovered the Mississippi. Crossing with their attendants, who carried their canoes, the narrow portage that divides the Fox river from the Wisconsin, they embarked upon the latter river, and in a few days to their great joy, entered the Great River. From the period of these labours there have been Indian Roman Catholics in Wisconsin.

All the Indians of the North-west believe in Chimanitou, the Great Spirit, and did not worship any idol in the human form. Some of them sacrificed a white dog, before entering on a hunting expedition as a means of success. The Rev. Mr. Marsh, a missionary among the Stockbridges, showed me an object of worship of an Indian, living amongst them, though not related to them. It represented an Indian woman—dressed in blue; and was about nine inches long. I sent word to the press, and the opinion was that it had a Catholic origin, and was intended for the Virgin Mary. The Indian name for a white man is chimocomon, which means a long knife, in reference to the swords of the soldiers, who were among the first white persons they saw. Many of the settlers pronounce this " smoke-a-man," thinking the reference is to the habit of smoking tobacco.

In commencing my labours in Wisconsin I had, as a co-worker, the Rev. Richard Griffing, of New England. Together we visited various settlements. He had a curious mode of hunting bees. Where he saw bees flying he would drive a stake into the ground, and place on its top a small piece of flat board. Having lighted a fire he would heat a stone, and with it burn some bees wax, which he placed with some honey-comb on the top of the flat board, and near it a piece of white paper. The fragrance of the wax arrested the attention of the bees, the white paper caught their sight. They came, took the honey from the comb, and went straight to their hives. He watched secretly, and learning their locality, suffocated the bees and obtained the honey. Some bee-hunters would at night cut down the tree, separate the portion of it occupied by the bees, and place it in the garden, thus securing both hive and bees. Wherever a few Baptists had settled, we visited the locality, and aided them to form a church. A meeting would be held, and they would present their letters from the churches of which they had been members. They adopted articles of faith and practice, joined in a covenant to live for the Redeemer, and we then gave them the right hand of fellowship. Each church adopted also two rules in reference to temperance and slavery. One was an agreement to abstain from intoxicating liquors as a beverage; the other was to admit no slaveholder to membership till he had emancipated his slaves. Many years since the latter rule was adopted by the Society of Friends.

About sixty Baptist churches in Wisconsin accepted these rules and carried them out. To the temperance rule few objections were made, because those who had been members of the churches in the Eastern states had been so well educated in this particular, that they thoroughly appreciated the danger and evils of the use of intoxicants as a beverage. To the other rule there were many objections. It was asked if we desired to introduce a human rule among the laws of Christ? We replied by showing that slavery was a sin, and that persons were required to repent of their sins before joining the church; that no one would be admitted as a member who enslaved a white person, and that to enslave a black one was equally sinful. We then asked them to make the case their own, would they regard that man as a christian who should seize and carry into slavery their own children? After full consideration, the rule was adopted in every church. In forming the church at the village of Mequanego, a new objection was presented, which led to my separation from the Home Mission Society. It was stated that the Society approved of slavery, and received subscriptions from slaveholders; perhaps the price of some slave sold in the market. Mr. Griffing considered that, for this reason, connection with the above-named Society could not consistently be retained. I determined to examine the question and do my duty. Ascertaining that the society sanctioned slavery, I wrote to New York, regretting to part with those who had treated me so kindly, but stating that I must decline to be their missionary so long as they supported slavery.

The society treated a slaveholding religion as if it were pure christianity. It elected slaveholding officers, and appointed slaveholding missionaries, who planted slaveholding churches; and it welcomed into its treasury the contributions of slaveholders, which had the effect of hush-money. From the Rev. Dr. Brisbane I obtained a list of twenty-eight names of slaveholders who were life-members or life directors of the Society. I will mention three. Jonathan Davis of Monticello, South Carolina, was a man without education, possessing a mere modicum of intellectual power, and distinguished for a childish vanity. In Boston, Massachusetts, he boasted that he was the owner of thirty human beings, and that he would wade knee deep in blood to defend his right to hold them. He speaks, in a letter, of the kind treatment he received at the Hamilton Theological College, where he spoke in defence of slavery; and concludes by saying, "God bo praised for sustaining me. I give him all the glory ; for without him, I can do nothing."

Another life-director was Richard Fuller. He had about one hundred slaves; and contended that Father, Son, and Holy Spirit sanction slavery. In the Secession he was one of the most active leaders, but escaped punishment by the influence of his northern friends. He was an able preacher, and often melted the audience to tears.

Jesse Hartwell was another life-director. He sold a slave woman, and received a higher price because she was known to be truly pious. His father charged him with selling the Holy Spirit. I called on the latter in passing through Pennsylvania, and dined with him. He told me he should feel as much pleasure as any father would to hear his own son preach, but he could not do so while his son held slaves. All the above were Baptist ministers.

Occasionally I would be censured for giving up my connection with the society and my salary. My reply was, I would rather, like Paul, labour with my hands than sanction slavery. Some other missionaries saw the question as I did, and resigned their connection with the society. The sanction it gave to slavery continued till the war broke out. It proved costly to the north, for it strengthened the slave system.

The Home Mission Society encouraged slaveholders; it ought to have reproved them. It kept back the northern churches from Anti-slavery efforts ; it ought

to have fostered those efforts. Had this society given
up its connection with slavery the effect would have
been felt throughout the United States. The system
of slavery would have tottered if it had not fallen.
Even now this society is more anxious to gain the
good will of the ex-slaveholders than to extend protection and religious benefit to the Freed-men.

Thus ended, after about three years service, my
connection with the Home Mission Society.

The census of the United States taken in 1840, stated
the population of Wisconsin to be 30,945, of whom
eleven were slaves. In the next ten years there
was a rapid increase both of Anti-slavery sentiment
and of population, the latter being in 1850, 305,391,
of whom none were slaves. Slavery had been prohibited in Wisconsin, by a law of the Territorial
Legislature, as well as by the Ordinance of 1787.
Few, however, thought the holding of these eleven
slaves deserved consideration. I wrote to Mr.
James, the marshall, and inquired how slaves could
be held in a free Territory like Wisconsin? For I
regarded this return of the census as giving the
Territory an unworthy name; bidding defiance to
the law; strengthening the slave power; and inflicting cruelty on the victims. He was an Englishman,
and courteously replied that persons brought slaves
to Wisconsin, held them for a term of years, and
then set them free. How far it was legal he was not
prepared to say. At this period I was appointed on a
mission tour by a missionary committee of Wisconsin;
and decided to embrace the occasion of calling on the
Governor, to bring the subject to his notice. Lead-

ing lawyers whom I consulted agreed that the slaves were held in defiance of the law. The counties, however, in which they were held were chiefly settled by southerners. This was a difficulty; for with true southern characteristics they would be ready to enforce lynch-law against any one who should propose to enforce Territorial law where it interfered with slavery. Besides, Governor Dodge, a Virginian himself, brought slaves with him to Wisconsin, and for a time held them. He was a democrat, and the whigs, through their newspapers, began to throw out the inquiry—" Is it proper for the Governor to hold slaves?" The Governor then emancipated his slaves, and gave each one a piece of land.

His mansion was modest and commodious, situated in a secluded valley, not far from the town of Mineral Point. I called on him, and was kindly received and invited to stay till the morning. Mrs. Dodge was a member of the Baptist Church. In figure the governor is tall and portly, his military air shows that he has been a soldier, and he evinces the frankness frequently exhibited by Southerners. In the course of conversation, he observed that he had received a letter from England, from Mr. Thomas Clarkson, urging him to do all in his power to have Wisconsin enter the Union as a free state, when it became a state. "Now" added the governor, " Wisconsin is already free from slavery." I then referred to the eleven slaves reported in the census— and taking from my pocket the letter I had received from the marshall on that subject—read it to him. He stated that some of the lawyers held that a slave who was brought to Wisconsin by his master, was not free till his freedom was legally recorded; but that his own opinion was that the slave in such case was free, as soon as he stepped across the boundary line of the Territory.

In continuing my journey the next day, I recalled with great pleasure the statements of the governor. I felt, too, greatly strengthened by the aid rendered by Mr. Clarkson and the British and Foreign Anti-slavery Society. I had commenced the contest single-handed. The friends of the slave in England were quite unconscious of the effort I was making, yet, how timely and powerful was the aid afforded by their appeal to the governor. The effect of English anti-slavery effort on the United States can scarcely be over-estimated. It was dreaded by the slave-party; and to guard against it—they disingenuously attempted to persuade the English public that its efforts to abolish American slavery did harm instead of good.

I called on Mr. James, the marshall, and obtained his permission to copy from the census the names of those who reported themselves as slaveholders. I then called on the person having charge of the census papers; and stated that I should feel obliged if he would allow me to see the returns in reference to slaves; as the marshall had allowed me to take a copy of them. He placed the papers before me—and gave me in addition—what I did not expect—a very large amount of reproach and vituperation; denouncing me as an enemy to the United States—and as seeking to destroy the American Union. He displayed his temper—and his authority as far as possible; but, being neither governor nor marshall, he could not prevent me from making a copy of the names. The storm had scarcely ceased when I wished him good morning. I consoled myself with the reflection that my list was a correct one, of which I hoped to make good use; and that the American Union could scarcely be destroyed by my having obtained a list of the Wisconsin slaveholders. I wrote to the *Genius of Liberty*—an anti-slavery paper, published in Illinois—giving an account of my interview with Governor Dodge—and sending also a copy of the marshall's letter. Both of which the editor kindly published.

The Rev. James Mitchell, a Virginian, connected with the Methodist Episcopal Church, was chaplain to the Wisconsin Legislature. Learning that he held two slaves, although they were not reported in the census, I called on him and stated to him my regret to learn that he held two slaves. He replied that he had no slaves, but his wife had two. I thought of Adam. Turning to Mrs. Mitchell, I stated that it was against the laws of Wisconsin to hold slaves. Mr. Mitchell responded, " My wife knows the law." He contended that it was not a sin to hold slaves, but added that he knew of no slaves who were not addicted to telling falsehoods. I enquired whether that was not owing to their position as slaves. This he admitted. I then contended that a system must be sinful that produced such effects. Crossing the Mississippi river, I preached at Du Buque. A strong pro-slavery sentiment prevailed. By means of the river they are in constant intercourse with the slave states Re-crossing the river, which is at Du Buque a mile wide—I visited Galena, on the Fever river, in the north-western part of Illinois. The Baptist Church wished me to become their pastor, if I would consent to keep in abeyance the slavery question. Several members formerly held slaves, and a still larger number were once slaves. Two coloured women desired to join the church. They were accepted. On Sunday a procession was formed at the place of worship. A coloured member—named Uncle Tom—gave out two lines at a time, and they sang till we reached the river. The mayor of Galena and several of the most respectable citizens walked in the procession. In the afternoon I administered the Lord's Supper, not recognizing any distinction on account of colour. I was somewhat surprised to learn that several of the members—having obtained their freedom—and having no hope of seeing their former partners again—had been married the second time. I inquired of Uncle Tom " Were you married in the south ?"

" Yes, and I was sold from my wife and nine children ; and my wife has been compelled to take another husband."

" Well, tell me how you obtained your freedom ?"

"I was the slave of Mr. Madan, son-in-law to Governor Dodge ; and always spent the Sundays in the woods in prayer to God. One Sunday my master came to the woods and said to me ' What are you doing here ?' I made no answer. He then said ' Go up to the house !' I stood still. He went and cut a stick and began to beat me about the head. I knelt down before him— clasped him round the knees—and holding fast, began to pray aloud to God. My master said 'Let me go and you may go where you please— let me go, and I will give you your liberty.' I un- clasped my arms, he made me free, and I put into a pocket handkerchief all I had—came to Galena, and began to black shoes for a living."   .

Uncle Tom has a remarkable gift in prayer, and is a tall and powerful man. Mr. Madan is neither tall nor powerful. "One Sunday morning," continued Uncle Tom, "Some young clerks came and said, 'Uncle Tom, just give our boots a brush.' I said no— it is the Sabbath. They pressed me—I said, What would you think of a man who having seven horses given him, on the condition that he should ride six himself and keep one for the person who gave them, if he should ride all the seven? Our divine master has given us seven days, six we are to keep for ourselves—and one we are to keep for him, and now you wish me to take his day for myself; there is not money enough in the bank to make me do it."

He was doing well in business and had a house, a horse, and some other property. I learned that his wife, whom I had baptized, had been sold from her husband at the south, and that her child had been sold for four hundred dollars. Inquiring how she became free, she said that she was brought to Galena from the south, and was about to be taken back to slavery, when she escaped from the house. It was finally arranged that she should have her liberty, if a certain amount of money could be paid. Uncle Tom came forward and agreed to pay the money, and was

then married to her. As the person from whose house
she escaped was a member of the church—I conversed with her—and suggested that no money ought
to be required of the coloured woman—as she was
legally free by being brought into a free state; my
effort in her behalf was unsuccessful. There was present a Baptist lady from the south, who held slaves. I
conversed with her—and she stated she held slaves
for their good. I inquired who should judge—the
slaveholder or the slaves—as to whether it was for
their good to be held in bondage? "Oh," she
replied, "the slaveholder of course." "Well, madam,"
I replied, "if a person should make a slave of me,
and say he held me for my good, your argument
would justify my enslavement."

I asked another member how he obtained his
liberty? He stated that his master always looked to
him for "de truth"—and for that reason he was set
free. He had a wife and large family in slavery, and
was married again.

Two others with whom I conversed—husband and
wife—told me, they had eight children, all in slavery;
and they could not tell where any of them were.
Family relations are obliterated by slavery. I heard
of a refugee slave who began to pay his addresses to
a young woman, also a refugee slave. He conversed
with her as to her early years—and ascertained that
she was his own sister.

I learned that the other coloured woman whom I
baptized was living with an Irishman who had bought
her, and that they were not married. The subject
came before the church, and I suggested that she

ought to be married to the Irishman, or run away, or be excluded. He declined to marry her—and as she did not run away—the church excluded her. The Irishman then took her to St. Louis and attempted to sell her into life-long bondage—she succeeded at great risk in making her escape.

I called on a coloured family in Galena, and a white man entered the house to search for his slave. The early laws of the state allowed of slavery, though contrary to the Ordinance of the North-west; and his slave had escaped. I took out my pencil and note-book to take down his remarks. He said something in an undertone, and evidently alarmed at the pencil, left the house which he had just claimed the right of searching.

CHAPTER V.

WHILE engaged in the foregoing labours, I became acquainted with Mr. Fulton, of Lowell, Illinois, a most zealous labourer in the Anti-slavery reform. Occasionally he would relinquish his lucrative busi- ness, travel extensively in the west, hold Anti-slavery meetings, obtain subscriptions for the Anti-slavery paper, and stir up the people to resist—by their in- fluence and votes—the slave power, which was coming in upon them like a flood. Visiting Wisconsin and learning of my Anti-slavery efforts, he came to me, and urged me to become an Agent of the Illinois State Anti-slavery Society. I soon afterwards re- ceived a similar request from the Committee of that Society; and as its origin illustrates the adage that

"The blood of the martyr is the seed of the church,"
I will briefly trace its history.

It was the design of the slave-party to make
Illinois a slave state. Hence while it was a Territory, slaveholders went to reside in it, and introduced
the practice of holding slaves, in disregard of the
Ordinance of the North-west ; they also subsidized
every newspaper in Illinois, with the solitary exception of the *Edwardsville Spectator*, published by
Hooper Warren, Esq., a sterling Anti-slavery man ;
who rendered good service to the friends of liberty
at that important period, aiding to save the state
from the curse of slavery. When Lovejoy established the *Alton Observer* it became the organ
of the Illinois Anti-slavery reformers. His death,
aroused them to increased activity, and they formed
the Illinois State Anti-slavery Society ; but they had
no organ. When the tragic intelligence of Lovejoy's
death reached the eastern states, two friends of the
slave—one in Pennsylvania, the other in Vermont—
simultaneously resolved that the work begun by
Lovejoy, and for which he was slain, should be completed ; and that an Anti-slavery newspaper should
be published in Illinois. Their names were B. Lundy
(referred to on page 33) and Zebina Eastman, the latter
is now the American Consul at Bristol, having been
appointed by President Lincoln. Visiting Illinois, Mr.
Eastman found that his design had been anticipated by
Mr. Lundy, who about two years after Lovejoy's death,
commenced the publication of the *Genius of Universal
Emancipation*, at Hennepin, in Illinois. Both became
associated as editors and printers, and by their united

efforts the paper was issued. But there were many difficulties, owing to the primitive state of the country and the hostile attitude of the inhabitants, so that but nine numbers appeared in a period of twelve months. A few months after the above union, Mr. Lundy was seized with a fever, which in three days closed his earthly labours. His obituary, written by Mr. Eastman, appeared in the *Genius of Universal Emancipation* of August 23, 1839. The following are extracts:—

"It has been our painful duty to announce to the friends of humanity, and to the patrons of this paper, the melancholy intelligence of the death of BENJAMIN LUNDY, long the faithful and persevering editor of the *Genius of Universal Emancipation.* * * * * The philanthropists of this state have unusual cause for grief in this signal visitation. It was but lately that they were called upon to lament the fate of one who fell by the hand of violence, and whose shroud is stained with blood; now another of the champions of freedom, permitted to labour for a season in this vineyard, by the inscrutable providence of God, has been taken away; he has finished his task and delivered up the trust committed to his hands."

Mr. Eastman, who afterwards occupied so important a position in the Western Anti-slavery movement, was the son of a Massachusetts farmer, in his youth fond of reading, and a perusal of the Life of Benjamin Franklin led him to desire to master the art of printing. After devoting some time to the business, he prepared to enter College, but applying himself too closely, was compelled by failing health to relinquish his studies. He then published a newspaper in Vermont. Mr. Shafter, who afterwards became a leader in the Anti-slavery cause, wrote a series of articles on the question—"Is the negro a man?" and although at that period scarcely a voice was heard in favour of the rights of the coloured man, these articles were published by Mr. Eastman in his journal.

After the death of Lundy, the paper was issued by Mr. Eastman for several weeks, and after an interregnum of a whole year, it re-appeared at Lowell, Illinois, under the title of the *Genius of Liberty*. In this enterprise he was joined by Mr. Warren, whose labours have already been noticed. This arrangement continued one year—when it was found that the enlarged area of the reform, required an enlarged area of action. By invitation of prominent citizens of Chicago, then in its infancy, and yet the thriving child of the great West—the *Genius of Liberty* was removed to Chicago. The most prominent of those engaged in procuring this removal was Dr. C. V. Dyer, now Judge of the Mixed Commission African Slave-trade Court, appointed by President Lincoln, as one of the leading abolitionists of Illlinois. The paper was now under the charge of Mr. Eastman alone, and the name changed to the *Western Citizen*. It had a wide circulation and was effective in checking the efforts of the slave-party. I have traced the press through all its changes to show that that party notwithstanding its violence, was defeated, and that the destruction of the life of the editor did not destroy the anti-slavery newspaper. I wished also to illustrate the faith and perseveranee of the anti-slavery party. Mr. Eastman published also monthly, for several years, the *Liberty Tree*, filled with important anti-slavery facts. When John P. Hale, the senator from New Hampshire, boldly resisted the slave-party, Mr. Eastman placed his name at the head of his columns, as a fitting candidate for the presidency, before this step had been taken in New England. When Mr. Lincoln was elected president, Mr. Eastman wrote him a letter of which the following is an extract:—

"I would frankly suggest that as all statesmen of both political schools have stumbled, as they were led to look at slavery as an institution to be perpetuated —always to be ignored—so also will the statesmen of to-day be led into a ruinous error for their prosperity, if they do not regard it as an institution, or evil, which must be destroyed. * * * I do have the boldness to thank God, that in my day, he has raised up a man, to whom, at least, he has given the opportunity and proffered the honour, of being the 'Saviour of his country,' by becoming its emancipator."

Mr. Eastman is now a member of the Arley Congregational Church, Bristol, of which the Rev. S. Hebditch is pastor.

An anecdote of Dr. Dyer occurs to me. Some refugee slaves having reached Chicago were arrested and secured in a room. Dr. Dyer visited the room, and being denied access to them by the guard, he knocked down the guard with his cane, opened the door and the slaves escaped. For this service the citizens of Chicago presented the doctor with a splendid gold-headed cane.

I once asked a doctor if he could explain how it was that so large a number of his class were willing to join the abolitionists? His reply was, " Do you not know that doctors are the best informed men in the world !"

Respecting the request of the Anti-slavery Committee that I should become an agent, I resolved to consider and decide upon it during a journey I was about to make.

In 1841, I paid a visit to the Brothertown Indians, comprising the remnants of those powerful and warlike tribes that once lived in New England; the Pequods, Narragansetts, and others, with whom the Puritans often came into conflict. These have united, hence the name of Brothertown. Having preached among them, several came forward for baptism, and believing they knew from experience the value of religion, I baptised them. It is their custom, after the sermon, to rise in succession and give an expression to their feelings. I never saw a Brothertown woman do this who did not hold her handkerchief to her face and weep during the time she spoke. The men did not weep. It is probable that when the early missionaries such as Eliot went among them and preached, that the Indians were very powerfully affected and wept when they spoke; and that among the women this habit has been perpetuated. Preaching on one occasion from the text Psalm cxviii. 25, " O Lord I beseech Thee send now prosperity," I made

reference to Peter; spoke of his backsliding, and
stated that he who wanders from the path of duty
might as well say to the waves of the sea "Thus far
shalt thou go and no farther," as to prescribe the
limits of his wandering. Peter denied his master
with oaths and cursing, but the Lord looked upon
him and looked him into repentance. At the close,
an Indian woman rose up and wept much as she gave
utterance to the following remarks:—"While the
servant of the Lord was going through, he spoke of
the Lord looking upon Peter and looking him into
repentance; and I thought there is a Peter here, and
I pray the Lord to look him into repentance." I did
not know to whom she referred, but soon after a
young man, her son, rose up, much affected, and
acknowledged that he had brought disgrace upon the
holy cause of religion; stated that he was determined
to pray for himself, and requested all those who had
praying hearts to pray for him. I afterwards learned
that having joined the Wesleyans he had gone, at
Christmas time, to a party of young people, and drunk
to intoxication.

Another Indian remarked upon his desire to make
a straight track. I should observe that after a fall
of snow the prairies look smooth as a sheet of white
paper, and the track made by the first person crossing
it in a sleigh, be it crooked or straight, is followed by
all subsequent travellers.

"I always try," said the Indian, "when crossing a
prairie after a fall of snow to make as straight a
track as possible; but when I come to look back I
find it is not near as straight as I intended; and so

of my Christian life—I have designed to make a straight track—but in looking back I find it not near as straight as I hoped to make it." In some cases after all had spoken, the first speaker would have some additional remark to make, and the second, and so perhaps all would speak the second time, before the meeting was dismissed. They have admirable nerves. I would suggest at the close that this made our meeting rather late. But they would reply, when we were in the service of sin we kept up our meetings till day-light, and now we are engaged in the service of the Saviour we do not deem a late meeting objectionable.

From Brothertown I set out for Sheboygan, a settlement of white people, where there was a Baptist Church, which I had assisted to organize. This was on the shore of Lake Michigan about fifty miles east of Brothertown. There was a good road by Green Bay, and one about one-third the distance, through the woods; the latter was an Indian trail, a narrow pathway wide enough for one person only. The Indians had no conveyances with wheels and made no roads. They did not travel two abreast but in single file,—men, women, children, and horses following one behind the other. I have known them as they approached me leave the path—on seeing that my horse was somewhat frightened—and hide behind the trees till I had passed by. The smell of the deerskins they wore might have produced this effect on the horse. I decided to reach Sheboygan if possible by the Indian trail. On Friday I started, having an appointment to preach in the evening. The day was

pleasant—it was in summer. In some portions of
the trail, the grass had grown—but I succeeded,
though not without some difficulty, in tracing it.
I passed through the oak openings. Many of the
trees were stunted by the fires that in the fall of the
year sweep over the country for hundreds of miles.
So dry is the grass that sometimes from lighted
tobacco from pipe or cigar it will commence burning
and continue many days.

There are two ways of guarding against it. One
is to plough a broad deep furrow round the house and
stack; another is to burn a circle round them.
Neither of these can be crossed by the fire. In
burning a circle two planks are laid down a little
distance from each other and the grass between them
is set on fire, it will not burn under the planks and
by a mop and a pail of water it is kept from spreading beyond their ends. I once saw a very large stack
of wheat burned which the farmer had neglected to
protect by either of these modes. Not far from his
house was what is termed a dry swamp; where the
grass was broad-bladed and grew luxuriantly. This
was on fire. Its smoke and flames seemed rolling
and leaping as they approached. It touched the
thickets and they were ablaze, and swept up the
bank. The farmer ran forward, but the fire mocked
his speed. Or ever he had taken breath the blue
smoke was curling up the sides of a large stack of
wheat, the flames followed; and the stack was at the
absolute disposal of its new and furious master. But
to pursue the trail, I passed the openings and entered
the thick forest. Here the trees on the trail were

blazed—this was an additional guide. The first travellers took with them an axe and cut off a little
bark from each tree on the way, and applied to the
wound a fire-brand, preventing growth and leaving a
permanent mark. The mark thus made by white
men is oval, that of Indians is pointed like an arrow.
Riding on with confidence, I was surprised to find,
near sundown, that the trail branched into two separate pathways. I took that most deeply trodden, and
hastened on, but after awhile observed that the trees
were not blazed. The wiser course would have been
to halt, kindle a fire, rest till morning, then return,
and follow the other branch of the trail. I supposed,
however, that I could not be far from Sheboygan;
and if I could make my way, should be in time for
the meeting and not disappoint the audience. So I
rode on. At some distance in the forest, on my left,
there appeared a large open space. Anticipating that
this was a settlement where the woods had been cut
down; probably the outskirts of Sheboygan, I left
the trail and hastened towards it; when, lo! it was a
large swamp in which no trees could grow; and as
my horse began to sink in the bog at its borders, I
leaped off to get him on to good ground, and while
doing so lost my reckoning of the direction in which
was the trail. In vain I tried to find it again.

The Sheboygan river, at the side of which the town
is built, rises in this direction. If I could but see this,
my difficulty would be at an end. Climbing a high
tree I looked in every direction; but no river was
visible; nothing but the interminable forest stretching away to the horizon, a prospect that made my

H

heart sink within me. The forest was a hundred and
fifty miles from north to south, and fifty miles from
east to west; and I had no compass. I hoped, however, by the sun, to be able to proceed to the east the
next morning. Descending, and tying my horse to a
tree, I kindled a fire, having dry wood in abundance,
and ate a supper of fine plums. In my journey I
saw a tree loaded with them, and had filled my pockets
with them to give to the children of the settlers.
Wolves and rattle-snakes were my only antagonists.
The former will not approach a fire, and the latter
always give warning before they bite. They are
readily killed by a stroke across the back with a
switch—I have thus killed many of them; considering
that by so doing I might be saving some one's life.
When the fire got low, I grew cold and awoke. I
replenished my fire, and was soon again in slumber.
The next morning there was a drizzling rain; and I
could not ascertain the east by the sun. I gave my
horse the rein, hoping he would find his way back to
the trail, but he made his way back to the place where
he had spent the night, and proceeded no farther.

By no expedient could I regain the lost trail. One
mode remained of judging of the east. A little moss
always grows on the north sides of the trees, near the
roots. Judging by this mode I proceeded eastward.
Descending a valley I hoped to find some water for
my horse, for myself I had found wild raspberries in
abundance, rich as they were ripe—and felt no thirst.
A small stream purled its course through the valley,
but so overgrown with thorns and briers, that it was
impossible without the aid of an axe to gain access to

it ; and I had no axe with me. Turning, however, down the stream, I at length came to an opening. My horse was now able to enter the stream, and while he slaked his thirst I observed the frame of an Indian wigwam on the opposite bank—the poles on which the covering had been placed. A wigwam is always built close to a trail. I rode up the bank and to my great relief found a trail. The trees were blazed—the marks were pointed, not oval. It was not the trail I left. Continuing my journey as long as light permitted, and reaching no settlement, I dismounted, and fastening the fore-feet of my horse together with a small chain having a strap at each end, I turned him out. He had never left me but once, when a man scolded him for endeavouring to enter a log-house where I was. A log served for a pillow—and wrapping my Boston comforter, a sort of over-coat round me, I lay down near the fire I had kindled, anticipating, however, that as the ground and log were wet from a recent shower of rain, I might take cold.

In the dead of the night I awoke, the owls were hooting; I listened and could hear the clank of the small chain, as my horse changed his position. My anxiety to know where I was amounted almost to an agony. I was lonely in its utmost sense. In the depth of that forest I thought of dear friends in Old England; of life as a probation; of great moral conflicts; of slavery and anti-slavery; and a voice seemed to say—" Great as your toils and anxieties are in this dilemma, they are not as great as those of the slave. You long to see a brother man; but,

were you an escaping slave, you would tremble to see
one; you are faint for want of food; but the escaping
slave, equally faint, may hear the blood-hounds baying on his track." I resolved to remember those in
bonds, as bound with them; and become Agent of
the Anti-slavery Society, should I escape from my
present peril.

With the earliest light I was on my way the
next morning. It was Sunday. The sun rose from
behind a cloud. My course was north-west. Emerg-
ing from the woods I came to an Indian hunting-
ground. There were level lawns and clumps of trees
—it seemed some English park. I reached an excellent spring of water, and there the trail ended. To
return and seek a settlement at the other end of the
trail was more than my strength could bear. Having
the sun to guide me, I decided to keep on in a north-
westerly course, hoping to strike the Wisconsin
river, when I should know my way. Before going
far, unexpectedly, I came upon another trail. Pursuing this I came to a level flat country. At my
right-hand were some hills. Passing these I saw in
the distance a log-house, and corn growing. These
the hills had hidden from view. Had the house been
built of polished marble, it could not have appeared
more delightful to me. I rode up to the door and
knocked. It was opened by a woman. I apologized
for my appearance, having been lost in the woods
since Friday, stating that I had left Fon du Lac for
Sheboygan, and should feel greatly obliged to learn
the name of the locality. The woman was from
Ireland, and replied "Faith, sir, then you are back at

Fon du Lac again." I was within four miles of tho place from which I started.

Writing to the Anti-slavery Committee at Lowell, Illinois, I soon received an appointment as Agent of the Illinois Anti-slavery Society. The committee had no funds. I was, however, to have a salary of about fifty pounds sterling, if I could obtain as much by subscriptions to the society.

I surveyed the field; the slave party seemed almost omnipotent. There was a great work to be done by exceedingly feeble means. Western Wisconsin differed as greatly from Eastern, in its population, as in its scenery. New England had chiefly given character to the latter, having furnished the larger class of settlers. This was indicated in the style of buildings, houses, shops, and churches; in the number of schools, and newspapers, and places of worship, and the strictness with which the Sabbath was observed; as well as in language and dress. Western Wisconsin in its public sentiment and habits bore the impress of the slave states. Such, however, was the intelligence, industry, tact, and moral and religious character of the inhabitants of Eastern Wisconsin, that if they had been animated by an anti-slavery spirit they would have abolitionized the whole of the Territory. The lack of this spirit was their great weakness. The whigs were the admirers of Henry Clay, a slaveholder; and were determined to make him president. The democrats must have a democratic president, and made no objection to his being a slaveholder. The presses were all under the influence of these two parties. No newspaper would advocate emancipation.

The Methodist Episcopalians were trammelled by a large southern slaveholding constituency and by pro-slavery bishops—in addition to a clique of Southerners in the Local Conference who sympathised with Mr. Mitchell—the chaplain of the Legislature, and Mr. Rountree, a member of the Legislative Council, both slaveholders in defiance of law, and yet members of the Methodist Episcopal Church. The Presbyterians were held in check by their slaveholding ministers and members. Some of the Congregationalists were out-spoken abolitionists, as were several of their ministers, who having offended their eastern congregations, by preaching against slavery, had come to the west to preach deliverance to the captives, where the public sentiment was more formative and plastic. The Free Missionists were untrammelled, but the missionaries, both Baptist and Congregational, who were connected with committees in league with slave-holders, were greatly restricted from anti-slavery effort, and some of them were hostile to it.

CHAPTER VI.

THE extent of agitation on the slavery question
measures the progress of the Anti-slavery reform.
This agitation was promoted in the Free States by
the Anti-slavery press, and by trials relating to
slavery in the Ecclesiastical and Civil courts, as well
as by Lecturing Agents.

With respect to the Anti-slavery press, the
Liberator was published in Massachusetts; the
Emancipator and the *Anti-Slavery Standard* in New
York City; the *Friend of Man* at Whitesboro, New
York; the *Philanthropist* at Cincinnati; and the
Genius of Universal Emancipation in Illinois. These
all contended that emancipation was the duty of the
master and the right of the slave; and their names
indicated the benevolent spirit that originated and
animated the movement. It was looked upon as a

great religious enterprize which the ministers and
churches would not fail to support.

The slave power, however, was soon revealed to be
a vast and mighty political organization—shaping, in
relation to slavery, the creeds of the churches—and
the activities and arguments of the Bible, Tract,
Sunday School, and other benevolent societies. That
to resist it, there must be a counter political organization. The very creed of the American citizen
committed him to the abolition of slavery. Hence
arose a class of papers advocating these views and
seeking emancipation; such as the *National Era*,
published at Washington, in which "*Uncle Tom's
Cabin*" first appeared, in chapters; the *True
American*, in Kentucky; the *Western Citizen*, in
Chicago; and the *American Freeman*, in Wisconsin;
and in the religious world the *Christian Reflector*
(Baptist), Massachusetts; the *True Wesleyan*, New
York; the *Free Presbyterian* Ohio, and similar
papers.

Of the Anti-slavery books published, were Jay's
"*View of the Colonization Society, and of the Influence
of Slavery over the Federal Government;*" Rev. A.
A. Phelps's "*View of Slavery;*" *American Slavery as
It Is, the Testimony of a Thousand Witnesses;*"
"*The Bible Against Slavery;*" "*The Power of Congress to Abolish Slavery in the District of Columbia*,"
the three latter by Theodore D. Weld; "*Emancipation in the West Indies*," by Thome and Kemble;
and the reprint of several English works, such as
"*The Life of Granville Sharp;*" "*Clarkson's History
of Abolition;*" and "*Wesley's Thoughts on Slavery;*"

also "*Narratives of Escaping Slaves;*"—and in these, woe to any slave who made some slight mistake in spelling the name of a slaveholder, as this would be made the ground for declaring the book utterly false.

As an illustration of agitation in the churches, Lewis Tappan was charged in the Presbyterian Church with disturbing its peace by forming an Anti-slavery Society among its members; being found guilty, the case was appealed from the session to the Presbytery, thence to the Synod, thence to the General Assembly. In the Methodist Episcopal Church, the Revs. E. Smith, L. Matlack, and other ministers, were tried and excluded from the church for preaching on the slavery question. Among the Baptists Rev. Elon Galusha, and other ministers were displaced from their positions as officers in the Missionary Society, for denouncing slavery as a sin. The question, like an unbidden guest, appeared in all the religious anniversaries, and would not down. By this means many became enlightened, and united with the abolitionists.

Then there were trials before the civil courts. The Governor of Kentucky demanded of the Governor of Ohio the surrender of John B. Mahan, charging him with stealing slaves, which means aiding them to escape. He was surrendered, and immured in prison in Kentucky. The Governor of Maryland demanded of Mr. Seward, then Governor of New York, the crew of a vessel, charging them with aiding a slave to escape; but Governor Seward replied, that by the laws of New York that was not a crime, and refused to give them up. Cases occurred of the arrest and

trial of fugitive slaves.   Much depended on the feeling of the people in the locality where the trial took
place.   If that were pro-slavery, the slave was returned
to bondage, if that were Anti-slavery he was safe.

The course of the Federal Government had been
moulded by the slave-party during the administration
of Jackson, and of his successor Van Buren, whose
term of service had just closed.   I will, therefore,
briefly review their administrations by comparison
and contrast:—

ANDREW JACKSON AND MARTIN VAN BUREN.

Jackson was a native of a slave state and a slaveholder; Van Buren was a non-slaveholder and a
native of New York—a state that in 1827 set free
the 10,000 slaves held under its laws.   Jackson was
a duellist.   In his duel with Charles Dickenson two
of his ribs were shattered; Dickenson was killed.
In his duel with Governor Sevier, of Tennessee, each
was armed with a brace of pistols; the Governor had
also a sword, and Jackson a cane, which he carried as
a spear; the interference of the governor's attendants prevented any serious mischief.   In his fight at
a public-house with Colonel Benton, a slaveholder,
his arm was fractured by a pistol shot.   Van Buren
fought no duel, and probably never went armed.
Jackson was a military man and a lawyer, Van Buren
a lawyer and not a military man.

When Jackson in 1814 was defending New Orleans
against the British forces, he called the coloured
people to his aid; and denounced the spirit that
would treat them as an inferior class.   When the
danger was passed, he praised their prowess, but did

nothing to secure to them their civil rights. When the constitution of the state of New York was being revised, in 1821, Van Buren, at first, voted that coloured people, equally with white, should have the franchise. But he afterwards voted that no coloured person should have the franchise unless he held a freehold estate worth two hundred and fifty dollars; while he granted manhood suffrage to white citizens.

When Georgia, in driving out the Cherokee Indians, made state-law paramount to federal-law, Jackson sanctioned the deed. When South Carolina in attempting to secede on account of the tariff, made state-law paramount to federal-law, Jackson resisted the deed, with the naval and military forces of the United States. The tariff question, however, was only a pretext. Jackson himself denied that dissatisfaction with the protective policy was the real incitement to the ambitious and restless attempt of John C. Calhoun at nullification. "The Tariff" he wrote in 1834, to an intimate friend in Georgia, "was but a pretext. The next will be the slavery or negro question." The free states were the principal contributors to the expenses of the government, because they were the principal consumers of the articles taxed. Senator Benton in his " *Thirty Years View of the Federal Government* " shows that the real ground of secession at that period, 1835, was not the tariff, but slavery; and that a secession avowedly for slavery was anticipated. This was the real danger. Slavery was to the Union what a train of gunpowder is to a magazine; Calhoun stood with the match lighted, threatening to blow up the Union unless the north submitted to the slave-party. A true statesman would have removed the danger by abolishing slavery, as far as he had the constitutional power; but Jackson and Van Buren increased the danger by increasing slavery.

Jackson in his message to Congress, took advantage of his position as president, to libel and slander the abolitionists, charging them with intending, by their publications, to instigate the slaves to insurrection. The American Anti-slavery Society publicly repelled the vile attack, and demanded a Commission of Inquiry. An honest man would have either furnished his proofs; or apologized for the slander; or agreed to an inquiry. But Jackson, though he never ventured to repeat the calumny, never defended himself for his guilty course; never apologized; and never consented to an investigation.

Van Buren, in his message to Congress, took advantage of his position as president, to eulogize slavery, and silence respecting it—as the two handmaids to the peace and prosperity of the Union. He charged abolitionists with imperilling American Institutions. In their simplicity they thought that whips, chains, and bloodhounds were not the best means of governing men. But Van Buren, pitying their ignorance, showed them the more excellent way; and he renewed the pledge of fealty to the slave-party which he had made before his election to the presidency.

Jackson desired Congress to make a law to prevent the transmission of Anti-slavery publications through the post-office; Calhoun brought in such a measure and confessed that his great fear was lest the truth should be known. Benton, and some other slave-holders in the Senate, voted against it—but Van Buren, who was chairman, gave a casting vote in its favour; it was, however, finally defeated.

Jackson in his message to Congress—encouraged the violence of the mobs against the abolitionists; so did Van Buren in his message. Jackson in support of his high-handed measures fell back on the com-promises of the constitution; so did Van Buren.

Neither Jackson nor Van Buren evinced any shame when a slaveholder rose in the Senate to encourage his fellow-slaveholders, by reading from the *Leeds Mercury*, published in England, a letter written by Mr. George Thompson, showing the opposition he met with in New England, as follows:— In Concord, New Hampshire, he narrowly escaped losing his life; in Boston, a short gallows was found on the morning of September 11, 1836, standing opposite his door, with two halters hung from the beam, and the words above them "By order of Judge Lynch." In break-ing up Anti-slavery meetings, the commercial cities —Boston, New York, and Philadelphia—led the way, and the smaller towns followed the example. In Boston, Garrison was dragged through the streets by a rope and thrust into prison; in New York, a meeting at Chatham-street Chapel was broken up, and the houses of Dr. Cox and Arthur Tappan at-tacked; in Philadelphia, Pennsylvania Hall, in which Anti-slavery meetings were held, was burned down. In " *Dr. Beecher's Life*" this is attributed to the con-duct of a white quaker girl walking arm in arm with

I

a black man—thus maddening the people with fury. It was not the case. The indignation of the mob arose from a mistake. Mr. Purvis, a light complexioned mulatto, was walking with his own wife, who was of a much darker colour; and he was supposed to be a white man walking with a coloured woman. The burning of the Hall followed.

When Jackson was president, the city authorities of Washington passed a law that whoever desired to trade or traffic in slaves for profit in that city, must first pay them four hundred dollars for a license. When Van Buren was president the same law was in force, and he did not make the slightest objection against it.

Jackson admitted into the Union the slave state of Arkansas, and the free state of Michigan; but Van Buren admitted no state into the Union, as none applied. Jackson commenced a war with the Seminole Indians. The following was the cause :—The wife of Osceola, one of the chiefs of the tribe, was the daughter of a runaway slave, and for this reason was seized as a slave. The tribe with their slaves numbered about 600 persons. The war cost forty millions of dollars besides many lives. In it bloodhounds, imported from Cuba, were employed. Van Buren, during his administration, continued this war.

It was a rule of Congress during both administrations, that all petitions referring in any way to slavery should be laid on the table unread, and that no further notice should be taken of them.

During both administrations the home slave-trade was vigorously prosecuted. Both presidents put forth their power to seize the trembling fugitive slaves, in order to return them to bondage. Jackson endeavoured to obtain from the British government the market value of American slaves, who being driven by stress of weather to the West Indies, had become free. The American ambassador to England, Mr. Stevenson, a Virginia slaveholder, intimated that a refusal to make the payment might lead to a war—nevertheless the demand was not paid. Van Buren, at the request of the Spanish minister, sent a United States ship to New Haven, to convey to Cuba some Africans, should the Judge, before whom they were being tried, decide that they were slaves. They had been stolen from Africa, were sold to Spaniards in Cuba, and while voyaging from one port of that island to another, they obtained the command of the vessel, and came to the United States. The judge pronounced them free. Van Buren, on behalf of the Spanish minister, had the case appealed to the Supreme Court. One of the judges died suddenly during the trial; of which an impressive use was made by John Quincy Adams, who pleaded for the slaves. They were again pronounced free; and accompanied by some missionaries returned to Africa.

Jackson and Van Buren were the mutual friends of Aaron Burr. At the trial of Burr, at Richmond, Virginia, General Jackson was summoned as a witness, but was not examined. Aaron Burr was the first to nominate Jackson for the presidency. (Jefferson had put both Burr and General Wilkinson on their trial for attempting to invade Mexico.) Jackson ordered General Gaines to march seventy miles into Mexico and occupy

Nacogdoches. Thus Jackson accomplished what Burr was prosecuted for attempting. At an earlier period Jackson had invaded the Spanish province of Florida.

Jackson offered Mexico five millions of dollars for Texas. The offer was refused. It is probable that but for the Anti-slavery movement he would have made war on Mexico. By dexterous management he succeeded in securing an acknowledgement of the independence of Texas by Congress.

Van Buren lost the nomination of the democratic party for the presidency, because he had expressed himself unfavourable to the annexation of Texas to the United States. Jackson and Van Buren both supposed that they could accomplish by the management of the revenues of the country, what could only be accomplished by the abolition of slavery. They aimed to make the people one, but slavery divided them; they wished to check monopoly, but slavery was the greatest and worst of all monopolies; they desired to secure state rights, but slavery despised those rights; they professed to be in favour of liberty, but by consenting to the enslavement of one sixth of the people, they dangerously imperilled the liberties of the entire nation.

During both administrations there was much distress. The sudden changes produced by their policy embarrassed men in business. Many banks failed. With reference to the distress I preached at Morrisville, a sermon from the following text: Habakkuk, iii. 17, 18. "Although the fig tree shall not blossom, neither shall fruit be in the vines; the labour of the olive shall fail, and the fields shall yield no meat; the flock shall be cut off from the fold, and there shall be no herd in the stalls: yet I will rejoice in the Lord, I will joy in the God of my salvation."

Jackson supported slavery to the last, and dying, left his slaves in bondage; Van Buren, changing his policy of fealty to the slave-party, was nominated for the presidency in 1848, by the Free Soil party, formed to resist the extension of slavery, and he received 200,000 votes.

CHAPTER VII.

THE journal of my labours as agent was published in the *Genius of Liberty*. From this I will make extracts showing the state of public opinion on slavery in the various parts of the Territory, and the treatment I received. Occasionally I will indicate the change that has taken place, and the progress that has been made.

In my tour in 1842, from Milwaukee to Green Bay, I preached at Granville, March 23, on the evils of slavery and the duty of emancipation. A few persons made objection because it was the Sabbath. Mr. Leonard Brown boldly defended my course, and advocated immediate repentance as the duty of all who supported slavery. The objection I met with throughout my labours; and I venture to state that during the war between the Federalists and the Con-

federates there have not been as many objections
made to battles on the Sunday, as were made previous
to the war to sermons against slavery on the Sunday.
Had there been more sermons there would have been
fewer battles on the subject.

At Mequon I preached two sermons on the Sunday
to attentive audiences. The same at Sheboygan. A
tragedy had just occurred at the Legislative Hall, at
Madison, the capital of Wisconsin, which arrested
public attention, and led to more serious consideration
of the slavery question. Mr. Arndt, formerly of Pennsylvania, had been elected a member of the Assembly
for Green Bay,—and was conversing in the Assembly
Hall, after the hour of adjournment, with James
Vineyard, formerly a Kentucky slaveholder, who had
been elected a member of the Assembly from Western
Wisconsin. The latter made some irritating remark,
and Mr. Arndt gave him an open-handed slap on the
face. Vineyard immediately took out his pistol, fired,
and Arndt fell a lifeless corpse,—his own father
witnessing the scene, saying " Oh, that I should live
to witness the murder of my son!" Such, however,
was the influence of Southern men, that Vineyard
was never punished. Of course the life of every
member of the Assembly from Eastern Wisconsin
was imperilled. Their relatives trembled for their
safety,—yet these members shrank from opposing
slavery, the source of such violence.

At Sheboygan, one member of the Church declined
attending meeting on Sunday because I preached on
slavery ; yet admitted that it would be right to lift
out of a pit a sheep on the Sabbath. At the close of

the services, however, Mr. Trowbridge, one of the most influential men in the settlement, rose and addressed the congregation. He said that any person who supported slavery was giving his sanction to the putting to death of Mr. Arndt. This legislator was a fair representative of northern legislators—few of whom, if any, ever went armed,—and this is, I believe, the only scene of violence that has disgraced a northern capitol. That Vineyard represented the Southern legislators may be questioned by those not familiar with their history, I will, therefore, quote a few facts from *"American Slavery as It Is,"* published in 1839, by the American Anti-Slavery Society, as evidence that James Vineyard was a Representative of Southern Legislators.

"At the session of the Arkansas Legislature, in 1838, Colonel John Wilson, President of the Bank at Little Rock, the capital of the state, was elected Speaker of the House of Representatives. He had been elected to that office for a number of years successively, and was one of the most influential citizens of the state. While presiding over the deliberations of the House, he took umbrage at words spoken in debate by Major Anthony a conspicuous member, came down from the Speaker's chair, drew a large bowie-knife from his bosom, and attacked Major A. who defended himself for some time, but was at last stabbed through the heart, and fell dead on the floor. Wilson deliberately wiped the blood from the knife with his thumb and finger, and returned to his seat. For this murder he received no punishment."

"Slaveholders," says the same work, "have converted

the Congress of the United States into a very Bear-
garden.   Within the last three years some of the
most prominent slaveholding members of the House,
and among them the late speaker, have struck, and
kicked, and throttled, and seized each other by the
hair, and with their fists pummelled each others faces
on the floor of Congress.   We need not publish an
account of what everybody knows, that during the
session of the last Congress, Mr. Wise of Virginia,
and Mr. Bynum of North Carolina, after having
called each other 'liars, villains, and d——d rascals,'
sprung from their seats, 'both sufficiently armed
for any desperate purpose,' cursing each other as they
rushed together, and would doubtless have butchered
each other on the floor of Congress if both had not
been seized and held by friends.   The *New York
Gazette* relates the following which occurred at the
close of the session of 1838 :—' The House could not
adjourn without another brutal and bloody row.   It
occurred on Sunday morning immediately at the
moment of adjournment, between Messrs. Campbell
and Maury, both of Tennessee.   Maury took offence
at some remarks made to him by his colleague, Mr.
Campbell, and the fight followed.'

"The *Huntsville (Alabama) Democrat* of June 16,
1838, gives the particulars which follow:—' Mr.
Maury is said to be badly hurt.   He was near losing
his life by being knocked through the window, but
his adversary it is said saved him by clutching the
hair of his head with his left hand, while he struck
him with his right.'   The same number of the *Huntsville Democrat*, contains the particulars of a fist fight

on the floor of the House of Representatives, between Mr. Bell, the late speaker, and his colleague, Mr. Turney, of Tennessee. The following is an extract :— ' Mr. Turney concluded his remarks in reply to Mr. Bell, in the course of which he commented upon that gentleman's course at different periods of his political career, with great severity. He did not think his colleague (Mr. Turney) was actuated by private malice, but was the willing—voluntary instrument of others, the tool of tools.' Mr. Turney—' It is false ! it is false!' Mr. Stanley called Mr. Turney to order. At the same moment both gentlemen were perceived in personal conflict, and blows with the fist were aimed by each at the other. Several members interfered, and suppressed the personal violence: others called order, order, and some called for the interference of the speaker. The speaker hastily took the chair, and insisted upon order ; but both gentlemen continued struggling, and endeavouring, notwithstanding the constraint of their friends, to strike each other.

"The correspondent of the *New York Gazette* gives the following, which took place about the time of the preceding affrays :—' The house was much agitated last night by the passage between Mr. Biddle of Pittsburgh, and Mr. Downing of Florida. Mr. Downing exclaimed, 'do you impute falsehood to me?' at the same time catching up some missile and making a demonstration to advance upon Mr. Biddle. Mr. Biddle repeated his accusation, and meanwhile, Mr. Downing was arrested by many members. The last three fights occurred, if we mistake not, in the short

space of a month. The fisticuffs between Messrs.
Bynum and Wise occurred at the previous session of
Congress. At the same session, Messrs. Peyton, of
Tennessee, and Wise, of Virginia, went armed with
pistols and dirks to the meeting of a committee of
Congress, and threatened to shoot a witness while
giving his testimony.'

" We begin with the first on the list. Who are
Messrs. Wise and Bynum ? Both slaveholders. Who
are Messrs. Campbell and Maury ? Both slaveholders.
Who are Messrs. Bell and Turney ? Both slaveholders. Who is Mr. Downing, who seized a weapon
and rushed upon Mr. Biddle ? A slaveholder. Who
is Mr. Peyton, who drew his pistol on a witness
before a committee of Congress ? A slaveholder, of
course. All these bullies were slaveholders, and they
magnified their office, and slaveholding was justified
of her children. We might fill a volume with similar
chronicles of slaveholding brutality. But time would
fail us. Suffice it to say, that since the organization
of the government, a majority of the most distinguished men in the slaveholding states have gloried
in strutting over the stage in the character of murderers. Look at the men whom the people delight
to honour. President Jackson, Senator Benton, the
late General Coffee, it is but a few years since these
slaveholders shot at, and stabbed, and stamped upon
each other, in a tavern broil. General Jackson had
previously killed Mr. Dickenson. Senator Clay, of
Kentucky, has immortalized himself, by shooting at a
near relative of Chief Justice Marshall, and being

wounded by him ; and not long after by shooting at
John Randolph, of Virginia. Governor McDuffie,
of South Carolina, has signalised himself also, both
by shooting and being shot ; so has Governor
Poindexter, and Governor Rowan, and Judge Mc
Kinley, of the United States Supreme Court, late
Senator in Congress from Alabama ; but we desist, a
full catalogue would fill pages.

"We will only add, that a few months since, in
the City of London, Governor Hamilton, of South
Carolina, went armed with pistols to the lodgings of
Daniel O'Connell, 'to stop his wind,' in the bullying
slang of his own published boast. During the last
session of Congress, Messrs. Dromgoole and Wise, of
Virginia, W. Cost Johnson, and Jenifer, of Maryland,
Pickens, and Campbell, of South Carolina, and we
know not how many more slaveholding members of
Congress have been engaged either as principals or
seconds in that species of murder, dignified with the
name of duelling. But enough, we are heart-sick.
What meaneth all this ? Are slaveholders worse than
other men ? No! but arbitrary power has wrought in
them its mystery of iniquity, and poisoned their
better nature with its infuriating sorcery."

Thus far from "*American Slavery as It Is.*"
Aaron Burr was a northern man and a duellist
But he was engaged with slaveholders in a scheme to
extend slavery, designing, as he stated to General
Eaton ; if the Federal Government stood in the way
to "assassinate the president, and turn Congress, neck
and heels into the Potomac." Mr. Giddings, a member of Congress from Ohio, advocated emancipation.

Certain slaveholding members went so far as to desire the hanging of Mr. Giddings and his friends, and so expressed themselves in their speeches.

I proceeded from Sheboygan to Green Bay, the town which Mr. Arndt represented, and in which he resided. I thought, as I approached it, surely the people will see in this loss of their member and townsman, that the welfare of the North requires the abolition of Southern slavery. I was informed that there was a revival in the churches; and as religion softens the heart, it was an additional reason why the subject of slavery should be considered:

> " Break every yoke the Gospel cries,
> And let th' oppressed go free,
> Let every captive taste the joys
> Of peace and liberty."

I asked for the use of the Presbyterian pulpit for two evenings to lecture on slavery; but it was not granted; because there was a revival of religion. One member of the Church went so far as to say, that he knew that if the question of slavery were brought before the people—it would put a stop to the conversion of sinners, it would turn the minds of the people away from the salvation of souls, and call out the latent enmity which was known to exist against emancipation.

In the evening I attended a religious meeting,— and was requested to give an address. The subject I selected was " Growing in grace." In describing the various graces of the spirit, I observed that "gentleness was one of them; and that an institution existed in our land exceedingly hostile to the

J

cultivation of this grace—an institution which fostered boisterous passion on the one hand, and degrading servility on the other. It was slavery. It educated the master to quickness of resentment; taught him to go armed, and thus exposed both himself and others to the most fatal calamities. His habits would be retained even if he removed from the atmosphere of a slave state, and resided where the influences of freedom were diffused. Yes, even then, he would be likely, if he were contradicted or corrected, to commit acts of the most appalling character.—That I was not describing mere abstractions, but sad realities, of which the recent loss of their late member was a striking evidence. The inhabitants of the Territory wept with the bereaved widow and father-less children, but slavery should be regarded as the real cause of the bereavement, and the same grave that received the chains of the slave, would receive also the southern bowie-knife and pistol, and the temper that employed them for the destruction of human life."

All this was borne quite as well as I anticipated. I called on the father of Mr. Arndt and expressed my sympathy with him in the dreadful trial he had been called to endure. I believe the dead body of his son reached the town before my departure from it.

As innocent blood had been shed, there ought to have been a public meeting of the town to express its detestation of the crime. But there was not one. Had there been, some punishment would have been legally awarded to Vineyard. The voice of Arndt's blood cried to God and to the whole Territory from the floor of the Assembly room. It was a loud call. But in Green Bay the people were deaf to it, because there was a revival of religion! As if religion did not recognize the relations which men sustain to God and to each other, and the duties growing out of those relations; and as if the power of religion could be manifested in any other way than in the faithful performance of those duties.

The slave-party ignored all duty so far as it related to the slave population; and required the religious and political parties to ignore it also, on pain of division. A pure Christianity demanded the separation of these parties from slavery, and their reconstruction on the principle of justice. But the churches and ministers sought a revival without such reconstruction. It was so in Green Bay. It was so throughout the United States.

Arndt was the victim of the slave-party. The Churches could not meet and consider the cause of his death, without acknowledging this fact. But they were in Church connection with slaveholders. To condemn slavery would be to condemn themselves for supporting it, and open the whole question of reconstruction. This they wished to avoid, and were glad of the excuse that discussion on slavery would put a stop to the conversion of sinners.

Reconstruction was desired neither by whigs nor democrats in Green Bay; hence they desired no movement in the case of Arndt's death; for the whigs were labouring to place Henry Clay in the presidential chair. If they had met and condemned Vineyard for going armed, it would be censuring Henry Clay also, for he went armed—as did every southern whig legis-lator—all of whom were slaveholders. If they had condemned Vineyard's hasty passion, it would have brought them into collision with the slaveholding whigs, and endangered the unity of the party. I have shown in the previous chapter the quick resent-ment and violence of slaveholding legislators. The whigs held their peace, lest their party should be divided. The democrats sustained similar relations to slaveholders, and fearing a disruption of their party, desired to keep in abeyance any movement which by leading to an Anti-slavery agitation, would lead to a collision with slaveholding democrats.

Besides, their leaders were then plotting for the annexation of Texas, and a war with Mexico, in order to obtain more Territory, and increase the number of slave states. A meeting to consider the death of Arndt would lead to an examination of this policy, and place the people on their guard against it. This would have proved inimical to the success of the democrats—hence they did not desire agitation on the subject.

A revival of religion conducted so as to require no reconstruction of the religious and political parties, as then organized, was of great advantage to Vineyard, and to the entire slave-party.

My design was to continue my efforts for the liberation of the slaves held in Western Wisconsin; to do this I must labour among Vineyard's con-stituents; and if he could take the life of a fellow-legislator with impunity, it would not be surprising if the mob should count on the same impunity in taking the life of an Anti-slavery lecturer. I felt confident, however, that the work would go on, and if my life were sacrificed, Providence would raise up and send into the field more labourers.

We often commenced our Anti-slavery meetings by the audience singing the following piece :—

" Let us raise our supplication
    For the wretched suffering slave,
  All whose life is desolation,
    All whose hope is in the grave ;
        God of mercy !
    From thy throne, O hear and save.

" Those in bonds we would remember
    As if we with them were bound ;
  For each crushed, each suffering member
    Let our sympathies abound,
        Till our labors
    Spread the smiles of freedom round.

" Even now the word is spoken ;
    ' Slavery's cruel power must cease,
  From the bound the chain be broken,
    Captives hail the kind release,'
        While in splendor
    Comes to reign the Prince of Peace."

FROM Green Bay I proceeded south-west to Brothertown; the road is near the eastern shore of Lake Winnebago;—this lake is fifteen miles from east to west, and thirty from north to south, and in winter is usually covered with one great sheet of ice, on which persons travel. In the states, the farther you advance west the milder the climate becomes. In New England the winter lasts six months, in Wisconsin three months, and at the shores of the Pacific there is no winter. But the winter in Wisconsin is severe while it lasts.

It was important to enlist the Brothertown Indians in the Anti-slavery cause, they had votes, and could elect Anti-slavery legislators; an effect would also be produced by their setting a good example to the white people. I preached to them in a large house, belonging to Mr. Dick, an Indian, one of whose daughters I had baptized. At the close, I gave them an account of the reasons which led me to become Agent of the Anti-slavery Society,—of my having, after visiting them, lost the trail at twilight in the woods; that during the forty hours spent there, as I reviewed my life, and as memory rested on some effort for the slave, it seemed a sunny spot; and hence I had decided to labour for emancipation. I announced that I should preach twice on slavery on the approaching sabbath.

In many settlements the people would hear me preach on slavery if I would give them a sermon on prayer, or the atonement, or some other kindred subject. This they called a Gospel sermon. The Rev. Mr. Manning, an Anti-slavery friend of mine, designated it as "buying the privilege" when I took this course.

Among the Brothertowns, as among the Stockbridges, there are different shades of complexion. I knew a man at Sun Prairie who had a Stockbridge Indian wife. There were several nice-looking children—faintly copper-coloured. He was, however, despised for having a coloured wife; so he sent her and the children to live among their Stockbridge relatives, and married a white wife. The difference of complexion can be traced usually to some act of similar injustice. But among the Brothertowns, negroes as well as white persons have intermarried

with the nation. Hence there are shades of complexion from black to red, and from red to white, and
the lighter the Indian the more does he esteem himself, and the darker he is the more is he despised.
The prejudice of the white against the black finds its
counterpart among the light and dark-complexioned
Indians.

The Sabbath came, and there was a large assemblage.
I preached on the sinfulness of slavery. There was
an intermission for refreshment before the next sermon, during which some of those who were light
complexioned wished to speak to me. They proposed
that the afternoon should be occupied by my preaching on some other subject than slavery. The aristoc-
racy of complexion is not limited to the whites. I
told them that the subject had been announced.
That if they preferred, however, a conference in the
afternoon, and each of them would make a short
address on religion, I would postpone my sermon,
and would leave it to the master of the house to
decide which course should be taken. He left me to
decide, and I decided to preach on slavery. I showed
that God had committed unto us the " Word of re-
conciliation." That if men were reconciled to God,
they would, as his children, be reconciled to each
other—the white, the red, the black, the rich, and the
poor. That thus national antipathies and class
antipathies would be removed, and they would be
all one in Christ. At the close of the sermon, I
felt very desirous to ascertain the effect on their
minds. By watching their countenances I learned
that they gave good heed, but nothing beyond.

They are trained to sit quite still, to look grave, and to control their emotions, and this they will do for three hours, making no demonstration. The negroes in the slave states go to the other extreme. In preaching to them, I soon ascertained their sympathies; and if they enjoyed the sermon they would rise when the last hymn was being sung, and shake hands, singing as they did so, throughout the chapel. After the close of the sermon I gave an invitation to any who were willing, to rise up in the presence of the audience and bear testimony against slavery as a sin. There was a pause; then Collins Fowler, a young Indian, and a young disciple of Christ, arose and apologized for speaking first. He stated that he had a mingled feeling of joy and sorrow in his heart; and while he mourned for the slaves he felt grateful for the mercies of God to himself; that he had been convinced by what he had now heard that the American nation was increasing in guilt daily before God; and whatever others thought, and he had no wish to injure their feelings, he was willing to offer his testimony against slavery, even if for doing so his life should be sacrificed.

Mr. Charles Bull, a white man, arose, and remarked that he had lived in the slave states, and had seen that the slaves were very great sufferers, and he believed that they ought to be set free. He was not particular as to the means employed, so that it was done. Mr. Cummach, who is a descendant of the Pequods, and something of a poet, arose. He stated that he would embrace the opportunity presented of testifying against slavery. He then referred to the enslavement of the Indians in the early history of the country ; to the efforts of Las Casas for their liberation, and the substitution of the negroes as slaves instead. " We see the slaves," he added " enduring that very slavery that, at first, was designed for us; they have, therefore, a strong claim on our sympathies." Another arose and said that ever since he had arrived at years of discretion, slavery had appeared to him to be a sin, and he designed in all his intercourse with others, to use his best efforts to promote emancipation.

Another arose and stated that he was of African descent, that he had been sold early in life, had spent a good portion of his youth in bondage; and thus had been deprived of an education; he mourned over the disadvantages of those in slavery ; he wished to see them all set free, that they might all be educated ; and he often remembered them in his prayers.

Another arose, also of African descent, and stated that his heart had often been pained at the thought of his brethren and sisters in bondage ; and one of his chief sorrows arose from the fact that the Methodist Episcopal Church, of which he was a member, had in many of its conferences restrictions by which the preachers were not allowed to preach against slavery.

Squire Mathews, an Indian magistrate arose, and said he thought it was the work of the Good Spirit to cause them to feel thus for the poor slaves. Squire Johnson observed that being a new thing they needed time to look into it, and that they ought not to be hasty. Another Indian arose and stated that as the slaves had been in bondage two hundred years, it could scarcely be called something new, and his mind was already made up on the subject. We agreed to meet the next night and form an Anti-slavery Society. We assembled the next evening. Mr. Cummach said he understood the movement was to change public opinion, as in the temperance reform; and that no weapons of war were ever to be used. I arose and stated that many of the abolitionists were members of the peace society, and would under no circumstances use weapons of war; that by our constitution we promised never to strike a single blow with any weapon of war, but to change public opinion by the press, the platform, and the pulpit.

Mr. Smith, an Englishman, and a Methodist local preacher now arose. I counted on his supporting the movement. He had told me in private conversation that the state of society at the south was neither creditable nor comfortable; and had quoted the golden rule as opposed to slavery. To my surprise, he objected to forming an Anti-slavery Society, because persons preached on the subject on the Sabbath; because those who joined the society would be published in the papers as abolitionists; because some abolitionists had said that they would accomplish their object though blood should flow; and because in some places colonizationists and abolitionists had disputed till blood had been shed. Finally, he admonished them that they had newly become citizens; that they had enemies, and should act with caution. I met his objections, showing that they were entirely dependent on God, that they should do his work, "Remember those in bonds as bound with them," and trust the results with Him. The subject was discussed till past midnight, but no society was formed. Whether sectarian rivalry, or the pro-slavery white people, induced Mr. Smith to take the above course I do not know. But we never had an Anti-slavery society among the Indians, though I doubt not many fell in the war.

A white man, a Wesleyan, passing through Brother-town, heard of my meetings and of the proposal to form an Anti-slavery Society. He stated that he thought the agitation would cause division, and in-quired what the proposed Society was to accomplish? Mr. Cummach, before replying, asked him what was the reason for the existence of churches; were they not formed in order to destroy the works of the devil? To this the white man readily assented. "Then," said the Indian, "the proposed society will have the same object, Slavery is the work of the devil and the Anti-slavery Society will be formed to destroy it."

At Aztalan, though there were many opponents, I formed a good Anti-slavery Society by the following arrangement. I gave notice that on the approaching Sabbath I should preach in the morning, and there would be no sermon in the afternoon, but a prayer meeting for the emancipation of the slaves, at the close of which I should form an Anti-slavery Society.

On Sunday there was a good audience. I preached in the morning, and announced the arrangements for the afternoon. Usually I had two or three invita-tions to take dinner after preaching, but that day there was no invitation, evincing that my proposal was not very well approved. However, I went for a gentle walk. In the afternoon there was a good audience, and very earnest praying by both men and women.

One woman pleaded thus—"Lord, how should we feel if our dear children were taken from us and sold in the market and sent into slavery; and the slave mothers love their children as much as we love ours. Oh break the chains and deliver them." The hearts of the people were melted. I was persuaded we should form a good society. But just as I was about to go round to take down the names, a person of considerable influence arose and contended that it would be the wiser course to postpone the formation of the society, as there were persons who were not prepared to commit themselves either way. I replied that I believed the sympathy with the suffering slave which pervaded the meeting was the work of the Holy Spirit, and that we should grieve that Spirit by delay. I then went round, and about thirty persons gave me their names as members of the Anti-slavery Society.

There was the trifling loss of a dinner, as I had not anticipated the feeling in that particular, but there was the great gain of an Anti-slavery Society; and its members did good service for the cause; the Rev. J. F. Ostrander was one of the most active members.

One person, Mr. P., had said that he would be one of six to tar and feather me, if I preached on Abolition and produced any excitement. Some time after, passing his house, I observed him lying down in front of it, having just come out, after a severe fit of the ague.   He accosted me thus—"Well, Elder," (in the west ministers are called Elders) "you seem to enjoy good health.   I expect that the business in which you are engaged (referring to my Anti-slavery labours) is such that the ague cannot take hold of you."

There was one democrat who was never wearied in opposing me.   He would go round and urge the people not to listen to a minister who preached " niggerology."   He was boarding at the house of a relative of his, who was a friend of mine, who invited me to visit him, take tea, and stay over night.   I went, and after tea, taking the bible, sat down with our democratic friend, proposing that we should together examine the scripture argument relative to slavery.   Instead of doing this, he said—"Where is my hat?" and taking it, he went to the barn.   He could not be persuaded again to enter the house.   His relative said—"If he is so warm as that he will not take cold."   He stayed in the barn all night.   The next morning, Mr. Merriam, one of our Anti-slavery friends. and a Methodist local preacher, heard the democrat uttering rather strong expressions in the house of a neighbour; and going in inquired what was the matter?   "Why," said the democrat, " Mr Mathews is preaching federalism ! yes, federalism !" " But," said Mr. Merriam, " what is federalism ? It is tyranny ! and what is slaveholding ? Tyranny of the worst description ! And what is democracy ? That all men are born free and equal ! And what does Mr

Mathews preach? That all men have a right to liberty. Why the fact is he is as good a democrat as you are!"

The democrat went to Illinois to visit his son, and found him a warm-hearted abolitionist. At once his opposition ceased. We were ever afterwards friends. I visited him shortly before his death, which was caused by a cancer in the face.

One day after riding through the woods fifteen miles, I came to a log-house and rode up to the door to obtain a glass of water. The farmer came to the door, glanced at me, and said—"Are you a minister or a doctor, Sir?"

I replied, "My labours are devoted to secure the emancipation of the slaves!"

"Then we don't want you here!"

"But I am here, so I have the advantage of you. Come please to let me have a glass of water?"

"You can have that, Sir." The water was brought, and the farmer continued :—

"My son has got the ague, that is why I asked you if you were a doctor."

"Well, go and peel some bark from the young poplar saplings, and make a good strong basin of tea with it."

For this and some other directions which I gave him he thanked me, so that in saying he did not want me there, he was mistaken.

At Sun Prairie I formed an Anti-slavery Society of thirty-four persons. Dining with Mr. Adams, a farmer, a pro-slavery neighbour came in, and observed that the slaveholders thought a great deal of their slaves, and he did not believe they treated them cruelly. Mrs. Adams replied—"Well, we thought a great deal of our cow—but we killed it, and are now eating a part of it. They might think a great deal of them as property, but we wish that they might think a great deal of them as members of the human family."

Passing through Madison, I called on an old friend, who had heard that I would marry persons who differed in complexion. He inquired, therefore, of me, whether I would officiate in marrying parties, if one was black and the other white. I replied certainly, unless he could show me that the bible forbade it. He showed me the door immediately. His wife wept the rest of the day at this conduct on his part. Passing through Madison again I attended a prayer-meeting. He was present, and came and made a handsome apology, requesting me to pardon him; I did so. He invited me to take tea with him. I accepted the invitation. We were ever afterwards friends.

Several slaves had been brought by their masters to Western Wisconsin—were held by them for three or four years—and had been sent back to the South as slaves ; usually passing through Galena, being there placed on board the steamboats. There were a few abolitionists in Galena, but their vigilance was not always a match for the cunning unprincipled supporters of slavery. The following letter from my friend Mr. A. H. Campbell, dated Galena, September 25, 1844, furnishes an instance :—

"About the 15th of May last, I was informed one evening, by a coloured man, that there was a coloured woman in the jail of this county (Jo Daviess), who wished for some assistance. My informant stated that she had been brought at midnight, of the night previous, in a wagon, secretly thrust into jail, and was expecting to be carried away under cover of the coming night. Efforts were forthwith made to get out a writ of *habeas corpus*, that she might be entitled to a trial for her freedom. These efforts occupied considerable time, and while they were in progress, a wagon with the woman, guarded by several men, and attended by the jailor, passed down toward the steamboat landing. The wagon was followed to the landing by one who observed it pass, where the woman was seen to be carried on board, the jailor attending. Before the writ could be issued, and the sheriff could get to the landing, the boat was gone. Thus our jail has been prostituted to the puposes of the slaveholder and kidnapper. The jailor, without any authority whatever, has taken upon himself to incarcerate a woman who, for aught we know, was as free and innocent as any of us. From all that can be learned of this woman's history it would seem that she was brought from Fort Winnebago (Wisconsin.) According to the primary law of the land, she was free, and was sent somewhere to the south, no doubt to perpetual slavery."

Mr. Madan, to whom reference has been made (page 72), resided at Elk Grove, in Western Wisconsin. He had purchased a slave woman, Hannah Brown, and after holding her as a slave some years, sent her, and her child born in Wisconsin, as slaves into Missouri. I received the facts from her husband,

who had formerly been a slave to Mr. Madan
Passing through Galena on her way to Missouri—
Hannah made an unsuccessful effort by a legal process to obtain her liberty. I resolved to call on Mr.
Madan. It was reported that he had threatened to
shoot any abolitionist who came on his farm. It was
my rule never to go armed, believing that He whose
will I was obeying was able and willing to protect
me. I called on Mr. M. and stated that I should be glad
to have some conversation with him with reference to
Hannah Brown, who I learned had been sent as a
slave to Missouri. His reply was " I allow no one to
interfere in my domestic arrangements." By this
mode, therefore, I could do nothing. He called it
"his domestic arrangements" to send into slavery
another man's wife, who was legally as free as himself.
I determined next to lay the subject before the
grand jury. In the United States any person, who
believes the law has been violated, may lay the case
before the grand jury. I obtained also from Galena,
a duly certified copy of the trial in that city, in
which Hannah attempted to gain her liberty ; for the
proceedings of the court in one state are recognized
as authority in the court of another state. It was a
proof that the woman was taken from Wisconsin. I
called also on the judge before whom the woman was
tried, to learn on what ground he could give up
one who was legally free, to a man who was about
to plunge her and her free-born child into slavery for
life. He stated that he had decided that he had no
jurisdiction in the case, and therefore gave up the
woman to the man claiming her as his slave.

The grand jury met at Mineral Point. I knew the danger I incurred, and had duly arranged my earthly affairs in case I should be dirked or shot. I went to Mineral Point. One of the Galena Aldermen had promised to send me up a person as a witness who was present at the trial at Galena, but he did not succeed in doing so. Lawyer Hyde, however, who was engaged at the trial of Hannah in Galena, happened to be at the time in Mineral Point. I waited on the jury and made a statement of the case; handed in a copy of the trial at Galena, and referred them to Lawyer Hyde as a witness who knew the facts. The foreman of the jury was a son-in-law of Governor Dodge, and brother-in-law to Mr. Madan. The jury, professing that the evidence was insufficient, did nothing.

I decided to take with me at the next meeting of the grand jury, John Brown, Hannah's husband. He resided at Galena, and was glad to accompany me. When the time came we started in company. It was a new occurrence for a white and a black man to ride side by side. Mr. Brown was mounted on a splendid black horse. We halted at the tavern to dine. The landlord informed me that the company had just sat down, and there was room for one. I told him if there was not room for two I could wait, as I wished to dine with my companion. He made some remark about "niggers dining with white folks;" but in due season the dinner was prepared for us. The landlord would be able to say that a black and a white person in his house ate at the same table! Then an attempt would be made to fathom the mystery. It was already reported that I was a British spy, receiving six hundred dollars a year. I had food and raiment and was therewith content.

I proceeded with John Brown to the jury room; was admitted, related the facts, and referred them to the woman's husband, who was waiting outside. The foreman of the jury was the editor of the leading democratic paper of Wisconsin. He asked me if I had any white witnesses ? I stated I had not—but the laws of Wisconsin allowed a coloured man to be a witness. The foreman stated that it was not their usage to receive the evidence of coloured persons, and they should decline doing it. I withdrew, and stated to Mr. Brown how much I regretted that the jury refused his evidence on account of his colour; that they would only hear a white witness. " Well," he replied, "Judge Dunn knows all about it, for when my wife found they were going to run her off to Missouri, she went and told the judge and tried to get the protection of the law." This was the judge who presided at the sessions then being held. I called at the judge's lodgings, and was ushered into the room where he was. I said I called for the purpose of asking whether he would kindly give evidence to the grand jury with reference to Hannah Brown, who had been sent by Mr. Madan into slavery in Missouri. He gave me an indescribable look. It was an assumed air of dignity thinly veiling a strong feeling of amazement. After a short pause, he said—" When the grand jury sends for me, I shall go!" I hastened back to the jury-room and stated that I had secured a white witness, that Judge

Dunn would come when they sent for him. The sheriff accordingly went and summoned the judge. I saw him go into the room. I never fully ascertained the results, but from what I could gather the judge told them to pass by the case. Such was the power of the slave-party. At noon Mr. Brown left me to get some refreshment. I told him to return to the grand jury-room and I would meet him there, as I had not yet given up all hope. When he went to the tavern he was so severely threatened that he left the town alarmed, and I think we never met again. I returned to the grand jury-room after dinner, and while waiting outside, William Schuyler Hamilton, a son of Alexander Hamilton, who fell in a duel with Burr, came up to me. He is a small man, with a cadaverous complexion, and has a sharp, shrill voice. The editor of the *Genius of Liberty* said of him "He often boasts of his descent, without considering how great that descent is." The following dialogue occurred between us.

"I understand you are an abolitionist."

"I am."

"Now, if you don't leave the town at once, you shall be tarred and feathered, and I will be the leader of a mob to do it."

"I think I can endure it."

He went away to try his power. At the end of the street there was a house which jutted beyond the others, so that a person from the window could see the entire length of the street. In it resided the Rev. Mr. Heaton, a congregational minister, a good abolitionist and a friend of mine. I went to him, told him how matters stood, and requested leave to watch from his window the effect of Hamilton's attempt, so that if the mob should come I might escape. He kindly consented. But Hamilton was unsuccessful. There were threats of throwing me into one of the miner's pits, but I came away unharmed. Mr. Madan in a revival at Mineral Point professed to be converted; but as he did not restore the woman and her child to the liberty to which God and the laws of Wisconsin gave them a right, I had no faith in his conversion.

Wishing to preach on the slavery question at Mineral Point, I made another visit, hoping to have the use of the Court House. The Presbyterians were without a pastor, and by invitation I preached for them in the morning. After dinner Mr. Messersmith, the sheriff, and Thomas J. Parish—who reported himself in the census as owning one male and two female slaves—called at my lodgings, but I had gone for a walk. The sheriff closed the Court House, so I resolved to hold an open-air meeting. Mr. Martin, an English miner, who felt a deep interest in the slavery question, borrowed a chair for me to stand upon.

The people assembled, and while I was selecting a chapter to read, the sheriff came up and urged me not to speak on so agitating a subject. I replied I should my duty. He then inquired of Mr. Martin, who stood by my side, if he was willing to sacrifice his standing in society for the sake of the negroes. Mr. Martin replied—"I own no property here, but if I did it would make no difference." After singing a hymn, reading the scriptures, and prayer, I commenced my sermon by drawing a comparison between the man who, journeying from Jerusalem to Jericho, fell among thieves—and the slaves.

Colonel Nicholls, who kept the principal hotel in the town, was standing near me, and a man named Crawford called out to him to throw me down. Mr. Martin requested that I might be allowed to proceed without interruption, and any who wished to reply could do so at the close." "Martin," said Crawford, "are you an abolitionist?" "I am," said Mr. Martin. "Then," replied Crawford, "you had better clear out from this place pretty quick." "Why," said Mr. Martin, "have I not been a useful and well-behaved citizen among you, why do you wish to drive me away?" Continuing my discourse, I showed that the slave had no right by the laws of the south to any religion, and gave an instance of a slave in South Carolina who was flogged to death for his religion. Colonel Dougherty at once pronounced it the biggest lie he had ever heard. Colonel Nicholls demanded my authority for the statement. I drew from my pocket "*American Slavery as It Is*." published by the American Anti-Slavery Society, and read as follows :—

"Testimony of Sarah M. Grimké, a daughter of the late Judge Grimké, of the Supreme Court of South Carolina, and sister of the late Hon. Thomas S. Grimké.

"A beloved friend in South Carolina, the wife of a slaveholder, with whom I often mingled my tears, when helpless and hopeless we deplored together the horrors of slavery, related to me me some years since the following circumstances. On the plantation adjoining her husband's, there was a slave of pre-eminent piety. His master was not a professor of religion, but the superior excellence of this disciple of Christ was not unmarked by him, and I believe he was so sensible of the good influence of his piety that he did not deprive him of the few religious privileges within his reach.

"A planter was one day dining with the owner of this slave, and in the course of conversation observed that all profession of religion among slaves was mere hypocrisy. The other asserted a contrary opinion, adding, I have a slave who I believe would rather die than deny his Saviour. This was ridiculed, and the master urged to prove his assertion. He accordingly sent for this man of God, and peremptorily ordered him to deny his belief in the Lord Jesus Christ. The slave pleaded to be excused, constantly affirming that he would rather die than deny the Redeemer, whose blood was shed for him. His master, after vainly trying to induce obedience by threats, had him terribly whipped. The fortitude of the sufferer was not to be shaken; he nobly rejected the offer of exemption from further chastisement at the expense of destroying his soul, and this blessed martyr died in consequence of this severe infliction.

"Oh, how bright a gem will this victim of irresponsible power be, in that crown which sparkles on the Redeemer's brow! and that many such will cluster there, I have not the shadow of a doubt.— Sarah M. Grimké, Fort Lee, Bergen County, New Jersey, 3rd month, 26th day, 1838."

A printer connected with the *Miner's Free Press* (!) ascended the roof of the Court House after I had read this, and was continuing my discourse,—and poured down water upon myself and Mr. Martin. Some scoffed, others mocked, but a number patiently listened to the close of the sermon, then without interruption I returned to the residence of Mr. Martin; there were, however, some who threatened to burn his house, but at that period no further violence was offered.

Miss Grimké was by inheritance a slaveholder—but she gave the slaves their freedom.

The subject of my preaching so much upon slavery was once discussed at a party at Aztalan, where I was not present. The Rev. Mr. T., a Baptist minister, censured me strongly for doing so. A lady, a member of my congregation, replied that as the ministers generally never mentioned the subject in their preaching, if Mr. Mathews preached on it the whole of the time, it would not make up for the deficiency of the other ministers.

CHAPTER IX.

I FORMED an Anti-slavery Society at Boice Prairie, near the Mississippi river. Mr. Laughlin and his family were the life of this Society. He was a native of South Carolina, and grieved that his sister was a slaveholder. Returning one day from an Anti-slavery meeting, we started a deer. It made for the river — but was caught, killed, carried to his home, and duly served up. He had the " *Life of Granville Sharp*," which he prized highly, and was never weary of talking of the labours of Clarkson, Wilberforce, Knibb, Thompson, Garrison, and other Anti-slavery advocates. He related to me the case of a tailor in

the south, who had been the means of making five
hundred people abolitionists ; he went round to work
at the houses of those wishing to employ him, was
well informed, and advocated emancipation wherever
he went.

The following incident shows how desirous Mr.
Laughlin was that persons should hear sermons on
the subject. He had a new neighbour just come
from the slave state of Missouri, and calling on him,
stated that on the approaching Sunday there would
be Anti-slavery preaching, and invited him to attend.
The Missourian objected that his clothes were with his
goods, and that they had not arrived, " Never mind,
said Mr. Laughlin, " go in your working dress, and
that you may not appear singular, I will go with you
wearing my working dress." On Sunday Mr. Laughlin
called for him, but he was not ready. At the close
of the service I heard Mr. L., relate to his friends
how it was he had come to the meeting in his working
dress.

His wife, Mrs. L., was ill. I called on her and found
that she was rapidly failing. I asked her whether —
in view of soon entering the world of spirits—she
considered that too much of her time had been
devoted to emancipation? " No," she replied, " I
have not done too much, would that I could have
done more ; though it appears to me I should have
liked to live and see the slaves all set free, but
the will of the Lord be done." She died peacefully,
having the blessings of those ready to perish.

I made an appointment at Plattville, and learning
that there were some threats to handle me roughly,

placed my horse at a safe distance from the town. There was an overflowing congregation. On the question whether an Anti-slavery Society should be formed, there was a discussion, which lasted till midnight, when the following resolution was moved by one of the pro-slavery party :—

" Resolved, that the best mode for abolishing slavery is—for abolitionists to lay by half their earnings to compensate the masters for the loss of their slaves." This was offered by Mr. Grey, a member of the Legislature, and was withdrawn in favour of the following :—

"Resolved, that it is dishonest and disorganizing to form societies in the north having for their object the abolition of slavery without compensation to the masters.

" Resolved, that we will not hereafter countenance, by our presence, any itinerant lecturer whose object is to form such societies."

These were passed by a large majority. I requested the friends of the slave to remain after the audience separated, that we might make arrangements to form an Anti-slavery Society; steps for this purpose were accordingly taken.

Returning to Mineral Point, I announced that I should preach against slavery on the Sabbath. This the *Miner's Free Press* strongly opposed in a most abusive article. The Court House was opened on the Sabbath. The people assembled, and I commenced the meeting. Planks were used for a ceiling above; in the midst of my discourse some of these were removed, and an abundance of eggs was showered down upon me. We adjourned to the outside, and I continued my discourse, being confronted by a large mob. The opponents were armed with clubs, and were led by a stout Irishman. Mr. Martin was severely threatened. In a short time I was interrupted, seized by some of the mob, whose grasp was painful, and dragged into a tavern. At length yielding to my remonstrances, they let me go, and I returned to the Court House. Many of the mob were standing around Mr. Martin, who requested them to bring forward their members of the bar, or their best informed men, and let them present arguments to show that slavery was right. We, on our part, would prove that it was a sin against God and man. We invited them to try by argument to defend slavery, and not rely upon violence.

They were about to seize me again, when a tall, stout New Englander took off his coat, and declared I should be protected. A pro-slavery man then took off his coat, and all began to form into two parties for a contest. Seeing this, rather than that there should be any fighting, I withdrew from the town, uninjured; my clothes, however, bore the impress of the eggs, which it was difficult to remove.

As Western Wisconsin approaches the Mississippi river, its chief features are deep ravines and sharp ridges. Two of the towns built in these ravines are Potosi and Fair Play. I will relate what took place during my visit to each of them. In the former town, I called on the Rev. W. E. Boardman (the work, the "*Higher Christian Life*," is from his pen), and asked permission to lecture in the Presbyterian

Church, of which he was pastor. His reply was "I have been praying in reference to the subject of slavery. We will go and see the members."

They favoured holding a meeting. It was arranged that Mr. Boardman should take my place at a Sunday morning service in the country, and that I should preach for him; and that my subject in the evening should be the slavery question; that at the close I should announce a lecture in the week, or a discussion, if any of the audience wished to defend slavery. This plan was pursued, and at the close of the evening service I announced a lecture, or, if any wished to defend slavery, I invited them to discuss the question at the meeting. Mr. Latimer, a lawyer, an Englishman—from Oxford, my native city, arose and remarked, that as one state could not make laws for another, he did not see how those who were endeavouring to procure emancipation could reconcile their movements with the doctrine of state rights. I observed " that the abolitionists held to the principle that each state must make its own laws; but they regarded laws as the embodiment of public sentiment; and that in various ways one state could influence the public sentiment of another state.

"Missionaries who went from America frequently found in the field of their labours that idolatry was established by law, and they created a public sentiment which led to a change of the law; that slavery, like idolatry, was a sin, and was established by law. One mode of reaching it, was through the various religious bodies of the south, who by Conferences. General Assemblies, Missionary and other organizations, were connected with northern religionists. The slaves were a nation of heathen, according to Southern ministers, and it was the duty of the American churches to see that they were supplied with the light of life." It was then announced that a discussion would be held. Arrangements were made, and in favour of slavery there were four advocates,—Mr. Latimer, Mr. Lord, and another person, all three lawyers, and Rev. F. Mitchell, from Virginia, brother of the slaveholding chaplain. The advocates of emancipation were Rev. Messrs. Boardman and Dixon, Mr. Mills, a lawyer from Kentucky, and myself. The evening came, a large and excited audience assembled; at least one half had formerly been residents in the slave states.

I dwelt on the sinfulness of slavery, and the duty of repentance—giving a sketch of the history of slavery and abolition. Mr. Latimer opposed emancipation on the plea of state rights. Mr. Boardman made an earnest appeal for emancipation on account of the suffering condition of the slaves. Mr. Lord unconsciously aided us by describing the agitation on the subject in the eastern states; an agitation with which he, a northern man, disclaimed all sympathy.

He stated that he had recently visited Boston, Massachusetts. A slave, named Latimer, had, by secreting himself in a vessel, escaped from the south and reached that city. The master was in Boston, determined to regain his property; the judges were in favour of giving up Latimer to the master, but a large portion of the Boston people were determined he should never be a slave again. A song had been

written, each verse ending with the words "Boston
boys! Boston boys! rescue the slave!" In fact, so
far had they gone, that there were pictures circulated,
which represented the judges as harnessed like horses
to a stage-coach, whilst the slaveholder was mounted
on the box of the coach and flourishing his whip over
them. He felt the greatest disgust at such proceedings.

The Rev. F. Mitchell followed; he said that the
chief point in the argument of the first speaker was,
that slavery should be given up because it was sinful.
He claimed, however, the propriety of following the
Apostle Paul, whose rule of life was expediency. He
then argued that it was expedient to hold slaves, and
therefore justifiable.

In following him Mr. Mills observed that he was
not accustomed to expound scripture, but he must
contend against the exposition that had been given.
When Paul stated that he did what was expedient, it
was in reference to things where there was no violation of moral law. For instance, it may be right for
a minister of religion to hold a civil office, yet it may
not be expedient. In such a case Paul would make
expediency his rule. But he would never contend
that he had a right to get drunk, or have two wives,
or hold slaves, for where moral law was concerned
that was his guide, not expediency.

The discussion lasted two evenings. The people
were obtaining light. This the pro-slavery party
feared, and offered a resolution at the close of the
second evening's discussion, which a majority adopted,
against any further agitation of the subject. I re-

mained in the place, and the pro-slavery party probably feared I should give another sermon on slavery on the approaching Sabbath. I may add that Mrs. Woolfolk, living in Potosi, who held slaves in the south, and attended the chapel I preached at on the subject of slavery, sent me word that I might have her slaves at half-price. Notices were posted up, stating—" That a resolution having been adopted that the agitation of the slavery question should cease, and Mr. Mathews still continuing in the town—a meeting would be held to consider what steps ought to be taken." I inquired of the person posting up the notices if any one who chose might attend. He replied " Certainly." I decided to be present. The reason of my delay was simply this. The horse of the Rev. Mr. Dixon, who lived at Fair Play, had strayed away. I lent him my horse to find it, and he had not yet returned it.

The meeting was held, but was not numerously attended. These friends of " law and order" elected a chairman, and appointed a committee to prepare resolutions expressive of the sense of the meeting. The committee reported a preamble and resolution as follows :—" That, whereas it had been resolved that agitation on slavery should cease in Potosi ; and whereas Mr. Mathews still continues in town,—Resolved, that this meeting will not be responsible twenty-four hours for the safety of his life." A friend of mine proposed that they should simply resolve that so far as they were concerned—no harm should come to Mr. Mathews,—and he thought there would be no danger. Of this, however, they entirely disapproved.

I now arose to speak, but they denied my right to do so. I stated that the person who posted the notices, had informed me that all were invited. Hence I had come. That if slavery had simply to do with this life, I should make less opposition to it; but when I looked at the slave as journeying with us to eternity, and yet deprived of the light that should guide him to everlasting bliss, I was resolved to do what I could to remove slavery, because it closed every avenue by which light could reach his mind; and that I believed if any one of the audience were on a dying bed—he would rather send for a minister to pray with him who was faithful to his trust—though unpopular for being so—than for one who moved with the stream of popular feeling and supported slavery.

The attempt to pass the resolutions failed; but my friends feared that I should be mobbed. They desired me to remain in the town over the night, if it were at all possible, not only for my sake, but for the sake of the cause. If I were compelled by the mob to leave, a precedent would be established, and the next Anti-slavery lecturer who visited the town would be waited on by a committee, announcing that the previous lecturer only saved his life by leaving the town; and, unless he followed the example, his life would be sacrificed.

As the sun was setting I walked out of town; my friends tried to ascertain the state of feeling in a quiet way. Soon after the moon rose I heard a whistle—this was the sign agreed on—I came out of the thicket where I was concealed, a friend met me who said—" We think you will be safe; but it has

been deemed prudent to change your lodgings. Stay
at my house." To this he led me by a circuitous
route. I retired to rest, and he went out to watch.
A company of men, near midnight, came near the
house at which I had lodged. They loitered about
some time, and finally dispersed, after going to a
tavern. My horse was sent the next morning, and I
rode out of town, sharply-eyed, but untouched.

Mr. Mitchell was connected with the Methodist
Episcopal Church. Mr. Lyon, one of his class-
leaders, an Englishman, had been before his conversion, a leading infidel. He was now highly esteemed
for his piety. When, however, he heard his pastor
defend slavery from the Bible, it recalled, in all their
bitterness, those feelings he once cherished against
the Bible as a pillar of tyranny. The night following
he had no sleep, but tossed upon his bed. The
conflict in his mind between his hatred of tyranny
and his love of the Bible was terrible ; but he settled
down in the conviction that the Bible was against
slavery. He called on Mr. Mitchell ; handed him
his class-book, and said, "Sir, you have defended
slavery by the Bible, I renounce for ever my connection with your church." This surprised Mr. Mitchell,
and he said, "Brother Lyon, you had better pray
over this subject!" His reply was "Prayer has led me
to see that the Bible is against slavery, which you are
defending, and I am convinced I am right."

I regret to add that Mr. Latimer died by the hand
of an assassin in Potosi.

Passing through Fair Play I observed that a neat
little Presbyterian chapel had just been built, and it

occurred to me, that the religious sentiment which led to its erection would be a sufficient protection for me if I lectured on slavery. I made, therefore, an appointment. Before the meeting took place, Mr. Butcher, one of the worst characters in the town, sent me word that if I came there I should be roughly handled by the mob. I thought differently I went, and put up at the house of the Rev. Mr. Dixon, the Presbyterian minister. The place of meeting was crowded, but they were all men. If it was designed to mob a lecturer, they usually persuaded the women to stay away. Hence women were termed the Quaker militia,—for if they stood between the mob and the lecturer he was safe. In commencing a meeting I would look round and if I could see a few bonnets, I considered myself out of danger. Mr. Dixon was at my side. We commenced the meeting in the usual mode, by singing and prayer.

I described the sufferings of the slaves at the south, and added " Such is the condition of our brethren in bonds." Butcher who sat opposite me, whispered a moment to his fellows, then rose and interrupting me said—" Now, sir, before you go any further, you must tell us who you mean by your brethren in bonds!" I wished to reprove him, and to find out how many friends I had in the audience. I responded " I will take a vote of the audience whether I shall finish the lecture before giving the answer, or answer it now ?" And added—" All those who desire me to finish the lecture before replying to the question asked by Mr. Butcher, please to say " Aye." There were a few "Ayes"—faintly pronounced. " Now," said Butcher, " all those in favour of my question being answered at once, rise up !" Nearly all the audience sprang to their feet. I thought—I am among my enemies, I will soften down the reply as far as truth will allow—and replied "All the human family are brethren, because they are all descended from Adam, and these slaves are a part of the human family—therefore, they are brethren. " You mean," said Butcher, "the niggers?" I replied " The slaves are negroes." He then gave the signal by throwing an egg at me, and the eggs came thick and fast from every part of the room—the mob came prepared and had found a pretext. A brickbat struck Mr. Dixon as he went out. As my cap and overcoat were at the other end of the room, I was compelled to wait till the fury of the storm was spent. Butcher then came up and reminded me that he had sent me word that I should be roughly handled if I came there. I told him I had not a particle of unkind feeling against him; I freely forgave him, but I should be glad to ask him one question—" Did not Jesus die for these slaves ?" This affected him, and for the moment the sympathy seemed to be turning in my favour. Some, seeing this, proposed further violence—one remarking that my throat ought to be cut. But Butcher restrained them, saying they had gone far enough.

After I arrived at Mr. Dixon's, a delegate from the mob made his appearance; he wished to be informed whether I would pledge myself to leave the town by ten o'clock the next morning. I replied that having to lecture twenty-five miles distant the next evening, it would be necessary for me to leave before ten. I

supposed there would be no further opposition. But
while we were attending family worship, we heard a
bell ringing in the streets. On rising from our knees
we opened the door, and by the light of the stars,
could see a black mass approaching the house. "Why"
said Mr. Dixon, "here comes the mob." I said "send
my horse to Jamestown to-morrow morning." Mrs.
Dixon was alarmed, and said "They will see you—
they will see you!" I darted out at the back door,
and over the fence, and ran along the base of the
ridge at the bottom of which the town is built; I
tried to keep the house, which was detached, between
myself and the mob, fearing to ascend the ridge, lest
I should be seen. But the ravine curved, and as I
ran on at its base, I looked back, the house did not
intercept the view of the mob. I could see them, and
feared they could see me. My heart sank within me.
A thrill of agony ran through my entire system. I
thought of the escaping slave pursued by the blood-
hounds; but I ran on, and then ventured over the
ridge; which now intervened between the mob and
myself. I could hear the ringing of the bell, the
yells and shouts of the multitude and the barking of a
dog. It seemed as if perdition had broken loose.

By the star-light I could see what appeared to be
two men; and feared my enemies had tracked me.
Stooping down to get a better view, I saw that the
figures were rapidly receding from me; and by the
sound of their hoofs I discovered that they were
horses and not men. This was a great relief. I arrived safely at Jamestown, and stayed at the house of
a gentleman who would receive me at any time; and

the next day my horse was sent to me. I saw Mr. Dixon afterwards, and inquired what the mob did? " Oh," said he, " they demanded you, and I informed them you were gone to Jamestown. They stated that had you been in my house they would have pulled the house down, unless I had given you up; when they neard that you were an Englishman, they scented for your blood like vultures;—and I do not dare pray for the slaves as my brethren in bonds, should I do so they would drive me also from the town."

On one occasion I called at a tavern after a long journey and engaged a bed. Before I had finished supper the landlady learning that I was in favour of emancipation, informed me that no abolitionist could be permitted to lodge there for the night. I told her there need be no difficulty; I could resume my journey. Paying for my supper, I departed. There was a river to cross. It was not so high as to require my horse to swim; though he had crossed some deep rivers swimming and carrying me on his back. Near midnight I reached the house of a friend, who received me the more cordially because, owing to my Anti-slavery principles, my journey that day had been extended several miles.

CHAPTER X.

A Meeting was held at the Camp-meeting ground, Boice Prairie, on the 1st of September, 1844, and I preached a sermon in the open-air on the immorality of supporting slavery. At the close the following Resolutions, which I had drawn up, were moved by Mr. Chauncy Jones, seconded, and after some remarks, unanimously adopted by the Meeting:—

"That the slave laws of the south are wicked and oppressive, and that the members of the various religious denominations in the slave-states might, by the proper exercise of their political power, almost, if not altogether, abolish American slavery.

"That those members of Churches, who pretend that the Holy Bible sanctions the 'sum of all villanies,'—American Slavery, are doing more to promote infidelity than the avowed advocates of infidel principles.

"That the professors of religion who aid the slave-holder by stating that efforts to liberate the slave are injurious to piety, have yet to learn that the services of the good Samaritan were as acceptable to God as those of the Priest and the Levite, who were so full of religion, that they had no time to do good."

These were published in the *American Freeman*, of November 1, 1844, and tended to check the vauntings of these who claimed superior piety because they stood aloof from the Anti-slavery reform.

On the 8th of September,—I preached a sermon at the Boice Prairie School House, on the " Indications of success from the present aspects of the Abolition cause." On the 15th preached at Edwardsville, on the " Influence of the Slave-power over the American Churches." Mr. Johnson, a Methodist local preacher, invited me to dine, and among other facts related to me the following :—

" I was formerly engaged," he said, " in the coasting-trade at the south, and made it a rule to cast anchor on the Sunday, and attend to religious duties. One Sunday, being some distance from a landing-place, and near a plantation, and observing a coloured woman tending cattle, I took an opportunity of conversing with her about her eternal interests. The tears started from her eyes and streamed down her cheeks, as she sobbed out, ' Sir, I had religion once,

but it was whipped out of me ; my master a Frenchman, compels the slaves to dance every Sunday; at
first I refused, but the strokes of the lash compelled
me to submit, and now I join in the dance.'" The
woman then went and told the other slaves, they
came flocking to the place, and Mr. Johnson published to them Salvation, in the name of the glorious
Redeemer. One slave had a hymn-book. He stated
that he formerly had other books, but they were
taken from him,—but, he added, the Lord blinded
the eyes of those who were searching for my books,
so that they did not find my hymn-book.

I proceeded from Edwardsville to Lancaster, to my
afternoon appointment. It had pleased the Arbiter
of life and death to summon to the spirit world Mr.
McCauly, a warm-hearted friend of the slave, formerly from a slave state. I gave an address at the
funeral, and pointed out his sympathy for the oppressed as a feature of the character of a true Christian.

Although I had not met with kind treatment at a
previous visit, when I lectured on slavery at Lancaster,
I announced that I should give a second lecture on
Monday evening. I will describe both meetings.
Mr. Laughlin accompanied me to the first meeting.
During my lecture in the Court House, we were
somewhat annoyed by pro-slavery persons running
up and down the stairs. We feared they would
attack us at the close of the meeting. Passing near
them on leaving the Court House, they threatened
us severely. We were not, however, further molested,
except by a few stones thrown after us ; and leaving
the town we arrived safely at Mr. Laughlin's house

When I commenced the second lecture at the Court House the audience was small, but increased to a goodly number. There was good attention till towards the close, when some noise was made outside, and while I was offering the closing prayer, the window being open, some one threw a stone at me from the outside—which struck me with great force on the leg.

On coming out the mob came near me, and poured forth a torrent of mingled oaths, abuse, obscenity, and blasphemy. It was horrible, and indicated the depth of that depravity without which slavery can-not be tolerated in any community. Mr. J. T. Mills, who assisted me in the debate at Potosi, kindly invited me to his house. I digress a moment to record with gratification that Mr. Mills is now a Judge. This I learn from the Rev. Dr. Holbrook, now labouring so efficiently in England for the Freedmen's Aid Society, and who has preached extensively in Wisconsin. To resume my narrative,—as Mr. Mills and myself walked along, large stones, thrown by the mob rumbled by, without striking either of us.

After conversing some little time on the over-awing influence of the slave-power, I retired to bed, but could not sleep on account of music and singing, which I supposed proceeded from a public-house near by. It seemed, however, so near the front of the house that I got up, and opened my room door, to ascertain the cause. To my surprise, Mr. Mills was standing as guard at the door. He said " Don't be alarmed, no one shall touch you in my

house!" The music and singing were from the mob
who had gathered round the street door. The
serenading of negro songs having ceased, a young
man came into the house, who stated that the per-
formers had gone to " the groggery to liquor up, and
that they designed to bring down a cannon to fire
off." We put up all the windows to prevent the
panes of glass from being broken by the report. A
cannon belonging to Mr. Banfils was brought, but
the men were so intoxicated that they had some difficulty in firing it; at last they did so several times to
their satisfaction. One of them then boasted that
he had been engaged in the scrape when Lovejoy was
killed, and wished to be engaged in just such another
scrape. As they were proposing to enter the house
and take me, I thought it prudent to retire to the
house of a friend at some distance. Mrs. Mills was
as calm and self-possessed as her husband. I wished
them both good night, and opening the window of a
back-room on the ground-floor, escaped into the
garden, and, unobserved by the mob, crossed the
garden and reached a grove of trees. By a circuitous
route I reached the house of Mr. Mahood, a Virginian,
and an abolitionist. He received me kindly, showed
me to a bed-room, and took my clothes to place by
the fire to dry, for in Wisconsin there are heavy dews,
and a portion of my clothes were wet with dew.

In the morning Mr. Mahood inquired how I slept.
I stated that I shut my eyes and opened them again
and lo! it was morning. I then inquired " How did
you sleep?" " Ah," he said, " I have had bad dreams
all night. In my dream I saw the mob approaching

the house. I went out and forbade any one of them to come within side of my garden gate. One came in ; I took the axe and mauled him up pretty badly. The others had now entered the yard. I then forbade any one of them entering my house; but they rushed in. I seized the saw and struck one in the face, and saw the blood spurt out. I took the shaving-knife and struck another on the arm. So in my dreams I was battling all night with the mob, using the axe, the saw, the shaving-knife, or any weapon that came first to hand." I had given him a description of the doings of the mob at Lancaster before retiring to rest, which had probably awakened his fears that the mob might follow me. The dream naturally followed. When I left him he said, " The people in Lancaster are anxious to sell their town lots, but I shall tell them that if they act in this disorderly way, no one will buy their town lots."

I was informed that the company were afterwards ashamed of their proceedings; and when I went again to Lancaster to enter a complaint before the grand jury against the Rev. James Mitchell, for sending his two slaves from Wisconsin into slavery in the south, I was not molested.

In a subsequent chapter I design to relate the means I used during six years for the liberation of Mr. Mitchell's slaves, including my visit to the Conference as a deputation from the Liberty Association.

At Lancaster there resided a minister, the Rev. Mr. Hopkins, belonging to what is called the Campbellite denomination. In another part of the county I was at a meeting where the Rev. Mr. Miles, a baptist

minister from Indiana, preached, and Mr. Hopkins
was also present. I have referred to a custom among
the slaves of passing through the audience and shaking
hands while the last hymn is being sung. This course
is sometimes adopted by southern white people. At
the close of the excellent sermon of Mr. Mills, Mr.
Hopkins arose and said, " Bless God for such hopes."
As they were singing the hymn he came round to
shake hands with each member of the audience.
Before coming to Wisconsin he held twelve slaves at
the south, and had sold them. I had learned this
from good authority. When he presented his hand
to me I imagined what the feelings of those slaves
would be if they were present, seeing me take the
hand of the man that sold them. He, who had made
and redeemed them was present. He counted their
tears, loved mercy and was angry with the oppressor.
Believing it would be well pleasing in His sight, I
nodded disapproval, and he took the hand of the next
person. An opportunity was then given for announcing meetings. I rose and gave notice that I should
preach at the camp meeting ground on the sinfulness
of slavery, and added that I would mention the reason
why I had declined to take the proffered hand of Mr.
Hopkins. He had sold twelve of my brethren and
sisters at the south, and if he would secure their
emancipation, I should be delighted to shake hands
with him. He was irritated at this, and stated that
he wished no association whatever with me. As the
people passed out there was much conversation as to
the course I had taken. Some said that learning
what Mr. Hopkins had done, they would rather go a

mile the other way than hear him preach. One told me that when I next visited Lancaster no one would hear me preach on account of my treatment of Mr. Hopkins. My reply was—"In five years the people of Lancaster will acknowledge I did right." Mr. Hopkins had no association with me. In less than twelvemonths I went to Lancaster, and inquired after him, and the reply was—he was taken ill, died, and is in the grave. So he lived but a short time on the profits of the poor slaves he sold.

In a settlement near Plattville, I formed a Baptist Church, of which Mr. Bresee, a Canadian, was an active member. It adopted the same rules as to temperance and slavery that the other Baptist churches in Wisconsin had adopted. Two persons came forward for baptism; I baptized them, and they united with the church.

Thus I have described the obstacles in Western Wisconsin to the Anti-slavery reform. Leading men in the political and religious parties were in favour of slavery; and some of them, as I have shown, were slaveholders in defiance of the law. The working classes were chiefly from the south, ignorant and bitterly pro-slavery. The leading men, through their newspaper organs, could have quieted the mob-spirit, but they employed the press to hound on the people, who having less light than their leaders, were less guilty. Gradually, however, the Anti-slavery movement increased in power; strengthened by the violence that was employed to destroy it; and the pro-slavery party defeated its own purpose.

From Western, I now turn to Eastern Wisconsin.

If the former field required faith and courage—the latter required faith and patience. In the former I was resisted by physical force—in the latter by mental power. Keen and cultivated minds vainly strove to defeat the operation of the laws by which the moral universe is governed. Equally wise would have been an attempt to stop the earth in its revolutions on its axis. The power of these moral laws was displayed in the defeat of the supporters of slavery.

In 1847, a meeting of the friends of the slave was held at Delavan, in Walworth County, and the Wisconsin Territorial Anti-slavery Society was formed This town was founded by two brothers—Samuel and Henry Phœnix, formerly from the State of New York. Both were earnest Anti-slavery men, and by example and subscriptions sustained the Anti-slavery cause.

They purchased the land and laid out the plan for the streets of the town; and being zealous temperance reformers, they named each street after some prominent temperance advocate; hence there is a Father Mathew street. The county also is named after Chancellor Walworth, a distinguished temperance reformer; the town, after Delavan.

Each person who purchased a lot in this town was required to engage that no building for the manufacture or sale of intoxicating liquor should be erected upon it.

Samuel, having visited the slave states as Agent of the Baptist Tract Society, had witnessed the sufferings of the slaves; these he desired to relate at the meetings of the Associations of the Baptists in New York.

But every effort was put forth by the friends of slavery to burke the subject. Taking out his watch, on such occasions, he would ask them to give him five minutes time to speak. To this they would consent. By his description of the woes endured by the slaves, the audience would be melted to tears before the five minutes had expired, and he would then be allowed to take as much time as he chose. To the Committee of the American Anti-slavery Society—he furnished a list of the names of religious slaveholders—and they were forthwith supplied with Anti-slavery publications.

Persuaded that some one who had recently visited them had furnished their names—these slaveholders never rested till they had ascertained who it was; and ultimately they procured the dismissal of Mr. Phœnix from his office as Agent.

His dismissal was an illustration of northern subserviency to southern dictation. A similar influence was exerted by the slave-party over almost all Northern religious bodies; and in this consisted the secret of the strength of that party.

In 1843, the annual meeting of the Wisconsin Anti-slavery Society was held at Racine. The presence of Mr. Eastman, editor of the *Western Citizen*, and the Rev. W. T. Allan, an agent of the Illinois Anti-slavery Society—cheered and strengthened the Wisconsin abolitionists. Mr. Allan was a very tall man and an admirable lecturer. His history is deeply interesting. In 1834, he was a member of Lane Seminary, Ohio, and took part in a discussion by the students on slavery, which lasted eighteen evenings.

N

He united with the Anti-slavery Society. His father, the Rev. Dr. Allan, of Huntsville, Alabama, was a slaveholding Presbyterian minister. Before the son returned home, intelligence had reached the family that he had united with the above Society; he was consequently received at his return with the greatest coldness.

After two or three days his sisters came to him and urged him to state what had induced him to join the Anti-slavery Society. He begged them to sit down and he would do so. "Suppose," he said, "that we were living in Africa, and armed men should, in the dead of night, break open the doors, rush into the house, drag us from our beds, load us with chains, take us to the sea-shore, and place us in the hold of a ship to convey us across the sea—would that be right or wrong?" Their response was "It would be, of course, exceedingly wrong." "Just in that way," he continued, "slavery originated."

He continued the comparison till he began to describe the auction, when their father would be purchased by one person,—and their mother sold to another—showing that in this way the slaves were treated, and that the difference was only in colour —when they interrupted him, saying, "Oh, brother, you need not say a word more, we see it all now, we are convinced that slavery is wrong." They then went to their father who was walking up and down the hall, and clinging to his knees, implored him to set free his slaves; declaring that they would not relinquish their hold till he consented. He yielded to their entreaties—and set free his slaves.

The further discussion of the slavery question having been prohibited by the trustees of Lane Seminary—the Faculty endeavoured to enforce the rule to this effect. Against this rule forty theological students entered their protest. "We have," say they, "scrupulously performed all seminary duties, as our instructors will testify. We are not aware of having done anything which could have been left undone, without a surrender of principle. On the contrary, we mourn that we have done so little for those who have lost everything in the vortex of our rapacity; and now all manacled, trampled down, and palsied, cannot help themselves." These students left the seminary—and one of the number was W. T. Allan.

Some of the pro-slavery men in Illinois, being unable to answer his arguments, determined to hinder Mr. Allan in his lecturing tour. Obtaining access by stealth to his travelling conveyance, they stole one of the wheels, and a new wheel had to be made before he could resume his tour.

The commencement of the publication of the *American Freeman*, in 1844, an excellent weekly Anti-slavery newspaper, indicated the rapid growth of the Anti-slavery cause. This was published in Milwaukee, by C. C. Sholes, who had previously published a democratic paper. He attended a course of fourteen lectures, each occupying two hours, delivered by Ichabod Codding in as many consecutive evenings, at the Congregational Church in Milwaukee. To these lectures I had the privilege and benefit of listening.

Mr. Cushing, an early labourer in the cause, seeing the chapel crowded, evening after evening, and the rapt attention of the audience, said, "This is the hour of the triumph of Anti-slavery principles." Of the lecturers who visited Wisconsin Mr. Codding was the most eminent. A native of New York, he studied at Middlebury College, Vermont. In his junior year, being familiar with the studies of the term, and wishing to replenish his purse, he obtained leave of absence, and became Lecturing Agent to the Vermont Anti-slavery Society. Mobs of ruffians assailed him, and the Faculty, more sensitive for the popularity of the College than for the outrages inflicted on the slaves, declared that he was away without liberty, and censured him. He returned to the college and demanded a college meeting, prepared the facts for the press, and threatened the officers with their publication in the public journals, unless they rescinded the vote of censure. Finally, they gave him a letter showing that he was not away without leave. Having established his innocence he left the college for ever.

In the State of Maine Mr. Codding had the honour of addressing the Legislature for three hours, upon the question of annexing Texas to the Union. It was afterwards said that it made more than forty members abolitionists.

In personal appearance Mr. Codding is rather tall, and has somewhat the air of a farmer. At a glance he is seen to be a man of mark; having a good forehead, fine, dark hair, a mouth somewhat large, and eyes of extraordinary mesmeric power. His gestures were graceful and dictated by his strong emotions. He has a rare voice, enunciates with great distinctness, infuses into his words meanings coming from the heart and reaching the heart, in a word—at his will he bids the smiles or tears of his hearers come and depart, or calls for the presence of both smiles and tears at once. I see him now, saying, "Slavery sweeps away the decalogue,"—and as he utters the word "sweeps," his right-arm gracefully but rapidly describes a curve, both voice and gesture leaving on the mind an impression not to be removed.

At Brighton, New England, a wild mob gathered to assail him. While he was offering prayer two of the boldest entered the church, rushed to the pulpit, seized him, and dragged him down into the aisle. Two young men who had known him at college being present, seized upon the intruders, overcame them, and binding them with handkerchiefs, placed them in the front pew, and thus they were constrained to hear one Anti-slavery lecture at least. He was mobbed at Brunswick; and with Judge Jay, at Bedford, New York.

While lecturing in Southern Illinois, he was seized by his neckerchief by a pro-slavery man, who was infuriated and presented a pistol at his breast; but the calm fearlessness of Mr. Codding overcame him, and at his bidding the pistol dropped on the floor. On one occasion, whilst he was lecturing, a perfect volley of eggs was thrown at him, and he was drenched with them. One eye was much hurt by a missile, yet he preserved his good humour through the treatment, and with excellent good nature, said

" Well, boys, I am fond of eggs, but I would like to have them done up in a little different style; may be in the haste of your generosity you did not take that into consideration." The "boys" roared with laughter at his reply to their peculiar arguments.

Regarding the publication of the *American Freeman* as vital to the progress of the Anti-slavery reform, I devoted much time to its aid. Mr. Sholes was an able editor, and the Rev. A. L. Barber and Mr. S. T. Taylor frequently contributed articles, so that the paper had a high literary standing. It passed through some vicissitudes, was removed to Prairieville, when Mr. Codding, who had become pastor of the Congregational Church, became the editor. Afterwards it was returned to Milwaukee, and the name changed to the *Wisconsin Republican.* Sherman M. Booth became its editor.

In his case the State of Wisconsin and the Federal Government came into collision. Joshua Glover, a slave who had escaped from St. Louis, was apprehended and imprisoned at Milwaukee. Mr. Booth, at the head of a company, went and released him from prison. For this he was tried before the United States District Court, and convicted of violating the Fugitive Slave law; whereupon, he was brought before the Supreme Court of the State of Wisconsin, on a writ of *habeas corpus*, sued out in his behalf, and Judge Smith decided the Fugitive Slave Law to be unconstitutional and void, and set Mr. Booth at liberty. This honor belonged to Wisconsin alone. No other judge having given a decision, on this question, so true and just.

But this righteous decision was overruled by that pliant tool, at that period, of the slave-party—the Supreme Court of the United States; which unanimously affirmed the validity of the Fugitive Slave Law; and also the right of a State Court to grant a writ of *habeas corpus* in behalf of a person imprisoned under Federal authority; but declared that the custodian, in such case, had only to make return that he *was* so held, and the State Court must be satisfied, and could proceed no farther.

Mr. Booth was liberated by President Lincoln.

Among those who visited Wisconsin, and by their advocacy strengthened the Anti-slavery cause, were the Revs. Lyndon King, H. McKee, and Mr. Martin Mitchell. Good service was also rendered by escaped slaves who told the story of their wrongs. Prominent among these were Andrew Jackson, and Lewis Washington. The former in escaping from the south was pursued by blood-hounds. Finding that he could not avoid them he provided himself with a large club. He was a Methodist. When the blood-hounds came up, he attacked them with his club, right and left, calling out at every blow, " Lord, help! Lord, help !" He overcame them, and reached the free states.

The former master of Lewis Washington, R. Erickson, of Missouri, offered a reward of one hundred dollars for " Wash," a run-away slave. " Wash " responded by advertising in a Chicago paper, a reward of one hundred dollars, for the recovery of twenty years wages of which he had been robbed by Erickson.

Samuel Daugherty, Esq., a New Englander, residing at Lisbon, near Milwaukee, took a deep interest in the Anti-slavery cause, which was fully
shared by Mrs. Daugherty, his wife. Knowing that
my salary was small, he gave me a room in his house
for a study, and desired me to be his guest whenever
I pleased, and as long as I pleased, free of all
charges.

A bright mulatto young woman escaping from
slavery in St. Louis, reached Milwaukee, but being
pursued by the slave-hunters, she was placed in a
flour barrel, the head being fastened down. Thus
concealed and placed in a wagon, she escaped detec-
tion and safely reached the residence of Squire
Daugherty. She told us a tale of the tender mercies
of slaveholders. Mrs. Daugherty, a truly motherly
woman, would have the slave take a cup of tea with
the family. While we were at tea, a pro-slavery
neighbour opening the door without knocking, saw
the slave, and reported her to the slave-hunters, who
came to the house and demanded her. She had taken
refuge in the cellar, but fearing the house might be
searched, escaped through the cellar window, and
concealed herself in the broom-corn—a corn planted
to make brooms of—and which, from its mode of
growth, was a safe hiding place. She was afterwards sent safely to Canada, disguised as a young
man.

CHAPTER XI

Slavery and Freedom in the Territories—Policy of the Federal Government—Policy of the Candidates for the Presidency in 1860—Slavery in Wisconsin Territory—The Slave "Alice" sent South by Rev. James Mitchell—Failure of an Attempt to Rescue her—Resolutions relating to the case adopted—A Deputation waits on Mr. Mitchell—His Presence, Confession, and Defence at the Anti-slavery Meeting—A Power of Attorney not a Deed of Emancipation—Report of a Committee on Kidnapped Persons — The Discussion — Mr. Mitchell's conduct denounced as Kidnapping—My visit to the Methodist Conference—The "Address" to that Body—The Trial—One of his Slaves gains her Liberty—Report of Conference Proceedings—Mr. Mitchell deposed from the Ministry—Reconsideration—The Power of the Slave-party—Presentment of Mr. Mitchell to the Grand Jury—The Foreman a Slaveholder—The Result—Position of the Methodist Church on Slavery.

THE ROCK on which the Federal Union split was not slavery in the states, but slavery in the Territories. A Territory is a state in the bud; a state is a Territory full-blown. The President appoints the governor of a Territory; the state elects its own governor. The laws of a Territory must be forwarded to Washington for the approval of the Federal government; state-laws require no such approval.

The Federal government left the slaves in each state to the entire control of the respective states' government. With regard, however, to slavery in the Territories, the Federal government claimed the power to prohibit it, or to sanction it, or to leave the subject in each Territory to the decision of its own inhabitants. The Federal government prohibited slavery in Ohio, Indiana, Illinois, Michigan, and Wisconsin, when they were Territories. It sanctioned slavery in Kentucky, Tennessee, Alabama, Mississippi, Florida, Louisiana, Missouri, and Arkansas, when they were Territories. By the Missouri compromise it prohibited slavery in all its Territory north of 36 degrees 30 minutes; and virtually sanctioned slavery in its Territory south of that line. Kansas was north of the line, and by the compromise free from slavery.

By its war with Mexico the Federal government acquired additional Territories; and it decided, after eight years of discussion, to refer the slavery question to each Territory, that the inhabitants might determine for themselves whether to adopt or prohibit slavery. The civil war in Kansas grew out of the two parties on this question.

In 1860 there were four candidates for the Presidency; and their respective positions in relation to this question were the chief points at issue.

Lincoln represented the policy of excluding slavery from the Territories; Douglas, that of leaving the question to each Territory to decide for itself; Breckenridge, that of establishing slavery in the Territories; Bell was prudently silent on the ques-

tion, avowing no policy in relation to it, at least till
the election was over.   He probably had a latent
policy, as he joined the secessionists.   After the
election of Lincoln those who claimed a right to
establish slavery in the Territories, seceded and
formed the Confederacy.

The war followed.   A law was passed excluding
slavery from all the Territories; and afterwards
slavery in the states went down in blood.   Wisconsin
was practically regarded as a slave territory by the
slave-holders ; first, by those who held slaves, as reported in the census; secondly, by those who having
for a period held slaves in the Territory had sent
them into chattel slavery at the south.

It was established by decisions in the Courts of
Louisiana, and other slave states, that a slave taken
by his master, or removed with his assent, to a free
state, or to any country wherein slavery was prohibited, became thereby free, and could not be returned or reduced again to slavery.   On this ground
I contended in 1840 that the slaves held in Wisconsin
were free.

(The Dred Scott decision was not made till 1856 ;
this declared that a slaveholder may carry his slave
to any Territory of the United States—and continue
to hold him as property.) If I could succeed in
obtaining a decision from a civil court in Wisconsin
that one slave was free—it would secure the freedom
of all the others who were held in the Territory ; and
show that those who had been sent south into
slavery were also legally free.   I have related my
unsuccessful effort for this object, in the case of

Hannah Brown;—and will devote this chapter to an account of my efforts to obtain the liberation of the slaves of the Rev. James Mitchell, referred to in page 71, who had been sent into southern slavery. In no other case did we succeed in obtaining evidence so full and clear; there was no other slaveholder in Wisconsin who was a minister; no other, who by his religious connections could be so well reached by Anti-slavery influences; no other, who, owing to his residence in Eastern Wisconsin, could be made to feel his amenability to its public sentiment; and no other, who entering an Anti-slavery meeting attempted to justify himself in trampling on the laws. I stood alone at the beginning of the contest, but as light was diffused and calmly reflected upon by the people, they united with me. Eventually, the Conference was induced, by outside pressure, to move on the question.

Owing to an agitation, continued for six years, one of the slaves obtained her freedom; the other was, I suppose, emancipated by Mr. Lincoln's proclamation. Although all that was desired was not accomplished, yet the rescue of one soul from the horrors of slavery abundantly repaid for the toil. The advantages however, of the agitation can scarcely be over-estimated. The public attention was arrested, and by degrees the public sympathy was enlisted in behalf of the slaves; afterwards no one ventured to report himself in the Wisconsin census as a slaveholder. Persevering anti-slavery agitation always secures the abolition of slavery. The weapons I used in this contest differed from those employed by Captain

John Brown. But I may appropriately make his defence my defence—" God is no respecter of persons,"—and " Had I so interfered in behalf of the rich, the powerful, the intelligent, and so called great, or in behalf of their friends, either father, mother, brother, sister, wife, or children,—or any of that class, and suffered and sacrificed what I have in this interference, it would have been all right."

The events illustrate the characteristics of the American mind, I therefore trace them in detail. A similar account from my pen was published in the United States by the Revs. Luther Lee and Lucius Matlack, the Anti-slavery Historians of the American Methodists, in their work showing the influence of the slave-power over the American Methodist Episcopal Church, giving an account of the secession, and the formation of an Anti-slavery Wesleyan Church.

Visiting Galena in 1842, the coloured people came to me and informed me that the Rev. James Mitchell had brought "Alice," one of his slaves, from Wisconsin to Galena, placed her on board a steam-boat, and " run her off" to the south—to perpetual slavery; and they besought me to endeavour to procure her liberation. The conversation I had held with Mr. Mitchell, page 71, made him apprehensive that the law would be enforced, and that the slaves he held would be declared free; and to guard against the expected loss he had sent one of the slaves to the south.

Promising the coloured people that I would do what I could, I visited Plattville, on the outskirts of which town Mr. Mitchell resides. Mr. H. Laughlin, son of the South Carolina Abolitionist, referred to on page 134, was the constable. Partaking of his father's spirit he was endeavouring to obtain subscriptions for the purpose of sending a lawyer to St. Louis, to restore "Alice" to freedom. The amount required was more than he succeeded in obtaining. Mr. Aiken, deacon of the Presbyterian Church, informed me that he had been to Galena, and conversed with the clerk of the steamboat on which the unfortunate "Alice" was taken south. The clerk stated that Mr. Mitchell brought the slave to Galena, placed her on board under the care of the captain, with directions that she should be taken to St. Louis, and left there, and that this had been done.

In 1842, when the Territorial Anti-slavery Society was formed at Delavan, Mr. Root, a Presbyterian minister, arose and stated that a slave had been sent to the south from Wisconsin, by a Methodist minister. When the name was called for, I arose and referred to the circumstances, giving Mr. Mitchell's name. It was, however, considered injudicious to move on the question, unless we were able to command a greater amount of evidence. I felt persuaded that Mr. Mitchell would rather restore the slave to freedom than lose his position in the Methodist Church. I related the facts to several members of the Conference, and earnestly requested them to lay the subject before that body, but they declined making any reference to it in the Conference. I believe, however, that just after Mr. Mitchell's character had passed, in one of the Conference Meetings, a member arose and referred to the charge, but the bishop told him it was too late, he should have mentioned it sooner. At the meeting of the Wisconsin Anti-slavery Society at Racine, in 1843, I moved the following preamble and resolution :—

"Whereas, the Rev. James Mitchell has sent a coloured woman into a slave state,—Resolved, that he is bound to inform the public whether he sent her off as a free person or as a slave, and if as free, whether he gave to her free papers." These were seconded, and adopted.

Mr. Mitchell had been sent by the bishop to Eastern Wisconsin, and he was preaching at Racine, and Southport. I therefore moved for a deputation to wait upon him and learn his reply. The deputation was appointed. For this step I was not only charged by members of the Conference with slandering Mr. Mitchell, but a communication was sent to Mr. Eastman, signed "Anti-Abolition"—stating that it was illegal to hold slaves in Wisconsin, and hence the statement relative to Mr. Mitchell must be false.

I forwarded to Mr. Eastman the list of names of those who reported themselves in the census as slaveholders, and pointed out that though they were held in defiance of law, yet public sentiment sanctioned their enslavement. I procured from Mr. Mitchell's neighbours statements of what they knew as to the sending off of the slave. The bishop removed Mr. Mitchell to Milwaukee, and he became pastor of the Methodist Church in that city.

In 1844, the Wisconsin Territorial Anti-slavery Society met at Milwaukee. This was the period when the citizens were so aroused by Mr. Codding's

lectures. All the ministers agreed to attend the
meetings of the Anti-slavery Society; Mr. Mitchell,
with the rest; but, judging from the course pursued,
I think that he made it a condition of his attendance
that I must not be permitted to make any inquiry
as to his antecedents on the slavery question; that
bygones should be bygones. The other ministers
probably thought that it would be so important to
have his co-operation, as he was a Virginian, that
it would be well to consent to this arrangement.
Certainly, this theory is quite in harmony with their
conduct.

The Executive Committee of the Wisconsin Anti-
slavery Society were the deputation to wait on Mr.
Mitchell and inquire about the slave. As soon as I
reached Milwaukee, I sought Rev. A. Gaston, the
secretary of the above-named society, and tendered to
him the certificates I had obtained from Mr. Mitchell's
neighbours. But how was I surprised to hear him
reply, " We have done nothing, and can make no
report on the subject !" I mentioned it to the Rev.
Mr. Foote, the Presbyterian minister, from Racine,
" Oh," said he, " let bygones be bygones, Mr.
Mitchell is now with us, and in favour of the Anti-
slavery movement."

The proceedings commenced. The secretary read
his report; it was ably drawn up, and sketched the
progress of the Anti-slavery cause all over the world.
But there was a fatal omission. There was no reference to the Wisconsin slaves, and no reply to the
inquiry as to Mr. Mitchell's slave.

A motion being made to accept the report, I arose,

and stated that before voting I wished to ask whether
the meeting would have the satisfaction of hearing
from the committee on a subject it was appointed to
investigate ;—the case of a young woman sent into
slavery by a Methodist minister ? I had no wish to
press the matter at that period of the proceedings,
provided the committee would give an assurance that
a report would subsequently be presented on the
subject.   An assurance was then given that the committee would make a report upon it.   The report
presented was then accepted and adopted.   I inquired
in the afternoon if the committee were now prepared
to report on the case of the slave sent south by a
minister; for the evening would not be so favourable
an opportunity, owing to other business, for the
report to be presented ? It was stated in reply that
it was too late, as the committee had been discharged!
I then begged leave to move the appointment of
another committee on the subject, and referred to
the promise which had been made and violated.   My
motion was violently opposed by what was evidently
a Mitchell-party in the meeting.   It was denounced
as inquisitorial to make any such inquiry of Mr.
Mitchell, and a motion was made to expunge from
the records the resolution adopted in Racine, calling
on him for an explanation.

Mr. Codding immediately arose, and showed that
the resolution was not inquisitorial.   That Mr.
Mitchell was a public man, and subject like all public men to public inquiries.   That the inquiry was
simply taking one step in the effort to rescue from
the horrors of slavery one of those very persons for

whose emancipation the society had been formed. The motion to expunge was lost. My motion prevailed, and the committee was appointed. Charles Durkee, Esq., (who has been recently appointed Governor of Utah), was a member of the committee. I took an opportunity of handing to him the testimony of Mr. Mitchell's neighbours. He kindly informed me that he had conversed with Mr. Mitchell, who had promised to give an explanation to the meeting.

The afternoon of the second day had nearly passed away. There had been no explanation. I knew that there would be a press of business in the evening, and ventured, therefore, to rise and suggest that an excellent opportunity was now afforded for Mr. Mitchell to give the explanation he had promised. This brought down upon me a denunciatory speech from Lawyer Finch, of Milwaukee, who observed that Mr. Mitchell did not wish to say any thing on the subject. Then there was more discussion and much excitement, and it became necessary for Mr. Mitchell to rise and give an explanation. He arose to do so, greatly to my relief. He commenced by complimenting the meeting on its candour, piety, and talent. He expressed the hope that justice would be done to him, even in an Anti-slavery Meeting—a hope that he had never heretofore indulged. He stated that an offer had been made him of property worth from 10,000 dollars to 15,000 dollars, which he declined to accept simply because he could not conscientiously hold property in slaves.

On leaving the south, however, two slaves were

given to his wife by her father; and in the deed of gift there was a proviso, that if she should ever part from them, she should send them back to her father. He then added—"I brought them with me to Wisconsin; and after living with me some years, they desired to return to the slave states. I took one of them in my buggy, carried her to Galena, and paid her fare to St. Louis; and afterwards, I sent back the other, and I would do so again to the tenth time." Then looking across the room at me he said, as he resumed his seat, "I could wish there were no sectarian feeling in bringing up this question."

By this speech he blinded the minds of the audience, so that when I arose to compare his own statement with the laws, and give the views of leading lawyers, and of the Governor of Wisconsin (already stated in page 69), I was prevented from speaking by the loud cries of Mr. Mitchell's friends of "question, question, question." I inquired "Gentleman, will you not allow me to speak!" but the only response was, "question, question." I sat down, observing "I do not call that justice." "Nor I," said one; "nor I," said another. I resolved to make Wisconsin ring with it. In the evening's proceedings, very late, Mr. Bean, the Methodist steward, arose, and begged to move a resolution—"That the pressure brought to bear on Mr. Mitchell, to induce him to explain his conduct relative to the two slaves, was ungentlemanly, unchristian, unkind, and unjust." Mr. Codding opposed this, and it was withdrawn. Another, however, was moved, exonerating Mr. Mitchell from all intentional wrong in sending back the slaves. I arose

and protested against the passing of the resolution,
contending that by both Divine and human law Mr.
Mitchell had been guilty of kidnapping.

The resolution was put to the meeting; the
Mitchell-party, about twenty in number, voted for
it—about fifteen voted against it; but the meeting
as a body did not vote either way. Many of them
were recovering their sight from pro-slavery blind-
ness, and saw men as trees walking. Their education
had begun, the lesson was difficult. I believed, however, that they would soon learn that the laws of ·
Wisconsin prohibited slavery.

Soon afterwards the Rev. Mr. Cross, connected
with the Anti-slavery Wesleyan Church, who had
seen the deed of gift relative to the slaves, wrote
from Illinois a letter, which he sent to Milwaukee,
stating that the deed provided that if Mrs. Mitchell
should die childless the slaves were to become the
property of Mr. James Mitchell, and the deed was
signed by Mr. Mitchell's own hand. Though the
freedom of the slaves depended on their having been
brought to Wisconsin, and not on the deed, yet this
showed that Mr. Mitchell had deceived the Convention respecting it.

Passing through Milwaukee a few days afterwards,
a friend of mine came to me in the street and con-
gratulated me on my salary. On my asking for an
explanation, he said "You have laboured persever-
ingly for the liberation of Mr. Mitchell's slaves;
they are now free,—what can be a better salary than
the consciousness of liberating from slavery two
human beings." He stated that to meet the new

difficulty arising from the letter of the Rev. Mr. Cross, Mrs. Mitchell had executed a deed of emancipation at the office of Lawyer Finch. This she had stated at a meeting of the Ladies' Anti-slavery Society, in Milwaukee; and also to Mr. Fowler, who conveyed her in his carriage from the office of the lawyer to the post-office, where she placed in the receiving box the deed of emancipation.

I called at the office of Mr. Finch, and asked him if he had drawn up a deed of emancipation for Mrs. Mitchell's slaves? He replied "No, but I have drawn up a power of attorney in reference to their disposal."

The bishop made Mr. Mitchell a presiding elder, an office somewhat similar to that of "preacher in charge" among English Wesleyans. As the slaves were not restored to freedom I resumed the agitation with voice and pen.

In reply to interrogatories proposed to Mr. Mitchell by some of the members of his church, he stated that one of the slaves had been taken ill in St. Louis, and the wages of the other had been absorbed in paying her expenses, except eighteen dollars which had been sent to Mrs. Mitchell, and she had received it. From this it was evident the slaves were hired out.

The St. Louis newspapers stated that one of the slaves had become the mother of a child. She was unmarried.

In 1845, the Wisconsin Anti-slavery Society met at Prairieville (now Wuakesha, the Indian word for Fox, it being near the Fox river); I attended, and called together a few earnest Anti-slavery friends, and stated my plan of effort, which they cordially agreed to support. I was to move for a committee on the case of persons kidnapped from Wisconsin and sent into southern slavery; and they agreed to nominate Rev. A. L. Barber, Jacob LyBrand, and Deacon Bacon, with myself, as the committee. Charles Durkee, Esq., was chairman of the meeting. I moved for the committee as pre-arranged, the names were mentioned, and the committee was appointed. Lawyer Finch saw that those appointed would make the liberation of the slaves the paramount consideration. He, therefore, moved that the subject of kidnapped persons be "referred to a special committee." This was carried. The chairman inquired —how shall this committee be appointed? Mr. Finch responded—" By the chair." " Then," said the worthy chairman, " I will appoint those just appointed." So Mr. Finch gained nothing by his motion. I called the committee together and read a report with some resolutions which I had prepared in advance.

The report showed that slaveholding was manstealing, which under the law of Moses, was to be punished with death; and by the Apostle Paul was classed with the greatest of crimes; that slaveholding was contrary to those principles of liberty and justice which the constitution of the United States was established to secure; that the Ordinance of the North-West for ever excluded slavery from Wisconsin. Extracts from the Ordinance were quoted as follows:

" And for extending the fundamental principles of

civil and religious liberty, which form the basis whereon these republics, their laws and constitutions, are erected; to fix and establish these principles as the basis of all laws, constitutions, and governments, which for ever hereafter shall be formed in said Territory; to provide, also, for the establishment of states and permanent governments therein, and for their admission to a share in the Federal councils on an equal footing with the original states, at as early a period as may be consistent with the general interest:

"It is hereby ordained and declared, by the authority aforesaid, that the following articles shall be considered as articles of compact between the original states and the people and states in the said Territory, and *for ever* remain unalterable unless by common consent." Then in Article 6 is the following:—

"There shall be neither slavery nor involuntary servitude in the said Territory, otherwise than in punishment of crimes, whereof the parties shall be duly convicted."

My report had in the next place a quotation from a law enacted by the Wisconsin Legislature, fining any one 1000 dollars who should hold a slave in Wisconsin, and declaring that whoever should send a free coloured person out of Wisconsin into slavery, should pay one thousand dollars; and that if the plea were made that the person consented to go into slavery, it must be shown that such consent was not obtained by fraud or force.

The statement made by Mr. Mitchell in Milwaukee was examined; and it was shown from his own statement that he had violated the law of God, the principles of the constitution, the Ordinance of the North-West, and the law of Wisconsin. The committee cordially agreed to the report. I then saw Mr. Codding; told him we should contend that "Slaves touch Wisconsin and their shackles fall," as Cowper said of England; and requested his able advocacy in supporting the report. "Yes," he replied, "you shall have it, and I will move that the report shall be the special subject of this evening's proceedings." He moved a resolution to that effect, and it was carried.

We met in the evening in the Methodist Church where Mr. Mitchell was accustomed to hold his quarterly meetings; and anticipated that he would be present. The place was crowded. The proceedings were opened by singing and prayer. As chairman of the committee I then read the report; and gave a brief history of the case, from the time when I called at Mr. Mitchell's house to the present time; and I closed by stating that whatever course the audience might think fit to pursue—I took them to witness that the blood of these slaves was not on my head!

The resolutions then came up in their order. The first was,—that the meeting rescind the resolution adopted in Milwaukee at the previous annual meeting, exonerating Mr. Mitchell from blame in sending the slaves into slavery at the south. This was unanimously agreed to.

The second was "That according to the Ordinance of the North-West and the laws of Wisconsin, no person can be a slave who treads the soil of Wisconsin, and whoever sent persons from its Territory into

chattel servitude, was guilty of kidnapping and man-
stealing, and violated the laws of God and of the
Territory of Wisconsin."

The discussion on this lasted till near midnight.
Several Wesleyan ministers endeavoured to excuse
Mr. Mitchell.

Mr. Peck, a Methodist Episcopal local preacher,
deeply regretted to see one minister attacking
another in this way ; he thought it was injuring the
Anti-slavery movement.

Mr. R. H. Deming, a Methodist Episcopal local
preacher, thought Mr. Mitchell must have known
that he was doing wrong ; he was too smart a man
not to know it, but he thought it would be far better
for the meeting to entirely dispense with the consideration of the subject.

The Rev. Mr. Clark, a Methodist Episcopal travelling minister, begged leave to say that one of the
slaves had been converted to God since she had gone
south.

Mr. John Hockings, a temperance lecturer from
England, said—"There are some persons who think
more of their political or religious party than of
suffering humanity." " Let us," he added, " hew to
the line, if the chips fly in our faces," (alluding to a
custom in the back woods of striking a chalk line on
the timber before hewing it square.) " Some persons
have the organ number ten, (and he placed his hand
on the phrenological organ of self-esteem on his own
head) very fully developed." He then urged the meeting to take sides with the suffering slave, and not
with the powerful slaveholder.

Squire Samuel Daugherty thought it was as great a sin to send these two young women into slavery as it would be for Mr. Mitchell to enter the chapel and seize two persons, as the chairman and himself, and send both into slavery.

Mr. Holton, a merchant of Milwaukee, said, " He who steals my purse steals trash, but he who filches from me my good name, takes that which not enriches him, but leaves me poor indeed."

Mr. Codding, referring to the power-of-attorney, thought it was giving up the power that might have been used to liberate the slaves. They had sunk down into slavery. The power-of-attorney cut the rope which might have drawn them up, and they had sunk to the bottom of slavery.

Rev. A. L. Barber wished to ask any lawyer present whether a married woman could make out such a power-of-attorney as had been described, without her husband's signature ; and it had only been signed by Mrs. Mitchell.

Mr. Tichenor, as a lawyer, wished to state that without the signature of the husband the document would not be valid in law.

Mr. Jillson, as a lawyer, begged to state that the slaves having been brought to a free state with the consent of all concerned, were legally emancipated.

Mr. Caulkins observed, that if the slaves really consented to go into slavery, then slavery had exerted upon them its most terrible effect.

The resolution was put to the meeting and unanimously adopted.

There were two other resolutions, one appointing a

committee to present the subject to the Conference; the other, appointing a committee to take legal steps to secure the liberation of Mr. Mitchell's slaves.

These resolutions, with the report, were recommitted to the committee and other members were added to it.

The annual meeting of the Wisconsin Anti-slavery Society was held in 1846, at Beloit. To show its identification with the political Anti-slavery party, its name was changed to the Liberty Association. I was present, and called the committee together to consider the case of Mr. Mitchell's slaves, who were still in bondage. I observed to them that Mr. Mitchell would rather restore the slaves to freedom than lose his position in the Conference, and if we could move the Conference, I had but little doubt the slaves would soon be free. I drew from my pocket an address to the Conference, and suggested that we should adopt it as a committee; that it would be adopted by the Anti-slavery Society I had full belief; it could then be forwarded to the bishop,—and I read the address. The committee objected because the Conference was an Ecclesiastical body. While I was pressing them to adopt the address to the Conference, Mr. St. Clair, an Anti-slavery lecturer from Illinois, happening to be in the room, asked permission to make a remark. This being granted—he said that the opinion of the Illinois abolitionists was that the Wisconsin abolitionists had failed to do their duty to a reverend kidnapper. This threw new light on the question, and aroused the committee. One of them, who had strongly objected to the adoption of the address to the Conference, said, "Why, we have driven him out of the Territory!" (Mr. Mitchell had been sent by the bishop to Illinois). Mr. St. Clair responded, "A few of you have been faithful to duty, but not all." These few remarks decided the question. Mr. Holton, a merchant of Milwaukee, strongly supporting the measure, the committee adopted the address. I reported it to the meeting. It was cordially and unanimously adopted, and a vote passed that it should be signed by the officers of the society, and forwarded to the Conference, with evidence of the guilt of Mr. Mitchell.

Soon after the above meeting, Mr. R. H. Deming, referred to on page 181, was put upon his trial before the Methodist Episcopal Court at Southport, charged with slander, in saying that Mr. Mitchell was a slave-holder, and had preached a sermon whilst he had in his pocket the title-deeds to immortal beings as property. He stated that he had made the remark, and that its truthfulness justified him in doing so. During the trial the chapel was crowded in every part. He furnished ample evidence of the truth of his statement, and was acquitted. The trial with a large portion of the evidence was published in the *Southport American*, the *American Freeman*, and numerous other newspapers.

Visiting Illinois in 1846, I learned that Mr. Mitchell was sorely trying our Anti-slavery friends by his pro-slavery opposition, I therefore, gave a lecture at Elgin. At the top of the bill advertising the meeting in large letters were these words:—

"The Rev. James Mitchell, a Kidnapper!" it then stated that I should lecture that evening, and show that he had sent into slavery two young women who were free. There was a large audience, including the Wesleyan minister and many members of the church. I related the history of the case.

The next Sunday it was Quarterly Meeting at Elgin. Mr. Mitchell was present as presiding elder. Outside the church a person sat in his conveyance who could see through the window of the Methodist Church the greater part of the audience, and they could see him; but he could not see the preacher, nor could the preacher see him. When Mr. Mitchell took his text, the person in his conveyance stood up, and held up to the gaze of the audience one of the bills headed "The Rev. James Mitchell a Kidnapper." So he was rebuked.

An adjourned meeting of the Wisconsin Anti-slavery Society was held at Southport on the 27th of January, 1847, in the chapel where Mr. Deming had been tried. In the order of business the Rev. A. Gaston made the following report from the Executive Committee:—" The persons whose duty it was made to forward the address of the Association to the Rock River Annual Conference of the Methodist Episcopal Church, in reference to the case of the Rev. James Mitchell, would report that the subject was duly attended to. The report signed by the President and Corresponding Secretary of the Association was placed in the hands of a suitable person, to be presented by him to the Bishop of the Conference; but by a providential hindrance, it did not reach him until after the session of the Conference. A very courteous communication has been received from the Bishop, intimating that had the report reached him in season, it would have been presented to the Conference.

All of which is submitted.

CHARLES DURKEE, } *Committee.*
A. GASTON,

I then moved the following resolution, "Resolved, that a committee of three be appointed to forward the Address referred to, to the Presiding Bishop, at the next session of the Rock River Conference, to be presented to that body, together with documents duly authenticated and witnessed, showing the agency of Mr. Mitchell in the transaction." This was seconded and adopted. The committee appointed were E. Mathews, C. Durkee, and R. H. Deming. I then moved the following resolution :—

" Whereas the case of the re-enslaving of two free young women by Rev. J. Mitchell has been before this body, and action has been taken upon it.— Resolved, that we, as an Association, have not yet performed our duty towards these unfortunate young women.

" Resolved, that a committee be appointed to make a presentment to the grand jury of Grant County, of Rev. J. Mitchell, in the coming fall.

" Resolved, that should the committee receive satisfactory evidence, before the session of the jury, of the restoration of the above-mentioned young women to liberty, that they may consider themselves discharged from the obligation which this appointment imposes."

The committee appointed were E. Mathews and Messrs. Tichenor, Chandler, LyBrand, and Revs. Messrs. Peet and Chaffee.

In 1847, the Annual Meeting of the Rock River Methodist Episcopal Conference was held at Chicago. No other member of the committee could attend, I therefore went to Chicago, carrying in my conveyance Mr. Peck—referred to on page 181—I gave him a history of the whole question, and handed him the "address" and accompanying documents. He sought an interview with Bishop Waugh, who presided at that session. When the Bishop read the documents, he shook his head and said—" If this be true, it is as bad as getting drunk." It was much worse. The bishop placed the subject before the Conference, and a committee was appointed to try the case. The following is the address ;—

THE WISCONSIN TERRITORIAL LIBERTY ASSOCIATION TO THE PRESIDING BISHOP AND MINISTERS COMPOSING THE ROCK RIVER CONFERENCE OF THE METHODIST EPISCOPAL CHURCH :—

" Esteemed Brethren :—We approach you in a Christian spirit, and feel justified in anticipating a reception marked by the regard which we entertain for you.

" Were you not avowedly enlisted like as we are in the elevation of the morals of the community; and like as we are, self-devoted to the redemption of the human heart from the darkness of sin, and the human mind from that of ignorance, we would approach you as opponents ; but as it is, we exhort you as friends and brethren.

" With deep regret we discover by the proceedings
of your last session, that you have exonerated the
Rev. James Mitchell from guilt in his agency in the
re-enslavement of the females whom he brought
some years since from southern slavery. The circumstances are so well known as to render re-capitulation
unnecessary. We need only refer to the fact that as
soon as those two females entered our Territory, the
contingent interests which different parties claimed
in them fell to the ground. The chains of chattel-
hood dropped from their limbs, they stood up 'free,'
and their rights were as much the object of the protection of the law as those of the highest officer in
Wisconsin.

" Being unable to perceive how you can draw a
different inference from these facts, we feel that we
only discharge a solemn and imperious duty, in
entreating you in the name of humanity, of our
country, of our religion, and our laws, to re-consider
the action you have had on the question; it is true
that no action of yours or ours may be successful in
recovering the representatives of God's poor from
the awful fate to which they have been consigned;
but humanity—grievously wounded by their exile
from freedom, happiness, and security—imploringly
demands some tribute of compassion.

" The high character of our Territory, as a land
whose inhabitants are secure, is impaired; and for its
sake, we remonstrate against any act that does violence to the sacred rights of her people with moral
impunity.

" Deep and lasting reproach has been cast upon

the name of Christianity, by an act involving in its consequences the physical and moral wretchedness, and probably, in addition, the spiritual death of the innocent and defenceless ; and we implore you not to throw the sanctifying mantle of our holy religion over an act of this character.

" The best of our laws, designed to paralyse the hand of tyranny, and secure to the weak as well as the strong the enjoyment of rational liberty, has been flagrantly violated ; and we invoke you by all that is valuable in social order, not to give the example—already fearful from the high standing of the actor—the still more fearful character that it would derive from your deliberate and solemn sanction. By your regard for the female character, we beseech you to withdraw your approval of the ungenerous excuse of Mr. Mitchell, that his wife was the holder of the freed women, and the principal actor in the tragedy. She could not, even if willing, occupy that place ; and if she would not, it is in strange keeping with his high professions, to compel her to bear the odium of a woman who was regardless of woman's rights and innocence.

" And we feel assured that after prayer and deliberation, you will hesitate much in sanctioning the trifling palliative, that these poor daughters of affliction were returned to the execrable brothel-house of the South, in compliance with an agreement made with the father-in-law of Mr. Mitchell.

" Awful thoughts are raised by the anxious apprehension, that on leaving the protection of our Territorial Laws, they went fast as time down to the gates

of death ; and it may be that even now the Lord of
Sabaoth hears the cry from their grieved spirits and
broken hearts—' No man careth for my soul.'

CHARLES DURKEE, President.

JOHN B. JILLSON,   } Secretaries.
R. H. Deming,   }

Adopted unanimously at the Annual Meeting of
the Wisconsin Liberty Association, January 27th,
1847, held at the M. E. Church, Southport."

Additional evidence was received from the St.
Louis newspapers. Mrs. Mitchell's brother went
from Virginia to St. Louis, and took one of the
slaves back to Virginia. When he returned to St.
Louis, to take back the other slave, his right to do so
was questioned, for the report of the discussion on
the subject going on in Wisconsin, had reached St.
Louis, and he was thrown into prison. To defend
himself he published a letter he had received from
the Rev. James Mitchell, authorizing him to take
the slaves to Virginia, expressing also some alarm
lest the Anti-slavery people should succeed in setting
them free. One of the slaves eventually, owing to
the agitation, obtained her liberty. The other
probably remained a slave till the period of the proclamation of emancipation by Mr. Lincoln.

The following report of my visit to the Conference
appeared in the American Freeman, published at
Waukesha, September 15, 1857:—

" Dear Brother Codding:—The following question
has been put to some of our brethren in the ministry,
who are members of the Methodist Episcopal Rock

River Conference—'What was done with the address and documents, relating to the enslaving of two young women by Mr. Mitchell, which the Liberty Association of Wisconsin forwarded by a committee to your Conference?' Some of the members of the Conference simply return to this question the following reply—'The committee that presented them, after the business had progressed somewhat, withdrew them.' This answer involved the matter in some obscurity to the mind of at least one of our leading Anti-slavery brethren (Rev. N. Miller). A brief statement of the facts of the case, however, removed the mists that were settling around it, and as other minds might labour under the same difficulty, and might be relieved by the same process, I propose, by your courtesy, to present to the public the statement I made to him; not intending by this to anticipate the report which the committee on the case will make at the next annual meeting of the Liberty Association.

"During the session of the Conference, in August, I visited Chicago, and through the kind agency of Brother Peck, of Southport, placed in the hands of Bishop Waugh the address and documents, agreeable to the arrangements of the committee, and the order of the Liberty Association. The bishop stated from the chair to the Conference assembled the character of the documents and address which he had received, and by a vote of the Conference they were referred to a committee, which committee had been previously appointed to investigate a matter of difficulty existing between Mr. Mitchell and the official members of the

Clark Street Church, Chicago. At this stage of the proceedings of the Conference, a prominent member of the Methodist Church, one who is an active liberty man, suggested to me the propriety of my withdrawing the documents which had been presented to the Conference, stating as a reason for my so doing, that a committee of the Clark Street Church had brought in before the committee to whom the documents were referred, eight charges against Mr. Mitchell, and that as a specification under one of the charges was ' that he had sent two free young women from Wisconsin into chattel servitude;' it was possible that Mr. Mitchell might denounce the whole movement as being abolition persecution, but he could not do this if the documents were withdrawn, and they might then be called up by way of evidence.

"In reflecting on the subject, it appeared to me that the efforts of the Clark Street Church would secure Conference action, which the Liberty Association were aiming to obtain, and hence that the withdrawing of the documents would be justified by the Association, if it tended to secure that action, provided that no unfavourable impression would be produced by such a withdrawal.

"There was danger, however, lest some minds should seize upon the fact of the withdrawal, and use it in such a manner as to bring odium on the Liberty Association, by asserting that it was unable to maintain the position it had assumed in relation to Mr. Mitchell, and had backed out in a disgraceful manner; and they might possibly adduce the withdrawal of the documents as a proof of the innocence of Mr. Mitche

"For the purpose of harmonizing, on the one hand, as far as I could consistently with our Methodist brethren who had undertaken in behalf of God's poor, I consented to the withdrawing of the documents for two or three days; and to guard on the other hand, against any unfavourable impressions which evil-disposed or uninformed persons might endeavour to produce, I stated expressly, that the documents might be considered as withdrawn for two or three days *only*, and at the end of that time they would be presented again, and that if it was necessary to obtain a vote of the Conference in order that I might do this, then I would on no account withdraw them, as I feared the impression that such a vote would create.

"The member of the Church who proposed the withdrawal agreed with this sentiment, and I proposed to him to take charge of the matter and act for me as agent.

"On entering the Conference the next morning, I was surprised to find a spirited debate going on, a motion being before the body that leave be given to the committee to withdraw the documents. Very greatly, however, to the relief of my feelings the motion was withdrawn. I was afterwards informed that a resolution was passed in the Conference, ' that the documents be copied,' and then returned to the committee who presented them.

"In the debate above referred to, Elders James Mitchell, John T. Mitchell, and Stebbins, strenuously advocated the necessity of retaining the documents and having a thorough investigation. When, how-

Q

ever, the committee came to *that* charge in the list of charges, Mr. Mitchell stated that he was not prepared to go into a trial. The committee reported this matter to Conference, stating that to *accommodate* Mr. Mitchell, they had declined going into an investigation of the matter, and recommending the appointment of a committee to try the case. The Conference proceeded to appoint a committee of five before whom the trial is to take place when Mr. Mitchell is ready, as the parties preferring the charges were ready at the Conference.

" Mr. Mitchell has been superannuated for one year. This, I believe, is the first instance in the history of the Methodist body where a member has been superannuated, with charges which he was not prepared to meet standing against him.

" It is the duty of the committee on his case to hear the statement of both parties, make a record of them, and report to the next Conference, when each party will introduce additional testimony, if they desire it, and address the body, and then the vote of the Conference will be taken. One additional thought —three speakers spoke in favour of retaining the documents, and urged as a reason for so doing, the publicity of the matter, and its extensive agitation. Three other speakers urged the appointing of a committee of five, to try the case, each of whom argued the necessity of it from the agitated state of the public mind in relation to it.

" From this it will be seen that the documents are to be copied, and the copy is to be reserved by the committee to be used at the trial."

The foregoing letter is dated Lisbon, Sept. 7, 1847. Mr. Codding observed to me respecting it—"Here is an illustration of what can be gained by agitation."

A meeting of the committee of the Conference was held, and Mr. Mitchell was put upon his trial. He was found guilty of kidnapping, and deposed from the ministry. I learn, however, that the pro-slavery party rallied its forces, called a large meeting, and passed a resolution condemning the Conference for this act; that the Conference, quailing under the censure, revoked its decision, restored him to his standing, and sent him to Missouri to preach, where he must have found many kindred spirits.

When the session of the grand jury in Grant County drew near, I set out to enter the complaint before that body. It was a long journey and no other member of the committee could spare the time to accompany me. On the way I held Anti-slavery meetings. Arriving at Lancaster I went to the room where the grand jury had assembled, and, having sent in my name, the foreman invited me in. I stated the whole case respecting Mr. Mitchell's slaves, and referred to various authorities by which my statement could be corroborated. I then retired, and waited in the town. The jury did nothing. The foreman of the jury was a slaveholder; his slaves were in South Carolina, and he was living in Wisconsin on their unpaid toil. Ten of the jury were in favour of slavery, two only were in favour of emancipation. They were bound by their oaths to take up the case, but they adjourned without doing so.

From the name of an officer I have met with in

the account of civil war in Missouri, I suppose Mr. Mitchell fought in the Federal army.

His mind, as a mirror, reflected the characteristics of ninety-nine out of every hundred ministers, of all denominations, in the slave states. Thus did slavery corrupt the ministers of religion.

During the foregoing struggle, I watched earnestly the proceedings of the General Conference of the Methodist Episcopal Church, knowing that if it opposed slavery, the Rock River Conference—its auxiliary—would speedily follow its example, and would aid my efforts for the rescue of Mr. Mitchell's slaves. But I found that as Congress was ruled by its slaveholding members, by their threats to dissolve the Federal Union; so was the General Conference ruled by its slaveholding members, by their threats to dissolve the Ecclesiastical Union. In the Rock River Conference, also, there was a clique of southerners, intensely pro-slavery, who influenced the bishops,— repressed anti-slavery effort in their church connection, and were resolved to sustain Mr. Mitchell in his slaveholding, at every hazard. So that in reality I was battling with this clique.

All the popular religious bodies were the auxiliaries of the slave power; but in each, there was an Anti-slavery minority working well for emancipation.

I will state the proceedings of the General Conference, and trace their effect on my own labours. It will be seen that there was an extended discussion on the influence of slavery, which resulted in a division of the body. The discussion furnished me with an argument against those who opposed discussion;—

but, as the division took place on a question, not of principle, but of expediency, that furnished me with no argument whatever against my opponents.

Some of the Methodist ministers would visit the deacon of the Baptist Church at Aztalan, and assure him that whilst Mr. Mathews preached so much against slavery no revival of religion could be expected. When he told me this I referred to tho command, " Open thy mouth for the dumb;" to the Seventy-second psalm, where it is said that Christ shall " deliver the needy when he crieth, and break in pieces the oppressor;" and to the Sixty-fifth of Isaiah, where it is promised that the " light " of those who " undo the heavy burdens" shall " break forth as the morning." On one occasion one of these ministers told me that he thought his congregation was larger than mine, and that this proved that it was a wiser course to be silent on slavery. My reply was that Isaiah preached the truth " whether men would hear or whether they would forbear;" that a pro-slavery people could only be sanctified by the preaching of anti-slavery truth, and that it was more important to save people from their sins than to have large audiences.

One Sunday after preaching on slavery, a minister of the Methodist Episcopal Rock River Conference came and said to me, " Brother Mathews, I should have trembled to have preached that sermon,—should I preach one sermon on slavery I should be excluded from the Conference." Some of the most talented and pious ministers had been excluded from the Methodist Episcopal Church because they preached

against slavery.   A rule was adopted at the General
Conference in 1836, which was construed to prohibit all preaching against slavery.   In 1840, a rule
was adopted at the General Conference, which prohibited coloured Methodists in the slave states from
giving evidence against their white fellow Church-
members in any Church-trial.   I preached a sermon
against this rule, and contended that the Conference
paid more deference to a white complexion than to
the work of grace on the heart; and that it practically denied that the Holy Spirit could induce
coloured Methodists to speak the truth.   Both these
rules aided the slave-party and strengthened Mr.
Mitchell's position.

But in 1844, the General Conference of the
Methodist Episcopal Church, in its Assembly discussed the slavery question during fourteen days;
thus furnishing me with an admirable answer to
these objectors to discussion.   I said to them—" If
your most learned and influential ministers, assembled
from all parts of the Union, in the great City of
New York, deem the slavery question of such high
import as to discuss it for fourteen days, as the representatives of all the Annual Conferences, and virtually
in the presence of the United States, surely you cannot object to a humble missionary on the frontiers of
the American confederacy following their example,
and discussing the question also."   The deacon,
Jeremiah Brayton, whose fears had been wrought
upon in regard to a revival, dismissed his fears, and
strengthened my efforts in the public meetings by his
able advocacy of emancipation.   In severely cold.

weather, in the winter, I have known him drive forty miles to attend an Anti-slavery meeting. Had all the ministers been faithful on the question there would have been no great difficulty with the people.

Respecting the division, this church, comprising a million of members, separated on a question of expediency. If the Conference had declared slavery to be sinful, the Methodist ministers would have laboured to abolish slavery; and those in Wisconsin would have aided me in my Anti-slavery efforts, and in the attempt to rescue Mr. Mitchell's slaves. But the Conference did nothing of the kind, as the discussions and resolutions show.

Bishop Andrew, by marriage and otherwise, had become a slaveholder. His office required him to travel in the free as well as in the slave states, and preside at the Annual Conferences. But, owing to the Anti-slavery light that had been diffused, no slaveholding bishop could be acceptable to the Northern Conferences. Hence, in the General Conference in 1844, the following preamble and resolution were proposed, and, after an extended discussion, adopted by a vote of 110 yeas to 68 nays.

" Whereas, the discipline of our church forbids the doing of any thing calculated to destroy our general superintendency; and whereas, Bishop Andrew has become connected with slavery by marriage and otherwise; and this act having drawn after it circumstances which in the estimation of the General Conference will greatly embarrass the exercise of his office, therefore,—

" Resolved, that it is the sense of this Conference,

that he desist from the exercise of his office so long as the impediment remains."

The resolution was carefully drawn up so as to avoid declaring slavery to be a sin, but it unmistakeably asserts that it is inexpedient for a bishop to hold slaves.

A discussion followed the proposal to adopt this preamble and resolution; it is published in the form of a large volume, which I have read attentively. Among all the speeches there is but one that declares slavery to be a sin, and that one was afterwards qualified by the person who made it—Mr. Cass. The following is a quotation from the proceedings:—

Bishop Soule, who afterwards became a slaveholder, presided; he said:—

"I know that some of my brethren of the North are involved in such a manner that I cannot apprehend; I see no way in which they can compromise this question. Why? For the obvious reason that it involves a principle. I will compromise with no man when a principle is involved in the compromise. * * * * It was advanced by my worthy brother Cass the other day. * * * * What is it? It is that slavery, under all circumstances, is a sin against God."

Mr. Cass interposed:—

"May I correct the bishop? I believe I did not say so; I said it was a moral evil."

Bishop Soule proceeded:—

"Well, I am glad to be corrected. This is not brother Cass's principle. A moral evil, a moral evil, and not a sin under all circumstances. It affords me a great deal of pleasure to hear my worthy brother's statement, for it greatly increases my hope that we shall have a compromise."

So the discussion did not declare slavery to be a sin. Subsequently the Conference adopted the following resolutions :—

"Resolved, as the sense of this Conference, that Bishop Andrew's name stand in the Minutes, Hymn-Book, and Discipline, as formerly. Yeas 153; nays 18.

"Resolved, that the rule in relation to the support of a bishop and his family applies to Bishop Andrew. Yeas 153; nays 14.

"Resolved, that whether in any, and what work Bishop Andrew be employed, is to be determined by his own decision and action, in relation to the previous action of the Conference in his case. Yeas 103; nays 67."

The Southern members voted against the last resolution, fearing, probably, that its adoption would weaken their argument for dividing the church. They also voted against the first resolution. It is clear, therefore, that Bishop Andrew, though a slaveholder, was neither deposed nor even suspended. But although slavery was not treated as a sin by the resolutions or during the discussion, yet the passing of the first resolution was felt by the southern ministers to be, indirectly, a censure upon them, as the great body of them were slaveholders. They immediately demanded a division of the church. The demand was agreed to. After the division thousands of slaveholding members in Maryland, Virginia,

Kentucky, Missouri, and Arkansas, preferred to retain their connection with the Northern division of
the Methodist Episcopal Church. They were allowed
to do so, and to retain their connection with slavery.
These states in the civil war were the scenes of many
battles. Had the Northern churches so willed,
slavery could have been abolished by canon-laws;
instead of which, however, it was abolished by cannon
balls. The former is the better remedy, and the one
which, as this chapter shows, I strove to apply to that
fearful crime.

As the Quaker Poet meditated upon the iniquity
of slaveholding ministers, he expressed his indignation in the following strain:—

> "Just God! and these are they
> Who minister at thine altar, God of Right!
> Men who their hands with prayer and blessing lay
> On Israel's Ark of light.

> "What! preach and kidnap men?
> Give thanks—and rob Thy own afflicted poor?
> Talk of thy glorious liberty, and then
> Bolt hard the captive's door?

> "How long, O Lord! how long
> Shall such a priesthood barter truth away,
> And, in Thy name for robbery and wrong
> At Thy own altars pray?"

CHAPTER XII.

THE PROGRESS of the Anti-slavery reform in
Wisconsin was greatly hindered by the connection
existing between several of the missionaries and pro-
slavery missionary committees in New York. To
guard the people against this unhappy influence it
was necessary to enlighten them; as their information on the subject was not equal to that possessed
by the Anti-slavery advocates. For this purpose I
moved in the Wisconsin Liberty Association that a

committee be appointed to prepare an "Address to those ministers and churches who, while they profess to be Anti-slavery, are receiving the gains of robbery and the price of blood, to sustain their religious institutions." A committee was appointed consisting of the Revs. E. Mathews, A. L. Barber, T. Tenney, N. Miller, and R. Cheney.

We prepared an Address, and in each instance where a religious body was charged with supporting slavery, the evidence was adduced from its own official documents. Having by a large amount of correspondence obtained this evidence, I classified and reported it in connection with the Address. Had the official facts not been published with it—the supporters of slavery would have emphatically denied that any connection existed between these bodies and slavery, the people would have been misled, and our labour would have been in vain in preparing the address. It was presented to the Wisconsin Liberty Association, at its annual meeting at Southport, February 10, 1847, and after full discussion was adopted. It appeared in the *American Freeman*, filling three columns, while the official facts filled nearly four. The editor speaks in the following terms, both of the Convention and the address.

"The meeting has been held. The weather was fine and the delegation large. It does not become us perhaps to speak too freely of the character of those who attended our meeting, but our opponents being judges, a more respectable, intelligent, serious, earnest convention of men and women, made up of all classes and professions, seldom, if ever, were brought together.

The sessions during the day were held in the Methodist Episcopal Church, which was crowded from morning till night with an audience moved to the depths of their spiritual being, with the great thoughts elicited, and the high duties enjoined by the deeply interesting discussions of the day, which were certainly very able, and called out a great variety of talent. * * * Mechanics and farmers, merchants and lawyers, physicians and ministers, all mingled freely in these discussions, and there were 'none to molest or make afraid'.

"The question—is it right to sustain missionary bodies which fraternize with slaveholders, and co-operate with them as Christians?—became the leading topic for discussion, and absorbed a large portion of the time and interest of the convention. A question this of great import. The discussion was warm, thorough, and protracted. It occupied nearly two days. It arose on the presentment of a report of a committee appointed at the Prairieville meeting, to remonstrate with those ministers and churches who continue to support pro-slavery missionary bodies. The report seems to have been prepared with great care, and was evidently written in a good spirit. After stating most clearly that these bodies were implicated in slavery, it asks the question solemnly, 'brethren can you any longer support them?' The report was adopted by a nearly unanimous vote; not over ten, at most, were heard to say 'no.'

"We can convey to those who were not there no idea of the unspeakable interest and depth of emotion which these discussions produced, and we are happy

R

to say that brethren of all parties—with very few exceptions, if any—seemed to arise from this discussion with subdued feelings, more in love with truth, with God, with one another, than before. The Revs. Messrs. Marsh, Hart, Bridgman, Miller, Mathews, Cheney, Lothrop, Gaston, and Messrs. Holton, Bacon, Smith, Hale and others, whose names are not in mind, mingled in the discussion. Mr. Bacon, while speaking in reference to the duty of ministers to cry aloud, said he loved ministers, but they ought to speak out; if they will not, *laymen must;* Christ will be represented. You look upon us here silent, but I tell you, Mr. President, we have got souls and can feel! At this moment we looked round upon the faces of the mechanics and farmers, and working men, and tears were filling their eyes."

"Resolutions were passed condemning the Mexican war, declaring the principles of the Liberty party, etc.

"Our noble Durkee generally presided though considerably out of health."

From the address a few extracts may be given. It commences thus:—

"We the movers, framers, and supporters of this remonstrance, believing that it is better to trust in the Lord than to put confidence in man, having long contemplated with amazement, and grief, the position and course of very many of our brethren and religious friends, in being associated in church connection, and through the relation of missionary societies, domestic and foreign, with those who practise and justify the heaven-defying iniquity of enslaving and making merchandise of their fellow-men and fellow

church-members, would once more, in the fear of
God, and in what we believe to be the charity which
His Word enjoins towards our brethren and fellow-
men, kindly, but most earnestly address to you our
remonstrance and entreaty, on this deeply interesting
and vitally important subject!"

Having shown the connection of various religious
bodies with slavery—and its demoralising effects, the
address proceeds :—

"The popularity of a practice, however it may
mitigate the guilt of an individual, can never wholly
excuse him.   It can never make any vice or intrinsic
moral evil a virtue ; otherwise there could be no hope
for the repentance and reformation of the sinner.
We are conscious also that professed Christians may
act under an *illusion*, and be led into practices, more
or less criminal, by the prevailing voice of the community.   Here, therefore, fidelity,—love in its best,
its Christian sense, may interpose her voice of alarm,
of rebuke, of expostulation, of entreaty."

The following bodies are then charged with supporting slavery :—

The American Baptist Missionary Union.

The American Baptist Home Missionary Society.

The American Board of Commissioners for Foreign
Missions.

The American Home Missionary Society.

The General Conference of the Methodist Episcopal Church.

This support to slavery is shown to be given by
each Society in six ways.   One of these refers to
heathenism at home and abroad :—

Exemplification the sixth :—

"These bodies are to a great extent made up of members and officers, who countenance, justify, and take part in a system which chattelizes and heathenizes at home, at a moderate computation, a hundred human beings, for each individual hopefully converted from heathenism by their missionaries abroad."

The appeal and remonstrance is then made on five grounds.

1. "That of now existing, extended and notorious facts.

2. That of "plain declarations from the inspired oracles of the living God." The following and similar texts being quoted, "For I the Lord love judgment, I hate robbery for burnt-offering."—Isaiah lxi. 8.

3. That of the "profession of sympathy, promises and vows of fidelity to the anti-slavery cause," which had been made by the parties addressed.

4. That of regard to religion. This appeal is thus urged :—"In the fourth place we make our appeal and remonstrance, from an earnest regard to the religious interests and prospects, and the salvation of our fellow-countrymen at the south, both the enslaved and the free. Without a pure religion, the only religion which God approves and blesses, individuals and communities may to any extent, assume the name and forms of religion, but will not thereby be led to refrain from the practice, and be relieved from the guilt of their sins. A sin-tolerating and sin-countenancing religion, can never honour God, purify society, or save the soul.

"Such to a fearful extent has already become,—

and such to a still more fearful extent is fast becoming—the religion prevalent in more than half the states of this great confederacy ; a religion steeped in iniquity, crimsoned and reeking with the guilt of monstrous and accumulated wrong to God and man. A religion that quails and keeps silent in view of wholesale cruelty, oppression, robbery and blood—which practically prefers the caresses and pecuniary liberality of the powerful and wealthy oppressor, and his abettors, to the favour of God and the rights and salvation of bleeding humanity—may well be regarded, as adapted to corrupt rather than to purify, to hasten blindfold to perdition, rather than to reform and save the subjects of its influence."

The fifth ground of appeal is on behalf of the purity of religion in the free states, which has been corrupted by the slaveholders with whom the northern churches fraternize, and thus the ministry had become to a " great extent a time-serving, popularity-loving, truth-compromising, and man-fearing ministry."

The Address closes with a reference to the increased moral power which the gospel, the church, and the ministry will possess when the system of slavery shall be abolished.

The spirit of the meeting and of western Antislavery men may be seen in the following brief extracts from four of the speeches :—

The Rev. N. Miller, a Congregationalist, arose, and said,—" Mr. President and Brethren—I am poor—I know that I am poor, and with me this is a practical question. When I came to the west, the question came up shall I receive aid from these missionary

committees ? In my imagination I took my wife and
children, four children, and placed them on the cotton
plantation at the south. I then took my station at
their side, and in the condition of a slave looked up
at the missionary committee. Was there pity ? Was
there willingness to aid ? No, their hearts were as
the adamant. The melting influences of the gospel,
the commands of God, the great principles of humanity,
as revealed in the gospel, all were powerless in the
missionary committee, they could fraternize with the
oppressor, but for my wife and children there was no
look of sympathy, and no willingness to aid. Oh,
brethren, brethren, I *could* not receive the aid proffered
by such a Board as this."

The church to which Mr. Miller preached had formerly received aid from the Home Missionary Committee, but he told the church to put the amount
down to him, and he would work on the farm for that
sum rather than receive it from such a source.

Rev. Mr. Marsh made a long speech. "While"
said he, "you are labouring with the missionaries,
why do you not labour with those who buy slave
produce ? Do you not preach out of bibles made
of slave-grown cotton ?"

Mr. Codding—"The Friends have bibles made out
of free-grown cotton."

Mr. Marsh—"Well ! give me a Quaker bible, but
I cannot agree with your report."

Rev. R. Cheney—"A commercial transaction must
not be presented as one in which Christian fellowship
is demanded and allowed. In purchasing cotton or
sugar of the merchant there is no expression of

Christian fellowship. But, when contributions are solicited from the slaveholders, the professors of religion among them expect to be treated as good Christian brethren. On this principle they furnish pecuniary aid. Were our missionary bodies to disfellowship them, not another dollar would be received from that quarter. If, in order to obtain the pecuniary aid of wicked men, we must acknowledge them to be Christians, then, it is morally wrong to receive such aid."

Mr. Codding—" These Missionary bodies sanction the slaveholder; they give him a Christian character, and hence are equally culpable with him. Now, brethren, you that retain your connection with these missionary committees referred to, you think the members of these committees good Christian brethren, do you not? (Replies of "Yes," "Yes.") Well, now, these committees think that slaveholders are good Christian brethren, and two things which are equal to a third are equal to each other. This report remonstrates against this position which you occupy, and it is perfectly right to do so. What have the Home Mission Society done in the case of John G. Fee? The Synod of Kentucky declares, that as John G. Fee is an abolitionist, therefore he shall have no support, and may starve to death. The Home Missionary Committee by its position says:— 'Abolition is just as correct as slaveholding, and we will not treat Mr. Fee in any different manner than we do the robber of God's poor—the slaveholder.' How much Anti-slavery is there in that! Here are these massive ecclesiastical bodies, resting with all

their overpowering weight upon the throbbing hearts
of our brethren—the slaves—and when we ask them
to remove their crushing power, and they refuse to
do so, and we turn to our missionary brethren and
ask them to withold their influence from these societies, they tell us that it is a remote application of the
principle! Oh! think of it; ought not these bodies to
cease to crush the bleeding victims of oppression."

I arose and traced the relations existing between
the Free and the Slave States in the Missionary
Societies; and referring to the case of John G. Fee,
showed that the Presbyterian Synod of Kentucky
was an auxiliary to the Home Missionary Society;
that its chairman was a slaveholder, and that he had
refused to recommend Mr. Fee to the Society as a
missionary because he was an abolitionist; that the
Home Missionary Society had many other auxiliaries
in the slave states; that it had doubled the number
of its churches in the slave states, all of them supporting the system of slavery and receiving slaveholders to membership, and I added—"That the work
which appropriately belonged to the Missionary
Societies was now being performed by abolitionists.
The moral and religious condition of the slaves can
never be ascertained from the missionary reports;
but go to the Anti-slavery periodicals and publications, and there the whole subject is amply spread
out; and who are endeavouring to remove the grand
impediment to the spread of the Gospel, and to
ameliorate the moral condition of the South? The
pro-slavery Missionary Societies? No! but the
abolitionists. Who are preparing the way to evan-

gelize the slaves? the abolitionists! Till the principles of the Liberty party prevail, the Gospel cannot
be given to the slaves.   By voting as well as by other
means, that party is aiding to open the way for
Sabbath Schools, such as we are now establishing
among the heathen, and such as we dare not now
establish among the slave population.   The missionary societies should consider the Liberty party as
their best co-adjutor."   The following are five of the
fourteen resolutions adopted at the meeting :—

"That we again reiterate our solemn conviction of
the sinfulness of American slavery, and that no circumstances can justify the chattelizing of a human
being, or his continuance in bondage a single hour.

"That the religion that can justify or palliate such
an outrage on the rights of man and the prerogatives
of God, is not from Heaven above, but from the pit
beneath ; we therefore call upon Christians of all
denominations to see to it that their garments are
clear from this abomination; that their testimony in
both word and deed be on the side of God and
humanity, and not staying up the hands of the
oppressor.

"That we seek not the destruction of the churches,
but their purification from slavery, believing as we do
that pure Christianity is democratic in all its tenden-
cies, recognizing in every individual essential equality
and common brotherhood; we therefore would not
thwart, but rather seek to promote that agency,
which, under God, we believe to be the most effective
in bringing this nation to repentance for the sin of
oppression.

"That the Anti-slavery fathers and mothers in Wisconsin should point their children to the late Thomas Clarkson, and bid them study his character and cherish his memory."

A resolution was adopted with reference to the war with Mexico, condemning it, and demanding not only the immediate recall of the army, but that reparation should be made for the injuries inflicted on Mexico.

The following resolution relates to the state constitution. The Territory of Wisconsin, having a sufficient population, was about to become a state; a convention had been elected and had framed a constitution, but through the influence of the slave-party it excluded coloured people from voting:—

"That the constitutional convention lately assembled at Madison—by acknowledging the equal right of all men to participate in the formation and benefits of government, and having by the same instrument restricted the right of suffrage—have not only committed a brutal outrage upon the coloured people of this Territory, but have stultified their own claim to democracy, showed their hypocrisy, and proved themselves willing co-workers with the slaveholder, in degrading the condition of the free people of colour to a level with the slave; and that to vote for such an instrument is to join hand in hand with the oppressor against the coloured race."

I will add but one of the official facts connected with the address.

The Rev. B. M. Hill, the Secretary of the American Baptist Home Mission Society, wrote as follows to the Rev. Mr. Blake, a missionary in Wisconsin, in 1841—" You will find in Wisconsin Territory an ultra-abolition spirit. Allow me to entreat you not to join it, or be moved by it. But while you entertain, as you should, opinions adverse to slavery, I beg you to remember that no moral evil can so effectually be removed as by gentleness, kindness, and persuasion. Let us maintain no other tests of communion in the Church of Christ than he has plainly established in the New Testament."

I came away from the meeting, cheered by the progress that had been made. The excitement of these meetings was so intense, and the mind so exercised, that I felt prostrated after attending them, and it was a day or two before my mind recovered its tone. Repose was the remedy. So earnest was the battle, and so strong the opposition, that for months together the cause of the slave was not absent from my mind for one hour, except during sleep.

Missionary committees, like civil governments, walk in the light the people possess. As many western men, owing to the discussion, understood the connection of the missionary committees with slavery, the power of these committees was weakened in opposing the Anti-slavery reform.

The Rev. C. P. Grosvenor published an extended report of the discussion, in his weekly Anti-slavery Journal, the *Christian Contributor*, Utica, New York; thus the religious bodies in the Eastern States felt the influence of the Anti-slavery movement in the west. Of the life-long Anti-slavery labours of the

editor of the above Journal I will speak in connection
with my visit to New York.

It will throw some light on the advice of Secretary
Hill to Mr. Blake, just quoted, if I add, that the
Baptist slaveholders had refused to subscribe to the
missionary cause unless the North would recognize
them as good Christians. Leading ministers had
signed their names to a paper avowing this recognition. The name of B. M. Hill, the secretary, is on
the list of names, which was extensively published.

The Anti-slavery men throughout Wisconsin determined to vote down the proposed state-constitution;
because it excluded coloured people from voting. At
that time each state-constitution was submitted to
the vote of the inhabitants of the Territory for approval or rejection. The state-constitution was rejected in Wisconsin. Another convention was elected
to frame another constitution. This was expensive.

The first constitution contained this clause—"Every
white male citizen may vote." We contended that
the word "white was the blackest word in the constitution; that "blue" was as good a colour as
"white," the sky was blue—and had the convention
declared that every blue male citizen might vote, then
no one could vote—and thus they would be robbed
of their rights. The second convention to frame a
constitution submitted the word "white" to a separate
vote of the people, to be retained or expunged. The
majority voted to expunge it—and the coloured man
was allowed to vote.

I should add, however, that other parties for other
considerations voted to reject the first constitution;

the Anti-slavery party alone would not have been able to prevent its adoption.

A person could be white in law and not white in fact. I knew a mulatto in Wisconsin whose mother was a white woman, his father was coloured. In law he was a white man, though slightly tinged by negro blood. He went up to the polls to vote when Wisconsin was a Territory. Those appointed to receive the votes, asked him if he could take his oath that he was a white man ? He replied " certainly," and took the oath and voted. On the other hand, persons could be white in fact and not white in law. If the mother had the least portion of negro blood in her veins the child was coloured, however fair ; and if the mother was a slave—so was the child. Slave-law was a bill of attainder. Yet the Federal Constitution declared—" No bill of attainder shall be passed."

To promote emancipation a number of large conventions were held, with special reference to the election of Anti-slavery men to civil office. One of these, which I had the satisfaction of attending, was held at Chicago, June 28, 1846. In the public square had been erected a vast tent, known as the Oberlin tent. Thousands of men and women, attracted by the strong influences of liberty, filled it to overflowing. Those who had laboured long and ardently in the Anti-slavery cause, whose lives had been laid upon the altar, and whose names had been cast out as evil ;—and those who had occupied seats in Congress, but had been looked upon with coldness for possessing the " heart that could feel for another ;"—

and those who from the sacred desk had sounded un-
pleasant truths to unwilling ears ;—and those whose
songs in favour of the cause had been sung to the
prejudiced, and charmed them to the favour of
liberty ; and those who handled the pen of the writer;
—and those who shielded the outcast and protected
the refugee slave;—and those into whose souls the
iron had entered, and on whose backs the tyrant slaveholder had made deep his furrows ;—from every department of life, from each sphere of usefulness,
from each point of the compass, they had assembled,
animated by the great, elevating, and glorious sentiment of Liberty.

A preliminary meeting was held on the evening of
the 23rd—Rev. C. Cook, of Illinois, presided. Prayer
was offered. Reports on the state of the Anti-slavery
cause being called for, responses were made by S. B.
Treadwell, general Anti-slavery agent, of Michigan,
and Rev. Marcus Harrison, and Judge Deming,
of the same state. Also by Mr. Crocker, of Indiana,
and Rev. W. T. Allan, from Iowa Territory. At
intervals the Liberty Choir enlivened the meeting by
their melodies.

The next morning the meeting was resumed at
eight o'clock. I made a report on the state of the
cause in Wisconsin, and was followed by R. H.
Deming, C. Durkee, and Rev. A. Gaston ; Rev. Mr.
St. Clair reported from Northern Illinois. From all
quarters the intelligence was of the most encouraging
character. A ball had certainly been set in motion
which could not be rolled back, but must roll onward
till every slave should be free.

The convention at ten o'clock, a.m., was called to order, and J. G. Carter, Esq., of Massachusetts, formerly a member of Congress, was chosen chairman. On taking the chair he made a brief speech. During the absence of the business committee, Henry Bibb, an escaped slave, addressed the audience, closing in the language of Patrick Henry " Give me liberty or give me death."

I then arose and moved the following resolution :— " That a special committee of five be appointed to prepare and present to the convention for its adoption, an address to the ministers of different religious denominations."

On this a discussion ensued as to the position of the ministers; I showed how important it was that as leaders of the people they should be foremost in resisting slavery. Remarks were made by Messrs. Durkee, Cook, Wisner, Allan, Torrey, Reynolds, Harrison, and St. Clair.

On the motion of the Rev. Mr. Gaston, the resolution was amended, so that the address should be to the people of the entire region represented in the convention.

Rev. W. T. Allan considered the Slavery question the great moral question of the age ; and the ministers, who should be the leaders of the people, had failed in their duty.

I arose and stated that the speech made by Mr. Allan would constitute just such an address as I desired to see adopted.

Mr. Bibb thought the address ought to be made to slaveholding ministers and their abettors. After some further discussion the amendment was carried.

The Committee on the Address were E. Mathews, L. Farman, Z. Eastman, G. Beckley, and Judge Deming.

Rev. Owen Lovejoy addressed the meeting. One of the remarks he made was, that—"Before the great work of emancipation can succeed, the religion of the churches must be regenerated. The ministry must be converted or crushed."

The Liberty Choir sung the following:—

"Oh, he is not the man for me,
   Who buys or sells a slave,
Nor he who will not set him free,
   But sends him to his grave ;
But he whose noble heart beats warm
   For all men's lives and liberty ;
Who loves alike each human form,
   Oh that's the man for me.

"He's not at all the man for me
   Who sells a man for gain,
Who bends the pliant servile knee,
   To slavery's god of shame !
But he whose god-like form erect
   Proclaims that all alike are free
To think, and speak, and vote and act,
   Oh that's the man for me.

"He sure is not the man for me
   Whose spirit will succumb,
When men endowed with Liberty,
   Lie bleeding bound and dumb ;
But he whose faithful words of might
   Ring through the land from shore to sea,
For man's eternal equal right,
   Oh that's the man for me.

" No, no, he's not the man for me
 Whose voice o'er hill and plain,
Breaks forth for glorious liberty,
 But binds himself the chain !
The mightiest of the noble band
 Who prays and toils the world to free,
With head and heart and voice and vote,
 Oh that's the man for me."

Several pieces were also sung by Mr. G. W. Clark, an excellent singer, and among them " The Yankee Girl," by John G. Whittier, the Quaker poet, and "The Fugitive Slave to the Christian," by Elizur Wright.

The first is a description of a slaveholder wooing a Yankee girl and rejected. Three of the ten verses are the following :—

" Oh, come to my home, where my servants shall all
 Depart at thy bidding and come at thy call ;
They shall heed thee as mistress with trembling and awe,
 And each wish of thy heart shall be felt as a law.

" Oh, could ye have seen her—that pride of our girls—
 Arise and cast back the dark wealth of her curls,
With a scorn in her eye which the gazer could feel,
 And a glance like the sunshine that flashes on steel.

" Go back, haughty Southron, thy treasures of gold
 Are dim with the blood of the hearts thou hast sold !
Thy home may be lovely, but round it I hear
 The crack of the whip and the footsteps of fear ! "

The following is from Mr. Wright's pen:—

" The fetters galled my weary soul,—
 A soul that seemed but thrown away ;
I spurned the tyrant's base control,
 Resolved at last the man to play :—
  The hounds are baying on my track,
  O Christian ! will you send me back ?

"I felt the stripes, the lash I saw,
 Red, dripping with a father's gore ;
And, worst of all their lawless law,
 The insults that my mother bore !
  The hounds are baying on my track,
  O Christian ! will you send me back ?

"Where human law o'errules Divine,
 Beneath the sheriff's hammer fell
My wife and babes,—I call them mine,—
 And where they suffer, who can tell ?
  The hounds are baying on my track,
  O Christian ! will you send me back ?

"I seek a home where man is man,
 If such there be upon this earth,
To draw my kindred, if I can,
 Around its free though humble hearth.
  The hounds are baying on my track,
  O Christian ! will you send me back ?

Of the twenty-four resolutions passed are the following. On the sinfulness of slavery and the duty of voting :—

"That we regard slavery as it exists in the United States, consisting as it does in the holding of men, women, and children, as property, and appropriating their persons, and all they have and are, to the use of another, contrary to their consent, as a heinous sin and the 'sum of all villanies.'

"That we regard the question of slavery as the greatest political question now agitated before the country, and are determined not to sacrifice the cause of freedom to any other political measure."

On the annexation of Texas and the war with Mexico :—

" That the annexation of Texas, for the express
purpose of extending and perpetuating slavery, was
an unconstitutional and void act, and that we will
neither regard the annexation itself, nor the terms
on which it was done, as binding upon us or our
children.

" That the attempt on the part of our National
Government to extend the boundaries of Texas to
the Rio Grande, for the purpose of bringing all that
vast country lying between its proper boundary and
that river under the dominion of the slave-power,—
and the making war upon Mexico, for that object,
and shedding the blood of hundreds of her innocent
citizens, is a high act of national robbery, which we
fear will draw upon this country the vengeance of
heaven, and which calls upon all good citizens to
humble themselves in dust and ashes, and exert the
uttermost of their power to arrest the Government
in its career of crime and blood."

On the duty of ministers :—

" That it is the duty of all men, especially of
ministers of the gospel, and all moral teachers, with
great boldness and plainness of speech to proclaim
far and wide the truth in regard to the sinfulness and
evils of slavery, and in the spirit and temper of the
gospel, to proclaim the duty of immediate repentance
and immediate and unconditional emancipation."

On the Union and Constitution :—

" That we love the Union, and desire its prosperity,
that we revere the constitution, and are determined
to maintain it, but the Union we love must be a
Union to establish justice, and secure the blessings of

liberty; and the constitution we support must be that which our fathers bequeathed to us, and not that which the constructions of slavery and servilism have substituted for it."

Some of the resolutions refer to the death of the Rev. C. T. Torrey, a Congregational minister, who died in a prison in Maryland, having been condemned to six years imprisonment for aiding some slaves to escape; other resolutions denounce colour-caste so prevalent, and others refer to the various evils resulting from slavery.

The last resolution was as follows:—

"That a committee of twenty be appointed by the chairman, for the purpose of corresponding with Anti-slavery men of all parties throughout the United States, on the propriety of holding a National Convention at Washington, or some other suitable place, and that they be empowered to call such a meeting."

Much talent was displayed in speaking to the resolutions, by Messrs. Codding, Lovejoy, and other speakers. The meeting indicated the approaching triumph of Liberty principles.

The proceedings of the Convention occupied two days, on the evening of each, Mr. Bibb spoke and gave us the history of his slave-life. He had been bought and sold several times. He told of a master who at one time owned him, who was deacon of a Baptist Church, and who was by far the worst tyrant he had fallen in with. He described the separation from his wife when he was sold by this master. Both he and his wife fell on their knees and prayed that he would not part them, but keep them both or sell them both. His master refused, tore her from his bosom, and bid her go to her work. She clung to her husband's neck, until her master dragged her from him, and applied the cowhide at the same time. Mr. Bibb stated that until he was out of hearing his wife was still screaming.

The audience were very powerfully affected. A rich man rising amidst the thousands present called out, "I will give three hundred dollars towards getting your wife again." Mr. Bibb sung some of the mournful songs sung by the slaves at the south. I have seldom witnessed such overpowering sympathy as that which seemed to affect every heart in that vast assembly.

In reply to the offer of three hundred dollars to rescue his wife, it was stated that Mrs. Bibb had been sold to a Frenchman, and had been compelled to live with him as his wife, and was the mother of several children. Mr. Bibb stated that he had been the slave of a Cherokee Indian, and that the churches in that nation, of all denominations, received slave-holders to membership.

This was a very important fact. The Cherokee Baptist Churches were connected with the Baptist Missionary Union; its committee residing in Boston, Massachusetts. I commenced an agitation respecting these slaveholding churches which ended in their separation from the Union. Thousands of people who contributed to the Union did not imagine that it supported slaveholding churches. I will refer to this again in the account of my labours in New England. Of the fifteen ministers in Chicago, but one, the Rev. Mr. Rice, baptist, attended the convention. The Chicago citizens kindly entertained all the people who came to attend it.

Many persons who listened unmoved to the most earnest appeals of the Anti-slavery advocates were deeply affected by the Anti-slavery pieces that were sung, and came forward and united with the Anti-slavery Society.

I heard in Chicago of a young man who on one occasion was exceedingly mortified in listening to one of these pieces. He had made a speech in defence of slavery; and several young ladies connected with the Liberty choir were present. At the close of his speech they commenced singing melodiously:—

"Oh, he's not the man for me,"

a piece quoted page 220, and they sung it to the end.

The Rev. Mr. P. an English Baptist minister, residing in Illinois, advised me to give the subject of slavery less prominence in my preaching. I reminded him of the course pursued in 1090 by Bishop Wulfstan, when the city of Bristol, in England, was a great slave-mart. Rows of young people, of both sexes, and of great beauty, were tied together with ropes and placed for sale in the public market. They were exported to Ireland—the young women having been prostituted. Wulfstan sometimes stayed two months amongst them, preaching every Lord's day; in process of time he induced them to abandon their wicked trade, and they became an example to all England. "Now," I inquired, "did Bishop Wulfstan do right or wrong?" To disapprove of Wulfstan's course would be an approval of the slave-trade which many slave-holders denounced as iniquitous ;—and to approve of his preaching would be a plea for mine. After a little reflection and hesitation Mr. P. said—" I do not know whether Bishop Wulfstan did right or wrong." My reply was " You must decide that question before you are qualified to advise me."

The Rev. I. T. Hinton, from Oxford, England, was pastor of the Baptist Church in Chicago, when Lovejoy became a martyr. He announced that he should preach a funeral sermon on the tragedy. The mayor begged him not to do so, fearing a mob. He replied " I am about to do my duty as a minister—I hope you will do yours as mayor." In his sermon he showed that God always punishes slaveholding nations. There was no opposition. The sermon was published. He received, however, and accepted call from New Orleans and became an apologist for slavery and a slaveholder. He died of the yellow fever. In the civil war one of his sons was in the federal, the other in the con-federate army.

CHAPTER XIII.

Anti-slavery Tour in Green County with J. LyBrand, Esq.—
A One Price Store—Visit to Dr. Harcourt—Anecdotes of
Father Craven of Virginia—Spring Grove—Justice to Whigs
and Democrats—Green Settlement—The Free Will Baptists
Anti-slavery—A Funeral—Rev. Mr. Stilwell on the Whig
Party—The Democrats and the Fourth of July—The Baptist
Denomination and Slavery—Musings in a Walk by Star-light
after being Mobbed—A Baptist Anti-slavery Society Formed in
New York—It declares Slavery to be a Sin—Wrath of Baptist
Slaveholders—They Require the National Baptist Societies to
Oppose Abolition— Meeting at Baltimore — The Command
Meekly Obeyed—Secession of Anti-slavery Members from the
Missionary Society—Formation in Boston of an Anti-slavery
Missionary Society—The Old Society refuses to send out a
Slaveholder as Missionary—Increased Wrath of Slaveholders—
They Form a Missionary Society with Slavery as its Corner
Stone—The Missionary Union Formed to Conciliate them—
United Opposition of both to Abolition—Meeting in Illinois—
Free Missions Approved—The *Georgia Index* on the Decline
of Abolition—A Free Mission Society Formed in Wisconsin—
Extracts from its Address—The Liberty Party in Wisconsin—
Praying and Voting—Anecdotes.

I RESIGNED my connection with the Illinois State
Anti-slavery Society for the purpose of becoming the
Agent of the Wisconsin Territorial Anti-slavery
Society. My journal was published in the *American
Freeman.*

A tour in Green County is thus described:—On the 2nd of August, 1845, I visited Monroe, the county seat of Green County. How beautiful was the scenery. As I travelled over the excellent roads,— woodlands, rolling prairies, and well-improved farms, successively delighted the eye and gladdened the heart. Monroe is pleasantly situated a little south-west of the centre of the county. A new Court House, about thirty-six by forty feet, built of brick and in the modern style, adds much to the appearance of the village. The lot on which it stands is a por-tion of forty acres of land presented to the county by Mr. Jacob LyBrand, who resides at Monroe, and is the candidate of the Liberty party for member of the Legislature. The village of Monroe contains two taverns, four shops, and about two hundred inhabitants, who are supplied with water from a mammoth spring.

On the Sabbath I preached on the slavery question, and on the 5th of August set out to visit the different parts of the county in company with Mr. Jacob LyBrand, whose early settlement in the place, as well as the character of his business, had made him generally acquainted with the citizens, by which means the object of our tour was greatly promoted. He has in front of his shop the words "The One Price Store." This indicates that in selling goods he asks a certain price and makes no abatement. Usually the tradesman has a private mark on his goods stating the cost price. In selling them he asks a high price, the customer offers a low one, and the intermediate amount on which both can agree is the price of the article.

Taking a southern course, we arrived in the evening at the house of Dr. Harcourt, a Methodist minister. I here spoke to an assembly from Matthew v. 4, "Blessed are the merciful, for they shall obtain mercy," pointing out the unmerciful character of those who support slavery, in contrast with the mercy of those who labour for emancipation.

At the close of the meeting we gratefully accepted the proffered hospitality of the doctor. He is from the south, and as an eye-witness, gave us his testimony of the peculiar atrocities of slavery. Among the southern characters which he described was that of Father Craven, an Anti-slavery Methodist Minister.

One Sabbath morning Father Craven stated to his friends that he wished to preach against slavery, but that he had no money to pay the fine. This was in Virginia, and by its laws at that period, the penalty for preaching a sermon against slavery was ten dollars. They immediately subscribed, and handed to him that sum. He ascended the pulpit and very faithfully delivered a sermon against slavery as the " sum of all villanies." At the close of the discourse, calling on those who were authorized to take the fine, and holding out the money, he vociferated, " Now, you blood-suckers, come forward and get the money."

In describing those who resided in the Free States, yet held slaves in the slave states, he would remark that " A pipe had been laid under the Ohio river, reaching from the free to the slave states, at which the slaveholders in the free states were drawing, and draining the life-blood from the veins of the slaves." Being sent for by a slaveholder who was seriously

unwell, to pray with him, Father Craven approached
his bed-side and inquired if he had in his will bequeathed liberty to his slaves? "No," said the
slaveholder,—"I have bequeathed them to my children." "Then" said Father Craven, "prayer will
be of no avail—God will not show mercy to those
who show none to their fellow-men."   So he bade him
farewell.   Soon after, a second message was sent for
Father Craven to visit the slaveholder and pray with
him.   He went and asked the slaveholder if he had
emancipated his slaves?   "Yes," said the slaveholder, "I have now emancipated them by my will.
Will you pray for me?"   "Certainly," said the good
man, and he knelt down and commended to God the
soul of the sufferer, who seemed near his end. Father
Craven agreed with John Jay, a leader in the
American revolution, who said—"Till America comes
into the measure (of abolition) her prayers to heaven
will be impious."

We conversed respecting Cassius M. Clay, who
had established an Anti-slavery press in Kentucky,
and though in daily danger of assassination from the
slave-party, was firm and self-controlled; when Dr.
Harcourt, using a southern phrase, said "Yes, the
feelings can be schooled to a vast extent."

On the 6th we proceeded to Spring Grove, and I
lectured on the influence of the slave-power over the
two great parties into which the people were divided,
the whigs and the democrats; and the rise, progress,
and principles of the Liberty party.   At the close a
democrat arose, and addressing me, said " I wish, Sir,
before the meeting separates, to state how true and

faithful have been the description you have given of the servility of the whigs to the slave-party." Immediately a whig arose and said "I also wish, Sir, before the meeting separates, to observe that the description you have given of the servility of the democrats to the slave-party is very true and faithful."

On the 7th we set out for Green Settlement. While passing the house of D. S. Sutherland, an ex-member of the Assembly, we observed a buggy at the gate, and soon met two gentlemen who had recently dismounted from it, to whom I was introduced. They were the Hon. James Collins and Lawyer Stewart. The term Honourable is applied to every member of the Legislative Assembly. The former had been nominated by the whigs as the Delegate to Congress—he was a man who on every test question that might come up at Washington was ready to take sides with the south and with slavery. Each Territory elects a Delegate, who may speak in Congress but is not allowed to vote. After dining at the house of Widow Pierce, where we were kindly furnished with a fresh horse, without which we should not have been able to fulfill our appointment, we hastened on, and were kindly received by the friends at Green Settlement. A respectable number had assembled, and I spoke on the question of slavery for an hour. The Rev. H. Hurlbut was present, who takes a deep interest in the cause.

We tarried over night at the house of Mr. Miller. The Free Will Baptists, of which body he is a member, exclude slaveholders from membership. Their organ, the *Morning Star*, is a thorough Anti-slavery

paper. Their General Conference has frequently condemned slavery and urged the members of the body
to act on Christian principles in voting for civil
rulers. In some religious bodies strenuous objections
were made to the introduction of resolutions of this
character, from a fear that they might open the way for
many evils. The objectors seemed to forget that by
voting for pro-slavery rulers, they were continuing
slavery and all its evils; such as depriving the slave-
woman of all protection, and the slave population of
the Word of God. Men, professing to tremble for
the Ark of the Lord, if religious bodies recommended
that there should be a divorce between the Federal
government and slavery, abandoned without scruple
millions of their fellow-men to the adversary. With
these Mr. Miller had no sympathy; and would vote
for no person for office unless he was opposed to
slavery.

On the 8th we proceeded to Exeter, and were
kindly received by Messrs. Willet and Calkins. The
land here, and the site on which Exeter is built,
resembles the waves of the sea suddenly stilled.
There are about one hundred inhabitants. Lead has
been discovered, but no mining was going on. I
lectured at the School House in the evening. Many
desire a public discussion, which we contemplate
having at my next visit. The rain fell fast as we
started on the 9th to the Pennsylvania district. We
arrived in time for the meeting at three in the afternoon. At the close of the lecture a note was presented requesting me to preach a funeral sermon on
the following morning, as a young man had died to

whom I had been introduced a few days before. His
mother, Mrs. Bowen, two years since left Pennsylvania
for Iowa Territory. On arriving there her husband
died and one of her children; removing to Galena
two other members of the family were called away
by death; Mrs. B. came to Green County, but death
kept close upon her track, two other children died,
and this young man was the third; making a bereavement in two years of a husband and six children. I
engaged to attend. At the funeral I gave an address
from Job vii. 17, 18, "What is man, that Thou
shouldest magnify him? and that Thou shouldest set
Thine heart upon him? And that Thou shouldest
visit him every morning, and try him every moment?"
I spoke of the insignificance of man whether considered as to his physical, mental, or moral nature;
and of the momentous relations which nevertheless
he sustains to God. He is magnified in being
placed over the lower creation, in having an immortal soul; in the union of his nature with the
Divine in the person of Christ—and in the discipline
under which he is here placed to form a character for
eternity. At the close I went to the bereaved woman,
and inquired whether under these mysterious and
afflictive providences, she was still enabled to trust
in the Redeemer's love and care. Her reply was
"Though He slay me yet will I trust in Him."

In the afternoon I lectured in the Pennsylvania
District on the influence of the slave-power over the
churches, and the impossibility of spreading the bible
among the slaves till they were free, which could
only be secured by voting for Anti-slavery rulers.

In the evening I lectured at the house of Mr. More on the responsibility the North assumed in sustaining slavery. The Rev. Mr. Stilwell, a Baptist, was present, and at the close he arose and made the following remarks :—" You must never expect, friends, that either of the two great parties, will emancipate the slaves, and here I will relate a circumstance, to show the dominance of the slave-power over the whigs. I myself have been a whig, and a gentleman of the name of Miller, a member of the same political party, intelligent and influential, belonging to the Presbyterian Church, made the proposition in Winnebago County, Illinois, where I resided, that the abolitionists should vote for the whigs, as they were so few they could do nothing alone, and the whigs might be relied on to carry out Anti-slavery measures. The abolitionists yielding to his advice voted with the whigs and placed Mr. Miller in the Legislature. A proposition came up in the House to pass a law prohibiting marriage between the whites and the blacks. Mr. Miller voted with three others against the proposition. For this he was treated with the most withering contempt and scorn. Deeply mortified he resolved to regain the esteem of his colleagues. The next morning he arose in the House of Assembly and asked if some more effectual mode could not be devised to prevent people from assisting slaves when they had escaped and helping them forward to Canada. In consequence of the introduction of the subject by this man and the co-operation of others, a law was passed sending to the penitentiary prison any one convicted of aiding a runaway slave; whereas before, the penalty was only five hundred dollars. This, then, is all the help we can expect from the whigs; and the democrats are equally servile to the slave-power."

On the 11th I lectured to an attentive congregation at Well's Settlement; on the 12th, lectured at Monroe on Temperance; on the 13th, lectured on slavery at the Douglass' Settlement; on the 14th, lectured twice at Janesville. The Rev. Mr. Murphy, a Baptist, closed the first lecture with prayer; and the Rev. Mr. Buckley, Congregationalist, the second.

The Anti-slavery friends always wished to read the reports of the labours of the Anti-slavery advocates. If there was opposition they were cheered, knowing that it would produce Anti-slavery agitation and progress; and if there was a favourable reception—they were cheered, because so many were willing to hear on the subject of slavery, and their zeal would thus be enlisted in the cause.

The slave-party in Monroe gave the following illustration of the means to which they would resort, to sustain the interests of the slaveholder.

At the time that Mr. LyBrand made a donation of forty acres of land to the county, it was in the highest state of cultivation, in the midst of a first-rate farming community. He also promised a hundred dollars towards erecting the Court House when the building should be completed, and paid the amount just as it was begun; and he was under an agreement to furnish a bell for the cupola.

At Monroe I organized a Liberty County Association—which was to meet annually on the fourth of

July. On the 1st of June, 1846, the annual meeting was announced to be held, in the Court House, permission having been kindly given by C. S. Thomas, Esq., the sheriff. At the appointed time the members of the Liberty Association accompanied by Mr. LyBrand repaired to the Court House, and found the door locked against them. The reasons as given in a letter from Mr. LyBrand published in the *American Freeman* are thus stated :—

"The 'Glorious Fourth' has passed. Not 'Glorious,' however, to three millions of our brethren who are groaning in southern bondage, although as much entitled to freedom as we are. The anniversary of that 'Declaration' which, when proclaimed to the world seventy years ago, caused the crowned heads of Europe to tremble on their thrones; that 'Declaration' which has since made us the scorn, the reproach, the bye-word, and the hissing of the whole world, whether civilized or barbarous! It appears, after it was known that the Green County Liberty Association had obtained permission to use the Court House, a pettifogger, S. P. Conde—'Simon Pure Democrat'— as one of his party addressed him in my hearing, a short time since, was desirous of displaying his oratorical powers on that day, in one of those sickening 'Fourth of July Orations' so current of late years; or some of the citizens wished to hear him, and consequently those who had the best right to the building, in every sense of the word, must be thrust aside. No gentleman of delicate and generous feelings would consent to address any people under such circumstances! A brother democrat (!) of the orator observed that Mr. Conde made his boast that he was suckled by a 'negro wench,' in the state of New York, a slave belonging to his father. The speaker, it is said, declaimed against Great Britain, as is common on such occasions. I am no apologist for that government, but on the contrary, greatly desire to see all tyranny banished from the world; but it ill become us, the most guilty nation upon God's footstool, to rail out against other people for acts of usurpation, while we are crushing to the earth one-sixth portion of our inhabitants, depriving them of every right, and then denying them the privilege (which all despots grant their subjects), of petitioning for a redress of their grievances. And yet we boastingly call ourselves the 'Free-est nation upon earth.'"

In my letters to the *American Freeman* I fully informed the friends of my efforts in the various towns; and it was only necessary at the close of the year's labours to give a general summary in my report, such as the following which I gave in 1846:—

" Having received on the 8th of June, 1845, a commission as agent for the Wisconsin Territorial Liberty Association, and performed Anti-slavery labour during the twelve months ensuing, allow me to tender my report.

" I made it a point to attend, as far as practicable, the Liberty County Conventions, previous to the last fall elections; and addressed the Conventions on such occasions, in Milwaukee, Jefferson, Dane, Rock, and Green Counties. I have laboured also to organize additional county societies during the past year, and

have succeeded in the counties of Dodge, Green and
Sheboygan ; I have lectured in the district which is
composed of Jefferson and several other counties,
and which has during the year nominated a Liberty
ticket for the Legislature.

"During the fall I held a series of Anti-Texas
meetings in Whitewater and vicinity, Spring Prairie,
Salem, Southport, Racine, Yorkville, Lisbon, Vernon,
Mequanego, Prairieville, &c.

"Protests against annexing Texas were put in circulation, signed and forwarded to Congress. During
the winter I visited the northern portion of the
Territory, and lectured at Mequon, Hamburgh,
Sheboygan, Manitowoc, and Green Bay. In this
part of the Territory but little labour had previously
been performed, and prejudice to some extent prevails
against the cause; mob opposition occurred, however,
but in one instance. In this section the leaven is
working well ; more labour is needed, but the
citizens generally do not feel a sufficient interest in
the cause to make sacrifices to obtain it ; there are,
however, some noble exceptions. Returning through
the inland counties, I addressed the citizen Indians
in Calumet County ; and by the aid of an interpreter,
Mr. Ostenfeldt, the Germans; by both parties the Anti-
slavery truth was favourably received. I addressed
the citizens of Taychedah, and found among them
some warm-hearted abolitionists ; as also in Osh
Kosh, though threats of opposition were thrown out
in the latter place ; but Justice Ford, a man of great
decision, announced that he should attend the meeting and order the arrest of the first man who violated

the law. In company with the constable, he attended the lecture, and a more orderly meeting has never been attended by your agent.

"From Osh Kosh I proceeded to Ceresco, and delivered two lectures before members of the Fourier Association. Proceeding to Dodge County I lectured at Beaver Dam, Fox Lake, Elder Cady's neighbourhood, Clauson's Prairie, Pratt's neighbourhood, Rubicon, Lowell, &c. There is a noble host of friends in this county. After lecturing at Aztalan and attending at the anniversary of the society in Beloit, I lectured at Burlington, Prairieville, Oconomowoc, Sun Prairie, Aztalan, Oakland, Janesville, Beloit, Waterloo, Sugar Creek Prairie, Hart Prairie, Johnstown, Lisbon, Warren, Hershey's Mills, New Berlin, Geneva, Southport, &c. I have also delivered lectures in Northern Illinois, one in Weston, near Galena, one in Elgin, and three in Halfday; travelling during the above period 2,030 miles.

"In conclusion I would remark that there is a dark and a bright side to Wisconsin. First the dark side. Slaves are held in our territory; ten or twelve have been sent south into slavery from Wisconsin; of nearly 200 ministers, at least 100 by their influence aid and abet slaveholding; there are about ten pro-slavery weekly newspapers. A number of the religious people are in connection with pro-slavery missionary societies. But there is a bright side;—There are Liberty organizations in at least ten counties in the Territory; the Anti-slavery votes last fall were between 700 and 900; wherever efforts were made results have been produced far better than could have been anticipated; a number of the ministers of religion are identified with the Anti-slavery cause; citizens almost everywhere are willing, and in a large part of the Territory anxious, to hear lectures on the subject of slavery; during the short time the 'press' has been in operation a very great change has been made in the public mind in favour of the cause; and the results compared with the means employed have been most encouraging."

I had the happiness to aid in the formation of the " Wisconsin Baptist Free Mission Society;" which was designed to separate the Baptists in their Missionary efforts from all connection with slaveholders. Its formation both indicated and promoted the progress of the Anti-slavery reform. Without a knowledge of the relations which the denomination sustained to slavery the value of such an organization can scarcely be appreciated. I will, therefore, take a brief glance at them, such as passed through my mind when walking along by star-light to Jamestown, after the mob had driven me from Fair Play for declaring that the slaves were my brethren in bonds. I mused thus:—Where is the sympathy of the Baptists, numbering in all the states, free and slave, 842,660? What is their influence, that the plainest truths of the Gospel are thus scorned, and their advocates persecuted? I will survey the denomination in all the states. I gaze south on the slave-states—Oh! ye 3,703 Baptist ministers of the south, are you all the defenders of slavery? Do none of you preach against slavery, not one? Echo answers —"not one." Oh! ye 403,000 Baptist members at the south who have no slaves, are there none of you that treat slaveholding as a sin, not fifty? Echo answers " not fifty." Oh! ye 100,000 Baptist slaves at the south, dare you not declare that you have a right to liberty? would it be death to do so? Echo answers—" death to do so." And you ye 20,000 Baptist slaveholders, holding 226,000 slaves, do none of you refuse to justify slavery as ordained of God, not one? Echo answers—" not one." I will then look to the free states. Oh! ye 3184 Baptist ministers, who claim that you have ever been historically the defenders of civil and religious liberty, are those of you that plead for the slave but a small number? Echo answers—" but a small number." Oh! ye 324,660 Baptist northern members do you, excepting a remnant, still yield to the demands of the slaveholder? Echo answers, " still yield to the demands of the slaveholder."

Then I look to the past. In imagination I see the assemblage of the Baptists at Washington in 1814. They are forming the Foreign Missionary Society. I observe present the subtle slaveholding Baptists, and hear them ask to be admitted as members. I listen to the reply—" You have deprived your own slaves of the Word of life, can you care for its diffusion in heathen lands?"—And to the response—" We hold slaves from kindness, and for their good." They become members. They elect a slaveholder as president of the society; and during twenty-one years out of thirty they elect slaveholders to that office. I see missionaries go forth, who are slaveholders, who plant slaveholding churches among the Indians. But hark!

a voice of remonstrance is heard. It comes from
Baptists in England; but it is hushed by the slaveholders. And now what mean the gathering of
Baptists in New York? They are men of faith and
prayer, who, touched with sympathy for the slaves,
have met to form a Baptist Anti-slavery Society.
The fate of the nation depends on the questions they
are discussing — what connection has the Baptist
denomination with slavery? What can Baptists do
to relieve the benighted and suffering slave, and to
disconnect the Anti-slavery portion of the denomination from a practical support of the slave system?

A Baptist Anti-slavery Society is formed. It
adopts an address declaring slaveholding to be a sin,
and that slaveholders are unworthy of Christian
fellowship. I look to the south, and mark the effect.
What large meetings are held! How bitter the
denunciations they utter against the Anti-slavery
Baptists! I see the slaveholders rush to the committee of the Foreign Missionary Society, and to the
other committees, for encouragement. They demand
protection on pain of withdrawing their subscriptions.
Will they obtain it? What a noble opportunity have
these committees of taking sides with the outraged
slaves and a pure Christianity, against religious man-
stealers. Will they embrace the occasion of doing
so? And now I see the gathering of Baptists north
and south in Baltimore. I hear an agreement read,
drawn up by Dr. Cone, of New York, recognizing
the Christian character of slaveholders. It is signed
by slaveholders from the south and non-slaveholders
from the north.

The sufferings of the slaves are ignored, the command to " break every yoke " disobeyed, and they sing—

" From whence does this Union arise ? "

My walk is completed, and my musings terminate I arrive at the house of a friend. All have retired to rest, for it is midnight. I am kindly received, and soon rest in security from the danger of the mob.

The remainder of the history may be briefly sketched. The Anti-slavery Baptists, seeing the influence of the "price of blood," assembled in Boston, Massachusetts, on the 4th of May, 1843, and formed a Free Missionary Society, separating themselves for ever from co-operation with slaveholders in the work of missions. They adopted a constitution, chose officers, raised a fund, and selecting Hayti as a field of missions, sent out several missionaries. The *Christian Contributor* became the organ of the society. Afterwards they sent missionaries and teachers to the refugee slaves in Canada, and commissioned myself to labour in Virginia and Kentucky. But the society from which the Anti-slavery Baptists had withdrawn, divided ; not, however, on principle, but as did the Methodists (page 201) on a question of expediency ; the question being was it expedient to send out a slaveholder as a missionary ? It came up thus :—

The Free Missionists learning that one of the missionaries of the Foreign Mission Society, the Rev. Mr. Bushyhead, a Cherokee Indian, was a slaveholder, published it among the churches. The Rev. Mr. Pattison, the Missionary Secretary, wrote immediately to Mr. Bushyhead, and seems to have suggested that he should quietly withdraw from the

society. But just at that period he died, leaving his
slaves to his widow. By some means the slaveholders
learned that such a letter had been sent. They
thought of the agreement at Baltimore, and demanded
of the missionary committee to state whether they
would send out a slaveholder as a missionary? The
committe replied—"We could not do so." "But," said
the slaveholders, "If we are qualified to preach at your
meetings in New York and Philadelphia, are we not
fit to preach to the heathen? We will now separate
from all your benevolent societies."

The missionary committee was now said to be
between two fires. It was certainly between two
fears. It feared the effect of the agitation of the
Anti-slavery Baptists and it feared the agitation
among slaveholders owing to its recent decision.
Large meetings were held in the slave states in which
the separation from northern Baptists in Benevolent
efforts was successfully advocated ; whilst the great
body of Northern Baptists highly approved of the
decision of the Boston committee ; and were glad
that they had not been disgraced by the appointment
of a slaveholding missionary. It required no little
disregard of northern sentiment in Baptist Churches,
and among the people generally, to brave this sentiment, and to attempt to roll back the Anti-slavery
reform by the strength of the Missionary Society.
The committee, however, seems to have decided that
to prevent division, the slaveholders must be con-
ciliated, and the northern Baptists managed. In
addition to the Boston committee there was a general
committee. The latter held a meeting at Providence,

Rhode Island, on the 30th of April, 1845. A humble apology to their lordships the slaveholders was made by the Boston committee. It meekly received a censure for its rash conduct in not having the fear of the slaveholders before its eyes. This was from the general committee; which granted absolution in view of the penitence manifested. All this humiliating work was done to conciliate the very men who afterwards led the south in the rebellion and caused the death of so many men in the war,—and I doubt not some of the sons of the men who made the above apology were among the slain.

Desiring to know all that was done at the above meeting at Providence, I examined the reports as furnished by the *Baptist Register*, a New York paper, the *Christian Reflector and Watchman*, a New England paper, the *Baptist Magazine*, and a paper published at Providence. From all these I could not learn what was really done at the meeting.

The key of the proceedings was a resolution offered by the Rev. Dr. Welch. For this resolution I searched in vain. This was the mode of managing the north. They were to be kept in ignorance. My colleague, the Rev. A. T. Foss, wrote to Dr. Welch asking him kindly to send him a copy of the resolution; having obtained this, the whole subject was explained.

The Boston committee in its letter to the slaveholders had declared that it could not approve of slavery; this it retracted at the meeting in Providence. Dr. Welch offered a resolution sanctioning the committee in its disapproval of slavery; but, says Dr. Welch, "after a protracted and somewhat piquant debate, the resolution was negatived." Yet the northern churches were taught that the Boston committee had not changed its position since it refused to employ a slaveholder as a missionary.

The Southern Baptists met at Augusta, Georgia, on the 8th of May, 1843, and formed a Southern Missionary Society, having as its corner stone the falsehood that slavery is instituted by the Almighty.

It was now anticipated that all northern Baptists would unite in one Missionary body, opposed to slavery. The great body of the people in the free states are farmers. They were prepared for the measure. But the commercial men, members of the Baptist Churches in Boston, New York, and Philadelphia, who traded with the south, had more intelligence but less humanity than the farmers. A meeting was held by the Baptists in New York, in 1845, to consider what arrangements should be made. There was a Baptist Missionary Society in the free states holding slavery to be sinful; and a Baptist Missionary Society in the south holding slavery to be heaven-ordained. The proceedings showed that the commercial men, and the ministers preaching to them had come to an understanding with the slaveholding Baptists, and that a society was to be formed which should fraternise with them. To accomplish this the first step necessary was to silence the voice of every member on the slavery question. This was difficult, because it was a body composed of delegates from the churches, and Anti-slavery Churches might instruct their delegates to move for a separation from slaveholders. The representative principle was therefore banished, and any person who would pay one hundred dollars could become a member.

The Rev. H. K. Green moved that no slaveholder should be allowed to unite with the body. The motion was rejected, and slaveholders with great glee paid in their money and became members.

The Rev. M. D. Miller moved that no slaveholder should be an officer. The motion was rejected.

The Rev. Dr. Welch moved to approve of the committee in declining to send out a slaveholder as a missionary. The motion was rejected.

A communication was made by the Free Mission Society, stating their desire to unite all Northern Baptists in one missionary movement, if a declaration were made by the assembly that it would have no connection with slaveholders. The communication was treated with contempt.

Thus was formed the American Baptist Missionary Union. The slave-party were preparing for a war with Mexico; and had this Union, instead of silencing the voice of every member on slavery, put forth its power against slavery, I do not believe the war with Mexico could have been entered upon by the slave party; and had there been no war with Mexico, there would have been no secession, and no war arising from the question of the extension of slavery to the Territories acquired from Mexico.

A meeting was held at Elgin, in Illinois, in the spring of 1846, to consider whether the Western Baptists could support the Missionary Union, in view of its position on slavery. I was present. Rev. S. Carr was appointed chairman, and Rev. R. R.

Whittier, secretary. A committee was appointed on resolutions. Two reports were presented, one from the majority of the committee, recommending co-operation with the Missionary Union; the other from the minority of the committee, recommending co-operation with the Anti-slavery Missionary Society. After an extended discussion the vote was taken, when twenty-four voted for co-operation with the latter society, and eight against it.

I preached one of the sermons at the convention. The text was Matthew xxviii. 17, 18. "Go ye into all the world," etc. I pointed out that the benevolence of the Gospel was universal, embracing the slaves at home as well as the heathen abroad.

The Rev. J. M. Peck, a pro-slavery Baptist minister, had assured the slaveholding Baptists that since the formation of the Missionary Union abolitionism had declined fifty per cent.

The *Georgia Index*, a Baptist paper, edited by a slaveholder, and defending slavery by the Bible, has the following article on the meeting:—

PROTRACTED MISSIONARY MEETING.

"A missionary meeting of three days continuance was recently held in Illinois, (the state of Rev. J. M. Peck's adoption.) A committee was appointed on resolutions, which brought in two reports. The majority reported in favour of contributing to Foreign missions through the American Baptist Missionary Union, at the same time they expressed regret that the Union had not excluded slaveholders. The minority reported in favour of contributing through the American and Foreign Missionary

Society, the Anti-slavery organization. After a discussion of two days, a resolution in favour of the Anti-slavery organization, in preference to the American Baptist Missionary Union, was passed by a majority of two-thirds! *Note.* Neither party were willing to recognize slaveholders on terms of moral equality! Is this evidence that Abolitionism has declined fifty per cent., as Brother Peck represented in the south, for the sake of effect we presume."
—*Georgia Index.*

For a time the formation of a Wisconsin Free Mission Society was delayed, because there was an expectation that the Baptist Missionary Society would separate from its slaveholding connections. When it became evident that the Society was determined to cling to slavery, a meeting composed of delegates from a number of the Baptist Churches met at Spring Prairie, in the Baptist Church, on the fourth Wednesday and Thursday of October, 1846, and formed a Society, for ever separating themselves from religious association with slaveholders. An introductory sermon was preached by the Rev. J. H. Dudley, of Delavan, from John xvi. 11. " Of judgment because the prince of this world is judged." After which he was called to preside, and Rev. S. Carr was appointed Secretary. A preamble and constitution were then adopted. The former states " We therefore solemnly pledge ourselves to God, and to one another, to unite in the support of a Baptist Missionary Society which shall be distinctly and thoroughly separated from all connection with the known avails of slavery in the support of any of its benevolent purposes, and to be

also in its operation wholly disconnected from those
societies that are in connection with slaveholders." A
committee was elected, and arrangements made to
promote the cause. An address which I had written
was adopted, stating the necessity for the formation
of the Society, the principles by which it would
be governed, and the work it proposed to perform.
The following extracts from the address throws light
on the policy of the slaveholders :—

"It may be necessary to advert to a great general
principle adhered to unflinchingly by every slaveholder. The principle is this—A slaveholder will
co-operate with no society, be it political, commercial,
literary, benevolent, or evangelical, unless that society
will tacitly consent to the principle of chattelizing
human beings. Slaveholders are life directors of one,
and life members of both the above-named societies
(Home and Foreign Mission.) Now let us observe
the mode of operation.

"Does a brother at the north plead for the dumb?
The slaveholder prohibits his election to the offices of
the society, and he is passed by as Galusha was.
Does a missionary give a trifle to help clothe the
trembling fugitive? The slaveholder thunders his
disapprobation, as in the case of Mason. Does a
member of the board attend an Anti-slavery convention? Again the lion is rampant, till a letter, meek
as that of Baron Stow, yet equally servile, appeases
his wrath. Does the Boston Board decline sending a
slaveholding preacher to the heathen? The South is
in commotion—the general board is urged to pass
sentence upon them, and they censure them forth-

with; and even that does not calm the tempest; the
air still resounds with cries of unconstitutional
action, treason, and division.   Are propositions made
to evangelize the slaves?   The face of the slaveholder
whitens with rage, and his eyes flash vengeance 'as he
points to penitentiaries, branding irons, and a gallows
as high as Haman's, and imperatively orders that
they shall let his property alone."

The Society contemplated sending missionaries to
the slave states.   The address proceeds:—

" Among the benefits of such societies, (Free
Mission,) we propose briefly to advert to their
influence on the slave states.   As Providence opens
the way, missionaries will visit the south who will
address the southern citizens in such language as this :
Brethren and Friends—We are far from having towards
you any feelings but those of the most friendly character.   We are interested in your welfare and desire to
do you good.   We live under laws which you have
assisted to make, and' have the same form of ecclesiastical government to which many of you profess to
adhere.   With you, we are going to the judgment.
There we shall give a strict account of all our conduct
towards you.   Aside from our desire to see the whole
south dotted with school-houses, your commerce flourishing, and your agricultural improvements rapidly
advancing, we long to see the rising generation, without regard to complexion, gathered into Sabbath-
schools, and enjoying the hallowed associations of the
Sabbath and the sanctuary.   But, that this may be
accomplished, you must give up slavery.   We proffer
to every inhabitant of the south the blessed Bible,

but it cannot be received till you give up slavery. We desire to see the marriage covenant honoured, and the domestic relations of each family protected, but this cannot be till you give up slavery. Slavery is the bane of your peace, the parent of crime, the cause of ignorance, and the work of the devil. Give it up, that you may enjoy happiness. Abolish it that you may avert the impending judgments of God. Righteousness exalteth a nation, but sin is a reproach to any people. Such is the message of the Free Mission Brethren to the south, and to the north also so far as it is implicated in the great crime."

How narrowly I escaped hanging in Kentucky for appeals similar to the above I shall yet show.

The *Christian Contributor* of December 23, 1846, published in full the proceedings, the constitution, and the address, with the following introduction:—

THE CAUSE RISING.

" Thanks be unto God, Wisconsin has set a noble example, worthy to be followed by every state in the Union. Most cheerfully do we comply with the request to copy from the *Western Christian* the doings of the Convention. Our eastern readers will peruse them with delight, and particularly the able, appropriate, candid, and truly Christian address."

Before bidding farewell to the west, I will briefly refer to the political Anti-slavery movement, and my connection with it.

At the commencement of the Anti-slavery reform the friends of the slave proposed questions to the candidates for office; and voted for those who promised to do most for emancipation. Owing, however, to the great influence of the slaveholders over both whigs and democrats, these promises were never performed. Hence it became necessary to organize a new party. A national convention was held at Albany, New York, April 1, 1840, "to discuss the question of an independent nomination of abolition candidates for the two highest offices in the Federal government." After a full discussion the Liberty party was organized, and James G. Birney, referred to on page 43, was nominated for President, and Thomas Earle for Vice-President of the United States. In the autumn the entire vote was a little less than 7000.

So rapid, however, was the growth of the Liberty party, that in 1844, the Liberty candidates, James G. Birney and Thomas Morris, received upwards of 60,000 votes. The other candidates were Harrison and Van Buren, in 1840; and Polk and Clay, in 1844; the two latter were slaveholders, and the two former openly opposed to the measures and objects of the abolitionists.

The choice of a President did not rest so much with the people as it did with the political party conventions that made the nominations. In 1844, after the whig convention had nominated Henry Clay, and the democratic convention, James K. Polk,—I asked a whig "How can you feel justified in voting for a slaveholder?" His reply was—he is not exactly the person I should choose, but it is certain that either Mr. Clay or Mr. Polk will be the next President; and as the lesser evil of the two I shall vote for Mr. Clay.

I asked a democrat the same question—and he re-

plied—" Well, I do not like to vote for a slaveholder ;
but we are in this position, Mr. Polk or Mr. Clay
must be the next President—and I prefer the former
to the latter." I said to one whig ; pray tell me if
you would vote for Mr. Clay if he held your wife in
slavery ? He replied—" No, I would shoot him
down as quick as I would a bear." I reminded him
that Henry Clay held other men's wives in slavery,
and that it was as sinful to hold coloured persons in
slavery as those who were white.

There was no hope of abolishing slavery without
disbanding the whig and democratic parties. This
will be seen if I refer to their conventions, presses,
philosophy, and party discipline.

A comparison of the questions agitated under the
different Federal administrations will show—that at
certain periods the slaveholders brought forward certain questions, chiefly referring to banks and tariffs,
and kept the northern mind occupied with them,
while they themselves were busily engaged in promoting the slave system.

The slave-party regarded these questions as the
dust of the balance when compared with slavery.
It boasted that when the slavery question was tested
—slaveholders knew no party—and that, which ever
party triumphed, slaveholders always ruled. Now
in what way was this done ?

First, by their conventions to nominate Presidents.
In the earlier history of the republic—the person
who filled the position of secretary-of-state was regarded as the fitting candidate for the presidency ;
next the members of congress recommended a candi-

date; then a plan was adopted which still continues, the election of a delegation from each state to meet in a national convention, and after consultation, to bring forward the name of some person for President.

This was an arrangement of the political parties— the conventions thus elected were neither legal nor responsible; yet so far as party-power was concerned —the nomination was an election. Slaveholding whigs in their convention would put forth every effort, even threatening to leave the party and join the democrats, to secure the nomination of a slaveholder. By the same arts the democratic slaveholders would secure the nomination of a slaveholder in their convention; and such was the discipline of the parties that the persons thus nominated would receive the vote of each member of the respective parties.

The presses connected with each party, would after the nomination, place the names of the nominees at the head of the columns of their papers respectively, and use every means to obtain success. Of course all discussion relative to slavery would be excluded, as this would obstruct the progress of the nominee.

James Cannings Fuller went to the south to emancipate some slaves by purchase, through the liberality of Gerrit Smith, and calling at Henry Clay's house in Kentucky, conversed with one of his slaves, and learned that all her children had been sold. This he published.

The northern whigs were particularly severe—not against Henry Clay for selling the slaves—but against Mr. Fuller, the quaker, for blabbing out the truth, and imperilling all their hopes centred in Clay's election to the presidency.

If, however, the northern whigs had gone to the national convention determined that it should pursue an Anti-slavery policy—they could have succeeded, as they were the majority. The southern whigs might have gone over to the democrats—but the union of the south publicly on slavery would have led eventually to the union of the north for liberty.

As an illustration of the policy of the slave-party in purposely dividing the north upon minor questions —I will refer to the course of President Jackson. The slaves during his administration were more than two millions. I have shown that he laboured to strengthen and extend the slave system. But any one who supposes that this could be gathered from his messages would be quite mistaken. His success depended on concealing his slaveholding policy and appearing earnestly engaged on other questions. His messages fill 266 pages of royal octavo, bourgeoise type; and not one single line is devoted to the slave. His proclamation in reference to South Carolinian nullification fills fourteen pages; his land veto message thirteen. Fearing that the facts of slavery and the schemes of the slave-party would be known he recommended the passage of a law prohibiting the transmission of Anti-slavery papers through the post-offices. The two words "the slaves" occur twice in the recommendation, which fills less than a page; also in his farewell address there are a couple of pages that may be applied to the nullifiers of South Carolina, or to the Abolitionists. Thus work-

ing men and men of business would have their attention absorbed by the banking and similar questions—
and would have no spare time to devote to the
slavery question. This was essential to the dominance of the slave-party.

Their leaders taught the people that the least of
two evils should be selected. This is true physically
—it is better to lose a limb than life itself—but it is
not true morally—of two moral evils we should
choose neither.

The following letter of Rev. Dr. Taylor, of New
Haven, is an illustration of the sentiments that prevailed generally among the ministers in the free
states :—

Edmund Tuttle, of Meridan, Connecticut, in a
letter to Dr. Taylor, proposed this question.:—

"Can a Christian, consistently with the word of
God, cast his vote, either for a duellist or for an
oppressor of the poor, for chief magistrate of this
nation?"

In an extended answer, sustaining the affirmative
of the above question, Dr. Taylor said:—

" To put a stronger case. Suppose that there is no
reasonable doubt that one of two devils, one of which
is a less devil than the other, will be actually elected,
let the Christian vote as he may; and that his vote
will therefore be utterly lost if he does not vote for
one of them. I think that an enlightened Christian
would vote for the least devil of the two.

"NATHANIEL W. TAYLOR.
" Yale College, October 5, 1844."

This letter was intended for the political advantage

of Mr. Clay, but it was at least a very equivocal compliment.

The *New Haven Register* stated that Elizur Wright, jun., of Boston, who delivered the poem before the Phi Beta Kappa Society, on Wednesday evening, in addressing the clergy, thought they should—

> "Find something better to do
> Than 'choosing the lesser devil of the two.'"

—At which some of the "old school" were observed to exchange significant winks.

The *Boston Chronotype* stated that the *Register* had not given the quotation from Professor Wright correctly.   It should be—

> "That in the gathering up of power,
> When Freedom's sons were wont to cower,
> And slavery gives the people's voice
> But just a double Hobson's choice,
> A righteous man has more to do
> Than thus to choose, in party's view,
> The better devil of the two."

The political creed of the Liberty party was— "Humanity first—everything else afterwards." There were persons possessing all the qualifications for office, who, if elected, would emancipate the slaves.   It was therefore the vote that released or that bound the slave.

Previous to the election in 1844, I preached a sermon at Aztalan on the duty of voting for Anti-slavery rulers, from the text Exodus xviii. 21, " Moreover, thou shalt provide, out of all the people, able men, such as fear God, men of truth, hating covetousness, and place such over them."   In pointing out the duty of the people, I showed that a slaveholder was not a man that feared God, or he would not, like Pharaoh, trample on the slave while so much light was being poured on the question; he was not a man of truth, for he classed human beings with property, and denied the distinction between man and property; he did not hate covetousness, or he would not deprive the slave of his liberty and earnings; and finally that the Lord could not abolish slavery by slaveholding rulers unless He first by His judgments drove them into an Anti-slavery position. Several of the people voted for the Anti-slavery candidate, Mr. Birney.

Previous to the presidential election in 1844, at a meeting of the Baptist Association at Spring Prairie, I moved the following resolution:—" That we pledge both our prayers and our votes to promote the deliverance of our brethren from bondage." I observed that many shrank back in their seats as I read it. The whigs intended to vote for Henry Clay; the democrats, for James K. Polk. A person arose and moved that the word "votes" be stricken out, stating that he felt sure that all present would most cordially join in prayer that the slaves might be emancipated, but as to voting for emancipation that was quite another question. I arose and asked permission to relate an anecdote which would, I thought, be a sufficient reply to the speaker who had just sat down. A shrewd fellow went to a priest and requested a dollar. " Why," said the priest, " surely the fellow is mad to think I should give my money away in such a manner." He then asked for half a dollar. This also was refused. Then he asked for one cent. " I tell you," said the priest, " I will give you nothing, so begone."

"Excuse me," said the other, "it was your blessing that I wanted." "Oh," said the priest, "kneel down my son and receive it reverently." "I find reverend father," said the other, "that had your blessing been worth one cent you would not have given it me." Now, Mr. Chairman, if we pledge our prayers for the deliverance of the slaves, and not our votes, it shows that we value the latter more than the former. The prayers offered for an object for which we decline to vote are not worth one cent, for he that prays in earnest will endeavour to bring about an answer to his own prayers.

Another resolution was proposed as a substitute in favour of using all lawful means for the abolition of slavery. This was adopted. After the meeting I was taken to task by a few friends for my proposal. "Now," said they "do you wish to make it binding on those who join our Baptist Churches that they shall vote for candidates of the Liberty party?" I replied, "I only ask them to vote in harmony with their prayers." "But," said one, "it is an unheard of thing to present a political question like this to a religious assemblage." I contended that we had the Wesleyan Conference of England as an example. He thought I must be greatly mistaken, I drew from my pocket a book published by the American Anti-slavery Methodists, and read to him a resolution of the Conference calling on every Methodist to vote for no legislator unless he was willing to vote for emancipation. He read this with surprise, and said no more against my effort. Usually I found that precedents had greater weight than to prove that a given course was right in itself. In all slaveholding communities there is a morbid deference to the opinions of others. Mr. Laughlin called once on a slaveholder and found his hands at dinner, the whites at one table, the blacks at another. He asked him whether he made the separation because it was right in itself or from deference to the opinion of others? He replied—" Solely from deference to the opinions of others, for myself I should not object to whites and blacks eating at the same table."

The Rev. Edward Smith, a Virginian Anti-slavery Methodist minister, excluded a person from the church for voting for a slaveholder for President. The person brought an action against Mr. Smith for lowering his character unjustly by the exclusion. The judge, however, decided that as one of the objects of the Anti-slavery Methodist Church was to abolish slavery; and the election of an Anti-slavery president was a very proper means to that end—he should give a verdict in favour of Mr. Smith.

I wrote an address on the subject of voting, which was adopted at the monthly meeting of the Liberty Association of the town of Lisbon, November 18th, 1846, and was published in the *American Freeman*, of which the following is a paragraph :—

" The term Liberty Association represents through all the north, those Anti-slavery Societies which hold that government should abolish slavery by legal enactments; and which by precept and example are urging the rest of the community to vote for men who will enact such laws, instead of continuing the practice of voting for those who refuse to do so.

Though all Liberty Associations are Anti-slavery societies, all Anti-slavery societies are not Liberty Associations. There are some who will talk and pray against slavery, but will not vote against it. Others will speak against slavery and yet vote for slaveholders. And others still, will sing, and print, and speak against slavery, and yet denounce all human governments. And these three classes are frequently members of Anti-slavery Societies, but till they have different sentiments they cannot join Liberty Associations. We believe that the elements of efficient Anti-slavery action are, praying, preaching, singing, talking, and voting. And that so long as voting is omitted, we neglect the means which God has appointed for the liberation of the slave, and have no reason to expect success."

In a journey from Madison to the Wisconsin river, I lodged for the night at a tavern. The landlord was a Pennsylvanian. In the morning when I asked for my bill, he thus addressed me—"It is a rule with me to entertain ministers of the Gospel free of all charge. I discovered, however, last evening, by your conversation with the other travellers, that you are in favour of the emancipation of the slaves. I can treat no person as a minister of the Gospel who holds such sentiments ; and shall, therefore, charge you one dollar."

I was treated on one occasion by a Scotchman in a similar way. He had been to the south and married a slaveholder's daughter.

In one of my visits to Green Bay, Mr. White, a local preacher of the Methodist Episcopal Church, made a subscription to the cause, and then said to me—" If the ministers throughout the land would but oppose slavery as you are opposing it, in a short time this terrible curse would be swept from the country."

On one occasion I preached at Aztalan from Revelation vii. 17, "For the Lamb which is in the midst of the throne shall feed them, and shall lead them unto living fountains of waters : and God shall wipe away all tears from their eyes."

I was pointing out that in Heaven the joy was universal, but on earth there was mourning as well as joy. "To-morrow," I observed, "will be the fourth of July, the day on which is celebrated the separation of America from England. One common joy will be felt by the aged, the strong, the young. There will be the procession, the feast, the music, the oration. And some who look upon this scene of gladness will contrast it with the scenes of sorrow at the south ; and will think of the anguish of those who are torn from their dearest friends—husbands from wives ; parents from children ; brothers from sisters, by the iniquitous slave system ; and as they think on these miseries they will pity the slaves and desire their emancipation, and such pity and desire is Christ-like. The Redeemer will contemplate the scene of joy here, and of anguish there ; and He counts the tears of the slaves ; He numbers the stripes of the cruel lash, and desires emancipation ; and such will be our sympathy and desire if we are the true followers of Christ." A person seized his hat and hastened out of the place of worship. He was sceptical in principle, so

I was not much surprised. Next a pro-slavery Methodist left. I said, "friends, is it not true that Christ sympathises with the slave? and ought we not to follow his example?" No others left, but there was much regret expressed by a few persons to me afterwards that I had alluded to the subject. They designed to forget the slave, and I designed they should remember him.

To show the change that took place, I will notice a large Anti-slavery meeting that was held on the fourth of July, at Aztalan, in 1846. An excellent dinner was provided, and the Rev. J. F. Ostrander gave an Anti-slavery oration. A leading man in the village boasted that he should give half a pig for the dinner at the nigger meeting. This coming to the ears of the abolitionists, they told him that in view of the remark he had made they could not allow him to contribute to the dinner.

In common with the western people generally, I had attacks of the fever and ague. The chief cause I suppose to be this—when the new land is broken up the strips of soil are turned quite over in the middle of summer, thus exposing to the sun the roots of the grass and flowers. Hence they decay and send forth noxious effluvia, which loading the air, and being inhaled by breathing, the ague was the result.

In 1846, a Baptist Association was to be held at Sun Prairie. A few days before the meeting, I was at Sun Prairie, and went one evening to the beautiful lake, which is about a mile in diameter, and nearly circular, and indulged in bathing. Afterwards, as it was moonlight, I went for a walk to mature my

W

speech for the approaching Association. I think my system was affected by the noxious miasma, for the next day I had a chill for a couple of hours, which was followed by a burning fever. It grieved me to think of the efforts that would be made by the friends of slavery to carry the example of the Association in a pro-slavery direction, and I besought the Father of mercies to enable me to attend. I remembered having heard that flour of sulphur was good for the ague; I took two tea-spoonsful, and felt relieved. The next morning I repeated the dose, and had no more of the ague. I found, however, that in consequence of bodily weakness, it required more effort of mind to bear the remarks of the opponents. A resolution which I had drawn up, pledging the influence of the Association to aid in removing slavery from the denomination, was, after full discussion, unanimously adopted.

Passing through Mequanego in one of my journeys, I was requested to preach, but the hope was expressed that I would not refer to slavery, because there was a revival of religion, and it might check the progress of the revival. It is customary in a revival to devote a day to fasting and prayer. I inquired if they ever knew a revival injured by a fast? The reply was "No, a fast always promotes a revival." I then asked them to bring the Bible, turn to the fifty-eighth of Isaiah, and read the sixth verse. They did so, as follows:—" Is not this the fast that I have chosen? to loose the bands of wickedness, to undo the heavy burdens, and to let the oppressed go free, and that ye break every yoke?"

I then stated that they had acknowledged that a fast promoted a revival, yet they feared to keep one of God's chosen fasts, lest the revival should be hindered.

In the above village resided Mr. Andrus, a Vermont Baptist. When passing that way I enjoyed his hospitality. We conversed on Free Missions, and I fully explained their principles and movements.

He died, and by his will bequeathed five hundred dollars to the Parent Free Mission Society, to be applied to missionaries in Wisconsin.

In the smaller towns and villages, usually, a long shed is erected to accommodate the horses of the members of the congregation during the time of worship. When a Baptist Association was held, the supporters of slavery on reaching the place of worship would go to the shed and survey the horses, and seeing my French pony among them would exclaim, "Ah! here is Mr. Mathews's pony, now we shall have to meet that slavery question again."

CHAPTER XIV.

Pro-slavery efforts of President Harrison—Presidents Tyler and Polk Compared—They lead the Slave-party—The African Slave-trade not Suppressed—The Slaver " Pons "—Ambassador Cass defeats the Quintuple Treaty—The Two Prisoners—Baker a Slave-trader and Rev. C. T. Torrey an Anti-slavery Minister—Tyler's Five Secretaries—Daniel Webster's early Anti-slavery Appeal—He claims from England Payment for Escaped Slaves —Secret Movements of Tyler to gain California—Death of Secretaries Legaré and Upshur—Secretary Calhoun's Power—The African Squadron—The Ashburton Treaty—Its Happy Effect on the Anti-slavery Reform—Texas Annexed—The Bank Question and Why the Cabinet was Changed ?—The Pretexts for the War with Mexico—Commissioner Trist Reveals the Secret that the War was for Slavery—Cost of the War in Life and Treasure—Governor Wise's Threat—Mrs. Tyler and the Stafford House Address—Joshua R. Giddings.

DURING the eight years I had been advocating emancipation there had been three Presidents of the United States—Harrison, Tyler, and Polk. They served the slave-party with an energy worthy of a better cause, as the following review of their labours will show :—

PRESIDENT HARRISON.

In 1803, William Henry Harrison, a native of Virginia, was appointed governor of Indiana Territory. In connection with its legislature he laboured totain a suspension, on the part of the Federal government, of the article of the North-West which prohibited slavery; so as to open that vast country to the iniquitous slave-system. He persevered in his attempt for several years, but without success. His public speeches at Vincennes and Cheviot show that he was one of the earliest and most violent of the opponents of the abolitionists. By this means, and by his letters to southern politicians, he gained so much favour with the slave-party, as to secure for himself the whig nomination for the office of President. The people were greatly demoralized by the means that were employed to elect him. Two great qualifications upon which his supporters expatiated were,—that he had lived in a log-house, and that he drank cider. To show his eminence in republican simplicity, small models of log-houses were carried round by them—and if there were any merit in drinking cider they could glory in having had more than their share of it.

Harrison was elected President in 1840; but in one month after entering upon his duties, he was called to the spirit-world to render up his account.

Tyler the Vice-President succeeded him. This was the first instance of a Vice-President taking the office owing to the death of a President.

Polk succeeded Tyler in 1844. The progress of the slave-party was rapid under both administrations, as is evident from the following review:—

TYLER AND POLK.

Tyler was a native of the Slave-State of Virginia; Polk, of the Slave State of North Carolina. Both were slaveholders, both were destitute of Anti-very sympathy, both were endowed with mental energ and force of will. and thus both were fittingly qualifi to fill their positions as leaders of the slave-party.

Both wielded the powers of the Federal government to strengthen, extend, and perpetuate the slave system.

Tyler was elected Vice-President by the whigs; Polk was elected President by the democrats. Tyler, before he became President, after being governor of Virginia two years, was elected to the Senate of the United States, where he was speaker *pro. tem.;* Polk, before he became President, after being governor of Tennessee for two years, was elected to the House of Representatives of the United States, where he was twice elected speaker. Both were lawyers and not military men. The term " Captain Tyler," which was applied to him in ridicule when President, was owing to his having raised a volunteer company, at the time the British forces were in the Chesapeake Bay, threatening to attack Norfolk and Richmond. His troops, however, were not brought into action.

When the admission of Missouri into the Union was proposed, Tyler voted against any restrictions respecting slavery. Polk was not then in Congress.

During both administrations the African slave-trade was prosecuted by the Americans. In the second year of Polk's administration an American slaver, the " Pons," was captured and taken to Philadelphia. In its hold were crammed 850 slaves. The hold was one hundred feet long, twenty-one feet eight inches wide, and six feet high. Captain Bell in his letter on this subject to Mr. Bancroft, who was then secretary of the navy, stated that he feared that the captain of the "Pons" could not be reached owing to the state of the laws on slave-trading. Tyler was satisfied with the laws as they were, as he was preparing to annex Texas to the Union, and probably contemplated re-opening the African slave-trade to supply Texas with slaves.

Polk was probably also looking forward to the reopening of that trade to fill with slaves the vast countries he was aiming to obtain from Mexico; hence he was satisfied with the laws as they were. During both administrations three-fourths of the American Ambassadors were slaveholders; and those who were not slaveholders aimed, by supporting the slave system, to obtain the political support of the slave-party. Mr. Cass, the Ambassador to France, is an illustration.

Although it is against the usual rule for Ambassadors to agitate, Mr. Cass wrote a pamphlet in France, which was circulated, in which he opposed the Quintuple treaty. This was a treaty entered into by the five leading powers of Europe, in which they agreed that if any ship bearing the flag of any one of the respective five powers should be found to be fitted up as a slaver, it should be treated as a slaver.

Tyler, in his second annual message to Congress, says:—"Taking the message as his letter of instructions, our then minister at Paris felt himself required to assume the same ground in a remonstrance which he felt it to be his duty to present to M. Guizot, and through him to the King of the French, against what has been called the Quintuple treaty; and his conduct, in this respect, met with the approval of this government." After this remonstrance the King of France declined to ratify the treaty his ambassador had signed. Thus Mr. Cass, a northern man, was bidding for the vote of the slave-party for the Presidency.

In the Maryland prison were two prisoners— Baker, who had been engaged in the slave-trade, and had probably reduced hundreds of free men to slavery; and Rev. C. T. Torrey, a New England Congregational minister, for helping three slaves to gain their liberty. Polk pardoned Baker, Torrey died in prison.

Tyler appointed in four years five secretaries of state in succession. Polk, in four years, appointed one secretary of state.

Pursuing the review of each separately,—Tyler first appointed Daniel Webster as secretary of state. In his early public life, before he was corrupted by the slave-party, Webster had said, " If there be within the extent of our knowledge and influence, any participation in this traffic in slaves, let us pledge ourselves upon the 'Rock of Plymouth,' to extirpate and destroy it—It is not fit that the land of the pilgrims should bear the shame longer. Let that spot be purified, or let it be set aside from the Christian world; let it be put out of the circle of Christian sympathies and human regards; and let civilized men henceforth have no communion with it.

" I invoke those who fill the seats of justice, and all who minister at her altar, that they exercise the wholesome and necessary severity of the law. I

nvoke the ministers of our religion, that they proclaim its denunciation of those crimes, and add its
solemn sanction to the authority of human laws.
If the pulpit be silent, whenever or wherever there
may be a sinner bloody with this guilt within the
hearing of its voice, the pulpit is false to its trust."

In visiting England he said, in a speech at Oxford,
that owing to the influence of England and America
over other countries, they were morally bound to live
in peace with each other.

Yet under Tyler's directions he virtually threatened
England with war unless the slaves of the "Creole"
were paid for. The case was this. Madison Washington, a slave, escaped to Canada; but returning to
the south to release his wife from slavery, was re-
taken, and was sent to the far south, one of a cargo
of slaves, his own wife it is believed among them, in
the brig "Creole." Led by him the slaves rose on
the crew, obtained the mastery of the vessel, and
reached the British West Indies, where they all
went free. Great Britain declined paying for the
self-emancipated slaves.

Webster wrote a menacing letter to Mexico, an
indication that a strong power was about to attack
a weak one if it resisted the progress of the slave-
party. After two years Webster resigned, and
Legaré, a slaveholder, filled the office; he died in five
weeks after entering upon it. Next, Judge Upshur,
a slaveholder, was appointed to the office. In 1829,
when a member of the Virginian Convention, he
pointed out to his fellow legislators—all of whom
were slaveholders—that the acquisition of Texas

would increase the price of slaves. He set to work as soon as he was appointed secretary of state, to annex Texas to the United States.

Seven months after Tyler became President, Commodore Jones, a Virginian, was despatched to the Pacific with a squadron; where he took possession of Monterey in California; and claimed the people as citizens under the protection of the American flag. The Federal government disavowed the act to Mexico, but never punished him. He had only mistaken the time to strike.

Another incident illustrates Tyler's policy. A professed exploring expedition under Colonel Fremont set out for Oregon; it was really designed to take California from Mexico. Arrived there, among the "American settlers," Colonel Fremont commenced his revolutionary movements a little in advance of those of Commodore Jones. The independence of California was proclaimed by the little settlement. After the republic had existed four days, the insurrection merged itself into Jones's proclamation of annexation to the United States. Colonel Fremont proved that he had acted in accordance with the designs of the Federal Cabinet—whose dishonest misrepresentations had produced the impression that Fremont had acted upon his own responsibility.

Before sending out these expeditions Tyler had, through the bank question, changed his Cabinet.

Upshur wrote to W. T. Murphy, chargé d'affaires of the United States in Texas, in 1843, "Few calamities could befal this country more to be deplored than the abolition of domestic slavery in Texas." So he aided to introduce a civil war to guard against the calamity of freedom in Texas. He was on board the steam ship-of-war, Princeton, which was in the Potomac river; and one of its long guns "the peace-maker" was being tried. Its guns were to overawe Mexico. This gun exploded, causing the death of Mr. Upshur, and of Mr. Gilmer, the secretary of war. Mr. Nelson, a slaveholder, performed for a month the duties of secretary and then Mr. Calhoun a slaveholder, filled the office. In his hands the pro-slavery people were as clay in the hands of the potter. He boasted that he annexed Texas to the Union.

A panic was produced by the report that England was about to obtain undue influence in Texas. The jealousy of the Americans against foreign inter-ference was aroused; but the chief actors afterwards acknowledged that it was a mere *ruse*, got up to promote the annexation of Texas.

Tyler without the knowledge of Congress, sent a large portion of the home squadron to the Gulf of Mexico, and assembled a large military force on the borders of Texas. Having thus menaced Mexico he negociated with Texas a treaty of annexation. This the Senate rejected. He then proposed that by a joint resolution of both Houses of Congress it should be annexed. For this there was no law; but it was done. He settled with England, through Mr. Webster, the dispute respecting the North-Eastern boundary. He agreed, by the Ashburton treaty, to keep a naval force on the coast of Africa, but as slaveholders were placed in command of the vessels, the slave-trade went on. He was willing to return to the British Government soldiers deserting from the army in Canada, if the British Government would return refugee slaves to the United States. But Lord Ashburton declined to give up one of them; and stated that if a slave in escaping to Canada should, to facilitate his flight, take a horse or a boat —and should be claimed by the Federal government as a thief, still the slave would not be surrendered by the British government—because taking a horse or boat, in such a case, would not be stealing, but incidents in his attempt to gain his freedom.

The treaty and statement gave additional strength to the Anti-slavery movement throughout the United States.

The course which Tyler took on the bank question was, to numbers of persons, a great mystery. The whigs were in power, and as a national bank was a whig measure, a bill to establish one was passed; special deference in preparing it being paid to Tyler's views. The bill passed, and he vetoed it. The surprised whigs prepared another bill in pursuance of his suggestions, after full consultation with the cabinet, and its provisions were made to conform to his views. It was passed, and he vetoed it. Whereupon all the cabinet but Mr. Webster resigned, declaring that the President " had forfeited his word " and treated them " unworthily." I apprehend that as the cabinet had been selected by Harrison for the objects of the whig party, Tyler wished to exchange it for a cabinet having for its object the annexation of Texas; and that other questions had but little weight with him. He did not wish, however, to avow his real policy lest it should be counteracted, so he got rid of his cabinet by the bank question.

Polk designed to make war on Mexico to obtain additional territory and extend the slave-system. To have avowed that as his object would have prevented its success. When he had succeeded in producing a collision of the Federal and Mexican troops, he sent a message to Congress declaring that war existed by the act of Mexico. John C. Calhoun said in the Senate—"We had not a particle of evidence that the Republic of Mexico had made war on the United States." Mr. Ingersoll, as chairman of the committee on foreign relations, made a report avowing that the war was necessary, in order to get possession of Territories that " every American administration had been striving to get by purchase."

Henry Clay, in a speech in Kentucky declared that the bill of Congress, of May 11, 1846, "attributing the commencement of the war to the act of Mexico," was " a bill with a palpable falsehood stamped on its face." A new House of Representatives fresh from the people, elected after the declaration of Polk of May 11th, 1846, resolved that the war was unnecessarily and unconstitutionally begun by the President of the United States.

The war has been rightly called a war of pretexts. One pretext was that Mexico refused to receive an American Envoy, Mr. Slidell; the same Mr. Slidell, the slaveholder, who, with his fellow-slaveholder, Mr. Mason, was taken from the Trent.

But a comparison of the letters of Mr. Slidell with those of General Taylor, then at the head of the

x

American army, shows that the warlike movements of the United States were pushed forward independently of the reception or rejection of Mr. Slidell.

The Mexican indemnities was another pretext. But the venerable Albert Gallatin states that before the annexation of Texas there was every prospect of securing indemnity, and they were in no shape the cause of the war. Judge Jay also states that the Federal government demanded of Mexico twelve millions of dollars, but could only make its claim good for a little more than two millions.

There was probably no general who could so well unite the Mexicans and accomplish so much by them as Santa Anna. Polk supplied them with this general. The following pass gave Santa Anna admission to Mexico.

"U.S. Navy Department, May 13th, 1846.

Commodore,—If Santa Anna endeavours to enter the Mexican ports, you will allow him to pass freely.

Respectfully yours,

GEORGE BANCROFT.

Commodore David Connor, Commanding Home Squadron."

The day that war was declared with Mexico was the day that the pass was written for Santa Anna, both are dated May 13th, 1846. A similar instance of promptness in supplying an enemy with a general is probably not to be found in history.

Santa Anna, who had been exiled to the West Indies, returning to Mexico, infused new life into his countrymen, and assembling an army of 20,000 men, led them against the Americans, and made many an

American bite the dust. Polk might have introduced him to Mexico with the hope of more readily obtaining California and New Mexico; or it might have been with the design to increase the complications in Mexico, which was already distracted by the two factions—one led by Herrera who favoured peace, the other by the warlike Paredes. They needed Bibles—not bayonets—and but for the slave-party the former would I believe have been sent from the United States instead of the latter.

I must confess to an affection for Blue Books. Poring over one of this class in America, I met with a letter which showed what the Mexican war was for. It was written by Mr. Trist, a slaveholder, and the commissioner of the United States to Mexico. When the American army drew near the city of Mexico— there was a truce—during which Mr. Trist had an interview with the Mexican commissioners, who wished him to promise that slavery should not be extended over the Territory that Mexico might cede to the United States.

"I assured them," says Mr. Trist in his official despatch to the secretary of state, "that if it were in their power to offer me the whole Territory described in our project, increased ten-fold in value, and in addition to that, covered a foot thick all over with pure gold, upon the single condition that slavery should be excluded therefrom, I could not entertain the offer for a moment, nor even think of communicating it to Washington." The subject was dropped.

This information was furnished by Polk to Congress and is published in its documents.

It confirmed what I told the people in my lectures, that every life lost in the war was as much a sacrifice to the Moloch of slavery as were the lives sacrificed of those Israelites who were offered up to Moloch. The war was resumed.

In the final close of the Mexican war, these Territories were obtained at a cost of fifteen millions of dollars, paid to Mexico in addition to the relinquishment of the long-contested American "claims" against that power.

The war cost the United States, directly and indirectly, at a moderate computation, two hundred millions of dollars, and it cost Mexico, directly and indirectly, an equal sum. To the United States the loss of life was about 20,000 to 25,000; and to the Mexicans about 20,000.

Governor Wise, of Virginia, who was the confidential friend of Tyler, and who, in 1859, hanged Captain John Brown, boasted in Congress that they would join the Texans and proclaim a crusade against the rich states of the south, "capture towns, rifle churches," and "plant the lone star of the Texan banner on the Mexican capital." "Let," said he, "the work once begin and I do not know as this house would hold me very long. Give me five millions of dollars, and I would undertake to do it myself"— "I would place California where all the powers of Great Britain would never be able to reach it. Slavery should pour itself abroad and find no limit but the Southern ocean." That speech gave me a heavy heart; but my sorrow has been turned into joy, for the slaves are emancipated; and the joy of Mr.

Wise has been turned into mourning for the same reason.

Tyler completed the attempt in which the slave-party had been for some years engaged, to rob Mexico of Texas, and annex it to the United States in order to strengthen the slave system. That was his chief work.

In 1829, Guerrero, the President of the United Mexican States, abolished slavery throughout the Republic. Texas was then a province of Mexico. After the above decree Guerrero was put to death by the consolidation party.

The Texan slaveholders, being chiefly from the slave states of the United States of America, aided by the Federal goverment, revolutionized Texas, separated it from Mexico, re-established slavery, and prohibited the Legislature from abolishing it.

Texas, as pre-arranged by the slave-party, was then annexed to the United States.

Polk by war and money obtained from Mexico the vast Territories of New Mexico and California for slave purposes. That was his chief work. Tyler succeeded in his measure without shedding human blood; Polk succeeded by causing the death of 40,000 of his fellow men.

But Tyler, aided by Wise, drove the confederates into war with the federalists, and caused the loss of more lives than did Polk. Authentic history declares that the southern slave states began to arm when it became certain that Lincoln would be elected President, and were arming for three months before Lincoln entered upon his duties. He was in Wash-

ington six weeks without calling for one regiment.
Botts, of Virginia, states that if Virginia had remained in the Union, Lincoln would have even given
up Fort Sumter and Fort Pickens.   On the 12th of
April, 1861, the Virginian Convention decided to submit the question of secession to a vote of the people
of Virginia.   Lincoln, who desired a peaceable solution
of the difficulty, was desirous that the Virginian Convention should disband.   This would have kept the
state in its former position,—would have been a protection to the capital from confederate troops, who
would have scarcely dared to enter Virginia ; and
would have furnished time for deliberation.   But on
the 12th of April the convention resolved to submit
to the people the question of secession.   This, according to the diary of Mr. Jones, a secessionist, was
chiefly through the efforts of Ex-President Tyler
and Wise.   Before, however, the people could vote,
the confederate troops, who were on their march to
Virginia before the above resolution of the Virginian
convention had been adopted, had, by the arrangements of the slave-party, entered the state.   The
people were over-awed.   James M. Mason, the slaveholder, who was taken from the Trent, virtually
ordered all Union-men out of the state.   On the
16th May he wrote :—" If it be asked—' What are
those to do, who in their consciences, cannot vote to
separate Virginia from the United States ?'—the
answer is simple and plain ; honour and duty alike
require that they should not vote on the question ;
if they retain such opinions they must leave the
state."

According to Mr. Jones, Ex-President Tyler and Vice-President Stephens were negociating a Treaty on the 25th of April, which was to ally Virginia to the Confederacy. This agreement was ratified by the Virginian Convention April the 25th, yet a month later the people were called upon to record their votes for or against secession! The slaveholders dared not trust the people, and decided in advance of their votes.

Such was Tyler's contempt for state-rights—yet he vetoed the Bank-bills from a pretended regard to them.

Mrs. Tyler, his wife, was from New York, who replied to the Stafford House Address on slavery; but omitted to state that her husband had always been a leader in the slave-party which had for its great object to sink man to the level of the brute.

In the Mexican war, Longstreet, Bragg, Lee, and Jackson fought side by side with Butler, Baker, McClellan, and Banks. In the civil war the former fought in the Confederate, the latter in the Federal army.

Tyler and Polk would not have moved one step in their career of guilt, could they have foreseen it would have ended as it has in emancipation.

Admirable service was rendered to the Anti-slavery Reform by several members of Congress. One of them, Joshua R. Giddings, commenced a series of speeches to show that the north was dragged into the support of the odious system of slavery. A rule was then established prohibiting Anti-slavery discussion. A few manly northern men determined to test its power. Mr. Giddings led off in an able speech on the Florida war, showing that it was a shameful slave-catching war. The slaveholding members called him to order; but the speaker, Mr. Hunter, a Virginian slaveholder, decided that it was in order to discuss the causes of the war, a decision that eventually led to the repeal of the odious rule.

In the case of the "Creole" the moral heroism of Mr. Giddings was displayed. In common with all the abolitionists, Mr. Giddings felt outraged that the Federal government, as the lackey of the slave-party, should demand of Great Britain payment for the freedmen. He, therefore, offered in Congress some resolutions, denying that the President had the right to make such demands in behalf of a nation, the majority of which did not recognize the right of property in man. These resolutions produced the effect of a bombshell.

Had the resolutions been adopted, not only would the inter-state slave-trade have been broken up, but every slave who had been carried out of one state into another would have been legally free. From the beginning, the great trouble in the Anti-slavery reform was, not want of law, but want of public sentiment. The following are the resolutions:—

"That when the brig 'Creole,' on her late passage for New Orleans, left the territorial jurisdiction of Virginia, the slave laws of the state ceased to have jurisdiction over the persons on board the said brig, and such persons became amenable only to the laws of the United States.

"That all attempts to exert our national influence in favour of the coastwise slave-trade, or to place this nation in the attitude of maintaining a commerce in human beings, are subversive of the rights, and injurious to the feelings and the interests of the free states; are unauthorized by the constitution, and prejudicial to our national character."

Not being able to answer his arguments, the slaveholders in Congress moved a vote of censure upon Mr. Giddings, which was adopted. He resigned his seat, but his constituents re-elected him; thus placing him above the censure.

He dared to visit Captain Dayton and his mate Sayers, who, by the schooner "Pearl," had endeavoured to rescue eighty slaves from the District of Columbia, and had been taken and thrown into prison. A mob surrounded the prison; some of them entered and demanded that he should leave the prison. Slatter, a noted slave-dealer, led on a mob without, and proposed to lay violent hands on him, but he escaped unhurt.

The slaveholders played upon the fears of the people; Mr. Giddings, by his boldness, dispelled their fears. The slaveholders swayed the public mind by keeping it in ignorance. Mr. Giddings enlightened the public mind and made such sway impracticable. The slaveholders misled the people by false views of law and religion; Mr. Giddings removed the false impressions, and diffused right views of law and religion. Is it any wonder then that the slaveholding members of Congress should threaten to hang him, especially as one of their fellow-slaveholders occupied the Presidential chair.

CHAPTER XV.

PREPARATIONS for an Anti-slavery tour to the Eastern states now engaged my attention; for, in connection with the Rev. Roswell Cheney, I had been appointed a deputation by the Wisconsin Free Mission Society, to attend the annual meeting of the Parent Society, to be held at Utica, New York, May the 10th, 1848.

I prepared a letter on the moral and religious condition of Wisconsin Territory. The number of ministers and members of each denomination, their operations, and the relations they sustained respectively to the Anti-slavery cause. The letter was adopted by the Wisconsin Free Mission Auxiliary, forwarded to the Parent Society, and published with its proceedings.

During my ten years labours in Wisconsin I had travelled extensively ; and there was scarcely a town or village in the whole Territory in which there was not some Anti-slavery friend ready to welcome me to his home in my lecturing tours ; to stand by me in my public advocacy of emancipation, and if need be to suffer for the noble cause.

Many of those who in my early efforts had opposed me as an extremist, now stood by me and strengthened my endeavours. The value, however, of efforts to obtain the liberation of the slaves held in Wisconsin was not fully appreciated. This was somewhat of a contrast with the zeal displayed throughout England when it was anticipated that John Anderson, the refugee slave, would be given up to the demands of the American slave-party, and when the writ of *habeas corpus* was despatched to Canada to bring him to England. Still the western people have displayed much zeal and self-denial in the Anti-slavery cause, and some of their ministers have shown their devotion to the Redeemer by the many sacrifices they have made for his outraged and suffering members.

By land the journey to New York was about six hundred miles. The voyage by the Lakes would have been more rapid ; but to promote the Anti-slavery reform I decided to drive my horse and wagon—a light conveyance with springs—and if possible hold an Anti-slavery meeting at each place where I stayed for the night.

Leaving Wisconsin, I drove to Chicago and thence to Michigan city in Indiana. There I spent the Sabbath, and held meetings—and was glad to meet Mr. and Mrs. Bigelow, friends I had known in Milwaukee. Crossing the southern part of Michigan, and the northern part of Ohio, I passed through Cleveland, through Erie in Pennsylvania, and reached Fredonia and Buffalo. On the way I held many meetings, and in some cases, found that the church-members were reluctant, till my visit, to express to their fellow-members their views on the slavery question.

I called, I believe, on every Baptist minister on the way. Some were warm-hearted abolitionists. Others were indifferent and I laboured to enlist them in the good cause. At Painesville in Ohio, through which I passed, Theodore D. Weld gave a lecture on slavery, at the commencement of the agitation; and announced that he would on the next evening lecture again on slavery. Whereupon General Paine, from whom the town is named, arose and stated that no such lecture should be delivered. Mr. Weld then stated that they had heard the statement of General Paine. He would now beg leave to give notice that he should lecture the next evening on this question " Shall General Paine rule the town of Painesville ?" The people assembled the next evening. In commencing Mr. Weld proceeded to define the rights of the citizens, and to show in what way they were invaded. Having thus introduced his subject, he gave the lecture he designed to give, under the heading " Ought General Paine to rule the town of Painesville ?"

From Buffalo I proceeded by railroad to Utica.

The Annual Meeting of the American Baptist Free Mission Society was held in the Eleutherian Hall. Delegates were present from Wisconsin, Illinois, Ohio, Pennsylvania, New York, Vermont, Maine, and the District of Columbia, who were all imbued with a sterling—earnest Anti-slavery spirit. Caste was unknown, and coloured delegates were treated with the same regard as those who were white. The discussions were animated. Missionaries had been devotedly labouring in Haiti, and in several of the states, and Agents had been travelling extensively and pressing the claims of the slaves on the churches.

It was cheering to meet those with whom I had become acquainted by correspondence—but had never known personally. Some of these I will describe.

One of the most influential officers of the society was Dr. C. P. Grosvenor, of New England. He knew what slavery was, having been pastor of a church in South Carolina. From a regard to the best interests of his own children he determined that they should not breathe the poisonous moral atmosphere of the slave states. Returning to the Free States he was one of the earliest labourers to promote emancipation. At the commencement of the Anti-slavery reform the slaveholders offered a thousand pounds for the head of the Rev. C. P. Grosvenor. This was an evidence of his faithfulness, and of their fears. He was a sub-scriber to Lundy's paper. An Anti-slavery sermon which he preached was approvingly reviewed, in 1834, by the editor of the *Baptist Missionary Magazine*. This offended the Baptist slaveholders and they required the editor to promise to keep silence on the slavery question. The promise was made and kept.

A discussion on the slavery question, through the press, took place between Dr. Wayland, the President of Brown University, and Richard Fuller, the slaveholder. Wayland, in the discussion, betrayed the cause he professed to defend, as was amply shown by the review of the discussion, from the pen of Dr. C. P. Grosvenor. Those who sinned he rebuked openly, that others also may learn to fear. His weekly paper, the *Christian Contributor*, was a sore trial to the worst class of men in America, the slaveholding editors of journals claiming to be religious but defending slavery by the Bible, as well as to their friends and abettors in the free states. He dealt justly with these men, as a pure Christianity required him to do. He had a skilful power of analysis, large learning, strong faith, and great industry, and to his labours the Anti-slavery reform, especially among the Baptists, owes much of its progress. He was active in establishing a College, where all complexions should be received, and his hopes were realized when New York Central College was established at McGrawville, New York. In this college he fills the office of President. During the war, in his visit to England, he imparted much information on the American question.

The Rev. Dr. Brisbane was one of the earliest Presidents of the Free Mission Society. Once a South

Carolina slaveholder—he was led to examine the slavery question—and becoming convinced that it was a sin to hold slaves, he emancipated those he held. Their market value was seventeen thousand dollars. The mob now gathered to murder him, but he escaped to the free states. At one time he terribly alarmed Calhoun and the few other slaveholding despots, who placed under their iron heel the people of that state. He wrote an address to these men pointing out the evils which slavery inflicted on South Carolina, and charging the blame upon the slaveholders. This was printed and the papers were directed to leading slaveholders. But it was a part of the scheme that they should be posted in South Carolina. A person went to the state to obtain names for a commercial directory—and he liberally posted these papers whereever he went. Calhoun and his brother mansteaters finding these papers coming to them from all parts of the state, were afraid. In the south the system of espionage is perfect—they watched—and soon ascertained who posted these appeals. They asked him what he meant by such an outrage! His reply was that he had not read these appeals, but posted them to oblige a friend. He was hurried to prison, but his health failing, he was liberated on bail. He died, however, before the day for his trial arrived. Slaveholding communities are readily alarmed. The fears to which they are subject are a part of the divine retribution for their sins.

When the war began Dr. Brisbane was placed in some office in South Carolina by Mr. Lincoln; two of his sons were in the Federal army. There were some other Baptist slaveholders who emancipated their slaves, and joined the Free Mission Society.

The Rev. A. L. Post was one of the sons of Judge Post, of Pennsylvania. Trained as a lawyer, he became a zealous and successful minister at the completion of his studies. He is one of the most devoted friends of the slave. His labours have been abundant. His pen has been constantly employed in almost every branch of the Anti-slavery contest—and many a poor slave has, by his assistance, succeeded in reaching Canada. His description of his tour to New Orleans was deeply interesting. He was the first to contend that the seceded states had reverted to the condition of Territories. This solved the difficult problem of reconstruction and has been advocated since by many leading statesmen. He arrived at this conclusion after poring for a number of days over the constitution of the United States.

The Rev. G. G. Ritchie became an Agent of the Society. He was a Scotchman. When a student at Hamilton, he published a journal called "The Hamilton Student." The articles were written by the students. When in 1846 the state of New York denied to the coloured population the right of suffrage on equal terms with the white—Mr. Ritchie published an article in his Journal truthfully but temperately animadverting upon it. For this he was excluded from the Institution.

George Curtiss, Esq., the Treasurer of the Society, was ever ready to devote time and talents to the emancipation of the slaves;—but what shall I say more? for the time would fail me to tell of J. N.

Barbour, Esq., who was the first Treasurer of the Society
—and of the Revs. Messrs. Hutchins, and Pease, and
Cheney, and Prescott, and Walker, and Warren, and
Van Loon, suddenly called away in his vigour, and
Miller, and Kenyon, and Tillinghast and Hayward,
and Howe, and Sawyer and Hawes, and Foss; and a
host of other ministers, besides thousands of lay
members—who were never weary in their efforts to
stem the mighty tide of pro-slaveryism; who spared
no labour to aid the slaves; and bore no incon-
siderable share of reproach and contumely because
they opened their mouths for the dumb. Nor can
the labours of our coloured brethren Revs. Messrs.
Newman, Davis, and many others be forgotten. With
one heart and will all co-operated to redeem religion
from reproach, the slave from his bonds, and the land
from its greatest curse.

At the close of the Meeting I was appointed
Agent of the Free Mission Society to travel among
the Eastern churches and present the claims of the
Anti-slavery Churches in the West.

Leaving Utica, I attended the meeting of the
Missionary Union, at Troy; the Free Mission Anniversary at Boston; held meetings at Albany and
various other towns in Eastern New York; in
Vermont I took the towns in their order on the
eastern, and the western side of the mountain; held
some meetings in New Hampshire; visited Boston
again; then New York city to attend the meeting of
the Bible Society; and Philadelphia to press on the
Missionary Union its duties to the slaveholding
Cherokee Baptists; and returned to Utica.

With the exception of two or three days I had the satisfaction of labouring every day and all day in preaching, or lecturing, or writing, or travelling, or by some other mode promoting the Anti-slavery reform.

The meetings I attended were missionary meetings at which I pressed upon them their duty to the heathenized slaves;—Baptist Associations, where I endeavoured to obtain the adoption of Anti-slavery measures;—meetings of delegations from Baptist Churches—specially called to consider how they could best promote emancipation;—ordinary meetings in which by sermons or lectures I tried to enlist the sympathies and engage the energies of the people in the reform; and Anti-slavery meetings comprising all who were willing to co-operate in the cause. At all the meetings I gave a full account of the Anti-slavery movement in the Baptist Churches in Wisconsin.

The meetings and my speeches were fully reported in the *Christian Contributor*, which had readers in all the free states and was also read by the slaveholding Baptist editors in the slave states; they would fill many pages of this work. An account of two or three meetings will indicate the questions involved in the struggle between the advocates and the opponents of emancipation.

Having learned at Chicago from Henry Bibb, a refugee slave (page 225), that slaveholders were members of the Cherokee Baptist Churches, I determined to bring forward the subject at the meeting of the Windham Baptist Association, which was to be held at Brattelboro, in Vermont, on the 20th and

21st of September, 1848. The statement which convinced me—would not convince those who despised coloured people, especially if the missionary committee should deny its truthfulness. I had, however, learned on good authority that one of the missionaries to the Cherokees had acknowledged to a Baptist member in Boston that some of the members of the churches were slaveholders. The Rev. Mr. Tracy, an Agent of the Missionary Union, would be present at the meeting, and might treat the statement as an idle tale. Then what should I do? I decided in this event to propose a resolution calling on the committee of the Missionary Union to state the facts of the case. I drew up the resolution before starting for the meeting.

In the course of the proceedings, Mr. Tracy made an appeal in favour of the Union, referring to its numerous labourers among the heathen.

It had been arranged by the committee of the Association that, as the Agent of the Free Mission Society, I should be the next speaker. I arose and addressed the audience as follows:—

Mr. Moderator,—The sentiment that ministers should fully inform the people as to the missionary operations will, I have no doubt, receive the hearty and unanimous support of this Association. There exists even among Baptists a degree of ignorance in regard to the religious organizations which they are sustaining. I may refer to those who sympathize with the slave and yet sustain the Missionary Union, not knowing that in the Cherokee Baptist churches, under the patronage of the Union, there are slave-

holding members. Now, I would ask how we should
feel if sheep-stealers were received into those churches?
Should we not infer that sheep-stealers had moulded
the character of our missionaries, instead of our missionaries moulding their characters and leading them
to repentance? And if the missionary committee
sanctioned the crime by sustaining the missionaries,
then, would not the character of the missionary committee be moulded by the same sheep-stealers? And
if the Agent of the committee defended it in such a
course, then would not the character of the Agent
be moulded by the sheep-stealers also? I have fears
that the slaveholders in the Cherokee churches are
moulding the character of the Agents of the Missionary Union. Here is our respected Brother Tracy,
who would not for any consideration sit down at the
communion table with a slaveholder, and yet I expect him to rise and defend the conduct of the
missionary committee in reference to the Cherokee
slaveholding churches. It is thus that a little leaven
leaveneth the whole lump; the evil spreads from the
slaveholding church member to the missionary, from
the missionary to the committee, from the committee
to the Agent, and from the Agent to the churches;
and thus the slaveholders mould the character of our
churches which are sitting at their feet; instead of
moulding their characters and leading them to repent
of the sin of slaveholding. Ought not the people to
understand the character of the organizations which
they are sustaining? But how shall we remedy the
evil? Do you say, we will send a delegate to the
Missionary Union, and instruct him to request the

committee to enforce the principle of disfellowship-
ing slaveholders ? Your delegate cannot be received
sent with or without instructions. The Missionary
Union has silenced your delegates. It has stricken
down the principle of representation. This subject
of slaveholders being members in the Cherokee
churches has for some years been discussed in the
meetings of the American Board of Commissioners
for Foreign Missions (sustained chiefly by the Congregationalists and Presbyterians), it having been
brought before that body by way of petition. As
Baptists, however, we do not petition missionary
committees. Our feelings towards them may be expressed by the greeting which Black Hawk, the
Indian chief, gave to General Jackson, when he said,
" Well, General, I am a man, and you are another."

The Rev. Mr. Tracy now rose and inquired of me
what proof I had that slaveholders were members of
the Cherokee Baptist Churches ?

I stated that Miss Macomber, a missionary to the
Cherokees, admitted the fact to a Baptist who resides
in Boston, and defended herself for uniting with a
slaveholding church stating it was the best she could do.
I received the intelligence from that Baptist in Boston.

The Rev. Mr. Tracy rejoined—" I can bid God
speed to the Free Missionary Society, and to the
brethren engaged in it; the Union, however, though
charged with being pro-slavery, is free from all responsible connection with slavery, and as to the
proof which has been given that slaveholders were
members of the Cherokee churches, it was like the
thousand and one flying reports which were being

circulated without authenticity. In regard to the
Rev. Mr. Bushyhead, as soon as the committee
ascertained that he held slaves, word was sent to
him that he could not be sustained, unless he gave
up holding them. He died, however, soon after, and
the inquiry from Alabama followed, and the action of
the committee upon it. The committee will not sustain a slaveholding missionary, nor sanction the reception of slaveholders into their churches. I am
Anti-slavery as much as the brother who has addressed
you. I will not yield to him in regard for the slave;
still I rejoice to bear some humble part in sustaining
the Missionary Union."

This denial was what I anticipated. I immediately
therefore arose, holding in my hand the resolution I
had prepared, and begged leave to observe, that as
remarks of a somewhat contradictory character had
been made, I would move a resolution which would
satisfactorily decide the whole question, as follows:—

"That this Association respectfully requests the
board in Boston, of the American Baptist Missionary
Union, to inform the Baptist public through the
columns of the *Christian Reflector and Watchman*,
whether there are any slaveholding members in the
Cherokee Baptist Churches, or in any other churches
under their patronage; and if so, how many?"

The resolution was unanimously adopted.

This troubled the missionary committee. To remove
the slaveholders from the churches would offend its
southern friends, and to retain them would offend its
northern friends. I wrote a letter to the Rev. Dr.
Sharp, who had been an active member of the com-

mittee—urging him to do his duty in removing slave-holders from the Cherokee Baptist churches.

I pressed the subject also on the attention of the Vermont Baptist State Convention, which held its Annual Meeting at Whiting on the 10th and 11th of October, 1848. The Rev. E. Bright, a Secretary of the Union was present. He pleaded ignorance on the part of the missionary committee, and promised that if there were slaveholding members they should be removed. The ignorance was most remarkable. The committee had superintended those churches for nearly thirty years. Mr. H. Lincoln, the Treasurer of the committee had visited the Cherokees, and had been the guest of Mr. Bushyhead; and it may be inferred had been waited on by his slaves. Besides, the facts had been stated by the Rev. Abel Brown in the *Christian Reflector*, in 1841, then edited by the Rev. Dr. Grosvenor, which one of the members of the committee received regularly. As the committee continued to plead ignorance for about eight months, I decided to press the subject on its attention at its Annual meeting in Philadelphia, which was to be held on the 15th of May, 1849.

On my way to that city I conversed with the Rev. Mr. Colver, one of the members of the Missionary Union, and offered to bring a witness who had resided in the Cherokee country—Henry Bibb—to prove that there were slaveholding members in the Cherokee Baptist Churches.

The committee of the Missionary Union met at the Sansom Street Baptist Church, Philadelphia, at nine o'clock in the morning for prayer. I was present.

The exercises closed at five minutes before ten. There was an intermission till ten o'clock. I arose, passed through the meeting, and gave to each person a hand-bill, of which the following is a copy :—

SLAVEHOLDING SUSTAINED
BY THE
AMER. BAPTIST MISSIONARY UNION.

THE BOARD CALLED UPON FOR LIGHT.

Resolution passed by the Windham (Vermont) Baptist Association, September, 1848.

"*Resolved*, that this Association respectfully requests the Board, in Boston, of the American Baptist Missionary Union, to inform the Baptist public through the columns of the *Christian Reflector and Watchman*, whether there are any slaveholding members in the Cherokee Baptist Churches, or in any other churches under their patronage, and if so, how many ?"

THE BOARD CONFESS THEIR IGNORANCE.

Extract from Eld. Angier's letter, describing the proceedings of the Vermont Baptist State Convention, dated Whiting, October 12th, 1848.

"Another fact was mentioned by Eld. E. Bright, of the Missionary Union. A short time since, Eld. O. Tracy wrote to the Board, informing them that the Free Mission Agents were publishing that there were slaveholders in the Cherokee churches, under the pastoral care of Missionaries of the Board. Upon this, the Foreign Secretary immediately wrote to those Missionaries to ascertain the facts in the case."—*Christian Reflector*.

Extract from a Report on Anti-slavery memorials
adopted by the American Board of Commissioners
for Foreign Missions, in Brooklyn, N.Y., 1845.

THE PROOF ADDUCED.

" The whole number of the Cherokee tribe is probably about eighteen thousand, and the number of
slaves owned by them about one thousand." * *

" The whole population of the Choctaw tribe, including the Chickasaws, is about twenty thousand. * *

" It may also be stated that our brethren of the
Moravian, BAPTIST, and Methodist denominations
have churches in both these tribes, to which many
both *masters* and *slaves* have been received."—*Missionary Herald*, 1845.

I now watched the effect. In the course of the
proceedings a report was presented on the Cherokee
churches, which described them as growing in grace,
and the belief was expressed in the closing paragraph
of the report, that the spirit of Christ would lead to
the removal of any evils with which they may be
connected.   The Rev. Mr. Colver arose and referred
to the expression; stated that he had ascertained
since he left Boston that slaveholders were members
of those churches, and if they excluded drunkards
from them, they ought certainly to exclude slaveholders also.   Other remarks were made, but the
Rev. S. Peck, a secretary of the Union, declined to
give any information, further than to state that a
correspondence was going on, and in another year he
would furnish the results.

The subject was difficult and delicate, " and required
time to elucidate it."   He intimated, however, that it

might come to the question—" shall we relinquish our connection with these churches?" One member of the Union informed me that he had heard that there were five slaveholders connected with these churches. Another, that it had been designed to kick slavery out of these churches, without having the matter brought before the public.

Thus the strenuous efforts to maintain silence on slavery in the Missionary Union proved a failure. This discussion was I believe the only one that took place on that question in its whole history, till the war broke out. Then the slaveholding Cherokees took sides with the confederates. Then the Missionary Union, which would not give up any one of its connections with slaveholders unless forced to it by such determined outside pressure as I have described, changed its course and thundered out its denunciations against the rebels.

To excommunicate the slaveholders from the churches was most distressing to the committee. To excommunicate the same Cherokees with powder and ball when they joined the confederates, seemed to be the hearty recommendation of the same committee.

I was anxious to learn the number of slaveholders in the above churches, and publish it; the missionary committee would not then be able to decline giving information on the subject.

The Rev. Mr. Jones, a missionary to the Cherokees, sent his son to Hamilton Institution, to study. The name had now been changed to that of Madison University. I visited Hamilton; as I paced the building I thought of the happy hours I had spent there. I found Mr. Jones, jun., engaged in his studies; and explained to him the object of my visit. He was frank, polite and communicative, and gave me a list of the slaveholders. Mrs. Bushyhead, the widow of the missionary, held twelve slaves, and four other members were slaveholders. He stated that his father had informed the missionary committee of this, six months previously; that the Rev. S. Peck had during his visit to Madison University acknowledged that the letter had been received; had expressed the wish that the father of Mr. Jones should join the Southern Baptist Convention—but he declined,—having for thirty years been associated with his northern brethren. Then it had been proposed that the Cherokee churches should sustain their own pastors, but they were too poor to do this. Mr. Jones, the missionary, had also been requested to persuade the Cherokee slaveholders to withdraw from the churches—but as this did not meet the principle, he had declined to do so.

Mr. Jones showed me a Cherokee newspaper; part of it was printed in English and part in the Cherokee language. One of the Indians had originated a Cherokee alphabet. I think he was named Mr. Guess from that circumstance.

Soon after I had published this, the missionary committee acknowledged that there were slaveholding members in the above churches—and at the next meeting stated that a separation had taken place, and the churches were not now connected with the Missionary Union.

The slaves were, I suppose, held till they were

emancipated by Mr. Lincoln's proclamation. From the first I felt persuaded that the northern churches generally would decline to sanction slavery in those churches; what they needed was information.

After the civil war had lasted one year the Missionary Union spoke out against slavery. A similar favourable change took place in all the popular religious bodies.

The *Providence Journal* in 1862 stated that:—

" The American Baptist Missionary Union, a body whose high intelligence and character every one must have been impressed with who attended its recent session in this city, has, if we mistake not, generally abstained from any severe expression against slavery. But on Wednesday night it declared with unanimity that slavery was the origin of the rebellion, and that a safe, solid, and lasting peace cannot be expected short of its overthrow."

The American Bible Societies strangely consented that the slaves should be deprived of the Bible. This arose from their connection with slaveholders. I was a member of the American and Foreign Bible Society, and decided to attend its meeting and move that slaveholders should not be appointed officers. At one of the meetings of this Society the Rev. Abel Brown was present—and a resolution having been adopted that the Society would furnish every family in the United States with a copy of the Bible—he arose and mildly asked if the resolution embraced the slave population? No sooner had the inquiry escaped his lips than the shout of " order! order!! order!!!" resounded from every part of the house. The President, S. H. Cone, clenching his fist and striking the desk, called out to him "Sit down, Sir, you are out of order."

By the Southern Baptist press it was declared that the Secretary of the Society had given a pledge that no Bible should be given to any slave. To the inquiry made to the Society whether this was true, no answer was returned.

I stated to five ministers in succession my intention to move that no slaveholder should be elected as officer, and requested each one to second the motion, but each one declined. I asked Mr. Noble, a lay-brother, and he kindly consented to do so. The remarks I made at that meeting were read by many a slaveholder in Kentucky; as they were copied from the *Christian Contributor* into the *Baptist Banner.*

AMERICAN AND FOREIGN BIBLE SOCIETY AND THE SOUTH.

"As much has been said in relation to the action of the American and Foreign Bible Society in the appointment of its officers, especially in 1849, we have thought the following might serve to shed some light on the subject. We find it in a recent publication of the American Baptist Free Mission Society, entitled "Facts for Baptist Churches." The article below was written by a Rev. E. Mathews to the *Christian Contributor*, in which it was originally published."—*Baptist Banner.* It reads as follows:—

"New York, May 12th, 1848.

" DEAR BROTHER GROSVENOR :—The business meeting of the American and Foreign Bible Society was held yesterday, in the lecture room of the Oliver Street Baptist meeting house.

" Soon after the opening of the meeting, a committee was appointed to nominate a list of officers. The writer then offered the following resolution :—

" Resolved, That the committee to nominate officers be instructed to present in their report the name of no person who is a slaveholder.

" Mr. L. P. Noble, the former publisher of the *National Era*, at Washington, seconded the resolution.

" In sustaining the resolution the writer remarked as follows :

" Mr. President—Allow me briefly to state some reasons in favour of the adoption of the resolution before this body. Slaveholding is a sin of awful magnitude. So long as we elect slaveholders to fill offices in this or any other similar society, they will feel that we approve of their course.

" I might prove this, were there time, by the resolutions passed by the Alabama State Convention; and by other Southern documents. It is our duty to rebuke those who sin. We owe it to the slaveholder to rebuke him; and if we decline to elect him as an officer of this Society, it will be a rebuke which will be felt.

" In the next place,—duty to the slave requires this at our hands. Suppose, Mr. President, that some one should take your family and should reduce them to chattel servitude, I ask would you be willing that *that* man should be elected to fill any office in this Society! I ask if there is a brother present who would vote that the enslaver of his family should fill any office in this Society? And if, from a regard to his own family, no one would do this, then it should not be done to the enslavers of the families of other individuals.

" But once more,—duty to the churches requires us to take this position. A great number of churches have declared that they could not, and would not, commune with slaveholders ; a regard to those churches should lead this Society to rebuke slave-holders, and to have no union with them.

" We owe it then to the slaveholders, to the victim of his oppression, and to the churches of our Lord Jesus Christ to elect no slaveholders as officers. With these remarks I submit the subject to the Society.

" Mr. Noble rose and desired to present a reason in favour of the passage of the resolution.

" The President hoped there would be no discussion, the time was short, and this subject is brought up every year.

" The Secretary of the Society, (Mr. Wyckoff,) wished to state that no member of the board elected the past year was a slaveholder.

" The President—brother Noble has the floor.

" Mr. Noble—The statement of the secretary has removed the objections I was about to make.

" The writer—The resolution embraces all the offices in the gift of the society.

" Mr. Warren Carter wished to understand the position of the society on this point, I am (said he) interested in slave property, though I set them free as opportunities allow.

" Mr. Noble—As the president has objected on account of time, I would inquire when will be an appropriate time ?

" The President—An adjourned meeting of the Society could be held.

" Elder Seaver—Agent of the Society—I would inquire, Mr. President, whether it is proper for a person who is not a member of the Society, to offer a resolution, and whether Mr. Mathews is a member of this Society ?

" The writer rose to reply, when the president remarked—We want no discussion. Mr. Mathews is known to me, the question will now be taken. As many as are in favour of the resolution will raise the hand. (Up went a respectable number). Contrary, by the same sign. (Up went a larger number.) The resolution is lost.

" Some feel persuaded that the votes in favour of the resolution would have been more numerous, had they not considered the explanations of the secretary sufficient. Had the resolution passed, it would of course have prepared the way to move,—to cut loose from slaveholding auxiliaries, and to decline to receive the price of blood.

" The committee made a report, which was adopted; the only slaveholder on the list, so far as I was in possession of evidence, was Elder Pratt, of Kentucky, I have been credibly informed that he married as his second wife one who was a slaveholder.

*   *   *   *   *   *   *   *

" A member of the nominating committee wished me to say, that it was the design of the committee to place no slaveholder on the list of officers, and he wished this to go before the public, when I forwarded the proceedings to the press, as a matter of justice to the committee.

" Yours, E. M."

On this the editor of the *Kentucky Bapitst Banner* comments thus:—

"With such drivelling nonsense and disgusting cant have all our societies in the north been annoyed for years past. All the good and great men of our denomination there have steadily and firmly resisted this silly twattle of the fanatics. But they have been overborne by numbers. The old Triennial Convention was overwhelmed by this influenee; and the American Baptist Home Mission Society has been subdued by it. Will the American and Foreign Bible Society be able to resist it? Thus far, that institution has nobly maintained its ground. God grant it may be able to stand at least a single and a solitary monument, of true and old-fashioned Baptist principles, amid the waste and ruin of fanaticism around it."

Mr. Waller, the editor of the *Banner*, considered every scriptural testimony against man-stealing as " drivelling nonsense," till the war began. One officer of the Federal army was the son of Dr. Cone, who presided at the above meeting. Mr. Waller did not regard the sword of steel as nonsense, however much he ridiculed the sword of the Spirit.

But before the battles in Kentucky, in many of which Kentuckians slew Kentuckians, Mr. Waller met with a severe reproof. Under the title of " A

Volume in a Sentence," the *Louisville Examiner*, published in the same city as the *Banner*, says :—We are informed that a very interesting discussion upon the subject of Emancipation was held recently in Woodford County, between Elder Waller and T. F. Marshall, Esq. Mr. Waller, who is a pro-slavery candidate for the Convention, undertook the somewhat difficult task of proving slavery a divine institution. In his earnest advocacy of the sacred cause, Mr. W. laboured to show that slavery has the direct approval and sanction of Jehovah. Mr. Marshall rose to reply. All who know the gifted man and his peculiar manner of speaking, can easily imagine the effect produced by his reply, as perfect as it was brief.

"The gentleman" said Mr. Marshall "has attempted to prove that the blessing of heaven rests upon the institution of slavery. I have too much respect for my God to defend him from such a slander."

This brought to my mind a discussion I once had in a stage-coach in Ohio with an Episcopalian minister, on the same question. He was returning from Bishop Polk, the same Bishop who when the war began doffed his canonicals and donned his regimentals—became Brigadier-General—fought at Columbus in Kentucky—and I suppose, gave the order to have it burnt when he left—fought at Island Number Ten, fought at Corinth—and fought at Chattanooga, and was killed. The conversation turned upon the Bishop's slaves, which the above minister declared were very happy, and would not be free if they could, when the following dialogue occurred between us.

"Then am I to understand that you, a minister, advocate slavery?

"Certainly—it is instituted by God.

"Well, a being claiming to be divine who should sanction slavery ought to be hurled from his throne, and I would help to do it.

"Who are you, Sir, to undertake to say what sort of a character God should have?

"Listen a moment—can you believe that two and two make six?

"Of course I cannot.

"Just so—you have a sense of number—and it is contrary to that sense to believe that two and two are six. But you have a moral sense; by which you are able to contemplate the character of God—the relation you sustain to Him, and the duties growing out of that relation; and it is as revolting to that moral sense to believe that a God of Holiness, Goodness, and Love, can be in favour of selling the husband from the wife and the parent from the child, and all the other unspeakable villanies and atrocities of slavery—as it is contrary to your sense of number to believe that two and two make six. A being, therefore, claiming to be divine, who sanctions slavery, ought to be dethroned, and when dethroned will turn out to be the devil.

"Then, sir, according to your argument I am a devil-worshipper!

"Well, your god is my devil.

"What a remark. I write for a newspaper, and shall send word what you have said.

"I write for three or four newspapers, and shall send word too."

A few incidents of my tour may not be uninte-
resting. At the meeting of the Missionary Union in
Troy, Mr. Briggs, the Governor of Massachusetts,
presided. The pastors of a large number of the
wealthy churches were present. An address from
the Free Mission Society was presented, requesting
the Union to express its disapproval of slavery.
The Rev. H. K. Stimpson moved that the address be
laid on the table, which was carried; this amounted
to a disregard of the request. From a name I have
met with in the history of the war, I infer that he
became an officer in the Federal army, as did some
others who constantly resisted the Anti-slavery
reform.

Governor Briggs really seemed to be an excellent and devout man. He related the following
anecdote, which deeply affected the audience. A
father gave his son a dollar, and told him to be careful of it and save it. The son passing through the
streets and seeing a little girl crying bitterly, inquired the cause, and learned that her mother was
ill and that they had no food. He went to the house,
found that it was indeed a case of distress, and gave
the woman his dollar. A few days afterwards the
father said to him—" Well, my son, have you the
dollar I gave you." " No father," he replied, " I
have lent it." He then inquired, to whom? and
learning the facts of the case said—" I do not object
to your having aided the distressed family, but you
should have been more candid, and not have said you
lent it. " Father," said the son, " the Bible says he
that giveth to the poor lendeth to the Lord." The

father was so well pleased with this smart answer, that he gave his son another dollar. On receiving it he said—"There, father, I knew I should get my dollar again, but I did not think it would come back so quick!"

Yet, as an illustration of the power of the slave-holders to corrupt and mislead men of benevolent minds, by means of their pro-slavery political party machinery, the course Governor Briggs pursued in the Mexican war may be adduced. Polk called on Mr. Briggs, in common with the Governors of the other states, to furnish troops for the war. Governor Briggs ought to have protested against this high-handed iniquity. Instead of doing this he called out some troops, and sent them forward to fight for the extension of slavery.

He died a soldier's death—for going one day to a closet in which was a loaded gun, as he opened the door the gun fell forward and exploded, causing his death.

I was at the meeting of the Missionary Union board ; and the members were discussing the practica-bility of raising for the coming year one hundred thousand dollars. When much had been said on the subject, I ventured to suggest that it would be im-possible to bring the churches to feel their obligation to the heathen abroad, so long as missionary bodies practically taught them to throw off all their obliga-tions to the heathenized and chattelized heathen at home. But I seemed as one that mocked at them— and when I attended at another meeting of the board, one of the members called their attention to the passage in Job, which spoke of the meeting of the sons of God, and Satan (and he looked significantly across the room at me) came also among them. According to this implication, they, the supporters of slavery, were the sons of God; and I, who was labouring night and day for its removal, was Satan.

At the Free Mission Anniversary in Boston some steps were taken to establish a college which should be open to coloured students as well as white.

In reference to caste the Rev. A. T. Foss said:—
" Look at the noble act of Mrs. Judson, in interceding for a wretched slave and aiding to lift up to happiness and hope one who was degraded and miserable. If God had made my skin as black as that of the blackest African, it would have been perfectly right; infinite wisdom would have directed it, and no person would have a right to find fault, or to despise me for it. Man is to be loved without regard to condition or complexion."

I arose and remarked that the lives of missionaries evinced their love to God and man. In the life of William Carey a striking evidence of this principle is recorded. While his son was passing through the streets, he saw a poor criminal bleeding on the cross, having been crucified for his crime. Mr. Carey went to the ruler, interceded for him, and obtained a pardon,—of course, according to the laws of the country, the released man became his slave. Having written to his father these facts, the venerable man returned a reply, urging him immediately to set free his slave.

Mr. Foss also observed—" I cannot advert to the

time when I became Anti-slavery. But I remember
all at once finding myself strongly and bitterly
opposed to slavery ; and soon after I found that the
Baptist denomination was deeply involved in it ; and
that our missionary operations were connected with
it. Deacon Lincoln, the Treasurer of the Foreign
Missionary Society, received fifty dollars as a subscription for missions, being told by the man who
paid it (for I will not call him a gentleman) that it
was part of the price of a slave-woman whom he had
just sold."

To show the interest which the coloured people
evinced in those meetings, I will relate an incident; it
deeply affected the audience. A coloured aged man
in a feeble state of health arose, and said, "I bless
God for what I see to day. Oh, I rejoice for what is
doing for my poor coloured brethren! I was once a
slave, I have taken a hundred lashes at a time, the
blood running in streams down my back. I was
three months in the woods when I was running away.
I almost starved to death. I used to pray to God to
help me, and blessed be his name he did help me. I
have four children in bondage—I don't know where
they are—I suppose I have many grandchildren in
slavery. Go on! go on!!—Oh it may be that what
you are doing will be the means of delivering some
of them! Oh keep to work till every body is waked
up! and till *the man* up there at the WHITE HOUSE
shall catch up the pen and write the word LIBERTY."
The last sentence was uttered with the deepest feeling
and earnestness.

The person referred to by Mr. Foss as having sold

a slave and with the price paid his missionary subscription, offered the first prayer in connection with
the confederate government for its success.   It was
the Rev. Basil Manly, pastor of a slaveholding Baptist Church at Montgomery, Alabama.   He was
called upon by the confederate government to perform
the office of chaplain.   For twenty years he had
been praying for the dissolution of the American
Union.   Many of his hearers were slain in battle,
and were taken back to the town and buried in the
graveyard adjoining Mr. Manly's church.   There was
a slave-mart near it, at which great numbers of slaves
had been sold.   In his church the white hearers met
in the morning, the coloured in the afternoon, the
latter in the basement, and were often addressed by a
coloured preacher.

In one of my communications to the *Christian
Contributor*, I wrote:—" I learn that Elder Wait,
the slaveholder (manstealer), from North Carolina,
not only had free access to the pulpit at Hartford,
but that he sat down at the communion table with
the Church.   Well! it will not always be honourable
among these Northern Baptists to hold slaves, nor
dishonourable to refuse the price of blood."

This was read by members of a church which had
given to Mr. Howard, the pastor of the Hartford
Church, a call as pastor.   A meeting of the church
was held, and a vote was taken, that in view of the
willingness of Mr. Howard to commune with slaveholders the church could not receive him as its pastor.

At Brattleboro, in Vermont, there is an Asylum for
the Insane.   I visited one of its inmates, Mr. Van

Husen. At the Hamilton Institution we were class-
mates. He was never apt in learning languages, but
as he desired to labour among the heathen the missionary committee of the Union commissioned him
to labour in the Teloogoo country. He commenced
to learn the language, and was attacked by the jungle
fever. While ill, he persevered in his efforts to learn
the language, and his brain became affected. He
recovered his health—but never spoke again except in
the language of the Teloogoos. It became necessary
for him to return to America, and he was placed in
the Brattleboro Asylum. I stated to the doctor of
the Institution that I should like to visit him, as we
had been fellow students. He was quite willing.
On entering the Asylum we passed through a large
hall, where several who where recovering were walking
up and down. One of them stepped immediately up to
me, and grasping my hand, said " Why, how do you
do ?" as if he had known me twenty years. Another
came up and said " Do you know what they put me
in here for ?" I looked at the doctor ; and the
insane man rejoined, " Aye, ask him, he knows."
After passing through the hall, and making an ascent
here, and a descent there, and several turnings and
windings, we at last came to a room which the doctor
unlocked, and we entered. There sat my former
acquaintance near the window, with a book in his
hand. The doctor arrested his attention by saying—
" Mr. Van Husen—do you know this gentleman ?"
He looked up, and in his eyes there was the gleam
of recognition. He grasped my hand and began to
converse. From what he said I could only under-

stand that the language he was speaking was on his part somewhat difficult to pronounce, and to me perfectly unintelligible. " I see," said the doctor, "that he knows you, and have no doubt that all that he is saying is most appropriate, only it is Teloogoo." I told Mr. Van Husen, that I had not studied the language in which he was speaking, and would be glad if he would kindly speak in English. This brought a rejoinder,—but not a word of it was English. I then bade him good-bye ; and felt saddened, in leaving him, to think that he, who was willing to devote the share of intellect he possessed to the good of his fellowmen, should be thus checked in his benevolent efforts ; while John C. Calhoun, having a giant mind, should devote the talents he possessed to extend the degrading and imbruting system of slavery ; and promote the misery of his race. " We know, however, but in part "—and there is more importance attached to the work of doing good to others than will be ever revealed in this state of existence.

In the discussion in the Vermont Baptist State convention—a committee made a report that after a deliberate and careful examination, "they discovered no connection between the Missionary Union, and the Home Mission Society, and slavery,—which countenances the institution."

Rev. A. Kendrick moved that the phrase " which countenances the institution" be stricken . out, so that the report should read, that the societies have no connection with slavery. I wish, said he, to test the committee, and see if they will approve of it so. He was an earnest friend of the slaves.

Rev. Mr. Thomas—"You know I referred to Mr. Crane's case. (He was a Baltimore slaveholder.)

Rev. A. Kendrick—"Yes, you have told us of a good many other cases. I have been perplexed in regard to this matter, and I expect to be perplexed about it till I die."

I attended the Baptist Meeting on Tower Hill, in Vermont, on Sunday, November 26, 1848. The pastor, the Rev. Mr. Smith, invited me into the pulpit, and desired me to preach, provided I would say nothing on Free Missions. I declined speaking under restrictions, and he preached. In his closing prayer he prayed for my "reformation, inasmuch as I was sowing discord among the churches." After the benediction had been pronounced, I requested the audience to pause a moment. They took their seats; and I remarked that I felt it to be a pleasure to meet with them for worship. I had been invited by their pastor to preach, and I thanked him for it; but as he desired to restrict me in regard to the missionary question, I had not accepted the invitation; that I should not have detained the audience, but I held that no person should censure or praise another in prayer, and that as Mr. Smith had censured me in his prayer "as one that sowed discord," and as I felt no consciousness that the charge was just, I thought he owed it to me to state in what way I was blameworthy. Mr. Smith said nothing, and the audience separated.

At the Woodstock Baptist Association, held at Weston, Vermont, September 28, 1848, I gave an address on Free Missions; just before the collection was taken for that cause, the Rev. Mr. Pearce arose, and wished to make a remark. He said—"I antici-pate a person will purchase four cows of me to-morrow, and I shall give the price of one of them to the Free Mission Society."

In the discussion at the Brandon Convention the Rev. Mr. Thomas said—"The Free Mission brethren were coming North instead of going South. Why do you not go to the South?

I arose and replied—"I will start to the South to-morrow if the Home Mission Society will withdraw all its missionaries who justify slavery, then I shall not have to contend against men there who are sup-ported with northern funds.

Rev. A. T. Foss—"The subject of sending Brother Mathews to the South has been under consideration. (He then remarked ironically)—I think we had better send him there, and let him be killed by the southerners for the satisfaction of some of our brethren."

Observing the state of society where I travelled, I considered that the religious and political leaders of the people were more to blame for the general truck-ling to the slave-party than the people themselves. These leaders were "too politic." The "follow your leader" policy was decidedly more general than in the valley of the west. It seemed as if they had im-bibed the teachings of Aaron Burr. "The American Statesman's Manual" says that "Among the maxims of Colonel Burr, for the guidance of politicians, one of the most prominent was, that the people at elec-tions were to be managed by the same discipline as the soldiers of an army; that a few leaders were to think for the masses; and that the latter were to obey implicitly their leaders, and to move only at the word of command."

Anti-slavery advocates had to deal with this spirit and this party machinery; hence the difficulty of their task. There was, however, wherever I went, an Anti-slavery minority working actively, and aiming to leaven the whole community with Anti-slavery truth. Their work demanded, and they evinced great moral courage.

Well-to-do New Englanders told me that, if by giving up the whole of their property they could see the curse of slavery removed, they would gladly sacrifice it all, and begin the world again without a dollar.

Some of their ministers too were earnest labourers in the Anti-slavery cause, exceedingly desirous to array all the power of the churches against slavery; and they bore much for the slave's sake. For the ramifications of the slave-power extended to every hamlet in New England.

I learned in Vermont that one minister had a sister-in-law who was married to a slaveholder—that minister was pro-slavery. In another case the son of a deacon had married a slaveholder's daughter—the deacon was pro-slavery. Pursuing my inquiries, I found that in nine out of every ten Baptist churches in Vermont, there was some case of social relationship with slaveholders. As a general rule, a person's judgment is somewhat influenced by his relations; and these relationships to slaveholders were obstructive to Anti-slavery progress, at least for a time.

The difference in the views of abolitionists was marked in the East more vividly than in the West. One class believed that the Federal Constitution was a " covenant with death, and an agreement with hell;" another class belived it to be an Anti-slavery document. These different views had employed much thought, and had been much discussed by voice and pen. In the West I never heard a public discussion on these different views.

Western abolitionists supposed that different persons would work out the slave's emancipation by different modes. That the cause required a variety of talent—and union. The tactics were to run out all our guns, and fire at slavery, designing after that was destroyed to see what spare ammunition remained, and how it could be best employed. We felt the need of an Anti-slavery public sentiment. Having this, if the Federal constitution were pro-slavery, we could correct it; and if it were Anti-slavery, we could enforce it—but we could do neither the one nor the other without such a public sentiment.

Wendell Phillips, one of the ablest of the leaders in the Anti-slavery cause, and one of the most eloquent of American speakers, regarded the power of an abolitionized public sentiment over the constitution as absolute.

In the seventh meeting of the New York Anti-slavery Society, he said " Now, there are men who spend their lives in lauding the constitution of the United States, which is merely the weather-cock on the steeple. I go for the wind, (laughter and applause)."

In creating an Anti-slavery public sentiment, western

abolitionists showed that slavery trampled on the Ten Commandments, the Golden Rule, and the Declaration of Independence ; and urged every man, woman and child to help to remove it.   By this teaching the west was prepared to unite with the east in the election of Mr. Lincoln to the Presidency in 1860.   Without this aid the slave-party would have triumphed.

In our travels the Rev. A. T. Foss and myself collected every document, fact, circular, and discussion that threw light on the connection of the Baptist Benevolent Bodies with slavery.   These we presented to the Free Mission Society.   The committee requested us to classify, arrange, and review them, with a view to their publication.   We did so, and I was requested to carry it through the press It formed a work of 400 pages, crown octavo.

It was entitled " Facts for Baptist Churches," and shows by official documents and by the discussions at their anniversaries, as well as by the resolutions adopted, that the following societies had been corrupted, in all their official relations, domestic and foreign, by their union with slaveholders—a union established at the formation of each society :—The American Baptist Triennial Convention ; the American Baptist Home Mission Society ; the American Baptist Publication Society ; the American Baptist Missionary Union ; the American and Foreign Bible Society.

The correspondence is given which was carried on between English and American Baptist Bodies on the slavery question ; also the history of the Rise, Principles, and Progress of Free Missions ; the history of the Anti-slavery College at McGrawville,

New York; and a chapter on the Nature and Evils of American slavery.

I was under appointment to labour in Virginia while engaged on this work. Sometimes after penning a paragraph on the iniquity of slavery, I would say to myself, "That might be read in Virginia and cost me my life, but the cause is worthy the sacrifice." I visited a large number of the churches in the vicinity of Utica, and preached against slavery, leaving Utica on Saturday, and returning to my labours on the above volume on the following Monday.

A pro-slavery person complained to Mr. Foss of this work after it was published, Mr. Foss asked him if it was not true? "Yes," he replied; "but it is just that kind of truth that ought not to be published."

The Rev. W. Goodell, in his work on The "Great Struggle between Slavery and Freedom" quotes largely from this Book in his description of the Baptists and Slavery and says:—"This book contains a mass of documentary information, chiefly concerning Baptists in America."

In the chapter on slavery I gave several extracts from "Stroud's Sketch of the Slave Laws." To this work every American Anti-slavery writer is indebted. As it illustrates the mode in which Anti-slavery friends on both sides of the Atlantic aided emancipation, I will mention its origin.

The Memoirs of William Forster, a minister of the Society of Friends, whose first visit was paid to America in 1824, contain the following from his diary :—

"Almost from the first of my coming to America I have wished to obtain a brief summary of the laws in all the different states, relating to slaves and free people of colour. A few friends in Philadelphia are now interested in the object, and I hope it will ultimately be accomplished, though it must be a work of considerable time, of no small labour, and probably of some expense. I know of nothing that would be so likely to arouse the people of the Eastern and Middle states into action as having these oppressive statutes brought before them in such a compendium."

This was written in Pennsylvania in 1824—In New York, soon afterwards, he adds:—"The work I have so long had in view, a digest of the laws of the different states, affecting slaves and free coloured people, is in progress. A young man, an attorney in Philadelphia, the son of my friend, Daniel Stroud, of Stroudsborough, has it in hand; he is hearty in the cause; I augur great things from its publication."

Mr. Forster paid three visits to America. In the last he was one of a deputation sent by the English Society of Friends, for the purpose of waiting on the Governor of each State and placing the subject of emancipation before him in the form of an Address. The deputation called on the present President of the United States, who was then the Governor of the slave state of Tennessee.

In a lecture on slavery which I delivered at Burleigh, near Otley, in Yorkshire, which was illustrated by a large map, I traced out the course of the deputation in the slave states, and its arrival in Tennessee; and described the illness, death, and burial

of one of the number—Mr. Forster—adding, he was
the father of our worthy chairman. Mr. William
Edward Forster, M.P., who presided, now (June, 1866)
the Under Colonial Secretary, rose, and with much
emotion said, " I regard my father as, in some sense,
a martyr to the Anti-slavery cause."

The Report of the Free Mission Society for 1850
refers thus to my labouring in the south :

"HOME MISSION OPERATIONS.

" ELDER EDWARD MATHEWS.—The Society at an
early period after its formation, felt the necessity that
was laid upon it, of sending the gospel to the benighted portion of our fellow-men, residing in the
southern portion of the United States. By whom
shall we send ? and who is ready to go there ? were
questions often asked.   It was felt that the man who
should go there to preach the gospel of Christ, in its
character of opposition to *all* sin, must be of rare
qualifications.   Moral courage, great firmness, and
much prudence, and strong faith in God, were all
seen to be necessary.   Often did prayer on this subject ascend to Almighty God, from the members of
this Society.   But it was not until the Anniversary
of the Society last year in Charleston, that anything
could be done.   At that meeting, our much loved
and efficient co-labourer, Elder A. L. Post, of Pennsylvania, offered the following preamble and resolution,
which were adopted by the Society :—

" ' Whereas we have had in contemplation for some
time past, the sending of missionaries to labour in
the slave States, whenever the man, tried and true,
could be found to enter upon such labour ; and where-

as, we have full confidence, that in Br. Edward Mathews, of Wisconsin, we have found such a man.

"'Resolved, That we recommend to the Board of Trustees of this Society, the appointment of Br. Mathews as a missionary, to labour in such of the slave states as shall providentially open the most favorable field for labour. And we pledge our prayers and contributions in support of such self-sacrificing mission.'

"At its first meeting, the Board in obedience to the expressed wish of the Society, appointed Br. Mathews to the important work of a missionary to the slave-holding States. Important duties, however, in connection with the progress of our cause, kept him from proceeding forth until January last. On his way South, he visited a number of churches in New York and Pennsylvania, and disseminated anti-slavery and Free Mission intelligence. The following extract is from his journal :—

"A coloured brother, pastor of a Wesleyan Methodist church in the State of New York, gave some account of scenes which he himself had witnessed. In Baltimore, the Georgia traders, when taking slaves to the South, would take little children from their mother's arms, and holding them up, would inquire, —'who will have this?' 'who will have this?' Persons would then come forward and take them, while the parents, in the lowest depths of wretchedness and despair would be driven to the South."

I held several meetings in Pittsburgh before leaving for Virginia.

CHAPTER XVI.

Arrival in Virginia—Appointment to Lecture on Slavery at
New Cumberland—Visit from the Sheriff—Danger of Fine and
Imprisonment—First Lecture—Origin of the Panhandle Portion
of Virginia—The Slave-party in Eastern, rules Western Virginia
—Meeting to Petition for Free Discussion — An Anti-slavery
Virginian—Discussion on the Wilmot Proviso—Origin of the
Term—The Newspaper Report—How Postage is not Paid in
the South—The Cross Creek Church Disfellowships Slave-
holders—Sermon—Wellsburgh—Proposed Discussion on Intem-
perance and Slavery—Protection Promised by the Sheriff—
Objections Made—Discussion Agreed Upon—A Threat to Lay
the Case before the Grand Jury — Sermon on Slavery—It
Violates the Decalogue—Its Contrast with the Redeemer—A
Demonstration—An Anti-slavery Prayer Meeting—Poetry—The
Fear of Emancipation.

" Two slaves only are held in this county."—Such
was the intelligence I received at New Cumberland,
when commencing my labours in that state. I had
left Pittsburgh by the steamboat on the 27th of
January, 1850, and descending the Ohio river, landed
in the afternoon at the above-named village. It had
been recently built; the population was about two
hundred, many of whom were "Disciples," to whom the
place of worship belonged. A hydropathic establishment, which was supplied with soft spring water, was
kept by Dr. Beaumont, an Englishman. I experienced

the value of this establishment. There were in the village two stores and a school-house, and in its vicinity three mill-seats, a coal-mine, and a brick-factory.

I attended a meeting in the evening. The Rev. Mr. Reglar was expected to preach a sermon—but as he was unwell I was requested to preach in his stead. Having done so, I announced to the audience that I should be glad to address them the next evening on the slavery question; and requested as many as were willing to hear me to show it by holding up the hand; the vote to hear me was unanimous. The next day I received a visit from the sheriff of the county; he kindly brought with him the "Revised Statutes of Virginia," by which I learned that " Any free person who, by speaking or writing, shall maintain that owners have not a right of property in their slaves, shall be punished by confinement in the county jail for not more than twelve months, and by fine not exceeding five hundred'dollars, and such person may be arrested by any white person, and carried before a judge or justice to be dealt with according to law.'

That to subscribe for or receive an Anti-slavery publication, was also punishable by law; and it was illegal to preach to slaves or free coloured people. Any slave or free coloured person preaching to an assembly of free coloured persons was to be punished with stripes not exceeding thirty-nine; and to instruct coloured people to read and write was punishable by six months' imprisonment and a fine of one hundred dollars. I had no desire to go to prison —and as to a fine of five hundred dollars—that was a greater sum than I happened to be worth ; but I decided to lecture. It was not probable that I should be presented to the grand jury till the spring ; and if I were out of the state no attempt would be made to enforce the law against me. So I comforted myself.

In the evening there was a good audience, a number were young men. Dr. Beaumont opened the meeting with prayer. I commenced by giving a brief view of Missions,—showing that with scarcely an exception a school was established at each mission station throughout the world ; yet that Virginia and other slave states had denied this blessing to the slave population ; that persons who could read and write could not long be held in slavery ; that the slaves were on probation for the life to come,—yet the light of life was denied them ; and that it was better for the slaveholder to lose his claim to the slave, than for both master and slave to be in peril of losing their souls. I spoke for one hour.

Two prayers were then offered, and the people, who had listened with great attention, quietly separated.

Such was my first meeting in Virginia. Respecting the locality, Hancock county forms a part of that singularly shaped portion of Virginia which runs north between the states of Pennsylvania and Ohio. It is called the " Panhandle," and owes its shape to the following circumstances :—

Between the heirs of Lord Baltimore and William Penn there was a dispute as to the boundary line of the lands which had been granted to the former by Charles the First, and to the latter by Charles the

Second. To settle this dispute two commissioners were appointed—Messrs. Mason and Dixon—and they surveyed the line which still bears their names. At the end of every mile a stone was set up with the letter P. and the arms of the Penns engraved on the north, and the letter M. and the escutcheon of Lord Baltimore on the south side. In 1849 many of these stones were still found upon the line. Prevented by the fears of hostile Indians from continuing their survey westward till they reached the Ohio river, the commissioners when some distance from it, turned northward, and intercepted it in that direction, thus leaving a gore-shaped portion of land to Virginia. In this my labours commenced.

I was less exposed to danger than in any part of the state, as on each side were the influences of a free state ; and if flight were necessary, the distance would not be great in escaping from Virginia.

Greely in his History of the American war speaks thus of this portion of the state :—

"West Virginia—but more especially that long narrow strip, strangely interposed between Pennsylvania and Ohio (locally designated the 'Panhandle'), could not be surrendered by the Union without involving the necessity of still further national disintegration. For this 'Panhandle' stretches northerly to within a hundred miles of Lake Erie, nearly severing the old from the new free states, and becoming, in the event of its possession by a foreign and hostile power, a means of easily interposing a military force so as to cut off all communication between them. If the people of the free states could have

consented to render their brethren of West Virginia
to their common foes, they could not have relinquished
their territory without consenting to their own ultimate disruption and ruin. West Virginia was thus
the true key-stone of the Union-arch."

From daily intercourse with the people, I found
that a very strong feeling existed in favour of a Convention to revise the constitution of the state. The
state is divided into four districts, two east of the
mountains and two west. Owing to the slave population, and to the rule of counting every five slaves
as three free white persons, the two eastern districts
had a majority in the legislature, and ruled the state,
notwithstanding the Western districts had a majority
of 100,000 white people over the eastern. I feared
that the Western Virginians would even consent to
a dissolution of the federal Union, rather than come
into collision with the Eastern Virginians on the
question of a Convention to revise the constitution.
But my fears were not realized. Western Virginia
refused to secede, and became a free and independent
state during the war.

On the 8th of February I lectured for two hours
at Holliday's Cove, and by invitation preached on the
Sunday. I drew up a call for a conference to con-
sider the present state of the law which prohibited
discussion on slavery; and visited several influential
men in the county, and obtained their signatures to it.
This was published by the editors of the *Wellsburgh*
(Virginia) *Herald;* it also appeared in the *Florence
Enterprize*, Pennsylvania; and the *Wellsville Herald*,
Ohio; both the latter circulated in Virginia.

The meeting was held. A Virginian lawyer in advocating a petition to the Legislature for a law securing free discussion, said that " in all governments there was a tendency to despotism; and the great check was free discussion." A Virginian, who had been an officer in the last war with England, strongly supported the measure. A member of the Legislature being present who had voted for the gag-law, I asked him whether the term " right of property in slaves " in the law—to deny which was punishable by fine and imprisonment—had reference to a "legal right" or a "moral right." He said the meaning was that persons should not go to slaves and tell them they did not belong to their masters. After full discussion, the vote was taken. It was against petitioning. The ex-officer was much affected. I tried to cheer him, and told him that after awhile we would try again; but he said he had but little hope, the slaveholders would make great use of the vote; and going out into the street and standing in front of the shops, he called out—" O, Virginians! you have opposed free discussion, and in doing so, you are putting chains on your own children." Probably some who heard him, became prisoners during the war.

A person from Ohio had engaged to discuss with some Virginians, the question of excluding slavery from the Territories. I decided to attend, take notes, and if possible obtain their publication in the *Wellsburgh Herald*.

The discussion took place in a school-house. The Ohio speaker did ample justice to the subject. There was a good audience and perfect order. The question being—"Was the Wilmot Proviso a justifiable measure?" The term originated from a motion made in Congress by Mr. Wilmot, a Representative from Pennsylvania. When Polk's war with Mexico had lasted about three months, he thought that, in its weakness, enfeebled by revolutions and torn by factions, Mexico could not effectively resist the American arms; and that by offering to its government a sum of money he might obtain the object he was fighting for—more territory for the extension of slavery. Accordingly he sent a special message to Congress, asking that a considerable sum of money might be placed at his disposal for this purpose. A bill was reported making an appropriation of two millions of dollars, for the use of the President in making a treaty. Then to the dismay of the slave-holders, Mr. Wilmot moved, that slavery should be excluded from the Territory that might be acquired from Mexico. This was adopted, and formed a part of the bill. Hence the term the Wilmot Proviso.

The friends of the slave rejoiced with trembling at this vote. Their labours were telling on Congress, yet, as the slave-party were wily and powerful, they might possibly move the northern members of Congress from their purpose in preventing the extension of slavery. Eventually a sufficient number of democrats were bought up by the slave-party to vote against the measure and grant the President three millions of dollars without the above Proviso; but no extension of slavery has taken place.

The effect on the clique of slaveholders who ruled the country, when they saw the Wilmot Proviso adopted, was like that which a commander of an army would experience, who having given his orders, should see whole battalions wheel about and march out of the field in direct opposition to those orders.

The "wise were taken in their own craftiness." They did not avow that their great object in the war with Mexico was to extend slavery, deeming it best to conceal their policy. They did avow this when Mr. Wilmot offered his Proviso. But the Northern political leaders said—"You are too late, we told our constituents that this war was not for slave Territory. If you deceived the people we did not."

The discussion in Virginia on the above subject contained many important Anti-slavery facts. Besides, the Ohio disputant denounced slavery as the "sum of all villanies." I was, therefore anxious that it should be published. Having written it out; I found it would fill nearly four columns of the *Wellsburgh Herald*. There was a little risk in publishing it, in view of the law. But the editors agreed to do so, and I took three hundred copies. They were to be sent me. I called at the post-office some miles from Wellsburgh, and inquired—"Have you any papers for me ?"

" Yes, a large bundle.

" How much have I to pay for postage ?

" Nothing, Sir.

" Then I am indebted to some friend for kindly bringing them.

" No, Sir, in Virginia it is the custom to carry the newspapers outside the mail-bags, and to make no charge for postage.

This enabled me to understand why the profits of the southern mail fell so far short of its expenses; a deficiency made up from the surplus which the north always had after paying its mail-expenses.

I distributed these papers after my next lecture, and the people were anxious to obtain them.

On the 17th of February I visited the Baptist Church at Cross Creek. Twenty years previously a slaveholder wished to become a member. The church examined the slavery question, and declined to receive him unless he set his slave free. This he consented to do when the slave had compensated by his labour for the price paid. He was received, but withdrew, joined the "Disciples" and kept his slave.

I preached on Sunday morning. A collection was made, which was handed me at the close. This I did not anticipate, but it is their custom when visited by a minister. I inquired if any slaveholder had contributed, as I could not take slaveholders' money; and learned that none but church members contributed, though ordinarily members of the congregation contributed liberally. They attributed this to a remark in my sermon that "God always hears prayer, and as Christians were praying that the slaves might be set free, they would be set free."

On the 19th I visited Wellsburgh, attended a temperance meeting, and by invitation lectured on that subject. At the close Mr. Barnes, the high sheriff, proposed a resolution that intemperance was a greater evil than all others. I arose and stated that I did not know how far they allowed latitude of expression in Wellsburgh; that I did not wish to experience any unhappy results from those who were prejudiced in favour of slavery; but if an opportunity were granted me, I believe I could show that the influence of slavery over the churches, the government, and the press, was a greater evil than intemperance. "How far," I inquired, "do you allow freedom of discussion here?" The sheriff arose and said "In this community we trammel no one,—we are all in favour of free discussion, and a person may express his sentiments without injury." I then proposed to show that slavery was the greater evil, and an evening was appointed for the discussion.

On the evening for the discussion there was not a large audience. A mesmerizer had created a sensation and attracted some of them,—besides, the slaveholders had been on the alert. It was proposed that the meeting be postponed. The sheriff arose and stated that it had been suggested to him that the proposed discussion would be a violation of the laws of Virginia, and might occasion serious inconvenience to the person who proposed to speak on slavery. "We ought," said he, (and he is a member of the Methodist Church), "to obey the laws of the land, right or wrong." I arose and adverted to the assurance given by the sheriff that there should be free discussion; and stated that I had come to the meeting with that expectation. If, however, they would prefer a meeting to ascertain how far the people were in favour of free discussion, or if they would be willing that a meeting should be held to petition the Legislature at Richmond for a law in favour of free discussion, I should be willing to postpone the subject relative to the comparative evils of intemperance and

c 3

slavery. The sheriff would not agree to either of these propositions, and I stated I was prepared to go on with the discussion and take the consequences.

Mr. Chester, the President of the Temperance Society, a Methodist local preacher, arose and stated that he had his misgivings when the subject came up at the first instance, but the assurance given by the sheriff kept him from expressing them. He could not on any account violate the laws; or be President of a Society that sanctioned doing so. If the discussion took place, he should resign his office. (In business he is in partnership with a slaveholder.)

Mr. Tibbits, in view of the assurance given by the sheriff in favour of free discussion, had hoped the question would come up. He felt prepared to show that the condition of the slave was a comfortable exchange, compared with his treatment in Africa; yet to the white people, slavery had proved an appalling evil,—they were the greatest sufferers.

Dr. Bricely thought that if it was wrong to discuss slavery, the Senate of Virginia should be prohibited from discussing it. Surely we might discuss it as well as the Senate. It could be triumphantly shown that slavery was not the greater evil of the two.

I arose and contended that no law was binding which violates the law of God, or the constitution of Virginia. That the law prohibiting free discussion violated both. The constitution of Virginia declared that "The freedom of the press is one of the great bulwarks of liberty, and can never be restrained but by despotic governments." The law prohibiting discussion on slavery violates this declaration of the constitution; and no conscientious jury would convict a person for discussing slavery.

The President resigned his office. Mr. Tibbits was elected in his place, and the meeting adjourned for one week. Mr. Chester threatening me as he left the House that he would present me at the next meeting of the grand jury.

On Sunday, March 17th, I preached at Cross Creek, on the influence of the slave power over the churches.

After the preliminary exercises I took for my text. Ephesians v. 23. "Christ is the head of the church." I showed that if we would see sinners converted, backsliders reclaimed, saints encouraged, and the church built up, we must preach Christ. That as King of kings he rules all agents and all events, making them advance His glory and the prosperity of His church. That the text implies the Divine nature of Christ, the spirituality of His church, and the intimate and vital union between the church and Himself. That He would not reign over any heart or any church in partnership with sin; and that the churches that sanction slavery as much reject Christ, as the man rejects Him who lives in sin.

I showed that slavery claims supremacy over the conscience, thus denying the first and second commandments, which claim that prerogative for God alone

It denies the third commandment, for men will pray that the will of God may be done, and sell his children for gold, thus taking his name in vain. It denies the fourth, for the slave has no legal right to the Sabbath—and must work seven days a week, if the master so require.

It denies the fifth, teaching the child to live in sin, if the slaveholder commands it, though the parents may command the child to live a virtuous life.

It denies the sixth, for the life of the slave is in the master's power, and in "American Slavery As It Is," there is the record of a hundred slaves who were murdered, and not one of the murderers was punished. This is also shown by the waste of slave-life, as revealed by the census of the United States, —and by the custom of hunting them with blood-hounds, by which many lives are lost.

It denies the seventh, by selling the husband from the wife; a Virginian minister told me that in marrying slaves he said "You are married till death or some other cause over which you have no control shall separate you." That other cause was the master's will.

It denies the eighth, for it is man-stealing.

It denies the ninth, for it classes man with brutes —thus bearing false witness against him.

It denies the tenth, for it covets the slave's body, time, earnings, wife, and children.

It is opposed to each attribute of the Almighty, each grace of the Spirit; and each doctrine of the Gospel.

It has controlled the praises of the churches, and has stricken from the hymn-books the line,

> "Let the Indian, let the negro,"

not permitting the latter to be referred to.

It has controlled the sermons of the ministers, and in all the slave states not twenty ministers, of the six thousand of all denominations, preach against slavery.

It has prevented prayer being offered for their emancipation, throughout the south. With few exceptions such a prayer would endanger the minister's life.

It regulates church-membership, slaves who escape, are excluded from the churches.

It regulates the ordinance of baptism, no slave is baptized without the master's consent.

It regulates the ordinance of the Lord's Supper, and separates the whites from the blacks, even at the Lord's table. It does not allow a slave to be taught to read the Bible.

It sells for gold the human soul, which is worth more than the whole material world.

It sells in the market the nature in which Christ made the great Atonement.

Its influence extends to the free states,—and it has controlled all the machinery of the churches, and its Bible, Tract, Sunday School, and missionary operations.

It has given tone to society. Where Christ is preached in the pulpit men are not offered for sale in the market,—but slavery reigns in the pulpits, and men are sold in the markets throughout the south.

In closing the sermon, of which the above is an outline, I drew the following contrast:—

There are many Antichrists, and slavery is one.

Jesus when on earth took little children in his arms, blessed them, and returned them to their parents—slavery takes little children from their parents, sells them for gold, sends them away, and they see their parents no more; Jesus loves the family circle, and raised Lazarus from the grave to make the home happy—slavery invades the family, and sells husband from wife, and parent from child; Jesus says of the marriage covenant—I hate putting away; slavery blots out marriage from the slave population; Jesus was without a home, that we might have a home in heaven—slavery makes millions homeless that it might live in a stately mansion; Jesus gave his back to the smiters, and his cheeks to them that plucked off the hair, that the guilty, if they repent, might escape punishment—slavery scourges the innocent that its own guilt might not be punished; Jesus comes a light into the world to enlighten every man that cometh into the world—slavery closes every avenue by which light could reach the mind of the slave; Jesus elevates humanity uniting it with Divinity—slavery places humanity on a level with the lowing ox and the neighing horse; Jesus reigns in mercy—slavery in terror; Jesus labours, and gives to us the reward of his labours—slavery lives on the unrequited labour of others; Jesus weeps with those who weep—slavery laughs at human nature and compassion; Jesus drank the cup of suffering and gives to us the cup of salvation,—slavery quaffs the cup of pleasure and taking the cup of misery presses it to the lips of the slave, and compels him to drink it to the very dregs;—finally, Jesus lays down his life for us—but slavery drives many to an untimely grave to prolong its own guilty existence.

None but those who exalt Christ on earth shall

praise Him in Heaven. Unite with me, brethren, to exalt Him and to dethrone slavery. Let Him reign in the heart, in the family, in the Church, and over all nations. He is King of kings, and Lord of lords, and He only has a right to reign.

While I was preaching several young men rose and left the place of worship and held a discussion outside. I did not know what the result might be. One of the church-members said to me afterwards "Brother Mathews, while you were preaching and those men were outside discussing—I felt in spots all over—and I went to them and told them that you were simply a missionary travelling through the county, and would soon be leaving it." As I went out these young men looked at me threateningly, but did not touch me.

Formerly forty slaves were held in this county,—many have escaped to the free states.

On Monday evening I met the friends at a private house, and gave an account of the Anti-slavery movement in the free states. Prayer was offered for the liberation of the slaves. I sung the following verses:

> "I saw him bleeding in his chains,
>   And tortured 'neath the driver's lash,
> His sweat fell fast along the plains,
>   Deep dyed from many a fearful gash:
> But I in bonds remembered him,
> And strove to free each fettered limb,
> As with my tears I washed his blood,
> Me he baptized with mercy's flood.

> " I saw him in the negro pew,
>   His head hung low upon his breast, ?
> His locks were wet with drops of dew,

Gathered while he for entrance pressed
Within those aisles, whose courts are given
That black and white may reach one heaven ;
And as I meekly sought his feet,
He smiled, and made a throne my seat.

" Then in a moment to my view,
    The stranger darted from disguise;
The tokens in his hands I knew,
    My Saviour stood before my eyes !
He spoke, and my poor name he named—
' Of me thou hast not been ashamed,
These deeds shall thy memorial be ;
Fear not, thou didst them unto me.' "

On Sunday I preached at the Methodist Church, Mount Horeb; and in the evening gave an address on slavery for two hours. The house was crowded. At the close I received an invitation to lecture at Freeman's Landing. The chief point on which the minds of the people were labouring was this—" Is emancipation safe?" To this inquiry, the work of "Thome and Kimball on the West Indies" was a most satisfactory reply.

I wrote in my journal the following as to the state of the public mind.

The people need information, the slaveholders fear its diffusion. Some Anti-slavery resolutions have been recently passed in New York ; they have great weight here. Many hearts respond to them, but the non-slaveholders have not the facilities of making known their views, which slaveholders command. The poorer classes are trained to hate intensely the coloured people, so they become the body-guard of slavery, and the influence extends to the north.

CHAPTER XVII.

PASSING the brow of a hill on my way to Wellsburgh, the village suddenly rose upon my view.
Forebodings whispered "you will be liable to be
arrested at any moment of the discussion; and to be
imprisoned for twelve months and pay five hundred
dollars." Conscience replied—" your course is in
harmony with the moral forces of the universe."
The voice of duty said "were you a slave this is just
the course you would desire to be pursued by your
brother-man who enjoyed his freedom."

The population of the village was about one thousand. Formerly it was a port where the poor slaves were shipped for the southern market. The aged citizens can remember when coffles of slaves were seen moving, with despairing looks, to the rice swamps and cotton-plantations of the far south. But Anti-slavery discussion has wrought a change. Slaves were once transported to the south by way of Pittsburgh, Pennsylvania, as well as by Wellsburgh, Wheeling, and other ports on the Ohio river. Now, even as far south as Louisville, we find the captain of a steam-boat refusing to carry slaves. The traffic is becoming disgraceful, and slaves are sent by the eastern route, where there is less humanity and less shame.

At the appointed hour I went to the Methodist Episcopal House of Worship. The congregation assembled. The President took the chair. Prayer was offered.

After a long pause, the sheriff rose and said:— "When I offered this resolution I did not expect it would bring forth remarks upon slavery, hence I do not feel under obligation to defend it, and I will speak while others are preparing.

"Intemperance is an immense evil; many of its injurious effects never meet the public eye. The question opens a wide field; the gentleman on the other side has a wide field also. I do not consider slavery a greater evil than all others. Intemperance injures the character, destroys all the finer feelings of the heart, makes domestic life wretched, brings sorrow into the family relationships, inflicts suffering in this life, and reaching forward to the life to come, sends a tide of misery beyond the tomb.

"I have not come prepared with historic facts, but it is a greater evil than slavery. I have been in the more southern states, and have seen what slavery is there. The slaves are better off than if they were in Africa. What would have been their condition if they had not been brought to this country? There they were degraded; here they are not. They have been brought within the influence of civilization, and have thus been benefited. I have seen a great number of evils in this world, but intemperance is the greatest of them all. It has produced wars, even civil wars. Its effects are hereditary, its evils go down from generation to generation. It is the cause of ignorance, and that produces poverty and crime. Thus I have briefly introduced the subject."

The sheriff sat down. I arose and observed that idolatry and papacy were great evils, possibly each of them greater than intemperance; but the evils of slavery were six-fold. These I would describe. The introductory, the direct, the reflex, the ecclesiastical, the political, and the retributive.

First, the introductory evils of slavery. The writings of Sir Fowell Buxton, Thomas Clarkson, and others, describe the wars in Africa in order to obtain the slaves; the terrible sickness and loss of life in the middle passage; and the numbers who die in consequence of changing climates.

Secondly, the direct evils. I hold in my hand a work entitled "American Slavery As It Is, the Testimony of a Thousand Witnesses." It contains

extracts from the speeches of southern legislators,
laws, and newspapers. Names, dates, places, and
authorities are all given. Now, while I grant that
you are better acquainted than I am with slavery in
this vicinity, yet, as coming from a free state, I
contend that our opportunities exceed yours to
become acquainted with slavery as a system. We
obtain information from every part of the south—
your papers are not allowed to discuss it, nor are
your ministers allowed to preach upon it. From this
book I am prepared to prove that the slaves in the
United States are treated with barbarous inhumanity;
that they are over-worked, underfed, wretchedly clad
and lodged, and have insufficient sleep; that they
are often made to wear round their necks iron collars
armed with prongs, to drag heavy chains and weights
at their feet while working in the field, and to wear
yokes, and bells, and iron horns; that they are often
kept confined in the stocks, day and night, for weeks
together; made to wear gags in their mouths for
hours or days, have some of their front teeth torn
out or broken off that they may be easily detected
when they run away; that they are frequently
flogged with terrible severity, have red pepper
rubbed into their lacerated flesh, and hot brine, or
spirits of turpentine poured over the gashes to increase the torture; that they are often stripped, their
backs and limbs cut with knives, bruised and mangled
by scores and hundreds of blows with the paddle,
and terribly torn with the claws of cats, drawn over
them by their tormentors; that they are often suspended by the arms and whipped and beaten till they

faint, and sometimes till they die ; that their ears are cut off, their eyes knocked out, their bones broken, their flesh branded with red-hot irons ; that they are maimed, mutilated, and burned to death over slow fires. All this is proved by southern, and much of it by slaveholding witnesses.

But among the direct evils of slavery are the effects of the system on their intellects and morals. Here we have Christianity, so called, and heathenism in conjunction, and the former affording no benefits.

Slavery deprives its victims of the blessings of the Gospel. They have not received it from their fore-fathers, for they were pagans in Africa ; nor from access to the Bible, for the law denies them a know-ledge of letters ; nor from their associates, for white persons will not associate with them, and free coloured persons are deprived by law of a knowledge of letters, as the slaves are ; nor from their masters, for their position as owners of human beings contradicts their teachings ; nor from the ministers, for they come to rivet the chains of the slaves, instead of breaking every yoke.

To show that the slaves were in this condition I quoted the testimony of Bishop Andrew, of the Methodist Episcopal Church ; Rev. Mr. Converse, editor of a Philadelphia paper ; Rev. C. C. Jones, a slaveholding minister ; Rev. Dr. Nelson (page 51;) Dr. Breckenridge ; the Synod of South Carolina and Georgia ; Rev. Mr. Poole, a Baptist minister of Ala-bama, and Mr. Berry, a member of the Virginian Legislature.

The third class of the evils of slavery are reflex.

Jefferson shows that the whole commerce between master and slave is boisterous passion on the one hand, and degrading servility on the other. Only One Being exists who is good enough to possess absolute power.

Fourthly, the ecclesiastical evils. The tendency of slavery is to wither the moral power of the church, and to divide it. Reference was made to the divisions which had taken place in each denomination.

Fifthly, the political evils of slavery. Look at the Seminole war, the Mexican war, and the other wars which slavery has caused.

Sixthly, the retributive evils of slavery. It is one of the laws of the moral universe that slaveholding nations shall be overtaken by the judgments of God, as the Egyptians were. Slavery is a greater evil than intemperance.

Dr. Bricely arose, and stated that he wished simply to correct an impression which had been made in regard to the South, which he deemed a false one ; but before doing so, he would briefly refer to the argument adduced respecting the retributive evils of slavery. A comparison had been drawn between Pharaoh's conduct and that of the Virginians. But the cases are not alike. The Bible states that the Lord hardened Pharaoh's heart. He had a design in view and it was His will that the plagues referred to should fall upon Egypt. This is not the case with Virginia.

Alcohol is of recent discovery,—calculate the number of deaths it has caused, the enormity of crimes it has produced, and it will be seen to be the greater evil of the two. Besides, while the evils of intemperance are so well known, God has given his sanction to slavery.

I have seen the condition of the slaves, having lived in a part of the south where great numbers are held; the north charges us with the great crime of keeping the slaves in ignorance of the Gospel; I ask the gentleman if that is a fair representation of the case? Slaves have the privilege of uniting with any church they please, and in many instances without asking leave of their masters. I have seen them receiving the Lord's Supper, yet an outcry is made against the church of the south. Does their reception into the church look like their being deprived of the blessings of the Gospel. Thousands of slaves are distinguished for their integrity, and their conduct is better than that of the free blacks in the northern states. Make them free and place them in northern cities, and they would not be in so good a condition as they are now.

Mr. Tibbits arose, and said he agreed with the remarks just made, and hoped that before the discussion closed much more would be said. There have been mistaken views of the condition of the slave. Slavery, in the order of Divine Providence, has been of great benefit to the slave; but no benefit has ever resulted from intemperance. He then described a number of cases of misery produced by intemperance.

The Sheriff arose, and stated that he differed from Mr. Mathews respecting slavery. As an evidence that the slaves had the blessings of the Gospel he

would refer to the very large coloured churches at
Richmond, the capital of the state. After some
further remarks, the meeting adjourned to meet the
next evening. On re-assembling, the chairman took
his seat and called the meeting to order.

The Sheriff arose and said—"We believe slavery
to be an evil but intemperance is a greater evil. The
gentleman has shown that there were wars in Africa
to obtain the slaves, but forty thousand American
citizens die annually of drunkenness. The gentleman
tells us that an effort was made in a missionary convention in Philadelphia to raise two hundred dollars
to purchase a coloured minister; but it appears they
did not do it. Why, it would have been but a dime
a piece, (ten cents.) Yet with all their love to
coloured people they could not afford that much.
He proceeded to speak of the evils of intemperance;
he had known men who had been brought to the
gallows by that vice. That, with scarcely an exception, was the cause. Having spoken of some other
evils of intemperance, he contended that the slaves
were better off than the free coloured people at the
north. He spoke of Bishop Andrew, whose wife
owned some slaves. The Methodist Conference took
up the case, examined and tried him; yet the responsibility was not his. It belonged to the Legislature. The Virginian Legislature were just about
to abolish slavery, but the abolition excitement began,
and now where is the Legislature? Every thing is
thrown back. In consequence of this abolition excitement an insurrection, led by Nat. Turner, a slave,
took place, hence the necessity of the increased

severity of the laws, and of denying the slaves a knowledge of letters. Look at the efforts made by the people of Ohio to steal slaves—what an unhappy state of things! At the same time I would not like to be a slave, and I regard slavery to be such an evil that were I a slave I should run away from the south.

I then arose and in reply to the statement that intemperance destroyed more lives than slavery, referred to the loss of life in obtaining slaves from Africa. Mr. Dayton, a member of Congress, from New Jersey, had stated in Congress that the slave-trade was as extensive now as ever. According to Sir Fowell Buxton, a member of the British Parliament, more than forty thousand are annually taken from Africa to Brazil; more than sixty thousand annually to Cuba; so that more than one hundred and fifty thousand slaves are annually taken from Africa. Again, forty thousand slaves die in the United States annually, whose condition generally is as hopeless as that of the drunkard.

The Sheriff inquired—"Would they not die if they were not slaves?"

I replied—Certainly; I never contended that freedom made men immortal; but I was referring to their preparation for eternity. I then presented the loss of life on the sugar plantations as proved by statistics, there being a loss of two and a half per cent., instead of an increase of two and a half per cent., making a difference of five per cent.

According to the census of the population of the United States the increase of slaves from 1820 to 1830 was 31 per cent.; but their increase from 1830

to 1840 was only 23 per cent. It was 478,312. By
the ratio of increase of the previous ten years it
should have been 622,803. The difference of these
two numbers is 144,491, and indicates the slaves
that ought to be. There were slaves sent to Liberia
and Texas; and slaves who escaped to the free states
and Canada; estimating these unitedly as 44,491,
still there are 100,000 slaves of whose fate the slaveholders have given no account. To the inquiry—
"where are they?" our answer is—"slavery destroys
human life!"

It had been asserted that Virginia and Kentucky
would have abolished slavery but for the formation
of the Anti-slavery societies. But the ablest and
best minds in those states declare that the only
reason why slavery was not abolished was—because
the public was not prepared for it. Slavery, from
the adoption of the Federal constitution, had been
moving forward like a mighty river, and the force of
the current was not seen till an obstacle was placed
in its way by the Anti-slavery societies to arrest its
progress. Another evidence that slavery destroys
life was the Mexican war. I then referred to the
evidence of Mr. Trist, that it was a war for slavery,
page 279. In regard to the Nat Turner insurrection, it occurred in 1831. Now John C. Calhoun
states the commencement of the present Anti-slavery
discussion was in the year 1835; but if we take
1833, the year of the formation of the American
Anti-slavery Society, that would be two years subsequent to the Southampton insurrection led by Nat
Turner.

As to the laws depriving the slaves of a knowledge of letters being the result of the Anti-slavery movement, the dates of their enactment prove that some of them were passed before the revolutionary war. These laws kept Nat Turner in ignorance. Had he been intelligent he might not have committed the deeds he did.

In reference to Bishop Andrew it was stated that the slaves belonged to his wife. This reminds me of Adam, who laid the blame on Eve. It is not to be supposed that the wife of the bishop loved slavery more than her own husband. Had he desired to emancipate them his wife would have consented. Permit me to read the remarks Bishop Andrew made before the Conference on the subject.

" It had been said I did this thing voluntarily and with my eyes open. I did it deliberately and in the fear of God, and God has blessed our union. I might have avoided this difficulty by resorting to a trick, by making over these slaves to my wife before marriage, or by doing as a friend, who has taken ground against the resolution, suggested—'Why,' said he, 'did you not let your wife make over these negroes to her children, securing to herself an annuity for them?' Sir, my conscience would not allow me to do this, for had I done so and the negroes had passed into the hands of those who would have treated them unkindly, I should have been unhappy. Strange as it may seem to our brethren, I am a slaveholder for conscience sake. I have no doubt my wife would, without a moment's hesitation, consent to the manumission of the slaves if I think proper to do it."—*Debate in the General Conference, by Robert A. West, Official Reporter.*

Another opponent has said that the case of Pharaoh differed from that of the Virginians, because the Lord hardened Pharaoh's heart. Now, the Lord hardens no one's heart by a direct process. He works by means; and the means in the case of Pharaoh were the removal of His judgments. For so long as Pharaoh was pressed to the earth with them he was submissive, and when these were removed he rose in rebellion. It was by the mercies of God that the heart of Pharaoh was hardened; and by his mercies your hearts have been hardened. He has given you ten thousand agricultural mercies; he has favoured you with commercial mercies, and numerous other mercies. But you have hardened your hearts and sold your brother for gold.

There were men too in the days of Pharaoh who contended that their slaveholding religion was just as good as the Anti-slavery religion of Moses; that they could work miracles by their enchantments. And the king saw what they did and believed in their slaveholding divinities, and his heart was hardened. So you have ministers who will defend slavery from every book in the Bible, who say that a slaveholding religion is genuine Christianity; and point to their revivals. And you have listened to these men, who with the Bible in their hands have forged fetters and chains for the slave, and you have received their message as the Gospel, and your hearts have been hardened.

But nothing is more certain from the Bible, and

the history of nations, than the truth that sooner or later the judgments of God overtake slaveholding nations. If we obey the Redeemer, who came to destroy the works of the devil, we must be opposed to slavery. Where the Spirit of the Lord is there is liberty, and where there is liberty slavery will be abolished.

It was now decided that the discussion should close. The vote, however, on the Sheriff's resolution was not taken.

I learned that a book which I wished to use in the above discussion was in the possession of a gentleman residing at Steubenville, Ohio. Crossing the river I called upon him, requested the loan of the book, and stated the purpose for which I wished it. He readily handed it to me. I proposed, as I was quite a stranger to him, to leave a deposit as security. He replied—"Your willingness to discuss the slavery question over in Virginia is ample security. I want no other."

CHAPTER XVIII.

Visit to Wheeling—A Pro-slavery Revival—Caste—Prayer for Emancipation—The Answer—Mode unlooked for—The War in Western Virginia—Death of a Slave through extreme Cruelty—Another instance—Sistersville—A School Teacher driven from Virginia—Parkersburgh—The two Methodist Churches, Southern and Northern—Treatment of Northern Methodist Ministers—Escape of Slaves—the Recapture—The Night gnard—The Law Suit, and Decision—Abolitionists Liberated—Preaching against slavery—Visit from house to house—Arguments with slaveholders—Danger of circulating Anti-slavery Poetry—Imprisonment of an Anti-slavery minister —" Massa " running out of Church—Visit to an Anti-slavery College—Agreement to eat with coloured passengers on Board the " Ben Franklin"—Handbills against Caste—Effect on the Passengers—Treatment of coloured Passengers.

I VISITED Wheeling and called upon the Rev. N. G. Collins, the pastor of the Baptist Chnrch. We were fellow-students at Hamilton. He received me kindly. For three months he had preached every evening—there was a revival, and about fifty persons had united with the church. He felt somewhat wearied, and invited me to preach. I consented to do so, provided I had full liberty to preach against slavery. This he declined to give, and I declined to preach.

In the evening the Lecture-room was filled by the audience. Mr. Collins preached from Luke xvi. 31. "If they hear not Moses and the prophets, neither will they be persuaded, though one rose from the dead." The sermon was listened to with much interest. In one part of it the preacher was showing that the Golden rule, reduced to practice, would make earth a paradise. "Vexatious litigation would cease, people would be kindly affectionate towards each other, every form of evil would be removed, and there would be a universal reign of righteousness, peace, and happiness."

But neither the slaveholders present, nor the supporters of slavery, were told that the Golden rule, reduced to practice, would emancipate the slaves.

At the close of the sermon Mr. Collins invited any who desired to be prayed for, to come forward and occupy the front pews, which had been vacated for the purpose. Fourteen white young people came forward and took their seats. He then said—"If any coloured people wish to be prayed for—they will come forward and occupy this side pew." Two dejected-looking free coloured people came forward, and a woe-begone slave, and sat in a side pew. Being requested to offer prayer I did so, and besought the Redeemer that "those who were seeking salvation might find it ; and that the audience might remember those in bonds as bound with them ; they had been purchased by the same great Atonement, and were journeying to the same solemn tribunal in the world to come ; yet in disregard of the Golden Rule, they were held as slaves, and liable to be sold, husband from wife, and parent from child. I prayed that every bond may be broken and every slave go free."

I had liberty in prayer. Never shall I forget the breathless stillness of the audience—for this I suppose was the first audible prayer for emancipation that had been offered in that place of worship. I felt conscious that though it might have grated on the ears of the slaveholders, it was acceptable to God, and music to the hearts of the coloured people. If at the conclusion of the above prayer a sketch of future events in Wheeling and Western Virginia could have been given, the answer to that prayer would have been the event most vividly depicted; though in a manner altogether unexpected. The prediction might have run thus:—

"In less than twelve years, in this city, a Convention will assemble to frame a separate state constitution for Western Virginia, securing the liberty of the slaves. At Fort Carlile just across the Ohio river will be stationed thousands of loyal Virginians enlisted in the Federal army. This city of Wheeling will be threatened by a rebel force at Grafton on the east. The Virginian and Ohio troops, crossing from Fort Carlile, and passing through Wheeling, will hasten to Grafton, pursue the enemy to Phillippi, and capture it. Generals McClellan and Rosecrans will take the field and fight the battle of Rich mountain, when the enemy will retreat to Monterey, occasionally halting and fighting, and in one of the contests lose General Garnett. Barboursville will be captured by the federal General Cox. The Ohio troops at Scarytown will be defeated by the rebels. The rebel

General Wise, pursued by General Cox, will race up the Kanawha valley, he will succeed in keeping ahead —the only military success he will ever achieve. Yes, the same Governor Wise, who some years prior to the war, will be politely invited to lecture in Boston, to advocate untrammelled his own views, for which he will be fully remunerated ; and whose chivalric reply will be " I will not lecture—I intend to fight."—He will retreat to Lewisburgh, and be re-enforced and outranked by General J. B. Floyd ; the latter will surprise the federal Colonel Taylor, who will be routed with a loss of 200 men. Floyd will be attacked by General Rosecrans, and after a battle retreat to Meadow Bluff.

" General Lee will then appear with a considerable rebel force, and take command of both Floyd's and Wise's troops, swelling his army to 20,000 men. Soon after General Lee will be recalled to take command on the coast. Colonel John A. Washington, one of his aids, will be killed in skirmishing near Cheat mountain. Guyandotte will be plundered by Colonel Jenkins and his rebel regiment. Rosecrans, after Lee's departure, will attack the forces of Floyd and Wise at New river, and compel them to retreat to Peterstown. General Kelly will capture Romney and drive out the rebel battalion, and thus nearly clear Western Virginia of rebels. Major Webster will close the campaign of 1861 in Western Virginia, by attacking and breaking up the rebel post at Huntersville."

Such have become the records of history.

Mr. Collins, whose hospitality I shared, related to

me the following case of cruelty, which he had just
heard on good authority.

In Alabama a slave ran away. The dogs were sent
in pursuit, overtook him, and so attacked him that
his tongue hung out of his mouth several inches.
The poor fellow was brought back. To punish him
he was compelled to stand upon his feet in front of
the house of the woman claiming him. All night he
was kept thus, all the next day, and the succeeding
night. Nature, however, gave way, and he fell down.
A fire was kept burning, and when he fell a hot brand
was applied to him, till he rose up again. His shrieks
were such that the woman owning him, who was a
member of the Baptist Church, being unable to
endure them, left the vicinity; and then the slave
was hung by the mob.

A member of the Cross Creek Church stated to
me, that in Eastern Maryland, a slave was tied up to
an apple tree and flogged till he died. An iron collar
was round his neck, and to obtain it his head was
chopped off; the head and trunk were buried in a
hole near the apple-tree.

In almost every neighbourhood some tragical case
of cruelty to the slaves was related to me.

At Sistersville, Tyler county, I called on the pastor
of the Baptist Church, who stated that a slaveholder,
who was a member of his church, set free his twelve
slaves to send them to Liberia in Africa. Before
their departure he engaged a teacher from Ohio to
instruct them in reading. But the neighbours raised
a mob, broke up the school, and drove the teacher
out of Virginia.

At Parkersburgh the Baptist Church was without
a pastor,—and being invited to preach on the Sunday,
I consented to do so. Several circumstances had
contributed to awaken special attention to slavery.
I have referred to the division of the Methodist
Episcopal Church. The line of demarcation runs
through this town. By a rule of the Conference,
all the Churches south of the line of division became
the property of the Southern Methodists ; hence the
members of the Southern Methodist Church became
the owners of the Church here. Those who adhered
to the Northern Methodists built a Church on the
Northern side of the line. Six slave-owners have
united with them, the same number have joined the
Southern Methodists in the town. Yet, though both
sustain slavery—the controversy between them has
been bitter in the extreme. The preacher to the
northern adherents had instituted a suit against one
of the citizens, to recover ten thousand dollars
damages. The crime was of a high grade. He is
charged with saying that the said minister was part
nigger. Probably the minister feels it the more, as
he seems to resemble a negro. His predecessor, on
going to Parkersburgh after the division, was waited
upon by a body of citizens, who required him to
re-cross the Ohio river. His reply was "gentlemen,
I shall remain here, and if you kill me, another
minister will be sent by the Conference to take my
place." He was allowed to remain.

Some slaves escaped from a Baptist slaveholder,
crossed the Ohio river, and were being assisted up
the bank on the Ohio-state side. A party of Vir-

ginians, who had been previously informed, and were in ambush, rushed out, seized the slaves and those who were assisting them, and compelled them to cross the river to Virginia. The whites were imprisoned for aiding the slaves. A meeting was held on the Ohio-state side of the river, and a resolution was adopted that unless these white persons were liberated—a party would cross from Ohio and burn down Parkersburgh; so that, night after night, sixty citizens guarded the prisoners, waiting for the attack.

The case was tried before a federal court. Virginia claimed the Ohio river and to the top of the bank on the other side. Ohio yielded the river as far as the water-mark, but claimed the bank as being in the state of Ohio; and contended that it was illegal for Virginians to take citizens from Ohio and imprison them. The Court took the latter view, and the white prisoners were liberated and returned to Ohio.

In my sermon on Sunday I bore the following testimony against slavery. "The prayers of Christians for emancipation will be heard. But in what way will God liberate the slaves? He will fill the heart of this great nation with so much love, pity, and goodness, that the people will feel willing that our coloured brethren should enjoy their rights. He will then influence the hearts of our legislative bodies to pass laws giving them their liberty. Thus, without bloodshed, anarchy, or disorder, they will pass to the enjoyment of their rights. Did I not believe this I should look for the judgments of God;—judgments such as, sooner or later, overtake every nation that makes slaveholding its settled policy. And when, at the last day, the Recording Angel shall unfold his book and read this sermon and these remarks, you will all be my witnesses that I have delivered my soul in testifying against the sin of slavery."

At the close of the exercises I paused awhile, expecting that some one would object to my preaching again; as no one did so, I announced that I should preach again at three o'clock.

Deacon Coffee, who was a slaveholder, invited me to dine with him. He was from Eastern Virginia ; had never given to slavery a strict and thorough examination; looked upon it as an evil of which he desired to be rid, thought emancipation unsafe, and favoured sending all the free coloured people to Africa. When I told him of the superior advantages of the heathen to the slaves, in that the former might be taught to read the word of God, while the latter though members of our own churches, were deprived by law of the opportunity of doing so—he stated that to his knowledge several slaves, most of whom were cooks, were being taught to read by the children of their masters.

The class of slaveholders represented by Mr. Coffee would, I think, have yielded to a strong religious Anti-slavery influence in the free states, and emancipated their slaves. What a mighty reformation might have been wrought out by such a movement throughout the South ! But, instead of such an influence being exerted—there was displayed at the north, a spirit of bitter persecution towards the friends of the slave, and a degrading servility to the demands of the slave-party. Hundreds and hundreds of slaveholders would, I believe, have been led—by such an Anti-slavery religious movement—to follow the example of Dr. Nelson, James G. Birney, the Misses Grimké, Dr. Brisbane, Mrs. Brisbane, his mother, and many other slaveholders—emancipate their slaves and unite with the abolitionists.

There was a good audience in the afternoon. I took for my text, Titus, ii. 14, "Who gave Himself for us that He might redeem us from all iniquity, and purify to Himself a peculiar people, zealous of good works."

In remarking on the manner in which Christ purifies His people, I showed that a specific application of the principles of the Gospel must be made to the sins of the people. That it had been said—that when Austin, the monk, went to England, he was introduced to the Anglo-Saxon monarch, who stood with his battle-axe by his side and his men of war about him. Austin glancing at the signs of the times, said to himself. "It will never do for me to come out against war here, I will preach the Gospel and say nothing about war." He proceeded therefore, to speak of the sufferings and death of Christ, and to urge upon the monarch the duty of repentance and baptism. "I repent," said the monarch, "and am willing to be baptized." Austin baptized him, and virtually baptized the battle-axe. From that time to the present the religion of England to a great extent has sanctioned war.

When, however, Elihu Burritt went to England, and applied the principles of the Gospel specifically to the sin of war, the people came forward, hundreds.

and thousands of them, and gave their pledges, and
signed their names never to engage in war.

The example of Austin has been followed in reference to another sin, that of slavery. (Here a man
rose and hurriedly left the church. I saw a smile
playing on the countenances of those sitting near
the pew he had occupied.) The Gospel has been so
preached as to countenance slavery. Ministers have
said to themselves—this is a slave-state, it will not do
to speak against slavery here—we will preach the
Gospel and say nothing about slavery.

I then contended that we should apply the principles of the Gospel specifically to the sin of slavery,
and put forth the same efforts to remove it that were
being used to remove intemperance. I showed, from
the history of emancipation in the West Indies, its
safety. The slaves held a watch-meeting on that
memorable night, and the ministers told them to
kneel down and receive the boon of freedom in
prayer. They were to be free at twelve o'clock.
The bell began to strike. Peal on peal, peal on peal,
rolled over that prostrate throng in tones of angels'
voices; and when the last peal had struck, there was
a flash of lightning, and the thunder reverberated
through the sky, God's pillar of fire and trump of
jubilee. Then they rose from their knees; they
threw up their free arms, they embraced each other,
they praised God who had come down to deliver
them, and since then emancipation had worked well
for all classes.

At the close, the deacon gave out a hymn, which
was sung, and after prayer and benediction, the

audience quietly separated. The sheriff was present.

After the service one of the members said—
"Brother Mathews, if this is Anti-slavery, I am an
Anti-slavery man."

He had supposed Abraham to have been a slaveholder on a large scale. He resided five miles out of
the town, and wished me to preach at his house.
Monday morning I set out to visit from house to
house. Called on Mr. S., himself and his wife were
both members of the Baptist Church. The latter
expressed the deepest regret that I had adverted to
slavery in my preaching. I pointed to the immoral
habits produced by slavery, and the injury to the
children of the slaveholders. All this she readily
conceded. She had a large family of daughters. In
her own house was a specimen of a slavery-formed
character. Her slave, a very black woman, unmarried, had recently become the mother of a bright
mulatto child.

At the close of the conversation she said—"I was
raised in Eastern Virginia, where slaveholding was
general, and I might be wrong in my views of
slavery."

Her husband then took up the conversation. "Do
you not know," said he, "that the Federal constitution guarantees to us our right to property in slaves?"
I replied that those who framed the constitution
never supposed that slavery would be perpetuated;
they expected it would die out amid such a blaze of
liberty; and I was proceeding to give the views of
Jefferson, when he turned the subject by inquiring—
"Are you aware, Sir, that I have lost niggers worth

two thousand dollars through these abolitionists? They might as well have stopped me on the highway and picked my pockets. I hate an abolitionist as I do a rattlesnake." I told him that if he would converse good naturedly, the conversation could be continued; that I wished to be treated with respect, and the question was an important one, as he would learn at the day of Judgment. He then turned to a man and inquired—"Do you not think that the niggers, that the abolitionists have stolen from this part of the country, were worth fifty thousand dollars?" "Oh, yes," said the other, "certainly as high as fifty thousand dollars!" "Now," said Mr. S., "look at that. You might as well come here and steal our horses as come here and preach that slavery is a sin, for if it be a sin the slaves will think they have a right to run away."

I called on another member, who had sold his wife's slaves. He thinks that the Parkersburgh people would kill an abolitionist as quick as they would a black snake, because they have aided the negroes to escape. He laments that I have destroyed my influence by attacking slavery. I gave him an account of my labours in Northern Virginia. "You violate our laws," said he. "Your laws," I replied, are "unconstitutional." "Persons," said he, "have no right to come from the free states to agitate against slavery here." I then asked a question. Suppose only one person in the world was doing wrong, would not all the rest of the human family have a right to unite and persuade him to do right? To this he agreed. "Well," I replied, "you are doing wrong in Virginia, in holding slaves, and we have a right in the North to unite and persuade you to do right." Finally, he thought if he lived in Ohio, he would not commune with a slaveholder; and he was willing to aid in correcting public sentiment, that the way might be prepared for better laws. He is a magistrate.

Thus I laboured till Wednesday, when I preached five miles from Parkersburgh. One woman was present who had just lost six slaves; they escaped to Ohio.

Learning that the resident of the next house had been required to give bonds of five hundred dollars to keep the peace for two years for circulating some Anti-slavery verses, I called to ask what the verses were, stating that I was an Anti-slavery minister, and wished to inform my friends at the North respecting it. The gentleman was absent; but his wife showed me the verses. They were in "The Liberty Minstrel," a book used in the Anti-slavery meetings, having the verses on one page and the music on the other. The verses were a dialogue between an abolitionist and a lost spirit, the latter, in its probationary state having been a South Carolina minister and a defender of slavery. One verse read:

> "They paid me well, they made me fat,
>   To preach down abolition;
>   I died—and now I am in hell,
>   How altered my condition."

I could learn of but one minister in Virginia beside myself who preached against slavery. The Rev. Mr. Bacon, an Anti-slavery Methodist, said in a sermon— "Slaveholding is man-stealing, and it is as much worse than horse-stealing as a man is more valuable than a horse." This was in Grayson County, where the slave-power was stronger than where I was labouring. He was arrested and sent to prison.

Two other Virginians who had circulated the verses above referred to, had also to give security to keep the peace.

I learned from the Rev. Mr. Rector that there are six churches connected with the Parkersburgh Baptist Association, not one of whom had a slaveholding member. All the remainder, except two, have in each one slaveholder, holding one slave. The two exceptions stand thus: one has a slaveholding member holding six slaves; the other has two slaveholding members, one holding one slave, the other holding six or eight slaves.

The person who left the church while I was preaching was a slaveholder. His slave was present and related the circumstance to his wife; they were both members of the Baptist Church. "We had," said he, "an abolition minister preaching to us on Sunday, and as soon as he began to show slavery to be a sin— Massa run out of the church quicker!"

If some of the slaveholders hated me as they did a black snake—with what feelings must they have regarded the federal Colonel Steedman, who, at the beginning of the war, crossed the Ohio river with his troops and quietly occupied Parkersburgh.

I wrote a series of letters on the state of the slavery question in North-western Virginia, while labouring there. These were published in the *Christian Contributor*, New York, and the *Western Christian*,

Illinois. I never ventured to post a letter in Virginia, but as a precautionary measure crossed the Ohio river and posted it in the free state of Ohio.

On one occasion, the law requiring the magistrate to burn Anti-slavery newspapers was executed in Parkersburgh. The papers were duly piled up in the street, the citizens gathered around; when one of them, whipping a paper from the pile into his pocket, said, "I will just take one to see what it contains," —another, following the example, said "yes, I should like to know, what it says"—so did a third, and a fourth, help themselves, and when the match was applied, there was but a small pile of Anti-slavery papers to be burnt.

I had distributed a large number of Anti-slavery tracts, with which I had been furnished by the Free Mission Society, together with copies of its Annual Report.

Leaving Virginia I visited Eleutherian College in Indiana; this was not far from Madison, on the Ohio river. It received pupils of all complexions. The originators of this College were the Rev. Messrs. Craven, father and son, and the Rev. Mr. Thompson, they were self-devoted to their work, and—like those who were identified with similar liberty-loving and slavery-opposing institutions—they had foregone lucrative posts, for their love to the suffering members of Christ. A substantial stone building had been erected, on the brow of a hill, commanding a splendid prospect in a fruitful country. Students had commenced their course. Two slaveholders had brought their own mulatto children with the slave mothers,—

had emancipated both the mothers, and all the children ; had purchased land near the College, upon which two neat houses had been erected,—and were rejoicing in the opportunity they had to elevate those whom they had degraded.

But just as the houses were completed some pro-slavery persons went in the night, set them on fire, and burnt both houses to the ground. I saw the ruins. Mr. Craven told me that as he saw the flames in the night he trembled for the College, fearing it also would be burnt,—for he had received a message from Kentucky, stating that five hundred men had agreed to cross the Ohio river and set fire to the College. But they did not come.

At College Hill we had full congregations. Sermons were preached by the Rev. Mr. Kenyon, the Rev. Mr. Fitzgerald, a coloured minister, and myself. The inhabitants of the vicinity showed a cordial hospitality. Dr. Tibbats, a neighbour, had in his barn a secret room,—and when in the night a poor refugee slave came to him, he placed him in this room till the next night,—when he was forwarded to the next friend on the way to Canada. The slave had only to ask " Is this the pilgrim's home ?" and he was provided for. These were the pass-words on the underground railway.

Mr. Fitzgerald, the coloured minister above referred to, visited St. Louis. At that time all coloured men who were strangers in that city were liable to be sent to prison. While walking down the street a policeman came, and demanded who he belonged to? " I belong," he replied, " to Mr. Fitzgerald." As

this was a somewhat aristocratic name, the policeman
was satisfied, and went away, little imagining that
Mr. Fitzgerald had claimed the right to belong to
himself. I inquired of Mr. Fitzgerald how he succeeded in bearing up under the constant ill-treatment
of the white people. His reply was—" I used to
grieve much about it—till I came to the determination—I will deserve respect, and then if I am not
respected it will be no fault of mine. Since then
the ill-treatment has but little effect upon me."

In April, 1850, a Christian Anti-slavery Convention was held at Cincinnati, invited by a committee
representing several religious denominations. As six
of our white friends from College Hill designed attending it,—I proposed that we should strike a blow
at caste on the steamboat, and eat with the coloured
passengers; and then distribute handbills among the
whites, showing that we had done right. I read a
copy of a handbill which I had drawn up. This was
approved,—they would eat with the coloured passengers,—and I was authorized to have two hundred
bills in readiness. They were neatly printed and
ready when we all went on board the " Ben Franklin,"
one of the most superb boats on the river. But in
common with all the other boats, a white gambler on
board was treated with more respect than a coloured
minister, however intelligent or pious.

There were but two coloured passengers, Rev.
Mr. Fitzgerald, of Columbus; and S. Tosspott, a
Congregationalist. The supper bell rang in due
season, and the first white company were served. It
rang the second time, and a second company of white

people took their seats. I and my Anti-slavery
friends were patiently waiting for the third bell. As
I was beginning to fear they never would finish eating, the whites rose from the table, which having
been prepared, the third bell rang for the coloured
passengers. Then was seen the remarkable spectacle
of whites and blacks eating at the same public table.
The steward and waiters were coloured persons. I
had apprised the steward of our plan,—so that six
extra plates were duly laid. We enjoyed the supper,
albeit several pairs of eyes peered upon us from the
end of the cabin, who perhaps imagined the comet
was coming, or some other unusual event—or why
should caste be thus disregarded.

But the attention and diligence of the coloured
waiters,—who were delighted to see their colour
respected,—could scarcely be excelled. Will you
take some fish, Sir? Shall I help you to a thin slice
of ham? Will you take some of this excellent pie?
Shall I change your plate, Sir, this is another kind of
pie." Why, if we had been Governors of States, or
members of the Cabinet they could not have waited
upon us with more assiduity. After supper we prepared to give the passengers a little Anti-slavery
dessert. Our Anti-slavery friends divided the boat into
districts, and each taking a number of bills, we gave
one to each passenger. The bill read thus :—

" To THE PASSENGERS ON BOARD THIS STEAMBOAT.

Respected Reader ;—Custom having established a
law, which requires coloured persons, whatever may
be their intellectual and moral worth, to wait until
white persons have eaten, on board our steamboats, etc.

We present to our fellow-passengers the following reasons against the continuance of this custom.

1. It is unjust:—Coloured passengers pay the same as others.

2. It is contrary to the word of God:—"Do unto others as ye would they should do unto you."

3. It is Anti-republican—All men are born free and equal.

4. It pays no regard to moral character:—Gamblers, if white, take precedence of ministers of the Gospel, if coloured.

5. It is oppressive to the friends of liberty;—they are expected to sanction the wicked prejudice on which slavery—the sum of all villanies—rests.

Should the reader desire to reply publicly to these objections, he will please forward his name to the person from whom he received this handbill, that it may be appended to a paper to be presented to the Captain of the steam-boat, requesting the use of the saloon for that purpose.

(Signed) Several Passengers."

This was received differently by different persons; Mrs. Craven whose district was the Ladies' Cabin, handed one to the wife of the Captain. She read it and instantly returned it, saying, "Take this back, my husband is perfectly competent to make rules to govern this boat." But her husband had not made the rule. The slaveholders had made it, perhaps she feared the loss of their custom, if caste was disregarded.

I handed a bill to a man sitting near the stove,— he read it and threw it in the fire. Another proposed to see the captain and have those who had distributed the bills set ashore at the first wood-yard. This is one of the yards were wood is piled up for the steam-boats, as they consume wood instead of coal; and perhaps no house could be found within twenty miles of it. So great was the excitement that though I endeavoured to look calm, I feared all our Anti-slavery friends would be thrown into the river together; a passenger came to me for another copy of the bill, to send to South Carolina. This I was happy to supply. A person said I am quite willing to eat with such respectable coloured passengers as we have on board. Here was a convert. But among all the passengers not one was found willing to come forward and publicly defend the ungodly practice of excluding coloured passengers from the table. Yet it was a hard task for them, after having been challenged, to say nothing.

Free coloured persons were not allowed to sleep in the state-rooms. Beds are made up for them on the cabin-floor. Many prefer to sit up all night. Yet when a slaveholder goes on board he occupies one berth in the state-room and his slave the other, to be ready to hand his master a glass of water in the night, if he should be thirsty. I took a state room, containing two berths, and told Mr. Fitzgerald he could occupy one of them. This was the first instance in the history of the boat where a free coloured person and a white man had occupied the same state-room. As I thought of his comfortable situation compared with sleeping on the cabin-floor my pillow seemed softer.

CHAPTER XIX.

THE CHRISTIAN ANTI-SLAVERY CONVENTION was held at Cincinnati in April, 1850. There was a large and influential attendance of members from most of the Middle and Western States, and a few delegates from Kentucky. I was chosen one of the secretaries.

Resolutions were presented, and after long and earnest discussion adopted in favour of withdrawing from churches, ecclesiastical bodies, and missionary organizations connected with slaveholding.

Before the close I gave an account of our attempt to break down caste in the "Ben Franklin," and proposed a resolution that the members, in returning to their homes, would eat with the coloured passengers on board the steamboats. As it was feared that such a course would place their lives in imminent peril, I withdrew the resolution.

The following resolutions were adopted at the meeting of the Baptist Free Mission Society :—

"Resolved, That the bill in relation to fugitives from slavery, which leading and venal politicians, both from the North and South are endeavouring to urge through the national legislature, is wicked, diabolical, treasonable to God, a most flagrant outrage upon the rights of every American citizen, and a wilful assault upon the sacred cause of Freedom and subversive of the American Constitution.

"Resolved, That we proclaim to the country and the world, our steadfast and unalterable determination, and we cordially invite all the Christians of the land to unite with us in the declaration, that said bill, should it become a law, will, with its aiders and abettors, be steadfastly opposed and treated as utterly null and void."

When the fugitive slave-law passed there was much to be done. Refugee slaves who had been comfortably settled in the free states were compelled to fly at once to Canada.

The British government kindly permitted many of them to lodge in some barracks not then in use, or they would have had no place of shelter. The Free Missionary Society employed all its means to aid them in their distress ; its Agents every where pleaded for the refugees, and solicited money, clothing, food, and whatever would contribute to their relief. These were forwarded to the missionaries of the Society labouring in Canada among the refugees, and were distributed among the most needy.

I took part in this work of mercy, and endeavoured to obtain from each congregation a pledge that they would never obey the infamous enactment.

An Anti-slavery Baptist paper, the *Western Christian*, was published in Illinois. Arrangements were made with its editor and the western friends to unite it with the *American Baptist*, to be conducted by the editor of the former, the Rev. Wareham Walker, who was a good writer, an excellent editor, and a most earnest abolitionist. Like many of those who laboured in the Anti-slavery reform he was content to bear reproach and to labour if his daily wants were but supplied. This too when the conductors of pro-slavery religious newspapers were growing rich. At least they claimed to be religious, but they injured religion far more than if they had openly avowed atheism or infidelity. Of this class was the *New York Observer*. Its editor boasted of his increasing wealth at a time when no Anti-slavery newspaper was self-sustaining. But the editors of the latter papers stated that they preferred to plead for the enslaved than to support slavery however well it might pay.

The passage of the fugitive slave-law showed that the slave-party still wielded the powers of the Federal government. The people voted for the democrats and had a war with Mexico; they then turned to the whigs and placed them in power, and they gave them the above infamous law. Polk and Dallas were the democratic President and Vice-President. Their whig successors were :—

ZACHARY TAYLOR AND MILLARD FILLMORE.

In 1840, the whig party and their southern friends, elected General Taylor to the Presidency, and Millard Fillmore to the Vice-Presidency.

Taylor was a native of Virginia, and held three hundred slaves; Fillmore was a native of New York, and a non-slaveholder.

Taylor was engaged in two wars for the extension of slavery, one with the Seminole Indians, the other with the Mexicans. In the former, by his advice and under his direction, bloodhounds from Cuba were employed. For his services in these wars he was rewarded with the Presidency of the United States.

Fillmore, before his election to the Vice-Presidency, when a candidate for a seat in Congress, avowed his willingness to abolish slavery in the District of Columbia.

Taylor, when a candidate for the office of President, declined to say whether he was for, or against, the extension of slavery to the Territories of the United States. His northern friends denied, and his southern friends affirmed, that he would extend slavery to the Territories. This duplicity was also practised by the democrats, in supporting Cass, but Taylor was elected.

In his Cabinet the slave-party was represented by Preston, Crawford, Johnson, and Clayton, four slaveholders from the slave states. The other members, Meridith, Collamore, and Ewing were opposed to emancipation.

On becoming President, Taylor despatched to California Mr. King, a slaveholding member of Congress, who was aided by Messrs. Gwin, Boggs and Burnett, three slaveholders, either volunteers or emissaries of the slave-party, and they urged the people to form a constitution for a state-government without delay; promising them admission into the Union as a state.

The Federal Union then comprised fifteen free, and fifteen slave states, the new state of California would therefore hold the balance of power. To promote the great scheme of the slave-party it was essential that Congress should be willing to annex slave Territory. That party intended to obtain Nicaragua as a nucleus; to acquire Cuba; and restore slavery in the West India Islands. Mexico was to be absorbed, and slavery to be extended first to the Pacific, and then to the Southern ocean.

If California should be annexed as a slave-state the slave-party would have a majority in Congress and could carry forward their plan, but not without.

It was essential to the success of this scheme that the slaveholders should be united. Henry Clay, however, opposed introducing slavery into free Territory; probably setting his sails to catch the Anti-slavery breezes of the north and be wafted into the Presidential office. Any slaveholder would readily emancipate his slaves to become President.

The submission to the slave-party by northern politicians evinced their desire to occupy that office; and that influence would be equally potent in abolitionizing southern politicians, when once the gift the federal offices should be in the hands of the Anti-slavery party. If the Union were to continue—this influence alone without any change of the law would abolitionize the South. At this period President Taylor, having on a very warm day ate fruit and drank cold water freely was attacked by the cholera. While suffering greatly, two slaveholders, Stephens, afterwards the Vice-President of the Southern Confederacy, and Toombs, visited him as a delegation from an ultra slavery-extending clique ; and warned the President that he was not doing enough for slavery, and threatened him with a vote of censure. After this his mental equalled his physical sufferings. To his medical attendant he said "I should not be surprised if this were to terminate in my death. I did not expect to encounter what has beset me since my elevation to the Presidency." He died the next day.

When at the head of the federal army he received from President Polk an intimation to move against Mexico ; but he declined to do so until he had received positive instructions, differing in this particular from General Jackson.

Taylor, when a candidate for the Presidency, was strongly opposed by his own son-in-law Jefferson Davis, afterwards the President of the Confederacy. On becoming President he offended the propagandists of slavery by issuing a proclamation against the filibusters who were attempting to gain Cuba. So that he never bowed so low to the slave-party as his successor Millard Fillmore. On the death of President Taylor, Fillmore succeeded to the office, he signed several bills, which having been presented altogether were called the Omnibus.

First the California bill. The people framed a state-constitution—and to the surprise of all parties adopted a rule excluding slavery from California. This offended the slave-party and they laboured unsuccessfully to prevent its admission into the Union.

Second a fugitive slave-bill, adapted to break down all the defences of personal liberty. Probably the signing of this act rivalled in infamy any act of any American President.

Third a bill for the Territorial governments of New Mexico and Utah, admitting the introduction of slavery to them.

Fourthly, a bill to prohibit slave-traders from bringing slaves for sale to the District of Columbia —but admitting the residents to trade in slaves.

Fifthly, a bill surrendering to the slave state of Texas ten thousand square miles of soil previously free—and giving Texas ten millions of dollars. By this vote several members of Congress became rich. It was the first bill carried by the influence of money.

Fillmore was an unscrupulous advocate of slavery. He refused to enter into an agreement with England that Cuba should remain unmolested ; and he held that the progress of the Anti-slavery agitation justified secession. His name will go down with infamy to posterity for the fugitive-slave bill, which in despotism exceeded any law of Russia ; and yet after all these efforts to obtain the support of the slave-party it turned away from him and preferred Buchanan. Among the gloomy facts of this period was the attempt of eighty slaves to escape by the schooner, " Pearl," from Washington, and their recapture.

The opponents of General Taylor in the presidential election were General Cass and Martin Van Buren. Cass was nominated by the democrats, and an attempt was made to put a new article in their creed, denying that the Federal government could exclude slavery from the Territories, but that party was not then sufficiently corrupted by slavery to accept it.

Van Buren was nominated by the Free Soilers. This was an Anti-slavery-made-easy party. The Liberty Party, page 254, rested on moral principle, the Free Soil Party on present Anti-slavery availability. The slaveholders recognized but little distinction between them.

It was in opposition to the latter that they seceded and made war. The Free Soilers also nominated Mr. Adams, the present Ambassador to England, as Vice-President. The discussions in Congress on the Wilmot Proviso threw open the entire question of slavery, and rapidly increased the Anti-slavery sentiment, so that the vote for Van Buren and Adams was 291,342.

The way was now prepared for me to labour in Kentucky, and I proceeded thither by way of Cincinnati. I landed at Maysville, Mason county, Kentucky, December the 27th, 1850. This city has 5000 inhabitants, and is the largest hemp market in the United States. Following up the Ohio river seven miles, and turning to the east, I arrived at the residence of the Rev. John G. Fee. Till I joined

r C *

him he was the only minister in Kentucky that preached against slavery as a sin. Many of the coloured ministers felt that slavery was a high-handed crime, but it would have cost them their lives to preach to this effect to their coloured audiences, —and white people would not listen to them. Mr. Fee was a missionary of the American Missionary Association, an Anti-slavery body chiefly sustained by Congregationalists. He warmly welcomed me to Kentucky as a field of labour. He is of medium height, stout, has a fine large forehead and a cheerful countenance, has written an excellent book, an "Anti-slavery Manual," of 250 pages—and presented a copy of it to each family in Maysville.

His father, a slaveholding presbyterian, declined to hear his son preach, and when he died disinherited him on account of his Anti-slavery principles. In company with the son I visited the father,—and finding that he was a regular subscriber to the *New York Observer*,—a paper that constantly alienated his affections from his own son—who was an example of piety,—I aimed to save the father from the evil influence of that paper,—by showing him that when the public sentiment changed, the editor of the *Observer* would change with it.

As the son on one occasion was returning from preaching, a slaveholder, who had waylaid him, rushed out and struck him over the head with a thick stick, but owing to the stout hat that Mr. Fee wore, he escaped with a slight wound in the head; for this brutal attack the slaveholder was not punished.

On one occasion he was dragged from the pulpit by

main force, by the pro-slavery party, and night after night threats came to him that the mob would attack his house.

At length the arrangements were all made for the mob to gather and attack him; that night, however, a most fearful storm swept over Kentucky, and they were appalled, and gave up the attempt. He had established fifteen Congregational churches in Kentucky, all of which required emancipation as a condition of membership.

We held a day of fasting and prayer. At the close of my sermon, Mrs. Barrett, one of his church members, arose and spoke impressively to the audience. After referring to the duty of Christians to follow Christ, she said, addressing those who were in religious fellowship with slaveholders—"How I long that you might come out, and have no communion with that infamous system. My female friends, you well know the influence of slavery upon female slaves. Bear with me when I call it infamous. Oh that you would come out and oppose that system which is inflicting on our land so much wretchedness and ruin."

In the course of the Anti-slavery meetings held in connection with Brother Fee, it was announced that I should deliver a lecture on the fugitive-slave law. On the occasion the place of meeting was crowded, chiefly by men. We sung from the "Liberty-Minstrel"—"We are for freedom through the land;" and "I pity the slave mother." Prayer having been offered, I took for my text Isaiah x. 1, 2. "Woe unto them that decree unrighteous decrees, and that write grievousness which they have prescribed; to turn aside the needy from judgment, and to take away the right from the poor of my people, that widows may be their prey, and that they may rob the fatherless." Having illustrated the declaration of the text by describing the woes brought upon the Egyptian and Jewish nations because they disregarded the " higher law," the law of God—I showed that a system of legislation based upon the truth that man is man, must be hostile to a system of legislation based upon the wild and guilty phantasy that man is chattel-property.

For the former does not tend from its nature to punish the innocent law-abiding citizen; the latter does. The Rev. Mr. Hawkins, of Rochester; James Hamlet, of New York; Mr. and Mrs. Crafts, of Boston, Massachusetts, and other escaped slaves, were law-abiding citizens. By the laws of the free states they were regarded as having been guilty of no crime in escaping from slavery. The title by which they were held as slaves originated in stealing their forefathers from Africa; this the federal government declared to be piracy. They had escaped from a piratic claim. They believed what the nation declared, that, " all men are born free and equal,"—and " were endowed with inalienable rights ;" and believing these truths, they had reduced them to practice and escaped from slavery. Yet the fugitive slave law required them to be returned to the horrors of slave-life. That law attempted to alienate those rights that the founders of the government declared were inalienable—when intending to lay the foundation of a free government, " to secure the blessings of liberty."

A sketch was then given of the origin of the Federal constitution ; the Ordinance of the North-West, and the mode by which emancipation was effected in the Northern States.

The fugitive slave law aimed to perpetuate the sum of all villanies. Again, the first-named system of legislation punished the magistrate who received bribes. The second held out to the magistrate a bribe of five dollars to send a man into slavery.

The former laws do not arrest a person without a warrant. The latter dispenses with a warrant in making an arrest. I related the case of Adam Gibson —arrested and sent south as a slave, but returned by the slaveholder to freedom, stating that he was not his slave.

After continuing this contrast through various other points, between the fugitive slave law and the law based on truth, I described the effect of the arrests of slaves on the public mind of the North, in Boston, Worcester, Syracuse, and Detroit, the organized opposition to those arrests, and the various efforts which were being made to repeal the fugitive slave law.·

Next, I adverted to the question of dissolving the Federal Union, showing that this cry had been used as a bugaboo, to frighten the non-slaveholders, and to enable the slaveholders to manage the national affairs to suit themselves. I contended that no Southern office-bearer dared carry before his constituents this issue " Slavery and Disunion,—Liberty and Union," —because the discussion of these questions would po ur such a flood of light on the minds of the non-slaveholders that they would walk up to the polls and abolish slavery. That those in the free states who advocated the dissolution of the Union were few compared with the entire number of abolitionists,—and that the great body of them were using the same means to remove slavery that were being used to remove intemperance; and anticipated ensuring the same success.

At the close Brother Fee arose, and after bringing additional illustrations of the points I had advocated, showed conclusively that slavery must be abolished by a change of public sentiment, produced through the spread of truth, or God would abolish it by his exterminating thunders,—that the people must choose judgments or mercies;—and he closed by earnestly entreating the audience to choose mercy. Prayer was then offered, and, though some slaveholders were present, the choir sang from the " Liberty Minstrel," a piece called " The Fugitive," of which the following are two verses :—

" A noble man, of sable brow,
Came to my humble cottage door,
With cautious, weary step and slow,
And asked if I could feed the poor ;
He begged—if I had ought to give,
To help the panting fugitive.

He fell upon his trembling knee
And claimed he was a brother man,
That I was bound to set him free,
According to the gospel plan ;
And if I would God's grace receive,
That I must help the fugitive."

The sacredness with which the marriage vow is re-

garded, is, in any community, an index to the state of
morals. Cassius M. Clay has well said, that "The
moral influence of slavery upon the marriage vow,
by unhinging all the instinctive ideas of right and
wrong, cannot but be disastrous."

Looking over the acts of the Legislature of
Kentucky at its three months' session, commencing
December, 1848, I found the following decrees
granted:—Husbands and wives both divorced, 24.
Wives who obtained divorces from their husbands,
73. Husbands who obtained divorces from their wives
72. Entire number of divorces granted, 169. For
the number of whites in Kentucky this was appalling.
Special efforts were made at this session for divorces,
as it was expected that by the new constitution all
such cases would be left for the decision of the
judiciary, where there would be a more strict investigation ; but at the preceding session between 70 and
80 divorces were granted, and the 169 were additional
cases.

In company with Brother Fee, I visited Bracken
county. In this region laboured in 1805 the Rev.
David Barrow, a Virginian slaveholder. Becoming
convinced that slaveholding was sinful he set free his
slaves—and he held a large number—and wrote a
pamphlet entitled "Involuntary, Unmerited, Perpetual, Absolute, Hereditary Slavery, examined on
the principles of Nature, Reason, Justice, Policy,
and Scripture." An Association was formed of
churches that separated themselves from slaveholding Baptists. There were at that time seven other
Baptist ministers holding these views, and they were

known by having on the Minutes of their Associations the term—"Friends to Humanity." I found scarcely any traces of these churches. Some members had been removed by death, and others driven away by persecution.

I called upon a Baptist slaveholder to obtain some historic information of the Emancipating Baptists, but he declined to furnish it.

His little daughter had taught all his slaves to read, and Brother Fee had supplied each with a Bible, but the master expressed his regret that they had been taught to read. It had spoiled their sale; no one will buy a slave known to be able to read. He will learn from books how to escape. This slaveholder had sold two slaves. Their mother is a member of the same church with himself.

I lectured at Crooked Creek. Called on a Baptist member who was ill and seemed near her end. Read a chapter and prayed with her. Her mother, a member of the same church, declined to come into the room because I was an Abolitionist.

Visited Union; the Baptist minister is a slave-driver. His employer says—"My overseer is a preacher, but I do not allow him to ask a blessing at my table." This preacher kindly gave out that I should preach at three o'clock, on the sinfulness of slavery.

About fifty assembled, and listened attentively to the sermon. I gave the people Temperance and Anti-slavery tracts as they went out. One person refused to take a tract. I learned that the same day he joined the church he sold a slave to the slave-traders.

At the end of January I visited Mayslick, and attended a meeting at the Baptist Church.

The Rev. Mr. Hawker preached, but made no allusion to slavery. He called on me to offer prayer, and I prayed for the emancipation of the slaves. I accompanied Mr. Hawker to the residence of Mr. M., a deacon and a slaveholder. I requested the use of the chapel for a meeting; but the deacon said "No, not after that prayer you offered that the slaves may be emancipated." The minister apologized for calling on me to pray, and stated that he should not do so again. I presented the deacon with a copy of the Annual Report of the Free Mission Society, and gave him an account of the movement for emancipation going on in the free states. I asked him to allow me to see the records of the church, as fifty years before there had been a division on the slavery question, and an Anti-slavery church was formed, but he declined to allow me to see them. The deacon thought that were my principles known I should receive a coat of tar and feathers. I suggested that I had counted the cost, and could endure it if they decided to proceed with it. Word was also sent me that I had better leave the place. The trustees of a school-house, at which I had agreed to lecture on temperance, sent me word that I should not be allowed to lecture, as they had heard of my praying for emancipation. One slaveholding member told me that the prayer went through him like an electric shock.

The church numbers about 400 members. In round numbers there are 100 slaves and free coloured persons, 150 slaveholders, and 150 white non-slave-holders. The coloured members of the church are not allowed to vote.

Mr. A., a member, was once a slave. He obtained his liberty, commenced to trade, and was then worth 100,000 dollars, and yet he cannot read. He employs two white clerks. He will stand at the counter and sell all day, and at the close will state every article sold, the amount or measure, and the price.

The white persons he employed could not eat with him without losing caste. A white man and a member of the church, related to me a sad grievance. "You know, Sir," said he, "that I and another white man were engaged to work for Mr. A. Well, at noon we were called in from our work to take dinner, which was placed for us at the end of a long table; and, would you believe it,—before we had finished, dinner was laid for one person at the other end of the table. Then Mr. A. came in, and addressing us, said, —'Oh, pray excuse me for sitting down to dinner with you—I am greatly pressed for time—have an appointment to meet and should be seriously dis-advantaged by a delay.'" There seemed to be no help for it, but it was a sore trial to the white workmen.

The same person gave me an account of a fearful struggle between an overseer and a slave; the former went armed with a pistol, and threatened to shoot the slave. Both were members of the above church, yet they declined to allow me to lecture lest it should disturb the harmony of the brethren.

Mr. Humphrey Marshall, a Baptist member resid-ing at Cabin Creek, had an interest in a coloured man. He was sold, and Mr. Marshall received forty dollars, his proportion of the property. It troubled his conscience, and visiting Mayslick he sought out the coloured man, paid back part of the sum he had received, and designs to pay back the remainder. But he found him in the greatest distress of mind— he had obtained his own liberty and married a slave-wife. They had two daughters who had just been sold, one to the far south, the other to a neighbour. One of the daughters was in prison when I was at Mayslick, waiting, I suppose, to be sent south. The owner of the mother was a member of the Baptist Church at Mayslick, as was also the poor mother of the slaves, who was almost broken-hearted.

Without an Anti-slavery press in Kentucky it was difficult to make progress. Brother Fee and myself drew up some resolutions, which we signed, as did many others, including one magistrate. Our intention was to have them published in the newspapers with the names; the following are the resolutions:—

"Whereas, in the letter of Ex-Governor Metcalfe to Mr. Foote, the former, in speaking of the fugitive slave bill, assumes that Kentucky, with an unbounded unanimity, will regard its repeal by the general government as a *dissolution of the Union.*

"Resolved, that the opinion of a slaveholder, as is Ex-Governor Metcalfe, or of the 31,000 slaveholders of Kentucky, can in no fair sense be regarded as the opinion of the 600,000 non-slaveholders of our state.

"That we should be happy to be furnished with the evidence by which the Ex-Governor learned the views of the non-slaveholders, in advance of their having expressed them.

"That so far as we are informed, intelligent and influential non-slaveholders regard the fugitive slave bill as unconstitutional and unchristian.

"That the admiration which we feel for free institutions leads us to believe that the North will remain firm in its purpose of repealing this bill in a legal manner, and that it will be as much opposed at the South as at the North when the light shines as abundantly here as it does there."

These resolutions were published at the North, and because the South was the recognised leader of public opinion, they produced a remarkable effect.

On one occasion I conversed with a slaveholder whose slave had recently escaped to Ohio. The following was the dialogue :—" How can you defend slavery ?

" By the Bible.

" What part of it ?

" Why, there is an account of a man, his name was Cain or Abel—I do not know which—for I have not read the Bible much—when my wife was alive she used to read it a good deal—and the Lord put a mark upon him, and that was this black mark, and was the cause of the blacks being made slaves.

" But there was a flood.

" Yes, I know that is in the Bible about the flood.

" Well, by that flood all the human family were destroyed except Noah and his family, so that all the present human family are descended from Noah. Now, if he had the mark, we have all received it ; and if he did not have it, no one has received it."

CHAPTER XX.

I VISITED the Rev. Mr. Holliday, a Baptist minister, near Blue Licks—having been informed that he was a non-slaveholder. To my surprise I found he had five or six slaves. I stayed over-night by invitation, and we conversed for some hours on the slavery question. The following dialogue occurred:—

G 7

" How can you justify slavery ?

" By the Bible.

" What part of it ?

" By the example of Abraham—do you think he was a good man ?

" Not a doubt of it.

" Well, the Bible says that he had three hundred and eighteen slaves—born in his house, or bought with his money—of course they were his property.

" If they were his property, by whom was the law made ?

" By the Almighty.

" But slaves are always held by a law made by men?

" Yes, well, Abraham made it.

" But, slave-law can never be enforced without an outside power—tell me who enforced the slave-law that Abraham made, for we cannot suppose that he and Sarah surrounded three hundred and eighteen persons ; and he had no bloodhounds to pursue them if they ran away ?

"The tribes that lived near Abraham enforced the law.

" But the Bible shows that they made war upon Abraham—and would have been glad to get away all his servants. Judging either by Abraham's principles, or by his circumstances, he was not a slaveholder,—for as to the former he was a good man, and a good man would not make another person work all his life for nothing ; and as to the latter,—when he sent out his men to feed the sheep they could run away if they were so disposed. Besides American slavery began by means of the slave-trade, which our laws declare to be piracy.

"I admit that it began wrong—but would you help one of my slaves to run away?" (This was a close question, two ministers were then in prison, in Kentucky, for doing this.) I told him I would, unless he could show a good title to him, which brought us back to the Bible argument. He told me that he was desirous his slaves should come in and attend family prayer—but they usually declined to do so,—no wonder—his position as a slaveholder neutralised his influence as a professed Christian. I visited his son-in-law, and conversed with him till the stage-coach came. He pointed to a small shop in the valley below; and told me that he missed his chickens and spoons, and was satisfied that the slaves took them in the dead of night and exchanged them at the shop for goods. He wished the shop was not there. I saw his difficulty. It is against the law to sell anything to a slave. But it is also against the law for a coloured person to testify against a white one. In the dead of night the shopkeeper would trade with the slaves ; and unless he told of himself, which was not very likely, the case could not be proved.

I visited Frankfort, the capital of Kentucky. It is encompassed with hills; and the Kentucky river, a wide, sluggish, and turbid stream flows past it. The population was about 3,500 of whom 810 were slaves, and 200 free coloured people. The coloured Baptists had a good House of Worship, which would seat 600 persons. Of the 360 members about 60 were free. The Rev. Mr. Monroe, the pastor, was the slave of

Mrs. Breckenridge, to whom he paid a given sum yearly for his time; he received from the church one hundred and fifty dollars as salary, devoted a part of his time to manual labour, and succeeded in purchasing the freedom of his wife, whom he supported, with three or four of his children, who were free-born; he wrote an excellent hand, and had made great progress in learning. On the Sabbath I attended their place of worship. The pastor was absent in Georgetown, but another member of the church, a ministering brother, invited me to preach. I took my seat in the pulpit with him, and ventured to officiate, though I believe no other white person was present. Usually a minister is not permitted to preach to the slaves unless two white persons are present. This is to guard against his preaching on slavery.

Before commencing the services I begged leave to be favoured with his name. "My right name," he replied, "is Wilkinson, but I am generally known by the name of Eperson, the name of the family that own me.

"Are you then a slave?

"Yes, but I am buying myself, I have paid 300 dollars,—and shall be free when I have paid 200 more. But I do not know what they will do with me; the law compels me to leave Kentucky as soon as I am free; yet how can I do so; here is my wife a slave, and all my children slaves! I shall remain here and suffer whatever penalty may be inflicted on me, but I will not leave!"

He was much affected, and I rose, gave out a hymn

read a chapter, and offered prayer. I prayed that the period might soon come when every yoke should be broken, and every slave go free,—when I was startled by a loud, fervent "Amen," from every part of the audience. There was a world of meaning in that response—but it occurred to me that if some slaveholder heard it I might have to suffer for my prayer. I preached to them three times that day; and at the close of the third sermon, called on a member to offer prayer. He had an excellent command of language, and prayed with the Spirit. I supposed him free, but learned he was purchasing himself. Mr. Wilkinson is a warm-hearted, eloquent, and pathetic speaker; reads rather well, and can write, but is not so highly gifted as Mr. Monroe. The clerk of the church purchased himself for 400 dollars. He writes well, and has kept the records of the church in a business-like style. When a free person joins the church the word "free" was written after his name. When a slave unites, "servant to Mr. ——," was added. This coloured church strongly desired me to visit them again.

The word Emancipator, or Emancipationist, is frequently in Kentucky applied to a slaveholder. It means one in favour of gradual emancipation, on condition that the freed persons go to Africa. I conversed with a deacon of the white Baptist Church, he was one of this class. He opposed emancipation without expatriation, and when I reminded him of the judgments which would fall upon slaveholding communities, he replied "When the judgments come we will look out for them."

In 1862 thousands of Confederate troops swept through Kentucky. Lexington was surrendered to them, and there was a panic at Frankfort. A million of dollars of the state, and the public archives were forwarded for safe keeping to Louisville. The Legislature also was transferred to the latter city. Now came the period when the deacon was to look out for judgments, but it was too late, they were upon him.

I attended the Annual Meeting of the state Colonization Society, held at the Presbyterian Church, February 6th, 1851. The building, which is Gothic, will seat one thousand persons, but not more than six hundred were present. The President of the Society, Judge Monroe, presided; the lecturer was the Rev. R. J. Breckenridge, a prominent Presbyterian minister. The former became a leading secessionist; the latter a leading unionist.

Mr. Breckenridge illustrates the vacillating policy of leading Southerners. Henry Clay began public life as a friend of emancipation, passed through it as a supporter and defender of the slave system and slavery extension,—and ended it by opposing the latter.

Stephens advocated continued Union with the North,—and then became Vice-President of the Confederacy.

Breckenridge began public life as an opponent of slavery, became a supporter of the slave-system and a slaveholder,—presented, as in his Colonization speech, the interests of the whites as opposed to those of the blacks; wrote a letter to Senator Seward, contending that to exclude slavery from the Territories would justify the South in secession and war; and when secession took place—became a leading unionist.

In his lecture he advocated the unity of the human race,—but contended that white people had the chief claim on the regard of the audience, and that the free coloured people ought to be sent to Africa.

When General Robert Anderson, who defended Fort Sumter, commanded the Federal troops at Louisville, and General Zollicoffer, the confederate troops at Barboursville; John C. Breckenridge, who had been the slavery-extension candidate in the Presidential election, Judge Monroe, and some other prominent secessionists, escaped to the rebel camps in Southern Kentucky, and passed thence into Tennessee and Virginia, where they openly gave their adhesion to the Southern Confederacy. Judge Monroe formally renounced his office and his allegiance, and was adopted—citizen of the Confederacy—in open court at Nashville, October 3rd, 1861. Breckenridge was promptly made a Brigadier-General. The Rev. R. J. Breckenridge, at a meeting in Cincinnatti in 1862, declared that Kentucky was saved from the black abyss of secession by her proximity to loyal Ohio, Indiana, and Illinois, whose Governors, it was known, stood pledged to send ten thousand men each to the aid of her Unionists.

On the 10th of February I visited Lexington, and called on the Rev. W. M. Pratt, the pastor of the white Baptist church. We had been class-mates at Hamilton, and I regarded him as the best mathematician in the class. By marriage he had become the

owner of two slaves. He was holding revival meetings. I attended one of them, and he preached on
"The Hope of the Righteous." A young lad professed to have found peace. There were some excellent points in his sermon. Returning to his house,
he inquired my views of the divisions of his sermon ;
I gave them, but added that having heard that a
slave had been publicly sold that day in the streets,
it was present to my mind during the entire service,
and prevented my enjoying it. He made light of this.
When, however, the Confederate troops took Lexington, Mr. Pratt was compelled to fly to the free states.

From him I learned that the Kentucky Bible
Society had declined to continue to be an auxiliary
to the American and Foreign Bible Society, and that
this separation was the result of my motion to make
slaveholding a disqualification for being an officer.
The discussion, page 305, had been read by them,
and it was found that Mr. Pratt's father-in-law, a
Kentuckian, had been displaced from his position on
the committee; and Mr. Pratt, a New Yorker, substituted. Both were slaveholders,—but this preference for a native of a free-state was regarded as a
step towards abolition,—and with characteristic slaveholding sensitiveness, they dissolved the union with
the American and Foreign Bible Society.

On the 11th I proceeded by the stage-coach to
Foxtown. As we passed near the residence of
Henry Clay, at Ashland, it was pointed out to me
by the passengers.

The mansion, instead of wearing an air of fresh-
ness and elegance, looked sombre. Its owner's pro-

slavery course had, by association, invested the estate in gloom. He held fifty slaves; and, as was shown by James Cannings Fuller, who had called at his house, had sold every child of one of his slaves. In the coach I had extended discussion with some slave-holders from Lexington. One of the passengers stated that Cassius M. Clay had a farm of 2,000 acres, worth fifty dollars an acre. That the previous year he had made ten thousand dollars by purchasing, fattening, and selling cattle. That his former slaves, after being emancipated, had become his tenants; that if the emancipators could obtain his consent they would nominate him for Congress, and he would probably be elected in that event.

I had watched with the deepest interest the course of Mr. Clay. He established a weekly Anti-slavery paper at Lexington, the *True American*, which I read. It greatly moved the North, the more so as a mob went to the office, and seizing the press and types, sent them to Ohio; it was a specimen of southern pluck, and that has been greatly admired. Few men were so useful to the Anti-slavery cause. He continued his paper, printing it in Ohio, but publishing it in Lexington. But when Polk began his infamous war with Mexico, Mr. Clay, carried away with mistaken views of patriotism, entered the army, and during his absence, the paper was discontinued. At the close of the war he returned, and I desired to see him for the purpose of reviving, if possible, the *True American*. The slaveholders hired a man—his name was Brown—to shoot him. He way-laid Mr. Clay, fired at him, but the bullet lodged in the silver sheath of his bowie-knife. He always goes armed. He then attacked Brown, who was wounded, and eventually died. Passing on to 1860, when Mr. Lincoln was nominated for President at Chicago, Mr. C. M. Clay received 101 votes for Vice-President. When Mr. Lincoln went to Washington, and it was threatened by malignant foes, "A spirited body of volunteers," says Mr. Greely—"temporary sojourners at, or casual visitors to the capital—under Cassius M. Clay as colonel, had stood on guard during those dark days and darker nights; and these, in addition to the small force of regulars commanded by General Scott, had constituted up to this time the entire defensive force of the Federal metropolis." Mr. Clay was afterwards nominated Ambassador to Russia.

Leaving the stage at Foxtown, and passing through a gateway, I walked a mile and reached Mr. Clay's mansion. It is a fine two-and-half story brick building, with a school-room near it. The surrounding country is rich and picturesque, the land undulating, near is a large orchard, a grass-plot, and a few trees —beyond, well-cultivated fields, and in the distance a forest of trees. I showed Mr. Clay my letter of introduction. He kindly mentioned that he had heard of my labours in Kentucky; and stated that he had been honored with two letters from Mr. Thomas Clarkson, of England. He was willing to take his weapons and defend me in my right to lecture. I thanked him, but stated that that course would not be in harmony with my peace principles.

It was Valentine's day, and he showed me what he had received,—a letter containing a large heart with a knife run through it; and I think it was accompanied with a threat. I drew up a call for a convention of emancipationists, to deliberate on the propriety of again establishing in Kentucky an Anti-slavery weekly newspaper, which he kindly signed.

My intention was to get it well signed and publish it widely, with the hope of having an influential meeting. I stayed over-night. Mrs. Clay fully sympathises with her husband; they had five or six children. The next day I visited a Baptist slaveholder, Mr. Jones, a neighbour of Mr. Clay's, to obtain permission to lecture in the Baptist church at Richmond, and if possible persuade him to emancipate his slaves. By invitation I spent the day with him, and he related the following occurrence of which he was an eye-witness. At the time of an election Mr. Clay made a speech in the vicinity, and was showing that a slaveholding, can never be an educated community, observing that some money which should have been applied by the state for education had been loaned, and that the bonds taken as evidence of the debt had been burned, adding that the person who burned them was the tool of Squire Turner. His sons were present and they declared it was untrue, and at the close of the lecture, drew their knives and approached Mr. Clay. He also drew his knife, and they fought "They intended," said Mr. Jones, " to kill Mr. Clay, because they stabbed in an upward direction." A man near Mr. Clay was severely wounded in the arm, Mr. Clay was wounded in the breast; the ligature which unites the ribs to the breast-bone being separated—but one of the Turners received a back-handed blow across the abdomen. He died the next day, it was supposed that Mr. Clay could not survive, but he did. He was not brought before a jury—as it was known that his death was contemplated by those making the attack. The next morning Mr. Jones introduced me to the Rev. Mr. Dudley, the Baptist minister, a slaveholder; and he agreed to place my request for the use of the chapel before a church meeting. I visited Richmond, and obtained some signatures to the call for a meeting of emancipationists. For the same purpose I went into the country.

Whilst I was on the journey the weather changed and soon the rain fell in torrents. I called on Colonel Rhodes, a relative of Mr. Clay, and he kindly invited me to stay for the night, for which I was grateful. He had thirty slaves. We conversed much upon the subject of slavery. He declined to sign the call,—but said he had observed that, as a rule, slave-traders died a violent death; and instanced the case of a slave-trader in the vicinity, who being about to visit St. Louis, cursed his wife and each of his children separately, as he left them, went to St. Louis, and in a quarrel with another slave-trader was killed.

The next day I visited the Rev. Mr. Dudley; in the afternoon the horses were saddled, and we rode to Mr. Detheridge's house, to hear Dr. Coffey preach. The doctor pressed me to preach that evening. I did so. He then requested me to accompany him to his next appointment and preach again. I thanked him, but stated that I was an emancipator, and had applied for the use of the Baptist Church at Rich-

mond that I might lecture on the moral and religious
condition of the slaves; the church was to consider
the subject, and wishing to be present, I could not
accept the invitation. Mr. Dethcridge invited some
of the friends to remain. A number did so, and I
sat down and gave them a history of emancipation in
the Northern States. Supper was announced. After
supper the subject was again taken up, the company
presenting such texts as "Servants be obedient to
your masters," which I endeavoured to explain. We
continued to converse till a late hour.

The next day I met with the church at Richmond.
The minister presented my request for the use of the
House, but stated that he was himself opposed to its
being granted, as it was a political question. Messrs.
Burnham and Jones made the same objection. I
stated that the moral and religious condition of the
slaves was a proper subject for a minister of the
Gospel to present to the people. It was true the
question had also political aspects,—but the same
was true of popery, marriage, and many other questions. The church, however, refused permission, as
did also the Presbyterian and Methodist ministers.
The "Disciples," also by a vote of the church, refused
the use of their place of worship. One of the ministers proposed discussing the question with me. I
accepted the offer, but he would not decide on the
time. The prevailing sentiment was that it had better
not be discussed. On Sunday evening I attended the
meeting of the coloured people, and was invited by
the coloured minister to preach.

As two white men were present I felt safe in

accepting the invitation, and took for my text, Phil-
lippians iv. 6, "In every thing by prayer and supplication with thanksgiving let your requests be made
known unto God." Having shown that those whom
the Spirit taught to write the Bible were men of
prayer; that the early disciples depended much upon
prayer as a means of success,—and that the Redeemer
taught them to pray,—I presented the following
reasons for the performance of the duty of prayer:—
That God is so worthy to be worshipped; that He
has a right to our prayers; that He has commanded
us to pray, it being the chief command; that it is a
suitable acknowledgement of our dependence upon
Him; that it is the appointed means by which we
receive His blessings; and that prayer greatly affects
the temper, the character, the habits, and the course
in life; that its influence upon us in these particulars
was greater than the united influence of early training,
reading, companions,—or the laws we live under in
the church, or in the state. Having illustrated these
heads,—I showed that the Bible was full of answers
to prayer, and in giving a general review of these
answers, referred to the Jews who were in bondage
in Egypt; who prayed and were delivered. On that
subject I should have felt a pleasure in branching
out,—but I simply added—" His ear is as attentive
to your prayers as to theirs. Whatever blessing
you desire of God—"Ask, and you shall receive."
" Trust in Him and He will be a refuge for you."
(There was a mob of white people in front of the
chapel,—this I did not know at the time,—who were
listening, with the arrangement that the first word I

should say on abolition, they were to rush in and drag me from the pulpit. Had I branched out they would have branched in; and this book would not have been written. My life would have been sacrificed, I should have been added to the hundreds who have been murdered in the slave-states for their Anti-slavery principles.)

I traced out the benefit of prayer on the church, the minister, and the progress of true religion; and closed by appealing to them to persevere in prayer because the days of prayer are limited;—in Heaven prayer will be lost in praise; and that our dependence for the acceptance of our prayers must be on the mediation of the Redeemer alone, whose name is ever prevalent with the Father.

At the close of the sermon, as soon as the audience commenced to sing, they were all moving from seat to seat and shaking hands while they sang. Here a mother shook hands with her daughter—there a brother with a brother, or a friend with a friend, one coloured man approached the pulpit, which was a low one, and hesitated, he evidently wished to shake hands with me, but I was white. I held out my hand, and he grasped it and bade me God speed in the way to Heaven. Then a slave came and whispered in my ear that there was a mob of white people outside the chapel. I looked to see if there were any back-door, but there was none. I went out—there was a large mob, many of whom were armed with thick sticks, and had handkerchiefs tied round and partly concealing their faces. They inquired:—

"What is your business in this community?

"I am a missionary of a Baptist Missionary Emancipation Society.

"Are you an Abolitionist?

"If by that term you mean one in favour of the slaves rising and resisting their masters,—I am not. But if you mean one in favour of using the same means to abolish slavery that we are using to remove intemperance, then I am one.

"What are those papers in your pocket,—we would like to see them if they are not private ones?"

I handed them a tract showing that it was the duty of ministers to preach on the slavery question —written by the Rev. H. W. Beecher, and published by the Free Mission Society. One of them examined it by the light of the moon, which was high and full, and, owing to a dry atmosphere, gives more light in America than in England. He said "I pronounce this a regular abolition tract." They now said "you must leave this place in fifteen minutes, or be tarred and feathered." I proceeded to the tavern. They shouted "Kentucky hospitality ;"—one said my throat ought to be cut,—and others used profane language. Arrived at the "Webster House," where I lodged, I found the landlord either unable or unwilling to protect me, I paid my bill,—the mob drank liquor, —and we started on the road to Lexington. One of them said to me "We heard your sermon,—and had agreed that if you should say one word about abolition, we would rush in, and drag you out of the pulpit." We came near a pond, an attempt was made to throw me in,—but I escaped, and a revolver was then fired five or six times. I was not injured, but was afterwards informed that the hat of one man was shot through with a bullet. When I reached the house of the Rev. Mr. Dudley, it was late, but I roused him from his slumbers, and was kindly furnished with a bed. The next morning before I left, Mr. Dudley's son, a lad of fourteen, was in an adjacent room, and was observing to his mother that it was a great shame for a minister to be treated so badly, simply for preaching to the blacks. " Oh," said his mother " depend upon it he has done something else, or he would not have been thus treated."

By such and by similar misrepresentations throughout the slave states did parents repress all true human sympathy when they saw it manifested by their children. To guard against such attacks I determined to write a letter to the *Richmond Chronicle*, giving an account of my labours in Kentucky, of the " Free Missionary Society," and of the mob on Sunday night. The next day I spent with Mr. Clay, wrote out a statement for the press, and he kindly wrote another to accompany it, stating that he thought the Richmond slaveholders would not sanction such violence.

(From the marked resemblance between Mr. Clay and Mr. Clayton in "Dred," I regard the former as the original from which the latter character was drawn.)

I wished to go to the Big Hill, and my nearest way was through Richmond. Both Mr. Clay and myself thought that the public feeling of Richmond would not sustain the violence of the mob, and that there would be no danger in going through the town by day-light; that the mob would have no

time to rally, and I could leave my communication
with the editor for the next number of the *Chronicle*.
I, therefore, pursued this course, leaving with the
editor, in connection with the letters, a copy of the
" Annual Report of the Free Mission Society," and
a copy of the tract of Rev. H. W. Beecher, and
pursued my way to the Big Hill. When a mile
beyond the town four horsemen pursued and overtook me. I looked at them ; they were in the mob
on Sunday evening. They required me to accompany
them, threatening me with instant death if I made
any resistance or any outcry. To refuse to go was
death, and to go could but be death ; so I reasoned,
and consented to go with them. Turning from the
main-road through a gate-way, we crossed a field,
turned down a lane, and crossing another field,
descended into a deep valley, a bye-place where no
one could see us. A small creek ran through the
valley. Fastening their horses to the fence of a
field, one of them, the bar-tender at the house where
I had lodged—the " Webster House "—seized my
arms, brought them behind me, and bound them
together. Then ranging themselves in front of me
they inquired :—

" Are you an abolitionist ?

" I do not believe that the slaves ought to rise and
resist their masters, but they ought to be emancipated,
and I am labouring to array the moral power of the
churches against slavery.

" Did you not tell the Methodist minister at Richmond that slaves could not get to Heaven unless they
ran away from slavery ?

"No; take me to him, and I will prove that I did not.

"Did you not say that you would help the slaves to run away.

"No."

They then took a handkerchief, folded it, and blindfolded me. I stood for some time; they seemed to be waiting for some one to bring them some tar and feathers. But no one coming, they asked me some further questions, and then discussed, in my hearing, whether I should be tarred and feathered, whipped, thrown into the water, or hanged.

As I stood there, every case that I had read or heard of, where ministers had suffered for the slave's sake, seemed to pass before my mind, in broad and vivid phantasmagoria. I thought of dear friends in Old England, and of how little they imagined the perilous situation I was in; and it seemed so mysterious to be cut off in this way, my end shrouded in obscurity and gloom. But I commended my soul to God.

Finally, the long agony of suspense was over. They decided to take me up to the pond, and I felt comparatively relieved. The bandage was removed from my eyes, and when we reached the pond, which was at some distance, my arms were unbound. We were on the farm of Mr. Turner, who came up as we approached the water, a brother to the one who fell in his contest with Mr. Clay, and cousin to one of those four men who took me from the high road. They consented to my leaving my coat, overcoat, bible, watch, and pocket book, on the bank:

and asked me if I could swim, I replied I could, but was not certain that I could with my clothes on. One of them remarked that a stone ought to be tied to me, that I might sink to the bottom. They now seized me, and threw me in as far as they could into the pond. Before rising to the surface I swallowed a considerable portion of water, and paused near the bank to regain my breath. They ordered me to come out instantly. On reaching the bank I was thrown in the second and the third time. They then required me to promise never to come to Richmond again. I refused, and was thrown in the fourth time, when I made the promise. They next required me to promise to leave Kentucky and never return. Refusing to do this, I was thrown in the fifth time. On returning to the shore I was again required to promise, but refusing, I was led to a tree and tied up, as they designed to whip me. A bandage was then tied over my eyes, so tight as to pain them exceedingly. Finally, without whipping me, one said "Let us try the water again." They did not seem to wish to kill me if they could compel me to leave Kentucky; I must leave or be drowned; but I went into Kentucky desiring to labour there till slavery was abolished. I was now unbound from the tree, and as I was being led to the water I raised my hand, removed the bandage from my eyes, and found Turner, the linen-draper, not the farmer, leading me. He censured me for removing the bandage. I was now thrown into the water five times more, being required each time on reaching the shore to promise to leave Kentucky, and each time refusing.

The tenth time, as I approached the bank, they announced their determination to whip me. I found my strength was becoming exhausted; a most pleasing sensation was stealing over my brain, and over my entire system, and I felt that I had only to yield to it, and I should soon be beyond the power of slave-holders to trouble me. But I rallied my feelings. I had promised my friends in the free states that if the Kentuckians would not hear me I should return. I thought of the vast amount of work needing yet to be done at the North; and if I told the people there of my treatment it would promote the opposition to slavery; I thought of the words, "If they persecute you in one city flee ye to another." So halting in the water, with what of life remained, I said—"I will promise." Seldom if ever have I seen men whose countenances evinced such a feeling of relief as was displayed by the looks of these lynchers. The bar-tender said—"Do you swear so help you God you will leave Kentucky and never return?" I replied—"I will solemnly affirm that I will leave Kentucky and never return." I then came up out of the water. They told me I should have men to watch me out of the state; that if I attempted to go to C. M. Clay's, or by the Lexington turnpike, I should suffer death; and that if I ever returned to Kentucky again they would hang me wherever they found me.

They said I must go by way of Lancaster; and might put on what dry garments I had with me. I made an effort to unlock my carpet-bag but so shook with the cold that I failed, and one of the lynchers unlocked it for me. My muscles gathered in knots with cramp. I put on dry under-clothing and by exercise kept the blood in circulation. They inquired if I was as cold the day I was baptized as now? I stated that when I came to leave the world the proceedings of that day would not be a thorn in my dying pillow. " Ah," they replied, "you think they will be a thorn in our dying pillows;" They now required all my Anti-slavery books. I handed them the Rev. H. W. Beecher's tracts, already referred to, " Wesley's Thoughts on Slavery," " Lewis Tappan on the Un-constitutionality of the Fugitive Slave Law," and the " Liberty Minstrel." One of them opened the latter and began to read a piece by John G. Whittier,— " The Lament of the Slave-mother whose Daughters are sold :"—

> " Gone, gone—sold and gone,
>   To the rice-swamp dank and lone,
> Where the slave-whip ceaseless swings,
> Where the noisome insect stings,
> Where the fever demon strews
> Poison with the falling dews,
> Where the sickly sunbeams glare
> Through the hot and misty air,—
>   Gone, gone—sold and gone,
>   To the rice-swamp dank and lone,
>   From Virginia's hills and waters,—
>   Woe is me my stolen daughters ! "

I told them I would give them the books. They thought as the " Liberty Minstrel " was beautifully bound they ought to pay for it. I bade them keep it; I wanted nothing for it. " Now," said they, "see here, we want this book and we want to pay for it.'

I told them it cost me half a dollar, and they handed me the amount. They inquired what was thought by different persons of the treatment I received on Sunday night. " Now," said they, " had you come to Richmond and pursued the same course in regard to slavery that other ministers pursue, you would have been treated with the greatest kindness and hospitality." I found that they had received some communication from Mayslick, stating that I had been threatened while there with lynch-law.

One of them told me I was thrown into the water ten times; I was too far gone to count at the time except at the beginning.

The bar-tender now took a pair of scissors and cut off a lock of my hair to send to the " Free Mission Society." Then mounting their horses they rode back to Richmond, while I commenced my journey to Lancaster, which was distant twenty-two miles, along a bye-road, which was muddy and crossed by creeks. I was faint and hungry, and part of my clothes were wet. Thus I had fellowship with the slave in his sufferings and could judge how terrible it must be to pass one's life under the tyranny of slaveholders.

If the expulsion of an Anti-slavery minister would give peace to Richmond, the people might have expected a large share of it.

But the pond into which I was thrown was crimsoned in 1862 with the blood of Federal and Confederate soldiers; and the whole course I traversed from the high road to the valley, and thence to the pond, was strewn with the dead and wounded. So I

infer in reading the accounts of the battles near this
town, which is named after Richmond in Virginia.

But to complete the narrative of my escape—I
walked five miles, the road branched, and it was too
dark to read the guide-board. My efforts to hire
a horse had been unsuccessful, so I called at a farm-
house and asked if I could be accommodated with
supper, the name always given in America to the
third meal. " Yes," said the slaveholding master of
the house, " Will you walk towards the fire." " My
clothes," I remarked, " are wet—I will state why
they are." I then gave an account of my labours in
Kentucky as an Anti-slavery missionary, described
the brutal usage I had received, and stated that my
future health depended upon his kindly allowing me
to stay for the night, and requested that I might do
so. He consented, adding " If I thought you were
come to help one of my slaves into a free state, I
would shoot you at once." We conversed as I dried
my clothes at the fire. He wished all the free blacks
were sent to Africa, and that somebody would kill
Cassius M. Clay, as he was always troubling the
slaveholders about their slaves. This farmer's children were exceedingly kind to me, and lighted a fire
in my bed-room, that I might finish drying my clothes.
His son sat up and conversed with me till midnight.
" I would," said he, "have certainly killed one of those
men had I been you." I reminded him that the others
could have killed me; and that vengeance belonged
to God. That the command of the Redeemer was if
we were smitten on one cheek, to turn the other also.
That night I did not sleep for one moment. The son,

early in the morning, made an unsuccessful effort to persuade his father to let me have a horse, for which I offered compensation, and he would accompany me to Lancaster and return with it. At five o'clock in the morning I resumed my journey; and by moon-light crossed a creek on a mill-dam, which was somewhat dangerous. At length I hired a horse—and a boy rode with me to Lancaster to take it back. I next hired a horse to Bryantsville, a slave accompanying me to return it rode near me and asked many questions, I think he imagined I was from the North.

Arrived at Bryantsville I engaged lodgings for the night, and began to feel more secure from danger. But the mail carrier from Richmond arrived and stayed also for the night. He related what had happened, and ascertained that I was the abolitionist to whom lynch-law had been applied. Making this known to the tavern-keeper, who was a Baptist, he became alarmed, as he had a number of slaves in the house each worth a round sum. "How did you find him out? how did you find him out?" were his repeated inquiries. To relieve his fears I told him that though I was wearied, rather than he should be so apprehensive about losing his slaves I would go on to Lexington. His son interposed and urged me to remain.

In the night I was awakened by a noise, and imagined that the lynchers were knocking at the front door. They had threatened me with death if I told of my treatment in Kentucky—and I had no alternative but to do so the first night, to avert any suspicion that might be caused by my clothes being

I 9

wet. As I listened, the blood curdled round my heart. It was no small comfort to me, however, to find that the noise was only a violent rain-storm beating against the windows.

The stage-coach stopped the next morning on its way to Lexington, the inside was full, and though it rained heavily I was glad to get a seat outside.

The company were duly informed that I was an Abolitionist, and of the penalty I had suffered for being so, by some party, unknown to me. Upon hearing this they cracked their jokes, and sang alternately hymns and ribald songs. They swore, drank, and denounced the Abolitionists. Arrived at Lexington I found some of my Richmond enemies were looking out for me, and that as I proceeded to Frankfort I was still watched.

I called at the Temperance House. The landlord, with whom I had formerly lodged, and who was very anxious I should lecture on Temperance in the city, stated that his house was full, as a whig convention would be held the next day. I told him I could sleep on a buffalo skin—which means about the same as "I can sleep on the sofa or on a mattress" in England—so he arranged for my staying. I had no wish to meet my opponents at an hotel where I had not lodged before. A Kentuckian slept in the same room; and I observed, placed his brace of pistols under his pillow.

At my previous visit to this house, a slave, a young man, used to come into my room and light the fire. One morning we had the following conversation:—

"Are you a member of any one of the churches?

" No, sah, too bad a boy to belong to de church.

" But no one is obliged to be a bad boy.   Tell me, can you read the Bible ?

" No, sah, but I've often thought if I could only read de Bible, I should not be so bad a boy.

Now gaining a little confidence he said—" 'Tappears to me, sah, you are doing a powerful lot of writing here."

I was writing letters on the slave system such as I saw it in Kentucky, for the *American Baptist*, but that was a secret to the slave, and there was greater safety to me in its remaining so.

The common objection to emancipation was—" It will involve the nation in ruin."   My reply to this was—" By continuing slavery you will bring the very ruin you desire to avert."   The people in Richmond clung to slavery, and the results exemplified the correctness of my statement.   On the 1st of August, 1862, the anniversary of the Emancipation of the slaves in the West Indies, a band of guerrillas, led by John Morgan, visited Richmond, and plundered the stores, houses, and stables of the Union men, slaveholders as well as non-slaveholders.   Morgan with 1500 cavalry ran riot in Kentucky; and Richmond was one of the numerous towns which suffered from his raid.   This was a part of a more extensive plan.   After the pro-slavery McClellan had by some means reduced an army of 150,000 men to 80,000 without gaining a single victory, the leaders of the confederacy, which had slavery for its corner-stone, took heart; and resolved to send Generals Bragg, Hardee, Price, and Smith, at the head of 150,000 .

infantry and 12,000 cavalry, in supporting distance of each other, to Northern Alabama, Eastern Tenuessee, and South-eastern Kentucky, to make concerted marches upon the front and rear of Buell's and Grant's armies, supposed to be less than 150,000.

The guerillas were to aid by cutting off Federal reinforcements, and destroying bridges, trains, and transports. Such was Morgan's mission to Richmond.

The Kentuckians were neither cold nor hot. Their sympathies were with the confederacy ; their interests, with the Union. Their governor Magoffin desired to see the state secede. Their legislative body adhered to the Union. Meantime the state was the scene of much contention, of many small, and several large battles. It was invaded by three confederate armies. One from the South-west under General Bragg ; one from the North-east under Humphrey Marshall, and one from the South-east under General E. Kirby Smith.

On the 23rd of August there was a battle at the Big Hill, and the federals were defeated ; and retreated to Richmond. The confederates demanded the unconditional surrender of the town, but Colonel Metcalfe having received reinforcements, refused to surrender it.

On the 30th of August three battles were fought in the vicinity of Richmond, between the Union forces under General Manson, and a numerically superior body under General E. Kirby Smith, resulting on each occasion in a defeat of the federalists, who in the third battle were under the command of General Nelson. Mr. Benjamin, the secretary of the confederacy, in writing to Mr. Slidell, stated that "Major General Kirby Smith, advanced rapidly into Kentucky, reached Richmond, defeated and utterly routed an army of 10,000 under General Nelson.

"The enemy's army was absolutely destroyed, not more than two or three thousand fugitives escaping from the battle-field." This is probably an exaggerated statement. But there were heavy losses on both sides. The hold, however, of the confederates on Kentucky was but temporary.

Mr. Simpson, who visited America as a deputation from the Freedmen's Aid Society, informed me that he visited Richmond, in Kentucky; that a portion of the town was in ruins, and that he was exposed to some danger while there, as a man drew his pistol on him because he had expressed sympathy for the coloured people.

Having spent one night at Frankfort, I proceeded by steamboat to Madison, in Indiana, and was glad again to tread the soil of a free state. The next Sunday I preached three times to the coloured Baptist congregation, and continued to labour in Indiana.

Shortly afterwards I attended an Anti-slavery Convention in Cincinnati, and related my experience in Kentucky. Cassius M. Clay was present; from him I learned that the tutor of his children had been fired upon, that he was in too great danger to remain in Kentucky, and had returned to New England. Mr. Parsons wrote an account of my treatment to Mr. S. Bourne at Andover Theological Seminary.

Fillmore, President of the United States, had just

issued a message declaring that the army of the United States should be called out to support the fugitive slave law. I believe that message was written the day I suffered. Mr. Bourne, writing to the editors of the *Boston Commonwealth*, says :—"The following is a part of a private letter I received yesterday from a highly esteemed friend in Kentucky. Will the President issue another message assuring the people of Richmond that the army of the United States shall be called out to support law?—

" Whitehall, Kentucky, Feb. 19, 1851.

" I have just returned from tea, and my soul is so full of sorrow at an event of recent occurrence in Richmond (Ky.,) that I must water this sheet with my tears. O God! is there no justice in heaven? No vengeance? Must the wicked triumph and the righteous fall! * * * Let me give you a brief, and, under my present feelings, necessarily unconnected and imperfect account of a transaction calculated to make the ears tingle and the heart bleed."

Then after describing my being mobbed on Sunday evening, he adds :—

" Mrs. C. has to-day brought additional news. Says that on reaching the town yesterday, he (Mr. Mathews) was seized by some rowdies, taken to a wood in the outskirts of the town, and there told they intended to hang him, the rope being prepared." He then describes my treatment, somewhat as given already, and continues :—" One thing is certain, the God in whom he trusts will never leave nor forsake him, but will deliver him out of all afflictions. In bitterness of soul I have prayed for him. The ruffians

are Bill Stone, Shelby Irvine, Zech. Malanahan, Sid.
Turner, Hatch—son of a New Englander—who
teaches, and occasionally preaches, is a graduate of
Dartmouth, and several others.   Not a man in R. has
moral courage enough to bring to justice these hell-
hounds.   *   *   *   Mr. Clay is very deeply affected;
his enemies have done this.   He said to me at tea if
testimony could be obtained he should prosecute
them.   What will be the ultimate results altogether,
I shall not divine.   Mr. M. has broken no law; is an
innocent, free-hearted non-resistant, adopting and ex-
hibiting the spirit of the Gospel."

This letter was copied from the *Commonwealth* into
the *New York Tribune*, which was taken in Richmond,
and hence became known to the lynchers.   Concluding that it was written by Mr. Parsons, he was
attacked when he went to Richmond, and a pistol was
fired at him.   Conscious of his danger he left
Kentucky.   In concluding the narrative, Mr. Clay
said:—" Thus my children have lost their tutor,
because a private letter which he wrote was published; yet its publication was without his signature
and without his consent."

I lectured at Manchester, Ohio; that night twenty
slaves crossed from Kentucky.   Armed Kentuckians
were searching for them.   Nineteen of them were
recaptured; among them were a mother and seven
children.   I was suspected of aiding the escape.
Proceeding to New York I held meetings on the way.
At Cazenovia, George Thompson gave a lecture to a
crowded audience.   He requested me to speak first,
and describe my Kentucky experience.   I did so.

He then, taking up the subject, contended that in no heathen nation were missionaries treated with such barbarity as in the slave states of America.

The committee of the Free Missionary Society now requested me to visit England, and enlist, as far as possible, the sympathies of religious bodies in the work of emancipation. This was regarded as an important aid to the cause; the committee knew also that I desired to see my friends after so narrow an escape with my life. I gladly accepted the appointment, visiting Boston before sailing, and attending a public soiree to take leave of George Thompson, who was also about to return to England. Many hundreds were present, and speeches were made by the Rev. Theodore Parker, William Lloyd Garrison, and other leading friends of the Anti-slavery cause. By invitation I gave an address.

Calling on Mr. Garrison we conversed on the principles of peace among other topics. I was in favour of sending a policeman after a man who should steal a horse; and approved of physical force to sustain the law. Mr. Garrison thought that this might lead to the destruction of life, and as that was sacred, he could not regard me as being a thorough non-resistant.

In June I left New York in a fine ship, the "New World," Captain Knight. The voyage was pleasant. Two other ministers were passengers—one the pastor of a slaveholding church in Richmond. We preached in turns on deck. In my sermon I referred to slavery as an evil. This offended a passenger, who was a slaveholder, as I afterwards learned. The fourth of July was celebrated on board. As they were not willing to recognize the claims of the slaves in any way in the proceedings, I declined to take any part in them. Then there was a grand dinner, after which the captain called on each one for a toast. The slaveholder gave—"A strict construction of the constitution the only means of preserving the American Union," which simply means, that unless the whole north turn slave-catchers, the slave states will tear the Union to pieces. My toast was the repeal of the infamous fugitive slave-law and the abolition of slavery. I had penned some reasons for this toast, which I begged leave to read instead of making a speech. I had proceeded but a little way when a pro-slavery New Englander began to denounce me.

"I appeal," said he to the captain. "Here is a day consecrated to liberty, and he has brought before us the nigger-question. Ought he not to be put out of the cabin?" A few oaths were now uttered by him, and the ladies alarmed left the table and looked for protection. The captain said—"Gentlemen, I shall not take sides." So the storm passed over; in a day or two we were all friends again. I sent to a New York paper an account of the proceedings and the reasons I read with the toast, which were duly published.

The captain gave me permission to lecture on temperance. I did so. The first and third mates took the pledge, as did some others, and one man threw a bottle of rum into the sea. The captain, who was a life tetotaller, told me how pleased he was that the mates had signed the pledge, for said he, "on shore you can think at your leisure, but at sea you must think quick or your ship is lost, and a man who would think quick must not drink."

After reaching Liverpool I was soon on my way to Oxford, from which I had been absent nineteen years. " Now," I thought, " will my parents know me. I will see. I entered my father's shop; and as he entered it, I said "Good afternoon, pray do you know me?" He looked at me, smiled faintly, and responded "No, I cannot say that I do." My parents, six brothers, and three sisters were still living, and I was kindly greeted by them.

Since the Presidency of Fillmore I have not referred to the Presidents. To complete the view of them I will notice his successors, Pierce and Buchanan, Lincoln and Johnson.

PIERCE AND BUCHANAN.

Franklin Pierce was a native of the free state of New Hampshire ; James Buchanan of the free state of Pennsylvania. Both, though non-slaveholders, outdid, from their love of office, any slaveholding President, in yielding obedience to the dictates of the slave-party. Pierce began and Buchanan continued the civil war in Kansas. The measure known as the Missouri compromise, while excluding slavery from Kansas, protected it from civil war.

Atchison, the leader of the border ruffians, by bullying and driving, obtained the aid of both Pierce and Douglass in repealing the Missouri compromise. With its repeal began the reign of terror blood, and death in Kansas. Douglass aided in the repeal, with the hope of securing the united support of the slave-party for his election to the Presidency. That party could have elected him. But it was playing a deeper game. It designed to form the confederacy ; and the introduction of slavery into Kansas, and the defeat of Douglass, were means to that end. Kansas was to form one of the slave states of the confederacy ; the defeat of Douglass would render the election of Lincoln certain ; and his election was to furnish the pretext for secession.

The fillibusters, knowing Pierce's character, set on foot in the United States seven expeditions against countries with which the federal government was at peace, within two years after he had entered upon his office,—one to make Sonora, against her will, an independent republic ; one to rescue Tamaulipas from the control of her own inhabitants ; one to aid imaginary revolutionists in Cuba ; one to give undesired succour to Ireland ; one to occupy a grant of land in Costa Rica which Costa Rica denied ever having made ; one to help foreigners to overthrow the national government of Nicaragua ; and one to perform the same office to Lower California,—All of these paraded the American flag, and declared themselves missionaries of freedom, and every one of them was made up, mainly, if not wholly, of the defenders and extenders of slavery.

The fillibusters, knowing Buchanan's character, set on foot an expedition to revolutionise the United States, and establish, instead of the Federal Government, one of the most terrible despotisms that ever existed. The members of Buchanan's cabinet were among the chief actors in the crime ; Floyd, his

Secretary of war, supplied them with the arms, and
Thompson, his Secretary of the Interior, with the
funds of the United States. Buchanan saw seven
states in succession rise, repudiate his authority,
unite and form a new government. He saw them
elect Jefferson Davis as President, collect an army
and prepare for a war—but as he anticipated they
would not invade Washington while he was President,
he was content to let them proceed unchecked. Thus
without a hair of his own head being injured did he
lay the foundation of a civil war, which for the rapid
and extensive destruction of life and property has
probably no parallel in history.

Pierce, in disregard of the decision of the Supreme
Court of the United States, urged Congress to pay a
large sum to the kidnappers who claimed the Amistad
negroes. Buchanan was profoundly respectful to the
decision of the Supreme Court, given during his
administration in the "Dred Scott" case, by which
Judge Taney nullified any restriction by Congress on
the boundless diffusion of slavery throughout the
Territories of the federal Union. Pierce approved of
the martyrdom of Senator Sumner; and Buchanan,
the martyrdom of Captain John Brown. Sumner,
distinguished world-wide as the advocate of peace,
while writing in the Senate-chamber, was attacked by
Brooks, a slaveholding representative of South Carolina, and beaten on the head with a cane till he fell
bleeding and insensible on the Senate floor. Captain
John Brown, for using the same means to deliver the
slaves that America had employed to secure her
Independence, was hanged by a slaveholder, Henry

A. Wise. To aid in capturing and to guard in executing John Brown, Buchanan sent forward the troops of the United States.

Yet in 1856 Wise had arranged with the governors of the slave states to destroy the Federal Union if General Fremont should be elected President. Wise proclaimed himself a revolutionist for slavery purposes, in a speech in Congress, page 280; and by his aid not only was Virginia inveigled into secession, but the arms that John Brown would have given to the slaves were furnished to confederate soldiers— and the federal soldiers who had stood guard at John Brown's execution were driven from Virginia, some of them being killed in the flight. On the day that Jefferson Davis, C. C. Clay, and other secessionists, abandoned their seats in Congress to take part in the rebellion, Kansas was admitted by Congress into the Union as a free state. Buchanan signed the bill.

In 1852, the democratic convention that nominated Pierce for President, pledged itself to maintain the fugitive slave law and to oppose the Anti-slavery agitation. The whig convention that nominated General Winfield Scott gave similar pledges. The Free Soil party nominated John P. Hale, who received 155,825 votes. A less vote than Van Buren received four years before. The Anti-slavery feeling, however, had not declined, it had been intensified by the fugitive slave law and other pro-slavery measures of Fillmore's administration; but many voted for Van Buren from sympathy with their party leader, while those who voted for Hale did so from sympathy with the Anti-slavery cause.

The whig party commenced to sink from this period, and never rose again. In 1856 the whigs nominated Fillmore for President, who received 874,534 votes; while General John C. Fremont, nominated by the Free Soilers, and pledged to free soil, free speech, and free men, received 1,341,264 votes. This proved that the fugitive slave law and the civil war in Kansas had promoted the Anti-slavery cause as efficiently as if ten thousand lecturers on slavery had been sent abroad all over the Free States. Buchanan, however, received 1,838,169 votes, and became President.

LINCOLN AND JOHNSON.

Abraham Lincoln was a native of the slave state of Kentucky; Andrew Johnson, of the slave state of North Carolina. Both were from the labouring and poorer classes. Lincoln was a farmer, Johnson a tailor. Lincoln was a resident, except in early life, of a free state, and never held a slave; Johnson never resided in a free state, and held four slaves; these were a sufficient number to bind him in sympathy to the slaveholding class that then ruled the nation; but not to give him rank among them. Lincoln, before he became President, was elected a member of the Illinois Legislature, and on the adoption by that body of some extreme slavery resolutions, he entered his protest on the journals, declaring that "the institution of slavery was founded on both injustice and impolicy." Johnson before he became President was elected governor of Tennessee, and in 1853 was visited by the deputation of the English Society of Friends. "It was urged upon him," says William Forster, "to lead public opinion in favour of

ameliorating their (the slaves') condition. He remarked that hundreds of slaveholders would be glad
to be quit of their slaves altogether if they knew how."

Lincoln was elected to Congress by the whigs;
Johnson by the democrats. Lincoln, when a member of Congress, proposed the emancipation of the
slaves in the District of Columbia; Johnson has proposed no measure to secure justice or protection to
the coloured people; and in adhering to the Union
and opposing secession he told the slaveholders that
it was the best way to protect slavery.

Johnson was appointed by Lincoln military governor
of Tennessee, and was elected Vice-President by the
republicans. Lincoln tried by every means that his
sense of duty as President permitted, to save the
country from war. Johnson has pursued a course
adapted to re-awaken the war feeling. Lincoln was
anxious to do his duty. Johnson is anxious to
stand well with the ruling class of the south. Lincoln
had right impulses, but in shaping his policy yielded
to his cabinet. Johnson has southern impulses, which
direct his policy and that of his cabinet. Lincoln's
great difficulty was slavery. Johnson's great difficulty is equal rights for all. Lincoln's cabinet, it
may be fairly inferred, was not chosen with reference
to the rebellion, but with reference to the issues of
the election of 1860. It was too much in sympathy
with slavery, though opposed to slavery extension, to
deal efficiently with the rebellion. Hence it was a check
upon Lincoln's Anti-slavery policy. If Lincoln could
have removed slavery from the Border States his chief
difficulty would have been removed; for as the London

Times, whose editor is not an abolitionist, in a leading article of August 8, 1862, most truly states. :—The Border States "are linked to the South by an iron band. In proportion as slavery is represented as the cause of the war, the Border States must be enemies of the North, unless they could be induced by some powerful motive to eradicate this institution from their territories. It was to no less a surrender than this that Lincoln invited them. He wished to make them free soil states instead of slave states, well knowing, and indeed avowing, that the result of such a resolution would be their final detachment from the side of the South. * * * Their decision would materially facilitate either separation or conquest."

The appeal of Lincoln to the Representatives of the Border States was unsuccessful. They were slaveholders, and preferred to see the land drenched in blood than promote emancipation. Had Lincoln appealed to the people of the Border States he would have been successful. He could not do this without offending McClellan, who would not allow a verse of Anti-slavery poetry to be sung to his army. He should have dismissed McClellan. He could not make this appeal without a change in the cabinet. He should have changed his cabinet. Early in 1862 Lincoln wrote a proclamation emancipating the slaves, but owing to the determined objections of McClellan he did not publish it; he thought of removing McClellan, but the threats of the slaveholders of the Border States to secede kept him from doing so. These slaveholders prevented the acceptance, for a time, of the services of 100,000 coloured men for the army ;

and prevented it from affording protection to refugee slaves. When a bill was passed by Congress for the confiscation of the slaves employed against the federal government, Lincoln hesitated to sign it, saying " If I do so I shall lose Kentucky."

This difficulty might have been met by Mr. Lincoln calling together his cabinet and saying—" Gentlemen, there is an armed rebellion. To quell it slavery must be removed from the Border States. Anti-slavery agitation in those states will lead to its removal by a vote of the people—but the slaveholders will not allow such agitation. Free discussion, however, is a principle of the constitution. I shall secure it to the people in the Border States with all the power I possess. Slavery cannot be sustained by argument—it shall not be sustained by violence. The people need information, free discussion will impart it to them; a vote for emancipation will follow; I shall be glad to see it; the chief difficulty I have to meet will thus be removed. I have sufficient military power to protect all meetings for the discussion of slavery and abolition questions, and I shall employ it for that end." Blair would have resigned—he preferred a federal military defeat, to a federal Anti-slavery policy, witness his treatment of Fremont. Smith would have resigned, for he urged the President to support slavery as a requirement of the constitution. Bates would have resigned. Chase would have warmly supported the President, for one reason why he left the cabinet was the offence given to its pro-slavery members by his active efforts to establish the Freedmen's Bureau. Cameron would have supported

the President, for the reason of his leaving the
cabinet was his public proposal to call the slaves to
the federal standard. Welles would have sustained
the President, and Seward would not have resigned.
With such men as Senator Sumner, Wade, Stevens,
and other friends of the slave, there would have been
no difficulty in forming an Anti-slavery cabinet which
both for its ability and its Anti-slavery policy would
have commanded the sympathy of the friends of
constitutional liberty in America and throughout the
world.

Notwithstanding the difficulty of his position,
Lincoln signed the following Anti-slavery laws :—

A law giving freedom to all slaves employed by
rebels against the United States ; a law abolishing
slavery in the District of Columbia ; a law prohibiting slavery for ever in all the Territories of the
United States ; a Proclamation of freedom for ever
to the slaves of all rebels on the 1st of January,
1863. Lincoln also proposed an amendment to the
constitution offering compensation to such loyal
slave states as should emancipate their slaves. The
laws against the African slave-trade were enforced,
the captain of a slaver executed, and the traffic
suppressed ; a treaty was made with England conced-
ing the right of search to aid in putting down
the slave trade; the coloured Republics of Hayti and
Liberia were recognized ; and regulations established
protecting fugitive slaves by the army. Hence his
assasination by the slave-party.

Johnson has vetoed the bills passed by Congress to
protect those in the South who were not protected

by Southern laws—one relating to electors; the other to the Freedmen's Bureau. But as they have been passed by a two-thirds vote they are laws without his signature. The seed-principle of secession is contained in the refusal of the South to allow the federal government to protect coloured people.

It is worthy of remark that although I was compelled to leave the south, the Society by which I was sent as an Agent has now twenty-nine missionaries labouring in the Southern States.

LABOURS IN ENGLAND.

My labours commenced by addressing a public meeting on the 1st of August, 1851, at the Hall of Commerce, London, in connection with George Thompson and other friends of the slave.

In Bristol, September the 4th, at a meeting held at the Broadmead Rooms, Robert Charleton, Esq. in the chair, after addresses by George Thompson and several ministers, a resolution was moved by the Rev. Stewart Williamson, seconded by J. C. Neild, Esq., and adopted as follows:—

" Resolved,—That we offer to the Rev. Edward Mathews (an agent of the American Baptist Free Mission Society, who has recently received at the hands of slaveholders the proofs of their moral degradation, and of his own fidelity to the holy cause he advocates), the sincere thanks due from the members of every Christian sect to one who has nobly defended the great principle of freedom, fundamental to them all."

The resolution proceeds to urge the British churches to disfellowship the slaveholding, and encourage the Anti-slavery churches of America.

At this meeting I gave an account of my labours in America, and showed the importance of its churches being separated from slavery.

The lectures I have given since number more than one thousand, in the Metropolis and in the following counties:—Devon, Somerset, Wilts, Gloucester, Berks, Oxford, Buckingham, Hertford, Middlesex, Surrey, Hampshire, Dorset, Sussex, Suffolk, Norfolk, Derby, Lancashire, Cheshire, Yorkshire, Warwick, Kent, Essex, Cambridge, Bedford, Worcester, Huntingdon, Hereford, Monmouth, and the Principality of Wales.

I have regarded it as most important to show to each religious body, that its American co-religious brethren, with the exception of the " Friends," and such other religious bodies as excluded slaveholders from membership, were divided into two parties, the majority supporting, and the minority opposing slavery; and I have solicited them to unite with the Anti-slavery minority, and thus impress their own Anti-slavery character on their American brethren.

In explaining the relations which the American churches sustained to slavery, I have written as follows:—

A brief description of the relations which each American religious body sustained to slavery and Anti-slavery—a letter addressed to the Bristol and Clifton Ladies' Anti-slavery Society. This was published by the Society and forwarded to each religious body in England. It was published also by the Edinburgh Ladies' Anti-slavery Society and sent to each religious body in Scotland.

Thirty articles for the *Anti-slavery Advocate*, on

the same subject, embracing also a description of the relation which the American and Foreign Bible Society, and similar benevolent societies sustained to slavery.

A statistical view of the same subject showing also the number of constituents which each religious body had in the Southern States, the number of slaveholding members, and the number of slaves held by them. This was published by the British and Foreign Anti-Slavery Society.

Six letters to the *Freeman* showing the relations of the American Baptists to slavery and Anti-slavery. These were published in the *American Baptist*, New York, with the offer of the editor of the *Freeman* to publish any reply that might be made. There was no reply.

Six letters to the *Bristol Advertiser* on the relations of the American Methodists to slavery and Anti-slavery; and the reciprocal influence of British and American Methodism in relation to these two questions. Five letters to the *Daily News* on "Clerical Slaveholders" being a reply to the Address of Southern ministers in behalf of the Confederacy. Three letters to the *London Statesman* addressed to Mr. Dallas, the American Ambassador, on the "Right of Search;" a reply to his speech on the question. A series of letters to the *Morning Advertiser* on the relation of the American Board of Missions to slavery.

A Series of letters to the *Nonconformist* on the American Revival, denying that it was genuine because it did not lead to emancipation. These were among the most important, though I have written

letters upon various phases of slavery and the
Anti-slavery movement, which have appeared in the
London and provincial newspapers—and I have addressed several hundred letters to America which
have appeared in the *American Baptist.*

I may add that I have published several pamphlets
and occasional papers on slavery, one on "Uncle
Tom's Cabin," of which 15,000 copies were sold.   On
Sunday afternoons I have met hundreds of Sunday
School children, and by means of a large map, explained the slavery question, and pointed out the
advantages *they* enjoyed.   In Argyle Chapel, Bath,
I addressed one thousand children, and fourteen
hundred in the Rev. Dr. Reynold's Chapel, Leeds.

My belief is, that had the Americans when the
rebellion began, sent to England twenty of its most
able and devoted Anti-slavery lecturers, to go through
the towns lecturing, with maps, explaining the whole
question of slavery and its connection with the rebellion, not a single vessel would have left Liverpool
to prey upon the peaceful unarmed merchant vessels
of the United States.

In Leeds I aided to form a Young Men's Anti-
slavery Society, and after I had given two hundred
lectures in Yorkshire, its members kindly showed
their appreciation of my labours by presenting me
with a Testimonial, accompanied by an Address
stating that :—

" We desire to express our high admiration of
your noble exertions in behalf of Civilisation and
Humanity ; and, in the name of the members of our
Society, we beg your acceptance of the accompanying

Testimonial, as a small tribute to the glorious cause of Freedom. and also a very slight expression of the esteem with which we and they in common with the whole body of British Abolitionists regard you personally." (A Writing-Desk was presented.)

The Address was signed on behalf of the Society by Wilson Armistead, President; William Bilbrough, Chairman of Committee; and Joseph A. Horner, John Wood, and E. Knipe, Honorary Secretaries.

Thus have I endeavoured, by describing my Anti-slavery labours in the United States, to throw some light on American institutions, and their influence in forming the national character.

I have given a sketch of the Presidents, to exemplify the obstacles placed in the way of the Anti-slavery reform by their pro-slavery policy which was the result of the compromises of the constitution. When the slaves were bound we were all bound from the President to the humblest citizen; and in emancipating the slaves we broke our own fetters.

I am earnestly desirous that the impression most deep, vivid, and lasting carried away by the reader, in closing this Autobiography, should be that the life, health, and defence of a commonwealth is freedom of speech. By this public opinion is created, which is stronger than armies or navies. For its protection the people should rally from the highest officer to the humblest citizen, because it secures the majesty of the law, the dignity of the government, and the loyalty of the people. The slaveholders destroyed freedom of speech from the necessities of their position. Then began the troubles of the republic. When President Jackson proposed to prohibit the transmission of Anti-slavery newspapers, through the mails, his heel was upon the federal constitution, and Jefferson Davis copied his example. When the Charleston citizens rifled the mail-bags and burnt the Anti-slavery newspapers. they set at defiance the Federal government as certainly as when they fired at Fort Sumter; and, when in Congress, Foote threatened to hang any Abolitionist that should enter his state, in defiance of the laws of the Federal government, he was virtually recognising that state as having seceded already. The Federal constitution and the constitution of each state, south as well as north, makes freedom of speech the basis of the laws.

The missionaries of a free Christianity demanded as one of its first claims freedom of speech—their sufferings for doing so are here recorded. With freedom of speech every slave would have been emancipated by the power of public opinion and there would have been no rebellion, no secession, and no war. With slavery in America no power could bring the states into harmony; without it no power can permanently disunite them. With Liberty as the bond of union, their sympathies, their hopes their interests, their hearts will be one; and by their immense natural resources, their free institutions and their purified Protestanism, they will become a leader of nations, and will unite with the people of England —and by co-operation, example, and influence give laws to the civilized world.